# SISTERS OF THE SNAKE

# SISTERS OF THE SNAKE

SARENA NANUA &
SASHA NANUA

HARPER TEEN
An Imprint of HarperCollinsPublishers

HarperTeen is an imprint of HarperCollins Publishers.

Library of Congress Cataloging-in-Publication Data

Names: Nanua, Sasha, author. | Nanua, Sarena, author.
Title: Sisters of the snake / Sasha Nanua and Sarena Nanua.
Description: First edition. | New York, NY : HarperTeen, [2021] | Audience:
    Ages 13 up. | Audience: Grades 10-12. | Summary: "A street thief and a
    princess discover they are twins separated at birth and must switch places to
    find an all-powerful stone and prevent a deadly war from taking place"
    — Provided by publisher.
Identifiers: LCCN 2020055699 | ISBN 9780062985590 (hardcover)
Subjects: CYAC: Sisters—Fiction. | Twins—Fiction. | Identity—Fiction. |
    Princesses—Fiction. | Robbers and outlaws—Fiction. | Fantasy.
Classification: LCC PZ7.1.N3615 Sis 2021 | DDC [Fic]—dc23
LC record available at https://lccn.loc.gov/2020055699

Typography by Chris Kwon
21 22 23 24 25    PC/LSCH    10 9 8 7 6 5 4 3 2 1
❖
First Edition

To our family, for all the support. And to all the brown girls who
want to see themselves on the page.

# THE MASTERS OF MAGIC

## SNAKE MASTER

*Magic of serpents and stories*

*Descendants: snakespeakers*

## MEMORY MASTER

*Magic of mind and visions*

*Descendants: mindwielders*

## EARTH MASTER

*Magic of stone and soil*

*Descendants: stonebringers*

## SKY MASTER

*Magic of air and wind*

*Descendants: currentspinners*

## FIRE MASTER

*Magic of flames and light*

*Descendants: flametalkers*

## TIDE MASTER

*Magic of water and storms*

*Descendants: tidesweepers*

PART ONE

# A Switch in the Stars

# 1

## Ria

I despise the heat.

But it's everywhere, choking my breath, wrapping its claws around me. I pull my scarf forward, hoping it will shield against the sun's relentless rays. The humid air prickles my neck, my forehead, the hollow of my throat.

*Keep going*, I think, pressing a hand to my rumbling stomach. A girl's got to eat. So I push forward, past alleys of beggars and vendors with today's street foods: potato samosas with tamarind and mint chutneys. Fried pakoras, like jewels, glistening with oil. Fresh naan, like steaming pillows. Close. *So close*.

Passersby, young and old, hold out their hands. Some ask for money, others food. Some simply pray. I wonder if they've tried to sneak past the border, too. The smell of war practically stinks up the air.

I was once in their place, before I began to steal with Amir. Or as he called it, sleight of hand, as if we were playing card tricks instead of thieving rupees and jewels.

I shove toward the back of the stalls, nearly stepping on a stray cat's tail in the process. Its ears twitch, once, twice, before it spins to hiss at me. I nearly hiss back. Its matted fur reminds me of Barfi, the cat in my old orphanage, whose own fur was the color of curdled milk. I haven't seen her since I ran away twelve moons ago.

When I'm behind one of the stalls, I wipe my neck with my chunni, and the scarf becomes sticky with sweat. I tighten it around my waist like a sash. I don't want it getting in my way when I run.

A new vendor is here today. I can tell because he keeps the hot naan behind him, slathered in garlic and butter, mine for the taking. The former vendor, Samar, would never be so foolish. He's sold his wares enough times to notice thieving.

The vendor is accompanied by a lanky boy, probably a lookout, though he's not doing much of a good job of it. The only thing between me and this new vendor is a thin veil, unzipped, meant to keep him cool while he cooks. I measure the distance between the naan and me, calculate the time it will take to slip one into my hand.

The vendor holds up one finger, then another, to a customer: *One naan? Two?* He spins around to pull out the batch of naan and hands them in exchange for a pile of rupees. After he refills the basket with more, I slip my arm through the curtain's opening and tug. *I'll take two, please.* One for Amir and one for me.

The hot flatbreads sting my fingers, and I blow on them to cool them down the way Mama Anita used to do at the orphanage.

Before I spiral into memories of her, the vendor turns, and his eyes lock on mine. He sees the naan in my hand, and I realize my face is stupidly uncovered.

"Get back here, girl!" The vendor shouts something at the lookout, probably to watch the naan, and then hobbles toward me, arms outstretched. I shake my head and grin. I can't help it. The thrill of a steal, a chase, is like a firecracker inside me.

I take in the streets around me, stragglers and beggars and villagers all minding their business. I won't make it out of the market on foot. Not like this.

A hut looms in the distance. Wait—that's it! A plan forms in my head.

I bolt, ignoring the oncoming shouts, and head for the nearest hut with a low, sloping roof. I jump onto a stray rickshaw and, with one quick glance behind me, launch myself onto the top of the hut. I run recklessly, roof to roof, until I leap back to the ground, feetfirst. I press the naan to my chest and speed through the market, fast like an Amratstanian mountain cat. *Left, right, left.*

Despite having been here for only two weeks, I know this village better than I know myself. I know its worn alleyways, squat wooden buildings, streets that curve like question marks. I know the travelers on rickshaws, lugging miserable passengers who look like Death's second self. They scream when I leap in front of them, just barely skimming the rickshaw and landing in a nearby alley. I roll and cough up dust before springing back onto my feet.

"Those're mine!" The vendor's voice is gruff, but I hear him slowing. He's not quick like me. They never are.

I rush into the nearest alcove and watch him pass. I pray he won't hear me holding my breath. I pray my grumbling stomach won't betray me.

The vendor stumbles past, but I don't allow myself a grin just yet. *Never let your guard down.* Amir's lessons sink into me the way I want to sink my teeth into this naan.

A steal-and-run isn't uncommon in the Dirt Village. If anything, I've given the villagers of Nabh a show. Amir showed me how to steal quietly, but I prefer a quick chase, even if it means cutting it close.

When I think I've lost the vendor, I make my way back through the alley, keeping myself tight against the brick wall. I pull my chunni low over my head and let it curl around my face, more for protection from those who might pin me as the thief than from the bright sun.

I turn the corner. All clear. But before I can leave, a pressure at the small of my back jolts me and I whirl.

"Amir!" I growl.

"Evenin', Princess," Amir jokes. I earned the nickname seven moons back, not long after we first met, after stealing petty jewelry from a merchant's stall. He doesn't say the nickname as much as he used to, but it grates on my nerves nonetheless.

"Prince," I jab back. "You scared me. I thought you were a . . ." The word doesn't slip off my tongue, but he knows. One of the king's soldiers—a *Chart*. "Find any jewels?"

"Nothin'. And if I were a bloodcoat, don't you think you'd've heard the thudding boots?" He lifts his legs up and down like a monkey, sandals slapping the sun-scorched footpath. To Amir, saying *Chart* aloud is like spilling a secret. He thinks speaking the very word will summon them. But if the soldiers heard him calling them *bloodcoats*, he'd be struck faster than a thief could run.

Amir keeps his hair shorn, and a scar across his brown face cuts perfectly between his eyes. He looks the exact same as when we first met in a dank alley eight moons ago. He had naan, and I was a starving girl who knew little more than how to pick a lock. I thought he was a sixteen-year-old looking to play a joke. Turned out he's eighteen, with no one to call a parent and no place to call a home. Without him, I would probably be dead—or worse, half alive, easy bait for bandits.

"Charts can be sneaky, too, you know. And I don't wanna hear another word about 'em."

Only once have I gotten a close glimpse of a Chart. That day is imprinted in my memory, a stain that'll never wash away. *Bloodred coats. Fingers chaining Mama Anita's wrists.* All without giving my caretaker the mercy of saying goodbye before they dragged her to the palace.

*The Palace of No Return*, Amir calls it.

*The Kingdom of No Escape*, I say in return.

Three times we've tried escaping Abai. We were naive, thinking we could slip into a crowd and sneak onto the next carriage out of this kingdom. One time we nearly made it past the border that connects us to the northern kingdoms—and the waters beyond. For the first time in my life, I tasted freedom: sea salt laced with second chances, humid air filled with hope.

No—*false* hope. A guard discovered us hiding in the back of a carriage, alerted by a baby's cry. A foolish attempt, and a mistake we won't make again.

"What do you think the Ruthless Raja is up to today?" Amir tacks on the moniker with ease, but it makes me shudder. I have this eerie feeling that the royals are always watching us, spying from their lofty towers.

"Beats me," I say, tossing a piece of naan at his chest. He catches it with deft hands, a grin lighting his face. Neither of us waits to tear into the food, the first we've had to fill our bellies all day. We devour the naan in seconds.

Amir dusts off his hands and cracks his knuckles when he's done. "In that case, the royals might as well not exist."

"Pfft. Yeah, like the laws are made from thin air, right?"

He crosses his arms over his chest defensively. "Might as well be."

A metallic screech comes from behind us. We spin and find a trolley rattling its way across Nabh's dirt-lined streets, holding all sorts of food: a basket of ripe mangoes and papayas; boxes of snacks, like golgappa; a barrel of sweet gulab jamun.

Amir spins to the alley's entrance, a frown on his face as he watches the cart meander away with its precious cargo. That kind of food could only be headed for one place: the ice-cold palace. Outside, guarded by a ring of Charts. Inside, a merciless raja, calling for executions like one might order a meal. And in front of the palace, a supposedly magical fountain they say can predict your future.

Amir must know I'm thinking about the palace, because he says, "What kind of raja lives so far north? It's as if he's trying to get away from his own kingdom instead of rule it!"

I let out something like a laugh. But even the thought of the palace, whose spiraling towers are just specks in the muggy distance, makes me sick. Amir is right—it's as if the royals would rather be quarantined than expose themselves to any of us. I would spit on the ground in disgust, but my mouth is too dry.

I can't remember the last time a royal stepped out of that place. The Charts do the king's dirty work, looking for traitors.

But I'm no traitor. I'd rather not draw attention at all. Invisibility is a cloak that separates me from them, us from the royals.

I move toward the lip of the alley, where a carpet of garbage and glass lies, left over from drunks drinking bitters in run-down taverns. The alcohol must be in abundance now that some tavern owners have disappeared, *left*, like so many others in this Masters-forsaken kingdom.

Have they fled across the border, or been taken in as prisoners?

A young newsboy rushes by, hollering about trade happenings in the North, followed by rumor of a sandtiger sighting. He continues, "Kaamans preparing for war with Abai! Just over a half-moon away! Cavalry is set—"

The bone-chilling sound of hooves breaks through the din. I

step out of the alley. The only people with horses around here are the royals and, worse, the Charts.

That's when the horses arrive, stirring up clouds of dust. One knocks over a cart of papayas, and they tumble and crack open against the ground.

The once-trickling villagers brew into a crowd. Running would be a fool's errand right now—better to blend in—so Amir and I ghost toward the dense cluster. When we near the front and see them—the *Charts*—we stop dead in our tracks.

"Don't. Say. A. Word," Amir breathes. I can't even nod. One Chart, a man sporting gold tassels and too many badges to count, dismounts his horse and strides past us. I catch a whiff of his scent, like death and skin and bones all wrapped up in one. Why are they here? What do they want with us?

A sickening thought comes to mind. What if they're here for recruitment? Sure, the raja usually selects people from poor families and turns them into soldiers or army lackeys, but I've heard horror stories of people being tossed into wagons off the streets and dragged to the palace. There are more every day, with the upcoming war. Some say the Charts' induction ceremony, when the soldiers are assigned their official numbers and given their bloodred coats, is painful to watch. I don't really want to know why.

I train my gaze on the Chart closest to me. His face is stone, his uniform too clean to belong in Nabh. He barely looks at the rest of us; we're all interchangeable to them anyway. One smirk at the rips in our clothes tells me that much. I want to dig into the wrappings around my waist and pull out my knife, but the Chart is quick to move on.

He pulls a length of burnt-looking parchment from his pocket and flips it to face us. Drawn on the page is a man's face—and not just any.

It's Samar's—the naan vendor who wasn't in the market today. That gap-toothed grin is a dead giveaway. I shudder when I read the words.

**BY ORDER OF RAJA NATESH OF ABAI, THE GREAT SNAKESPEAKER, RULER OF THE OLDEST KNOWN MAGICAL KINGDOM**

**WANTED ALIVE: SAMAR BANGA, PREVIOUS TUTOR OF THE FUTURE RANI**

**CRIME: TREASON**

The words, written in a too-polished scrawl, make my eyes go wide. *Samar.*

It's no wonder he wasn't selling naan today. He was hiding.

Even the other words surprise me. Samar once tutored the *princess*? Everyone thought he lived a simple life. After all, that's the only life we know.

And that line—*Ruler of the Oldest Known Magical Kingdom*—nearly makes me vomit. I'm no believer in magic, but when Mama Anita was alive, it was all I thought about. Everything I know about the world outside of Abai came from her. She told me of the continent's four kingdoms—five, if you count Pania, now nothing more than a desolate wasteland. Kingdoms like Kaama, rumored to bloom fresh fruit year-round. Retan, with sand dunes cresting like a golden sea. Amratstan, where mountains' peaks graze the clouds.

My thoughts unwind as the Charts' eyes cut through the crowd. Mama Anita's voice disintegrates, the same way it had the day she was taken. The day she was killed.

"Anyone seen this man?" another Chart asks. Her black hair is tied into a tight bun, face shadowed by the black-and-red cap she wears.

Amir and I hold a collective breath. The Charts' horses stay steady, trained like the raja's lethal weapons.

"Speak up," another Chart spits, the number *213* gleaming on the badge hooked to his collar. "This man is a traitor. First one to find him gets a prize." Two Thirteen smirks and reveals his pristine, pointed teeth.

No one dares to speak, let alone breathe.

"All right, then." The next few moments blur together: the Chart grabs the nearest woman by the arm, ripping her chunni from her neck. He brings his knife out and presses it to her throat, silencing her screams.

Another woman steps forward, but an identical Chart knocks her aside with an elbow to the jaw. I hold in a gasp. My feet begin to move forward instinctively. My veins ignite. My whole body is coiled, ready to fight, but before I can, Amir wraps a hand around my wrist. He pulls me back, eyes fear-flecked.

"Amir," I whisper. He only shakes his head. The Chart digs the knife's point deeper, drawing blood.

Noise sounds behind us, and we all turn. Someone is shoving their way through the crowd. Before Amir can say *Raja's beard*, a man reaches the front.

My muscles melt when I recognize him. He's missing more than one tooth now. His hair is tousled like he just got out of a fight.

"Stop!" Samar yells. "Get your hands off her."

The Chart shoves away the woman, whose blood trickles down her neck in rivulets. "On your knees," he orders.

Coolly, Samar does as the Chart says, and the other soldiers rope the man's hands behind his back.

"What shall we do?" The Chart chuckles, curving the sword against Samar's throat. "Your obedience is shocking, I must say. To think you were once one of us, in the palace. . . ."

Samar fiddles with a golden band on his ring finger. A wedding band. I think of his wife, hidden somewhere far away, clinging to her husband's memory.

Samar's lips twitch. "You won't find Irfan."

Wrong answer.

The Chart grips him even harder. Another Chart marches up and strikes Samar across the face with the back of her hand, leaving a quickly purpling bruise.

*Rule number one: never talk back.*

Amir and I swap glances. The only sign of emotion on the first Chart's face is the slightest sneer of his lips.

Stale air and sweat curls around me. Silence—there's only silence.

"Up," says the Chart, removing his sword from Samar's neck. A small mercy.

But Samar's fate will be left in the raja's hands. And that is no mercy at all.

As easily as they came, the Charts shove Samar into a rickety old carriage. Another takes a scroll of parchment and slams it against a lone sandstone hut, then pins it in place. The still-bleeding woman cries out when she glances at the writing on the scroll. "My son!" she wails. "Oh, my son . . ."

My heart flips in my chest. Could that scroll be . . . ?

I glance at the carriage and watch the Charts pile up on their steeds. The horses clop away, kicking up dirt and despair in their wake.

A few people immediately turn to the injured woman, calling for cotton and gauze. I rip my gaze away and whisper to Amir, "The scroll. D'you think that's a . . . ?"

I don't need to finish my sentence for Amir to understand. "Let's find out."

We approach the scroll with bated breath, pushing through the crowd to reach the front. Some people cry out when they see their names. Amir gasps, color draining from his cheeks. I follow his gaze, finding the scroll's endless list of names and family identification markers. For the orphans, instead of last names, there are black strikes.

"It's a conscription list!" the newsboy from earlier announces. "Raja's callin' for more help!"

"He doesn't need our help!" a different woman cries.

At the same time, Amir murmurs to himself, "This can't be."

Skies be good. If Amir's name is on here—

The villagers' words blur together as I gaze at the scroll again. *Please,* I think, *not Amir, not Amir—*

More people squeeze in, blocking my view. Amir ushers me out of the crowd. Bile snakes up my throat, burning me from the inside out. Amir begins talking, telling me to remain calm. But I don't hear him, not clearly anyway. I hear what he told me moons ago, the day we first met, about what happens to those who try to defy the raja's orders.

*His executions are more painful than a sword through the chest. The royals use snakes. They twist their fangs in your gut and don't let go.*

It's not just snakes that send a jolt of fear spiking through me. It's not even the raja, or the Charts. It's that I finally understand the look of horror on my friend's face.

It wasn't Amir's name on the list.

It was mine.

# 2

## Rani

Everything I say turns to gold—or dust. On a good day, it's gold. It's power, sung in my mother tongue and listened to by many. On a bad day, it's dust. Derelict. Unheard.

Today is a bad day.

"Rani, come down," Mother calls from the base of the double spiral staircase. I twist my body over the railing to spot her figure. Mother is short, as if she stopped growing when she was no older than ten summers. She twists her own body, mirroring mine, to look up at me. "Quickly. This is important," she adds, the words a slap to my ears.

I pull at the threads that hang loose from my once-pretty sari and mutter a curse under my breath. I can wrap a sari with ease, but if I have to wear one more under Mother's orders, I'll lose every thread of the quickly waning patience I have.

I take my time strutting down the steps. Mother awaits, wearing a pink-and-orange fabric that mimics the sunset. She smiles, pale lips thinning. "Rani, beta. Come here." She spreads her arms open as if to give me a hug, but I know better. She wants me to twirl. I'm her own personal doll, ready to play dress-up, to bend to her every whim.

I follow her command. Twirl, bow; twirl, bow. Suck in a breath; don't loosen the stitching. For a moment, I wish for a thinner waistline but remove the thought. I won't let Mother's voice enter my head.

"Beautiful," she says, clapping as if I've just put on a show. "Saeed, isn't she beautiful?"

Saeed appears from the corner of my eye, sashaying down the hallway as if he's the prince himself. Once he's close by, he pops something into his mouth—a whole gulab jamun. He chews, swallows, and licks the saccharine syrup from his fingers.

"Beautiful," he finally agrees, the sunshine that pours in from the lower-level windows giving him an ethereal glow. His curly hair bounces against his head. His lips, once perfectly kissable according to my fourteen-year-old self, spread into a smile.

"Want one?" Saeed says, pulling me from my reverie. He wiggles his sticky fingers. "They were just delivered. Mangoes, too."

"Where are those manners Amara taught you, sweet boy?"

Saeed grins, and Mother pats his cheek as if he were her son. But she only has me, and so far, I'm more disappointment than daughter.

I clear my throat, bringing Saeed's attention back to me. "Beautiful? Beautiful enough to bow for?" I ask, hiding an impish smirk. I'd like to see Saeed squirm under my gaze, but today he won't have it. He bows, keeping his hazel eyes on me the entire time. Something in my stomach flares.

He purrs, "Always."

The air charges with heat. A false spark. I've had enough. "I'm canceling all future lessons."

"Rani!" Mother scolds, placing a hand to her chest. "That is no way to talk to your instructor."

"Or your betrothed," Saeed adds, his back now perfectly straight. That flare reaches my fingers, and for a moment I wish our lessons were comprised of sword-fighting and knife-wielding, rather than mathematics and chemistry. At least then I would have something to use against him.

"I will leave if it is your wish," Saeed says. His words are quiet enough—innocent enough—to Mother, but I know better. What I told him last night, at midnight in my bedroom, was not what he wanted to hear.

Not after three years of this. Of us.

"Yes," I reply regally, like the princess I'm supposed to be.

"Not without a kiss first, my boy," Mother orders. "You two are to celebrate your engagement in less than a half-moon. It is time you started acting like it."

With the faintest hesitancy, Saeed complies, striding toward me and placing a light kiss on my cheek. His lips caress my skin for a moment too long. As if I might fall into his arms like I had three years ago. Or just last moon.

I seethe against his haughty arrogance. Struggling to loose a steady breath, I stare at him with a venomous gaze. *He* is no prince. I, on the other hand, descend from a bloodline destined to rule. My role has forever been princess, to safeguard my people—and continue my line by marrying well. The last bit, however, is not quite working out as planned.

Before I can gather up the courage to tell her the truth of what happened last night, Mother begins to strut through the palace, past its bone-white walls and icy spires. "Hurry now, Rani. You are expected in the throne room," she commands. "Your father is waiting."

My gaze flits curiously to Mother's, but she keeps her expression curtained. I have no choice but to suck in a breath, press my damp palms against my sari, and follow Mother's shadow.

For eighteen years, I've walked these halls. Cool marble floors, paisley-patterned carpets, and a frosted-glass exterior. Ornate jalis, latticed screens that filter out the hot Abai air. Domed ceilings painted with sweet flower blossoms that belong nowhere near a raja like my father. The flowers are ornaments, distractions from what my family truly is. Royalty with nothing more on our minds than fatal justice—my father's specialty—and what our next meals will be.

The palace towers into the very clouds of Abai's capital, Anari. I know little of the world outside this home, this confinement. Its walls squeeze in on me as I walk, threatening to echo every horror of my existence. *Stuck here, forever. No way out. Princess of a kingdom you barely know. A kingdom on the brink of war.*

Every green-clad servant I pass bows, as if their spines are cemented in an arch. Mother's heels burn staccato footsteps into the cool marble tiles. When we reach the throne room, another servant heaves open the wide, gilded double doors.

Three chairs are perched at the front: one each for Father, Mother, and me. They are covered in soft velvet cushions and crowned with jewels, the silken thrones so spotless they look allergic to dust.

The deafening chatter withers away in the crisp air. Nobles from Abai's richest families, including elderly women—aunties—from the women's room with nothing more than gossip on their tongues, fall deadly quiet at my entrance. No—the raja's entrance through the door directly opposite this one. I wring my hands behind my back and face him.

Father is king in every sense of the word. In one hand, he carries his staff. A talisman, I've been taught, that's been passed down from raja to raja, rani to rani, imbued with our snake magic. His clothes, adorned with endless badges, make him look like he's been through battle, though he's never experienced any form of combat in his life. A royal-purple turban is perched atop his head, and two golden chains wrap around his neck, with minuscule beads that look like they've been plucked straight from the sand of the continent's lushest coastal beaches.

Samvir, Father's snake familiar, slithers patiently at his side. Today the snake sports glimmering obsidian scales streaked with gray. The king of cobras for the king of Abai.

I clear my throat, snagging Father's attention. His gaze cuts toward mine, tiger eyes flashing.

"Rani," he greets. "Just in time." Father heads for his throne just as Mother takes her seat. Queen and king, rani and raja.

I might be named Rani, but I am no queen. Not yet.

"Father," I say, tilting my head forward. "What occasion is this?"

But Father pays no mind to my words. He spins to the center of the throne room, where Father's Head Chart, Two Thirteen, hauls a man into the room. He dumps him onto the marble. There, I examine the figure crouched on both knees, clad in clothes dirtier than Nabh and covering his face with dirt-stained fingers. My heart thumps with understanding. This is a trial.

Removing his fists from his face, the man unveils nails both chipped and soiled. His eyes are a soft blue, the color of the rivers that shape and border our lands. He does not tear his gaze away from Father's, even when my own jaw collapses to the floor at the sight of him.

*Tutor.*

Before Saeed became my teacher, I was taught by this man— science and stars, algebra and fortunes. But he taught me more still: to wish for a stronger world, a world rid of war and hate. A world that does not exist.

He once had a clean face and all of his teeth, too-large ears and an ever-present smile. When I was no more than fourteen, he defied Father's iron-fisted rule and deserted the palace completely. Rumors flew—he left to join rebel groups or went off to live quietly with his wife. Father branded him Traitor instead of Tutor. He would forever be an enemy in the mind of the king.

I never learned his real name.

On the floor, weak-kneed and clothed in dirt and woe, he looks nothing like I remember. He is emptier, somehow. Perhaps that is what Father thinks will happen if I step outside—that I will change in some way. Or that I will become a traitor to the raja and everything he stands for.

"Your sentence is clear," Father states. His voice bellows through the throne room, curling into every corner. "You have been found guilty of treason, keeping information about rebel intelligence while tutoring Abai's future queen, fleeing the palace, and thus colluding with the enemy."

Tutor's facade does not give way, even at the sight of the snake slithering under Father's throne. It's Shima, my own snake familiar. Tutor never did like snakes. She is coiled like a spring and camouflaged so well I nearly mistook her for an intricately designed snakeskin rug. Her blue-green scales and vicious fangs echo the feelings of my own cold-blooded body, like a reptilian twin. It is our snake magic, my father's and mine, thanks to the Snake Master, that gives us the ability to bond with serpents. I glance over at Shima and, with a mental tug, unlock the wall I've built between her and me. Tonight, I need her in my mind. I need her fierceness and her strength.

"Rani," the raja calls, forcing my gaze back to his.

I clear my throat. "Yes, Father?"

"As princess, you know what must be done."

He stares at me a beat too long. It is only then that I register what he is asking of me.

My skin turns to ice. I think of the Snake Pit, humming beneath my feet. Of Shima, diving after Tutor's lifeless body. All at my simple command.

Just one word: *kill*.

To the spectators, tonight is a performance. A display of power. To me, it is a reminder of how I imagined this moment—Shima's fangs showered in red, screams twisting in the air like an arced blade—but never had I thought Father would ask it of me so soon.

His gaze trails over to Shima, who now slithers across the tiles, examining the traitor with bared fangs. She's hungry. I can smell it, taste it, *feel* it in our blood bond. She is ready for this. Tonight, Samvir is a bystander and Shima, the killer.

The Pit is alive beneath me—hundreds of snakes, waiting. They are ravenous. Starved, just like Shima.

I turn to the snake, but she is already moving. This is routine to her. A dance. Nothing more.

She circles around the traitor, making a complete loop. Her emerald-sapphire scales ruffle, pronouncing the hint of rose gold around her eyes. I approach him with caution and pause, my anklet surrendering its song. Tutor's hands don't need to be shackled for me to see he is a prisoner of fate.

But something niggles at my heart, chipping away at the icy cage I've drawn up around it. A memory. His gentle hands clapping out a song—one made to help me remember my lesson on one of the first queens of Abai.

They called her the Gem of Abai, the queen who passed
  so young
A ruler who commanded Abai to treat no one unjust
For Amrita was a woman of love, a woman of power as
  well
She gave so much for so little, and so we tell her tale

"Do not forget what I taught you, Rani," he whispers now. "You can be more than what the stars wish for. You can be like Queen Amrita. You can do what I could not."

My chest tightens. Time freezes as my eyes lock on his, as those words roll over in my mind.

"Find it," he tells me in a low voice, his words ominous. He reaches out, pressing the inside of his hand into mine. Something sharp bites into my palm. His voice becomes a whisper. "The stone."

I freeze. *The stone?* My eyes dart down to the object in my palm—a ring inscribed with a foreign yet familiar symbol—and I try not to glance back at Tutor with confusion.

"Rani," Father warns. He slides off his throne with ease, glaring at me as he approaches, then pauses a few paces from Tutor.

A fiery tingle grips my chest. "Father," I say. "Please. He was my—"

Before I can finish, or even utter a prayer to Amran, Father bangs his staff on the ground. That sound resonates through the room, sending spiderwebbed cracks along the marble floor.

One second passes. Another. The ground beneath Tutor

crumbles to ash, unveiling a pool of snakes. I grip the folds of my sari and hold back the gasp in my throat.

"A ruler never hesitates," Father's voice booms. The next command slips from Father's tongue.

"Kill."

Shima dives into the Pit, followed by Samvir close behind. My eyes seal shut at the first *crunch*. I don't have to look to know what is inside. Fang and flesh, blood and bone.

A hunger sated.

I blink my eyes open, peer over the Pit, and find the snakes writhing in contentedness. A coppery tang swells in my mouth—the taste of magic, blood, death. Over the years, I've learned to numb it. But now, as I hover over the Pit itself, the taste floods my mouth.

I twist away, covering my lips with my free hand. I could not speak Father's command. But I didn't stop Tutor's fate from being sealed, either.

*He is Tutor no longer. He is a memory.*

My body numb, I march toward my throne. Mother watches me with her eyes narrowed. Whether in fury or simple irritation, I cannot tell.

*This* is why she wanted me dressed up. Not for her but for this game. To show that the princess is capable of more than just wrapping a sari. *Which you are*, Shima hisses, her voice slipping into my mind. She glides out of the Pit, and in a blink, the marble tiles are back, sleek as silk. As though they had never crumbled. As though nothing happened.

The Charts branch out, heading to their posts. Mother dusts her hands off and stands, sighing. This is the third execution in one month, but Mother seems more preoccupied by her manicured nails than the smell of death.

"I'm going to go talk to Amara. There's much to be prepared for tomorrow," she says, and leaves.

*Tomorrow.* Diwali. This year, the celebration is midway through autumn, and will be held outside the palace beneath a starry sky in the courtyards. It will be my first taste of fresh air—*real* Abai air—since last year's celebrations.

I try not to think of all the guests who will be pouring into the palace, and focus instead on what Mother just said. She's going to talk to Amara, Saeed's mother. I shiver at the thought of my future mother-in-law, her bloodred lips, her mehendi-streaked hair—

"Daughter."

I start at the sound of Father's voice. Father's back is straight, scepter in hand, his head only just tilted in my direction. "I did what was necessary. And one day you shall, too," he says.

My body grows cold. I nod back, the ring searing my palm. "Of course," I reply.

Because no one is allowed to say no to a king, least of all me.

## 3

### Ria

*Curfew is for those who don't wish to dream with their eyes open.*

Mama Anita's mantra refuses to let go of me tonight. She used to recite it every night before she tucked me into the Vadi Orphanage's scratchy blankets. Once, the idea of wielding magic, being a princess, was all I really wanted. Dressing up, pretending the world around me was perfect. Falling in love.

Like any of *that* is possible in Abai.

I'm walking along Nabh's dusty streets, numb and nauseated and unable to utter a single word to Amir. I push reality aside. I might've turned eighteen recently, but I'm not about to throw my life away for the raja or his throne.

Minutes pass before I spot the back of a woman sporting a purple chunni. For an instant, I see Mama Anita: graying hair, fine wrinkles, thin lips that told endless stories.

But then the woman turns around. Her face is square instead of round; gaunt instead of plump. *Not Mama Anita.* I should've known better than to fantasize. To muddle dreams and reality.

Still, Mama Anita's stories cling to my memory. She'd recount how Abai hadn't always been this way, cruel as a knife's point, ruled by a snakespeaker's fist. Whenever she told me a story, she'd lean in conspiratorially, like she was telling a secret. This one always began the same:

"Over a thousand years ago, at the beginning of time, our Creator, Amran, made life. He sprouted trees from barren ground, gave rain to the hottest deserts. Not long after came six special beings, the first people to walk our world. But they were no mere humans—they were like spirits visiting from the sky. Collectively, they are known as the Masters of Magic, because each was born with a special kind of power."

Mama Anita taught me that all magic came from Amran and these special beings—the Masters. Amran's magic came in the form of gifts bestowed upon the world: the blessed Var River, where promises are forged in blood; the Fountain of Fortunes, perfumed with sweet scents; among others. On the other hand, the Masters' magics were tied to their blood. There was the Master of Fire, whose flames could grow hot enough to singe the soul and burn kingdoms to the ground; the Tide Master, who controlled disastrous monsoons and wicked floods; and even Masters of Earth and Sky. But there were others, two whose magics were considered the most unique and powerful of all: the Master of Memory, kind but persuadable—and the Master of Snakes, who possessed untold cunning.

The first time Mama Anita told this story to me, I interjected, looking at her wrinkled hands compared to mine. Her twine bracelet shook as she demonstrated a sweeping wave from the Tide Master's floods, or bursting fires from the Fire Master's fingertips.

"But Mama Anita, I don't understand. Where is this magic? I don't see it!"

Mama Anita chuckled. "The magic was passed on through the Masters' direct descendants. The Snake Master's bloodline—now Abai's royals—became known as snakespeakers. The Tide Master's children were tidesweepers; the Fire Master's children flametalkers. Their blood was bound to their Master, and when the Master's magic was gone, so was theirs."

Mama Anita glanced past the curtains that shielded me from the humid evening air. "If our world was a quilt, then magic was the threads that bound it together. Magic was as much a part of our kingdoms as the air we breathe."

I always loved that metaphor. It made me cozy inside, even during a brutal windstorm. But it was the next part of Mama Anita's story, the part she refused to repeat, that made my blood curdle.

*The way we lost magic to the royals.*

It was the Snake Master, the Great Deceiver, who took magic away from us.

"Long before the lines of our world were drawn and borders patrolled by soldiers, many of the Masters lived in harmony, like brothers and sisters of sorts. But like most siblings, some did not get along. The Master of Snakes was a known trickster, and for much of his life he was never trusted by anyone."

"Why not?" I questioned innocently.

Mama Anita pursed her lips. "It all began when the Snake Master asked the Master of Memory to search for a missing relic—something that could bring peace to the world forever. Something that could grant any wish—except bring back a loved one from the dead. It was called the Bloodstone. Made from the Creator's own blood, it was the most powerful of Amran's many gifts." She leaned back so she could look me square in the face. "Of course, the Memory Master agreed, using her mindwielding abilities to access the memories of everyone who'd touched or seen the Bloodstone before. She searched for moons before she found the stone, hidden away in a cave deep in Retan."

"Then what?" I bounced on the bed, begging Mama Anita to continue the story.

"Things fell apart," Mama Anita said simply. "The Snake Master never truly wanted the stone for peace. At the time, there were no kingdoms, no rulers. Once the Snake Master took the stone from the Memory Master, intending to use it for selfish purposes, the other Masters retaliated. And so began the Great Masters' Battle. The battle ended quickly, thanks to the Snake Master's possession of the stone. He used its powers to banish his siblings one by one. As a result, the other Masters became trapped, their physical forms stripped away while their souls drifted to the skies. No one knows where the Snake Master went. Soon, *his* bloodline ascended to what became the Abaian throne, and the stone was passed down from king to king, queen to queen. Until five hundred years ago. The stone was lost—or perhaps hidden."

I hung on to Mama Anita's every word like a bee to honey.

"With their magic fading away," Mama continued, "the Memory Master's descendants created their own kingdom, Kaama, becoming their own royalty and nobility. And soon after, new countries were born. Retan, Pania, Amratstan . . ."

I shivered but held her arm tight. "It's just a story, Mama. Right?"

She brushed my hair back. "This is no fable, dear Ria. After what happened to the other Masters, their descendants noticed their magic beginning to fade, until it all but disappeared. Those Masters have never returned from the heavens. There are rumors that they can appear in times of great need as spirits . . . just rumors, of course." Mama Anita swept my hair into a single knot. "Because of the feud between the Snake and Memory Masters, Abai and Kaama were at war for a long time. The two kingdoms' royalties haven't forgotten—and they haven't let the hate of the past go."

*The hate of the past.* I didn't understand what she meant back then.

"What happened during the war?" I asked.

"Many years of bloodshed and violence. A hundred years ago, the raja of Abai at the time, King Amrit, tried to find the Bloodstone. He thought he could use it to win the war and destroy

Kaama, but wherever it was, it was untraceable. Then he noticed that his kingdom began to change. There were lightning storms, a drought across the country, signs of ire from the Creator. Eventually, King Amrit proposed a treaty to the Kaaman king, Rahul. Both kingdoms were running out of resources, spending everything on battles, and everyone could feel Amran's anger. So the kings agreed on the Hundred-Year Truce. No war, no trade, for one hundred years. In just over a decade, the time will come for the truce to end, and the treaty with it."

"And then what?" I asked, standing. I remember jumping on my toes in anticipation, waiting for Mama Anita to continue. All she did was close her eyes, shake her head just slightly.

"And then it will be time for another story."

The hazy memory of Mama Anita's stories should mean nothing to me now. But some stories are true. And too many don't have happy endings.

Reality sets in. Mama's voice is gone. I never found out why she was taken away, even spent months wondering before realizing the answer would never bring her back.

A biting wind makes me shiver. Until I realize there's no wind. I'm shaking with such ferocity that Amir has to hold me up, but I fall to my knees and clutch my churning stomach. The world spins. I heave, trying to let something out. But there's so little there. A sob lurches its way out of my mouth.

The war is coming.

*My name on a conscription list.*

*My life, my future, gone.*

Amir offers me water from his canteen and helps me stand. He tells me we need to move fast, forget what we saw. I don't know how long it takes me to get moving. To stop thinking about what'll happen if I become a solider.

What'll happen if I don't.

*Imprisonment. Death.*

We know better than to stay in Nabh any longer. Hours ago, we escaped the dense crowds and headed for the outskirts of the Dirt Village. By tonight, we should reach the Moga Jungle, if I don't buckle to the ground first.

I tell myself the Charts won't find me there. In the jungle, I'll become a ghost. I'll make a new life, change my name if I have to. Anything but join a pointless war.

Before we left, Amir and I packed up what little we had stashed away: a jar of tangy lemon achaar, a bottle of sweet lassi, and a handful of now-crumbled besan. We pocketed a pile of rupees Amir snagged last week, and I stuffed coins into my now-bulging pockets. They expose me for who I am: a thief, and nothing less.

Blisters bloom on our soles. A caravan rustles past, hordes of people huddled inside. I've seen enough caravans rushing south-ward these past few moons to know where they're headed. These people must be rich enough to get through the border unharmed, passports in hand. A woman's eyes lock on mine with suspicion. Maybe she sees my bulging pockets, or hears the chime of coins. Maybe she can sense that I would rob her if I had the chance. Take her passport and run for freedom.

Amir gently nudges me in the arm. "You think they have mangoes in Kaama? Wait—stupid question. Of course they do. What about pomegranates? I've dreamed about those, lemme tell you."

"Never tasted one." I think of what lies beyond Abai's borders, where we'll go. Kaama won't work. I don't want to be in Abai *or* Kaama when war erupts in just over half a moon's cycle. Maybe Amir and I'll find a way to the North, where snowbirds drift through the Amratstanian mountains. Or south to Retan's desert dunes.

Everyone knows what happens to those conscripted from the lottery—they either follow the law and head for the palace's official induction ceremony, or they are eventually found and dragged to the Pit. Which means I need to get out of here, out of Abai, one way or another.

It's barely nightfall when Amir and I spot it: a rickety box-shaped cart on wheels. It's attached to a horse, but there's no owner to be seen. Painted on the side of the cart is Abai's crest, a snake slithering toward a crown.

"Royals." The word sticks to my throat, scrapes along my tongue. This cart is for King Natesh and Queen Maneet.

Amir takes a cautious step toward the cart, but I pull him back with a forceful hand. "What're you doing?"

Amir only smiles his trademark smile, mischief swirled with a dollop of anticipation.

Before I can speak, he's picked the lock with the tip of his blade. The back doors of the cart swing open from a gust of warm wind, revealing piles of fresh kharbooja.

My eyes bulge. The melons make my mouth pool with saliva.

Amir takes another step forward. "Must be for Diwali. You know, the party." He eyes me and mock-gags.

"Some party." I roll my eyes just thinking about it. Diwali is a time of celebration and good fortune. But only Abai's richest will attend, even the ones who despise the raja. And not just for his politics either—it's the tension that flares every time Kaama is brought up in a conversation, the hearts that pump at the thought of the princess ever showing her face.

She hasn't in years. Not once has she left the grounds of that pristine palace. In turn, the royals have become little more than a myth. Nearly, because if there's any proof of them, it's Mama Anita's stories. And the Charts.

Some say the princess doesn't show her face because she's half snake, half human. Some say instead of teeth, she bares fangs that drip scarlet blood, that she can rip hope from your soul with just one puncture.

If the rumors are true, I'd rather not know.

Amir strides toward the cart and reaches inside, pulling out a piece of fresh fruit. Its skin is clean, with no rot or dent marks to be found. As if the entire cart has been untouched by filthy villagers' hands. Hands like mine.

I shake away the thought, survey the wide array of melons, and gather up a few in my palms. Amir joins me, takes a few into his hands, and gives me a look, complete with a dipped eyebrow and a single dimple on his cheek.

"What's your plan? Steal a couple of melons and sell 'em? You know these are dirt cheap, right," I say.

"Not *dirt* cheap, exactly," Amir says. "After all, we are in Nabh. But . . ." He brings his gaze to the white mount. "Ever thought of stealing a horse?"

*Stealing a horse?* "Afraid not."

Eyes gleaming, Amir leans back and rests a hand on the cart door's wooden handle. "What about stealing this cart and riding the horse to the border? We'll pretend we're delivering the melons to Amratstan—"

I jab an elbow into his ribs, and he presses a hand against his torso, feigning hurt.

"Yeah, and when the Charts see Abai's crest, we'll be good as dead. Weren't *you* the one who told me about the king's snakes? Worse than a sword through the chest . . . gut-ripping . . ."

"Think about it," he offers.

To my surprise, he's as serious as I've ever seen him. "You're not kidding." I tap my foot and say, "Let's say we *did* steal this horse. We don't have identification markers. And we'd need fake passports."

Amir laughs. "So we steal some jewels and use those to pay for fake passports before we reach the border! No big deal. Did you forget? You knew how to pick a lock better than me before I taught you the tricks of the trade. You're the best damn thief in Abai, Ria.

Small and nimble as a mouse. No one notices a mouse."

"Unless you're a cat," I point out. "And where would we get the jewels from, anyway?"

Amir eyes the crest. "No place better for a heist than that raja-damned palace."

Now I'm the one laughing. "Didn't you see my name on the conscription list? If I go there, I'll just fall into their hands. And what about that Diwali party tomorrow?"

Amir's eyes sparkle. "It's the perfect opportunity. The royals will be too distracted with the party and all the extra people there. They'll never know you were one of the hundreds of names on that list! We get in, we get some jewels, we get out."

"We? There is no *we*," I retort. I think of all those pretty jewels locked up in the palace and nearly drool but snap out of it. "You're not gonna risk *your* life—"

"I'd rather risk my life here than never escape," he cuts in, gaze unflinching. "I'd rather fight weaponless than never try."

I'm quiet after that. Nothing except the sounds of our ragged breathing, of the thought—or maybe even thrill—of a heist. The biggest we've ever pulled. Am I insane for thinking that way? For wanting to believe him, for just a moment?

Stealing naan is one thing. But jewels from the palace itself . . .

Who knows what I might be able to snag in there? A pocketful of rubies? With those, we could get a boat to Amratstan or a cara-van to Retan. We could get those fake passports, pretend my name was never on that conscription list.

It's no secret Abai's border is closing the day the truce ends. Some say the treaty will be renewed, that we don't have a thing to worry about, but I know different. I know war is on the way, can taste it like salt on a sea breeze.

My stomach growls as I think about the melons inside the cart. *Just one bite . . .*

"If we're gonna do this, we've got to be smart about it," I say. "We need to get there soon, before the Charts expect all their recruits to arrive in Anari. Now, I can run fast like nobody's business. You, on the other hand, are noticeable. Good at distraction. If one of us can get in and out, it's me."

"Now we're talkin'." Amir jumps aboard, and the cart sways. I suck in a gasp, but the horse doesn't move. "C'mon," he urges.

I follow. Leaping onto the cart, I hunch down so I don't hit the wooden ceiling with my head. My trousers ride up, revealing the scar on my left leg I got five months ago. I was on the run outside of Nabh and given a lashing for stealing a petty bowl of paneer. Instead of evading my captor, I'd turned around to taunt him and instantly tripped over a bucket full of bathwater. Now the feeling of the scar is a reminder: Don't look back. Never stop running.

In seconds, I hear it: the huff of an old man, trudging his way across the dirt-laden grounds.

"Hide!" I whisper. Amir moves to close the cart doors. When the rickety doors are shut, we shift to the corners of the cart, where there are just enough slits for air.

The next thing we hear is a lock latching closed, wheels beneath us screeching forward.

"Raja's b—" Amir begins, but I clamp a hand against his mouth before he can say more.

The melons skitter to one side as we round a sharp corner. Amir and I fall back, and my spine connects with the door. I peer through the slits between the slabs of wood.

After a good while, the roads change. They're not the dark, gritty ones of Nabh. No—they're clean. Lotus flowers and plants bloom along the streets. There are no weeds here except for Amir and me.

I shut my eyes, but all I see are those damned Charts, their coats red as blood. The raja's snakes, hissing at his side. We're in Anari, the capital of Abai.

I wipe my sweat-stamped palms on my legs and swallow down my thoughts, my heart *thump thump thump*ing. My breath shudders in—and saws out. *Steal the royal jewels. Get out of Abai once and for all.*

This is it. We're headed to the palace.

# 4

## Rani

My earliest memory of Tutor is also my fondest: a night wrapped in the stars, Tutor and I tucked in the courtyards beneath a gauzy mosquito net. The net made me feel safe, as though nothing and no one could touch us.

"Your kingdom belongs to its people," he told me after a long lesson on historic Abaian rulers, closing the pocket-sized book in his hands, "as much as it belongs to you."

"I thought everything belonged to Father," I replied matter-of-factly. Eight-year-old me didn't mind being so outspoken, especially when Father was away on one of his official trips to Amratstan like he had been that night. I toyed with the tiara Mother had given me a few days prior.

Tutor put down his book, the cover a luminous jade, then took the tiara from my hands and gently placed it on my head. "You are to be queen someday. That is a great responsibility."

I scrunched up my eyebrows. "I don't want responsibility."

Tutor's laugh was brash and melodic all the same. "Did I ever tell you of Queen Amrita?"

I shook my head.

"She ruled hundreds of years ago as one of Abai's first ranis. Her first rule as queen was to provide education widely across her land—new schools and books made for the youth, and for young girls especially. She wanted to create change. You, dear Rani—you can make whatever change you desire. Always remember this: *You can be more than what the stars wish for. More than you ever dreamed.*"

Tutor's mantra echoed in my ears. "More?"

He touched his ring, almost absently. He once told me his wife had a matching band. Though he did not know it, I thought him my true father, someone who wrapped me in warm hugs and wove stories from thin air until I fell asleep. Someone who believed in me and the queen I could become. The queen I fear I'll never be.

A clang from the palace kitchens and the smell of simmering daal jolt me back to the present. I berate myself for daydreaming in the throne room.

The place where everything went wrong yesterday.

*Kill.*

One command to seal his fate. That word meant death. That word meant falling into the Snake Pit. That word meant Tutor shall never breathe again.

His last words to me echo like a clanging bell. *Find it . . . the stone . . .* Perhaps he was speaking of a simple gemstone in the treasury, but something tells me he meant something greater. His mentioning Queen Amrita must be important, too; or perhaps it was the panicked ramblings of a man about to die. Perhaps I'm reaching for something that is not there.

I swallow down my guilt and glance around the throne room. It's early evening of Diwali now, and frilly decorations fill the air. Servants glide past, carrying trays of fruit and lavish foods for tonight's meal. The palace has completely transformed, lit up for the Diwali celebrations.

More servants swarm around the throne room, and some decorate the double doors leading to the Western Courtyard. I catch sight of the grand map of our world along the eastern wall. In the northeast sits Kaama, above the strict line bordering its kingdom and mine.

*Soon to be* my kingdom; I do not want it to be mine anytime soon. I am no Queen Amrita, even if I'm meant to marry Saeed. He may have been a good teacher, but love was different altogether. Love, unlike history, is unteachable.

*Is it?*

Shima's words slip into my mind as easily as Saeed had once slipped a promise ring onto my finger. I spin around to find her lying across the threshold.

"Eavesdropper," I tell her.

She smiles a viper's smile. *Thought I couldn't hear you?*

I arch a brow. "I never said that." Or thought it, for that matter. Shima always glides into my mind without warning. There are boundaries to our bond—communicating only when Shima's

SISTERS OF THE SNAKE

near, for one. When I first chose her as my familiar and began my training, I lost control of her, thinking of ripping up the out-of-style lehengas in my closet. Not long after, Shima's fangs had torn through the precious skirts. I learned my lesson that day, that keeping my mind shut off from Shima is just as important as keeping it open. Even now, controlling snakes is something only Father has mastered. There's a reason people call him the Great Snakespeaker, one of the most gifted kings in centuries. I, on the other hand, have not earned such a title.

Shima exhales and finally uncoils herself. She slithers and slides toward me, her forked tongue flickering. *Good*, she replies.

The air chills around me, and an icy current sweeps through my blood. Shima twists her body to face the throne room entrance. Where Saeed stands, eyes drenched with memories of first love.

First love gone wrong.

I once ached to see Saeed every morning, holding towers of books for the day's lesson. At twenty, two years my senior, his frame is tall, his curly hair bouncy, tempting my fingers to tangle within the curls. His thick eyebrows are two curtains that sweep over his hazel eyes, dip with concern, or—this one I liked the most—lift when I would give him surprise kisses in the palace's hidden corridors.

My heartbeat rises to my ears and a flush grows over my cheeks.

*Looks like you're not as icy as you think, Princess.* At my blush, Shima's scales tint pink, and petal-sized patches of rose bloom along her scales.

*Quiet*, I snap as I stalk past her and toward Saeed. He leans against the doorway with an air of arrogance.

"I haven't seen you all day," he says once I'm within earshot. "The servants have been avoiding you too, it seems."

"They've always been scared around me," I snap, more a confession than a retort. "If they think me the Snake Princess, then cold-blooded I'll be."

Saeed narrows his gaze. "You don't mean that."

"I do. And I told you I don't need any more lessons, didn't I?" My words are bitter with hatred, burnt like the prospect of my freedom. My future is sealed, locked, the key thrown into an abyss of lies. "I turned eighteen just a moon ago."

He fingers an unclosed button at his collar, feeling the seashell between his fingertips. I remember a time when I once held those fingers, when they'd run their way through my hair, when they'd grazed my lips with the gentlest touch.

"You don't need lessons?" he asks. "Or you want a new tutor?"

"Both."

"The two are mutually exclusive."

"I'll *un*make them mutually exclusive."

"Despite the number of lessons we've had in probability, I'm not sure you remember what that term means."

I huff. Just because Saeed is right doesn't mean I'm going to give him the satisfaction of it.

Saeed arrived at the palace at two summers of age, around the time I was born, with his mother, Amara. His father had just passed, and Mother allowed him a place to stay with Amara in the palace. It wasn't long before the two of us were promised to each other. Neither one of us had any say in it.

My future mother-in-law has been Mother's friend for longer than I have been alive, even longer than my parents have known each other. Although Saeed and I were bound for betrothal once we grew up, our lives were anything but similar.

At first, we were playmates, scrambling around the palace, climbing like monkeys together into the rafters.

Then, when we grew, Saeed was taken away. Homeschooled by his mother in candlelit corridors, while I had a private tutor and towers for classrooms. Saeed chatted among noblemen with ease, while I was told to hold my tongue at the aunties' palace gossip. We lived in the same palace but might as well have resided in different kingdoms.

After Tutor left four years ago, Father instructed Saeed to become my new tutor. By then, we were strangers. I can hardly remember our first lesson; I was too distracted by how much he'd grown. After a few lessons, I asked Saeed to teach me outside. It wasn't long before Father's stipulations grew harsher than usual. Horseback riding and fencing became dangerous sports; the Abai sun would burn my skin; if I were seen, commoners would manipulate my image. Better to stay away from a world that ridicules us. A world filled with untold dangers.

At the time, Saeed's hair was shorn, barely displaying the crown of curls he wears now. I remember the way he looked at me the night of my fifteenth birthday—like I was one of the world's first

Masters, a being above all others.

His superior.

"You know I've never had an affinity for arithmetic," I tell him. I dare a glance into his eyes, and I remember exactly what I saw in him all those years ago. It took but a half-moon for his lessons to become spells, each one drawing me closer to him, until I thought about him daily.

*He* would be my adventure, I decided. A worthy one, with the way his hair shone in the light. The way his hazel eyes lingered on my own. And not long after, the way his skin felt against mine—the softness of his full, full lips.

Saeed clears his throat. "Then, may I ask, Princess . . . what—or whom—do you have an affinity for?" His cheeks rouge, mirroring Shima's scales. My heart flips in my chest. I do not know what to tell him. When I was younger, his mother, Amara, began taking me to the women's room to talk. She started with easy questions—my birthdate, my astrological sign. Then came the harder questions: *How many boys have you kissed?* Zero. *What are your aspirations?* I was unsure. *Would you be a faithful spouse?*

Saeed Gupta. He was always destined to be my husband and king consort. I would write his name in my notebooks when he wasn't looking. I would draw frivolous hearts around his initials. I would write my own name in ink, its permanence a sickening thought now, using Saeed's last name as part of my own, Singh.

I berate myself for thinking of it. "No one," I tell him firmly. I adjust the gold necklace my parents gave me as a present. It once felt light, but now it weighs a hundred pounds.

Saeed brings a finger to it, thumbing the precious jewels. He leans forward, his lips dangerously close. He is playing at something—another one of his games. I used to like them. Now they mean nothing.

He breathes against my ear, his hand gently coming down to my wrist. He leaves his fingers there for a moment, and I wait for that jolt of heat, that inexplicable feeling that filled my chest for so many years.

But no—instead I feel ice. And that's exactly what I want to feel.

"You're scared," he whispers, resting his eyes on mine. I don't waver in my gaze. He rests one hand on my cheek, and for a moment I close my eyes and relax against him. "What happened to us, Rani?" His voice cracks with hurt.

I splay a hand on his chest and push back gently. "Nothing." *Everything.*

He moves to cradle my neck but does not kiss me. His breath is perfumed with mint and candied fennel seeds.

Gently, he pulls away, something deeper than disappointment behind his eyes. I recognize it, the hesitation before he says something I don't want to hear. I should have known his banter was merely a way to hide his true feelings. He is covering something up. "What's wrong?" I ask him.

Saeed sighs. "Rani, I've been meaning to tell you something. I knew last night wasn't a good time, and now . . ."

I hold my breath. The words I've wanted him to say, finally. *I love you, Rani. I love you more than the stars love the sky.*

"I . . . ," he starts before courtiers bustle into the room. Whatever Saeed wanted to tell me, the moment is over.

I conceal my disappointment. "I must go."

Saeed takes my hands. "Rani, wait—"

Unable to handle another moment of his traitorous touch, I push past him and run up to my room. I move to shut the door and notice Shima has already beat me to it. She blends herself into the purple carpet and hugs her body tight, her scales mirroring the lilac-colored confusion filling my heart.

"Come here," I say, hating the way my voice cracks. A labored breath spills from my throat as I sink into my bed's silky cushions, letting Shima wrap around my right arm. For the first time in the past few days, my heart calms.

Ever since my Bonding Ceremony five years ago, Shima has been my snake familiar, the snake with whom I have the deepest connection and companionship. As a child of a snakespeaker, I could communicate with other snakes before I bonded with her but never felt quite a kinship with them. Shima is the only being in this palace who knows my true wants and desires, as if they are hers, too. Deep down, she knows the question I ask myself every night: Will I ever be like Queen Amrita? Or will I end up like Father?

I dig my fingernails into the bed's sides. I reach into my magic the way I was taught, envisioning the subsets of snake magic like a chest of drawers, each a compartment filled with a different force. I tug on the one I want, the one that allows me to channel my will to Shima's. *Don't constrict. Obey.*

The maids have left me a snake venom tincture on my bedside table. A numbing agent to help me rest before the party tonight. I take a long gulp and fall back on the bed.

It's not long before I drift to sleep. In my dream, I imagine Saeed's soft lips, his hair, his forever-tanned skin. I see him falling into the Pit instead of Tutor, Shima's fangs sinking deep into him—

I jerk up in bed and clasp my wrist, finding the empty space where Shima was curled around me.

"Shima?" I call. There is no answer.

What was I dreaming of? The snakes in the Pit, preparing for a fresh kill . . . No—it had been Saeed in the Pit, his flesh punctured with Shima's two fangs.

I gasp. In seconds, I'm sprinting out of my room, bare feet slapping against marble. Ashen pillars flash past me on all sides, and I feel Shima slithering through these halls, silent save for her hiss of death.

*Stop*, I think. I can speak to Shima easily, but when her bloodlust takes over, it's as though she's shed her skin for something unrelenting. Something crueler.

I pause in the middle of a hall studded with gems, red and rich as crisp apple rinds. I spin around and search everywhere for my snake familiar. But I'm too late.

Shima is going to do what I imagined. She's going to poison Saeed.

# 5

## Ria

Amir and I wake to light piercing the sky through a break in the wooden ceiling. As the carriage made its way across uneven plains last night, we eventually found sleep. But now we've stopped moving, and as I peer out the slats of wood, I know we've arrived. Far gone are we from Nabh, from the clanking of steel cups holding fresh lassi, from the smell of dirt after rainfall. From the world of villagers and peasants, grimy roads and sunken eyes.

A cool breeze slides through the wood's cracks. The sun is sitting far past its zenith, and I guess it must be early evening. How could Amir and I have slept for so long?

"Wake up," I say, shoving Amir's shoulder. He's way too groggy to function, like he always is after a long nap. I fiddle with the back door, but it won't budge.

I shove my pack aside and start throwing melons at the back door. After a few heavy throws, it begins to creak. Split. It pains me to throw this perfectly good food, but we need to get out of

SISTERS OF THE SNAKE

here. I don't know how long we've been sleeping and wasting time, or when the owner will be back.

Amir's eyes finally flutter open. "Hey! That's our lunch."

"Grab a melon and help," I snap. Taken aback, Amir does as I say. The doors are ajar now, the space in between allowing me to view the heavy chain binding us to this prison. I pull the chain toward me until the lock tumbles inside, fiddle with it using one of Mama Anita's plain hairpins, but the lock won't budge. I practiced picking locks with fervor at the orphanage—to Mama Anita's dismay—but now my hands are trembling, an ache of hunger in my stomach as familiar as a friend.

I throw the lock back out in frustration just as an idea springs to mind. I take a few deep breaths as wind slides through the wooden slats. Then I start banging on the wooden doors, rapping my knuckles so hard they nearly bleed. After I hear a sharp intake of breath from outside, I stop.

Amir glances at me like I've grown a third eye. "Please tell me you're not trying to get us thrown in the Pit."

"Just grab a melon and wait," I tell him. I roll one into my hand and hold my breath as shadows eclipse the doors. A man comes into view, shoving a key into the lock.

As soon as the doors creak open, I leap out and toss the melon. Target hit.

The man crumples to the ground. "Raja's beard!" he swears. Before he can get a good look at me, Amir grabs me by the arm and we pump our legs into the thick of the Moga Jungle and away from the palace road, where coconut trees jut into the sky like fists and tamarind plants litter the nearest clearing. I dive between the leaves, taking in the scent: musk and sap. My chunni catches on a two-pronged branch, sharp as fingernails. There's a gap in the fabric, like a fatal wound. Too bad. It's my favorite of my nonexistent collection.

Amir and I pause only when we're sure it's safe, the man nowhere in sight. When I look up, gasping for air, the tip-top of the palace comes into view, sharp and cruel and knifelike.

"We shouldn't stay in the jungle long." I wipe my hands on my trousers. "There're tigers and—"

"Snakes. I know." Before he can lock his mouth shut, Amir says, "C'mon—are we stealing jewels or what?"

I shrug the pack off my shoulder. It's too bulky to run with, but I've sewn hidden pockets into my salwar. A suit made for a thief. "We don't have much time. I've heard rumors about the jewels in the palace. Maybe if I can find the queen's chamber, I can swipe what we need and get out fast." I toss my pack to him. "You keep watch."

"Keep watch?" he says. "Those bloodcoats will be so preoccupied with *my* distraction that your part of the job will be easy." Then he tightens his mouth. "Are you sure you want to go in alone?"

"Did you hit your head on a melon? I'm quick on my toes, and much smaller than you. No one notices a mouse," I tease. Amir might be lanky, but he's roughshod, and his scar'll get him noticed just about anywhere. "So, what've you got in mind?"

He whispers the plan in my ear. I hesitate, searching for Amir's single dimple or his traitorous grin to tell me this is all a joke. That going into the palace is truly a death mission, one I shouldn't risk.

But then again: no risk, no jewels, and definitely no way out.

My stomach swirls. "Be safe. I'll be back soon."

Without turning back, I head to the palace courtyards, where servants are busy setting up ivory tents. Beyond that, gardens of fresh fruit and flowers adorn the palace's exterior, as if the lavishness could cover up the rot inside. I scurry through the long alley leading up to the palace, a sidewalk crammed with beggars and open hands. Beggars aren't only in Nabh, I realize; they're here, by the palace, seeking a way in but always pushed out.

*No. There's still a chance. Like Amir said—strike fast. Get in, get out.*

I continue on, using the trees as cover, and peer out for Charts every few seconds. When I'm close enough to the palace gates, I spot a boy no older than me approaching a Chart, head lowered as he hands something to the soldier. Behind the boy, a man and woman weep, hands clutched fiercely together. The boy's parents, I suppose. The Chart leads the boy off to the side, where he inspects the family crest sewn onto a spare bit of cloth. It's an identification marker, and he flips it over to read the boy's name on the back. Almost everyone in Abai has one, along with a passport if they're rich enough. But not me, not Amir.

The Chart nods as he finds the boy's name on a scroll. I hold in a gasp. This boy is here for conscription.

I stumble away from the scene, trying to push aside how young the boy looked, how tightly his parents clung to each other, turning to the gates. A long line of women protect their eyes from the sun with chunnis. I shield my own face with my chunni and step out to see a fountain—*the* fountain. The Fountain of Fortunes.

I called it the Fountain of Lies and Illusions as a child, thinking it to be an old wives' tale. The story goes that the fountain was forged by Amran and granted a sliver of mindwielding abilities thanks to the Memory Master, before the kingdoms were created and back when the Masters shared their gifts and powers. Now the royals use it as a fortune-teller, offering visions of the future to those who dare look into its waters.

I roll my eyes. As if any of *that* is true.

I bring my gaze to the fountain. It's double my size, with gold inscriptions of all-seeing eyes drawn over the marble. I peer inside, expecting to see a waste of coins swimming at the bottom, ones I could pluck as easily as ripe fruit. But instead, there's only rippling water clear as crystals. I haven't ever seen water like that: untouched, pure. A woman beside me shudders and rushes off in tears.

Maybe her fortune wasn't as lucky as she thought.

"Follow the raja's orders!" A row of gold-sashed Charts bark commands at palace servants. "Only a few hours left until the Diwali celebration!"

I glance down and see that the water has become a rippling mirror. Lit diyas float on the water's edge, and I grasp the edges of the basin as my reflection shimmers away to reveal a man I've never seen in my life. He has curly hair tucked behind his ears and . . . his eyes. They're hazel-gold, like fresh lemon achaar. I find myself inching closer to the water.

His face vanishes as quickly as it came, replaced with a mysterious voice, penetrating my mind:

*Danger lies before you. A switch in the stars' alignment, a change of fortune, could lead you to great peril.*

I nearly jump back. This fountain must be some kind of prank. A trick on us villagers. But then how can I hear this strange voice so clearly, telling prophecies inside my head?

"This fortune is absurd," I mutter. As absurd as me wearing an elegant sari, or Amir wearing a crown fit for a raja. As absurd as believing Mama Anita could ever come back to me, whole and alive.

A servant boy approaches, sneaking a glance at the fountain.

"Hey!" a Chart shouts, nearing the boy. I freeze, pull my chunni lower to cover my face. I'm reminded of Two Thirteen yesterday, the gleaming pins on his coat, the neatly arranged tassels. The Chart saunters over, grabs the servant boy by the collar, and dumps him on the ground. The boy hits the stone with a thwack, scraping his bony knees. "What were you doing over there? You should be in the palace."

Then the Chart pulls out a whip.

I don't think I'm breathing. I'm thrust back to five moons ago, the lash whipping against my leg so hard it broke skin. I blink away the sound, the memories, the blood. The Chart moves to bring his whip down on the boy's legs—

Until another servant rushes to the boy's side, apologies tumbling from his cracked lips.

Everyone stares, mouths agape at the servant's audacity. But the soldier must be in a giving mood, because he returns the whip to his side and jerks his chin to the palace's front gates. The servants are smart enough to run off, just as the Chart turns to the line of wallowing villagers by the fountain. To me.

I stumble back, rush away from the fountain and into the nearest brush, and remind myself of my mission. Without these jewels, there's no way we're getting out of Abai before the treaty ends and war breaks out. All week, vendors in Nabh have been gossiping about the war—about how the treaty will never be renewed because the raja's a war-hungry animal. But we won't have to worry about war once we're gone.

Out of the corner of my eye, Amir appears. "*Go*," he mouths.

Quick as lightning, Amir leaps out of the forest brush, cutting through the Charts' path. He turns to the soldiers, sticking out his tongue and wiggling his fingers next to his head, taunting them. People stumble back, mouths agape.

"Over there!" a Chart yells. The soldier rushes after him. But Amir's fast, weaving through the trees and taunting the Charts all around the palace gates. For a moment, I break into a smile, until I find Amir again.

Running toward *me*.

I pull myself away, cover my head with my chunni, and sprint. Past children, past a cluster of gossiping elderly women, until I'm close to the front gates. I grab onto the nearest tree and lift myself up to the lowest branch, then the next, moments before Charts barrel through the brush below me, just an arm's length away.

I pick up flecks of their conversation: *Diwali . . . fountain . . . peasants . . .*

My arms grow weak as I struggle to hold the thin branches.

"Oy," a Chart calls. "What are you doing up there?"

A harsh tug on my leg. I crash to the ground face-first. Pain explodes across my skull, rattling my teeth.

*I'm dead. I'm worse than dead.*

I cover my face again before the Chart pulls me up, clasping his hand around my wrist like a cuff. Words spill from my mouth. "I—my—s—"

Without a word, the Chart drags me through the gates, up the front steps of the palace. There, his brows narrow, and the Chart releases me, eyes finally finding mine. He does something bewildering.

He bows.

*What in the—*

My thoughts deflate. I don't have time to think of the Chart's idiocy. Or was it mockery? Did he take one look at my clothes and think a bow would be funny?

But then the Chart does something even more astounding. He gestures at the arched front entrance and says, "You should be inside."

Skies, am I hearing right?

He probably thinks I'm another servant. But if that's true and the servants aren't meant to be outside, why hasn't this Chart pulled a weapon on me like the other soldier did to that boy?

*Doesn't matter*, I imagine Amir saying. *Use this to your advantage. Get in, get out.*

I duck my head low and do as I'm told—run into the one place I've always hated, and that's always hated me.

# 6

## Rani

I rush through the halls, legs burning, craving a moment to relax my strained muscles. I can smell the Pit, worse than ever.

*Stop, Shima*, I think, though I can taste the bloodlust she feels. Her thirst is my own.

I call upon the Snake Master—every snakespeaker knows invoking the Master's name helps one connect more strongly to their magic—but it's no use. I am too late.

Amara is standing outside Saeed's door. With one hand, she blots a tear from her cheek with the fabric of her sari. Pinned to her blouse is her favorite flower, a rose with razor-like thorns. Her eyeliner is precise, sharp enough to cut. "*You* did this," she says.

I push past her into Saeed's room. My heart thuds, thuds, thuds in my chest.

*Shima, what have you done?*

Saeed is sitting on his bed, wearing the same outfit I saw him in hours ago. What shocks me is not Shima. She wraps around his throat but does not constrict. What shocks me is my parents, both here, eye bags heavy.

Father growls. "Rani, what is the meaning of—"

"I—I didn't think Shima was listening—"

"But what? She read your deepest thoughts? It is not enough to say that, daughter." Mother approaches me in three short strides. She raises her hand as if to slap me but then lowers it, her voice like sugar. "Rani, beta, you have a gift. Shima listens to you. Shima understands you. You must learn to *control* her."

"I know." I glue my eyes to the floor, tears blurring my vision. I detest looking weak in front of my mother. The woman who has always reminded me that magic is a gift, that being born in the royal bloodline is a blessing like no other. That my learning snake-speak has taken long years of practice and hardship.

Mother married into this life. She shall never know what magic tastes like: the coppery tang that hits the back of my cheeks, the iron-salt aftertaste when Shima's had a bite of a new kill.

Mother will never understand. Magic is not a gift. It is a burden.

*Shima, please stop*, I tell her. I bring up that wall again in my mind, not to block her out this time but to keep her in. It isn't until then that Shima slithers back to me. The entire room lets out a sigh of relief, as if the tension were cut with a talwar. Amara dashes over to Saeed, blabbering and clutching his shoulders with more drama than necessary.

My mother and Amara have been friends for nearly twenty-five years; as Mother's closest confidante, Amara is always present in the palace. Still, she was seen as a black sheep among her husband's family: half Kaaman, half Abaian, caught between two distant worlds. The last choice for a wife, silt among diamonds. She would routinely leave Kaama to visit Mother, while her husband was on missions in the Kaaman army. It was Amara who prodded Mother into meeting the raja while he first searched for suitors. Father knew Mother would be queen as soon as he met her—a fated fairy tale. A repulsive one, I realize now: I owe Amara my very existence.

She brought my parents together. My parents, who have become cold, distant, merciless.

"This shall not happen again, Amara." Father spins to me. "There's always something with you, isn't there, Rani? If I am in a delegation meeting with Retan, or . . ."

I want to roll my eyes. Father cares for no kingdom but his own and despises Kaama most of all. It doesn't matter that Kaama is known mostly to be a peaceful kingdom. For the past hundred years, war has stalled but never stopped. It's been simmering below the surface, and now it is about to burst.

Father stands taller, breathing through his nose the way Mother tells him to when he's frustrated. He continues, "We have everyone—and everything—under control."

"Yes," Amara says after a sniffle. "Except for *Rani*. A Chart just informed me she was outside the gates. Probably trying to put distance between herself and the scene of the crime." Her gaze hovers on Shima.

"You were outside?" Mother asks.

"No, I was *not*." Another one of Amara's lies. Mother and Father turn to me. Even Saeed bores his eyes into mine, except they're not questioning or cold. They're pitying. Why would Saeed pity me when I almost—accidentally—took his life?

"Look at how Amara pays attention to the world around her," Father scolds me. "Look at how she notices. And you? Thinking of snake fangs when you should be preparing for tonight."

My blood boils. "Father, I—"

"Amara has always had a great interest in politics," he continues. "And so I have named her my new adviser as we begin to prepare for war. She is the only person in this palace who has shown the interest, or aptitude, to aid me in my endeavors." There's a wistfulness in his voice as he says it.

"What?" I start. *Father's adviser?* "But Amara—"

"As such," he cuts in, "neither she nor I will have time for this nonsense in the future. Make sure it doesn't happen again."

"And you will do as Amara says to make up for this. She is Amara-*ji* to you. Do you understand?" Mother emphasizes the honorific, eyes leaving no room for remorse. Neither do mine.

"Fine," I relent. One word. Clipped. Harsh.

"Good," Mother says. "Now let's forget this ever happened and enjoy the party."

Amid the drama of Shima's near-kill of Saeed, I forgot about the celebrations downstairs. Father and Mother filter out of the room. When they're gone, I turn to Saeed, ignoring Amara's piercing stare behind my back, and reach out to him with a hand to his elbow. "I . . . apologize," I say, though the words are half baked. "I was having a dream. I never meant for things to go this far."

Though the words are but a whisper, they hold more than one meaning. *I never meant for Shima to hurt you. I never meant for us to reach this point in love.*

Love. That word does not feel right. It does not feel truthful. Saeed gazes at me now, but even still, his eyes are distant. It isn't the first time I've seen this from him—a gaping hole between us that will never be filled, no matter how sweetly his lips call to mine.

Saeed swallows but does not answer me. He leaves the room like I haven't said a word.

Heat reaches my cheeks. Amara reaches me in quick strides, tears entirely dried. If there were any to begin with.

She grabs my chin and digs sharp nails into my cheeks. I bristle but stand firm, having dealt with this before. "You mean to hurt my son, but it is not working."

"I never meant to hurt him," I retort.

Amara lets go and gently thumbs the decorative rose on her blouse. Roses are a gift in Abai, grown and cultivated in the royal gardens for oils, baths, and of course, love. It is no secret to palace gossips that Amara received a basket of roses from her husband on her wedding eve. She keeps them close to this day.

She puckers her red lips stained with betel nut. "You know, Rani, you're not much different than I. You have drive. Ambition. Desire."

*A kingdom to rule*, I add silently. A flawed destiny. Blood of royalty—a life Amara could never understand.

"You are no princess. Your decisions do not weigh as heavily as mine, or Father's, or Mother's," I sneer. But perhaps her decisions *do* matter now, as Father's adviser. How could Father trust the word of Amara more than mine?

"I am the royal adviser now. You will do as I say, *Rani*." She says my name as if I'm nothing more than a child, as if my name bears no weight. Sometimes I wish I was named anything other than Queen. That my name did not mark my fate.

"Now," Amara huffs, "that was quite a feat yesterday, I must admit." She examines the wealth of rings on her fingers. Her golden cuffed bracelets wink in the streaming moonlight. "The execution. The way you avoided snuffing out that tutor's life."

Something cool and sharp stabs at my chest. She's taunting me, telling me what I already know. I could not kill Tutor. And yet the gravity of Father's order sits like a weight on my chest. Tutor's death is as much my fault as it is his.

"It is as you said," Amara continues. "Your decisions weigh heavier than mine."

"Stop," I spit, bile lodged in my throat.

"A princess's first kill is never easy to forget. And against your own instructor, no less." A twisted smile spreads over her face. "Shame you couldn't spare him entirely. But I suppose you spared your conscience."

I think of Tutor, of his wife filled with grief. Of the ring he gave me after his final words.

*Find the stone.*

My throat is lined with glass. "Don't waste another breath, Amara-ji."

She only grins and saunters out the door to join the party.

I gather the folds of my hem, rush back to my room, and throw on a blue sari. Its threads itch at my skin, but I ignore them, if only for what just happened—Amara's chat with me, Shima nearly poisoning Saeed.

*Do you still love him?* Shima says from behind me.

I ignore the question. "I was only looking out for you. What if you killed Saeed, and Amara ordered you to death?"

*If I were to die, your soul and body would weaken, Princess Rani. You would not be strong enough to survive it. They wouldn't harm me*, Shima states. The snake slithers closer to the door. *Perhaps you should tell Saeed why you left him.*

"I left him because we only loved each other on the surface."

*Not entirely*, she hisses. *You left him because you were afraid he never loved you. And even truer, Rani, is that you want to part from the life being handed to you.*

I bite my tongue. Abai's sun, how I hate Shima's ability to read my thoughts. No—her ability to read my *emotions*. The difference is infinitely big.

I dash to my window and breathe in the balmy air, remember the feeling of warmth drenched on my skin like honey. Outside, the fountain gurgles. The only day the villagers can peer into it and see their futures is on Diwali, the day the fountain's fortunes are strongest. Father says it is the Memory Master's voice that imparts these magical predictions.

I don't need a fountain to tell me what my future will hold.

I turn away. Tutor's ring sits on my vanity, burnished gold and glaring at me. I take it into my hands, turning it over in my fingers. A symbol—a stalk of leaves—sits in the center. Once again, familiarity flutters in my chest. Where have I seen this symbol before?

I rush into my closet, flipping through an endless stack of books. Their pages are yellow, worn, the titles beginning to fade. Some are dry old history books. Instructions in mathematics.

Some are filled with old fables Tutor read to me before bed.

My eyes well with tears, but I move onward. No distractions. I must pursue Tutor's last wish. I must learn what he meant when he gave me this ring.

Peering out from the end of the stack is a pocket-sized, jade-colored notebook. Shock floods my veins when I catch sight of the cover.

It's the same plant on the ring. A stalk of leaves with a burst of sun hidden behind it.

I rush through the pages. It's a botany journal—a study of plants that Tutor and I kept many years ago. I flip until I find an exact copy of the image, and when I do, I sigh. This is no regular plant. It's one that grows only in the cooler northern climate. *The Mailan Foothills are known for their abundant plant-producing fields, among their grassy backdrop,* the book explains in minuscule font. On the side of the page is squished handwriting that I recognize immediately as Tutor's, along with a strange set of symbols and numbers I cannot decipher.

It all hits me at once. Is this where Tutor ran away to? The Mailan Foothills? He'd spoken to me of the life he'd left behind, of the fields where he'd first fallen in love.

He gave me his ring for a reason—did he mean for me to find this page? This writing? This place?

Clearly he was hiding something, but I can't quite figure out what these symbols, this code, means. Father says he was a traitor. If that is true, shouldn't we know his secrets?

Tutor's wish has spurred something within me. A longing to prove myself to Father. *I* could show the interest and the aptitude to help him in his endeavors. I could be more than idle Princess Rani.

I decide. I will follow Tutor's greatest wish, not just for him, not just for my kingdom—but for *me*.

I push the rest of the books back into the closet. With my plan firmly set in place and Tutor's notebook in hand, I rush to the throne room and search for Father. It's full to the brim with people wearing saris and lehengas, tunics and kurtas. When it's clear Father is not inside, I head for the Western Courtyard, where Father will make tonight's speech to his guests. Manicured shrubs and flowers greet me, followed by a cascading waterfall to my left. Candles and diyas, holding fistfuls of flames, are laid out across the grounds. More servants rush past me and bow, wearing verdant clothes to signify their devotion and subservience to the king and queen.

I head deeper into the courtyard. But before I can find Father, whispers strike the air like a slap.

"Is that . . ."

"It cannot be . . ."

"The princess . . ."

Women with too-big earrings and ostentatious necklaces halt me with manicured fingernails. "My dear girl, so pretty . . . Why not show that face of yours more?"

I bristle at a woman's touch. Only nobles and a few Charts in the palace have seen my face, which makes me tonight's biggest attraction.

"I have the perfect boy for you!" another says.

"No, no, *I* have the perfect one. Just you see."

More aunties find me, parroting one another like mynah birds.

I reel back in disgust. Don't these women know what *privacy* means? I'm the princess, not some farm girl raised for a bride price.

They hiss and chatter more, but their words only rot in my skull. I spin away, rushing deeper into the courtyard, and stop when I catch sight of him.

Father strolls toward me with a false smile. "Your mother is looking for you."

"I need to speak with you privately."

"What needs to be said can be done here." Father's voice is firm. "I have other matters to—"

"You must listen to me!" Every inch of me is hot, fiery. "You cannot shelter me from the outside world forever."

Father's smile is mirthless. "You could not last one night in Abai's jungles, daughter. It is for your protection."

I breathe protractedly as Tutor taught me. I speak as though I am Queen Amrita, confident and sure and a rightful Rani:

"Father, I know how deeply this war with Kaama has weighed on you, and I want to help. Let me prove myself. Let me help renew the treaty. The world is not only armor and crimson coats—"

"Rani." Father chuckles, placing a hand on my shoulder. I bristle at his laughter, and the easy way he shrugs me off. "You must understand something. I am the raja, and my word is final. Renewing the treaty is simply not an option."

My words pour out like a monsoon of rage and indignation. "Why not? Because you want to be like *him*? King Amrit? That isn't what our citizens need. Let me prove myself to you, Father. War will turn our kingdom to ashes."

"We cannot," Father booms, all laughter gone. Servants still around him. At the sudden silence, Father puts on his best smile and sweeps into the nearest outdoor alcove. Reluctantly, I follow, barreling forward with newfound confidence and anger. Of course he would deny me. My voice, to him, is nothing unless I utter his favorite word: *kill*.

In the alcove, Father looks moons—no, *years*—older. He expels a sharp breath, then speaks. "War is a complicated thing, and something you do not understand." Father laces his fingers together, and the silence of the alcove turns thick.

"I have been meaning to tell you this, Rani, when you came of age. I cannot wait any longer."

"What cannot wait?" I am bursting with confusion, a pot over-boiled. "Father, tell me."

Father braces himself. "The treaty was no simple contract—it was a pact forged in magic. The raja of Kaama and King Amrit both made their pact over the Var River."

"The Var River?" I picture the stretch of rippling water that divides part of Kaama and Abai, blessed by Amran, with waters both holy and magical all at once. "But a pact made over the river would last—"

"A century," Father finishes, "to the date. Promises made over the Var's blessed waters are bound to their makers like secrets. It was my father who taught me this when I came of age. And your mother has learned, too. The pact was clear, and a treaty was drawn with an important stipulation: *Blood must be spilled on the battlefield in one century's time.* Any discordance of this agreement would result in a consequence. A curse. Should King Amrit have broken this pact, his entire bloodline would be rid of magic, his kin left for dead. This is not a pact to be taken lightly, and neither is the Hundred-Year Truce."

Father's words ring in my ears. He is not lying.

"Kaama will not rest. War is inevitable. I cannot change what King Amrit did, and I do not want to. We must fight this war. As king, I trust you to agree with this sentiment."

I stifle the pang in my chest and shake my head. "You think war is the right thing, but it is not. You don't want me involved in any of these decisions. You never did!"

"That is not true." Father's eyes flare. "And you know of my mantra, Rani."

I hesitate before whispering the words Father has said over and over. *"We move like a king cobra. We strike first."*

He nods, pleased, though the mantra is not truly his. According to Father, the words were first said by King Amrit, then passed on to each king and queen. "One day you will learn, daughter, that war may cost lives, but it also brings victory. *They* will come for us if we do not seize the moment. *They* will be ready to fight even if we are not. And I will not let my kingdom fall."

My heart hammers in my chest. "You never cared about Tutor, did you, Father? I remember you respected him. I even remember you laughing with him on occasion. But you never cared about him. Do you care about anything outside of the kingdom?"

*Do you care about me?*

"He was a traitor, Rani. One of many against us. Traitors must be rooted out and destroyed."

"No," I whisper, stepping back. "Not *us*. They're against you."

I rush back into the throne room, shoving aside gawking onlookers. I skip the steps upstairs, burst into my room, and bang the door behind me.

My head pounds as every painful memory surfaces. I rush over to the vanity and drop Tutor's book, inspecting myself in the mirror. Tears well in my eyes. Instinctively I combat them with shuttered blinks, a tactic Mother shared with me to keep myself composed—to keep the kajal I wear from running down my face. But right now I want nothing more than to stop being a perfect princess. I want to be a little girl again, curled under the night sky, awaiting Tutor's astronomy lessons. I want Father and Mother to listen to me. And most of all, I want to *feel* again.

I let out a sharp sob, the first I've allowed myself in weeks. Tutor's face fills my mind—alive, whole, and healthy. Another sob pours out of me, and I hear a gasp.

I jolt away from the mirror. "Who's there?" My eyes fly to the closet doorway.

Through its shutters, I see something—someone—shift.

I stalk toward the closet. Closer. Closer.

"Come out!" If it's one of my servants, I'll give them double cleaning duties tomorrow. And if not . . .

"I am not going to say it again," I spit, voice unwavering, but the room is eerily quiet.

Whoever is hiding won't obey my bidding, and I'm in no mood to be toyed with.

So I wipe my eyes, charge for the closet doors, and thrust them open.

# 7

## Ria

My first step in the palace echoes off every wall. Through the thin soles of my shoes, the ground feels icy, and the jalis around me sift out the hot Abai air. The space around me is cold, too cold. Nothing like any air I've breathed before. It's pure, clean, even. But I want to exhale it all back out, because this is the air the raja breathes.

That's when I freeze. Across the corridor sits what looks to be a glass terrarium, housing snakes and other reptiles. I shiver, recalling nights at the orphanage when I was twelve. That year, every night, a small garter snake would slip over branches of the trees above the orphanage and rest on my windowsill when I was asleep. It would follow me home when I left the orphanage for scraps. I thought I was a magnet for bad luck, and that the snake was an omen.

I peel my eyes away from the terrarium and begin my search for Queen Maneet's chamber, climbing the nearest staircase, careful to keep hidden from all angles. My body is alert, always watching, eyes cutting every which way. Life on the street hasn't left me empty, it's built me up.

I spot a vase of blossoming flowers and hide behind it, looking around again. The vase tips forward when I rise, and before I can save it, it crashes onto the ground.

"Raja's beard!" I whisper. I tumble into the nearest room I can find. Jewels are strewn across the bedroom vanity along with makeup, powders and blushes that are all too foreign. I stuff whatever I can into my pockets and sneak out. They're heavy, but light enough that I can run. If it comes to that.

It's not long before I spot the back of a Chart. Badges and tassels wink up at me. I freeze and back into the same room, pressing up against the wall. I dig my nails into my palms and shut my eyes.

*Breathe.* In. Out. In—

"Tell the truth or the raja shall personally see to it that you rot in the Snake Pit."

I peer out. A girl stands across from the Chart. She's small, probably half my size, with twin braids on either side of her head. Her gaze finds mine. She sees me. I'm caught. I nearly crumple on the spot. But then she says:

"*I* did it. I'm sorry. I was—"

"I don't want to know what you were doing. Clean it up. You've got double kitchen duty next week, understand?" The girl nods. With that, the Chart leaves.

I'm crouched in the doorway, but her eyes remain on mine. "Miss? Please come out. I know you didn't mean to do it."

Sure as the skies I didn't mean to do it. That doesn't mean I'm going to take the blame.

"Please, miss, we have to get ready!"

I laugh inwardly. Oh, I'm ready . . . to leave Abai forever!

I step out of the room. The girl moves toward me—and bows. She's either knocked her head on a melon, or—

Or something is seriously wrong.

"Food is out for the guests, and your father will make remarks in the Western Courtyard. The queen wanted me to brush you up on the itinerary."

"*What?*" I pause. The staircase is far, but I can easily outrun this girl. "D-do you know who I am?"

Fear crumples her face. "I'm sorry, miss. The last thing I wanted to do was sound condescending."

"You . . ." *You're confused.* Clearly she thinks she knows me. My face isn't special—it can be swapped with anyone's from Abai. I take in her tiny frame. "How old are you?"

"T-twelve."

Twelve. When I was her age, I was only just beginning to understand how to steal. I would sneak out of the orphanage after meager dinners and impersonate a girl picking up samosas from the market for her family. Once, I even impersonated an orphanage teen who'd been selected for adoption, just to grab some rupees and run. It was the only way to get by.

NANUA & NANUA

And it's the only way I'll get to safety now—impersonating whoever this servant girl thinks I am.

I stand a bit taller, puff my chest out, and make my voice hard and demanding. "Lead me." The words roll off my tongue with ease, like second nature. If she thinks I belong, that I'm a noble, I'll be that much closer to finding the jewels.

"Of course," the girl replies, bowing.

I knit my brows. "Thank you. Er . . ."

"Aditi, miss," she says, as if whoever I'm supposed to be forgets her name all the time.

"Aditi," I say, sounding the name out on my tongue. She leads me past a wall of gems, and I want to pluck them right off. But there's no time. The girl walks so quickly, braids flying behind her, it's hard to keep up.

When the girl leads me to a bedroom, I exhale. There's an open window I can easily climb out of. Facing the Charts or whoever else comes my way once I do so is another matter entirely.

"I'll see you downstairs, miss." With another bow, Aditi heads off.

The girl must believe I'm a guest. Some foreign dignitary. But even that simple explanation makes my stomach knot. Time to grab and go.

The room is drenched in royal purple, a gaudy color compared to the soft pinks of Abai's sunset. I approach the four-poster canopy and run my fingers across the silken blankets. I wrap them in my hands and find I can't resist. I sink into the bed. It feels like a dream. The pillowy softness of these cushions, the jewels weighing down my pockets.

*If I blink, I might end up in Nabh. If I blink, I'll wake up.*

The bed feels as if it'll devour me in softness, and I'm tempted to give in. But a sparkle from the corner of the room catches my eye.

Next to the window sits a gold-encrusted table laden with jewelry boxes. Could this be one of the queen's chambers? If so, I don't know why that girl brought me here, but it doesn't matter. I've got the best jewels in all of Abai sitting in front of me, and I plan on using them to pay my and Amir's way out of this forsaken kingdom.

I rush to the table and pocket as many jewels as I can. I'm reaching out, ready to rearrange the ones left over to look like none are out of place, when I hear the sound of heels clacking down the hall. Getting louder, closer.

Adrenaline spikes through my body.

"Skies be good!" I whisper, my feet tripping over one another in panicked retreat.

A nearby closet offers refuge, and I shove myself as far in as possible, pushing back a pile of books tossed haphazardly on the floor. I watch through the shutters as a girl rushes in and slams the door. Her breathing is ragged, like she's just made her own escape from . . . somewhere. She flutters her eyelids—for what purpose I can't begin to understand.

But at that moment, I take her in. This isn't a servant, or just any noble.

She's young, and she's wearing a crown . . .

I peer closer.

*Princess Rani.*

I gasp without thinking, immediately slapping my hand across my mouth. But it's too late.

She whirls toward the closet. "Who's there?"

No. How can I ever escape this place if she finds me? How will I tell Amir to run? To never look back?

He won't leave without me.

"Come out!" she demands. But I stay still as a boulder in the White Mountains. I lick my lips, praying that I possess the magic to be invisible.

"I'm not going to say it again," she warns.

She's close enough that I can make out her night-blue sari, the tiny mirrors laced into the hems. My gaze moves up, up, up . . .

The princess swings open the closet door. "How dare you—" she begins, but when our eyes meet, her words fall flat. She can't find a way to finish her sentence, and I can't find a reason to run.

Because it's not just the princess of Abai before me.

It's a girl who's my mirror image.

A girl whose face is the same as mine.

# 8

## Rani

"Who in Raja's—" the village girl begins, but the words are caught in her throat. She blurts, "Who *are* you?"

"I am Princess Rani," I snap. "What are you doing in my closet?"

The girl widens her eyes. "You don't look like a snake," she says, avoiding my question.

I raise both plucked brows, but it's not her comment that's shocking to me. It's the fact that this stranger is an exact copy of me, from her face to her skin to her obsidian tresses.

I fumble back, grasping at a pointed corner of my canopy bed. The girl steps out, her face illuminated by moonlight that slips past the gauzy white curtains. A frisson trembles down my back, skittering and skirting around my spine.

I am unable to move my gaze from hers. Is she a trick of the mind?

Abai's sun. What is happening?

I take in the rest of her. This girl looks plain, a villager in a house of royals, wearing a half-ripped chunni and a suit I would never dare clothe myself in.

The girl lets out a sharp laugh. "I'm dreaming, right? I must've hit my head when—"

But I don't let her finish. In one swoop, I grab this replica girl by her dirty clothes and push her against my armoire. Her chunni falls to the ground. Behind her weight, the dresser rumbles, followed by the telltale sound of bangles tumbling to its wooden base.

"Who are you?" I snarl.

"None of your business."

"Do you think that's any way to speak to your future leader?"

The girl's mouth curls. "You're not the leader. You're the Snake Princess."

"And you are a girl who does not like to listen. Do you want to land in the Pit? I said, *who are you?*"

"I'm not telling you anything until you release me." The village girl's face is stern, her voice sharp, her whole attitude riddled with spikes and barbs.

With reluctance, I release the girl carefully, stepping back. I regard each of her features with attentive eyes: she has a carefully hooked nose; lips that, unlike mine, turn up sneakily; eyes that are both sunken yet alight with mischief.

"Ria," she admits, a scowl etched on her face. "My name is Ria."

"How is this possible?" I whisper under my breath. I peer

deeper at Ria while wringing my fingers. "A girl who looks exactly like me . . . in the palace? What kind of trickery . . . ?"

"I never thought I'd share your face, either," Ria snaps. I can tell she is just as perplexed as me. Her wide eyes comb my body, searching for any detail, any difference, anything to illuminate the truth.

I stare at Ria in return, lips parted, heart thrashing in my chest. My face, plain of birthmarks or spots, contrasts her skin—sun-darkened and worn. Her clothes are made of rags and patches, unlike the lush sapphire of my sari.

"And you're so . . . ordinary," I say slowly.

"So what if I am," Ria bites back, face red. "I've been through more than any of you damned royals."

"Is that so?" I counter. "Like what?"

"Beatings," she says curtly. "Whippings, lashings from the Vadi Orphanage's headmaster." At the dawning horror on my face, she adds, "Did the raja not tell his precious princess daughter that? I'm sure he never took one look at Abai's orphanages and thought of how we were treated. Like dirt."

I open my mouth to respond, but nothing comes out. All I can say is, "You don't know what it's like to never see the sun. To never feel it on your skin—"

"Oh, please. You live in a literal palace." Her voice is one of disgust. But then she furrows her brows and gulps, taking a step toward me. "But this." She gestures toward her body, then mine. "There must be a logical answer to this." Though she does not say it, I can tell what she's thinking.

How could two girls who have never met—two girls from different worlds—look exactly the same?

"Maybe there is a logical answer," I say. I take an equal step toward her as though pulled by a magnet, yet confusion pulses in my veins. "Where were you born?"

Ria crosses her arms defiantly. "Definitely not here."

I arch a brow. "You never learned?"

She shrugs, though her face betrays the truth. "I lived in the orphanage my whole life. I don't have a passport, a crest, or anything to mark where I'm from."

"You never knew your parents?"

"In case you didn't know, that's what being an orphan means."

I harrumph. "Then tell me, Ria. *When* were you born?"

Her gaze flicks to mine. "Diwali night."

"Eighteen years ago?" I ask, heart thumping.

At my words, Ria steps away from me. "How'd you know that?"

I shake my head and carefully touch her cheek, taking hold of her chin before she can flinch. Her face is sallow yet still reflects mine nearly identically, save for the birthmark next to her eye, missing from my face, and the hollowness of her cheekbones.

"There's something about you," I say. I see it in her face, her eyes, her words. "Don't you see? We're—"

"No! Don't say it," Ria cuts in, pulling back and knocking my hand away. She plants her fingers to her temples. "Just . . . don't."

"Why not? The answer is as plain as—"

"No," she interrupts, cupping her mouth as though about to vomit. Shaking her head, Ria whirls away, fists tightening in her hair. "It's impossible. Lots of people probably look like me. There're thousands of people in Abai—"

"There was only one of me, or so I thought," I tell her. "As confused as we both are, I think you know what this means. We—we must be sisters."

Ria swallows in revulsion, though I feel, deep down, that she knows the revelation to be true. I reach out, but she jerks back, a few precious rubies sliding from her pockets to the floor. The crystals shimmer like the eyes of a hungry tiger.

I glance at my dresser, void of most of my jewelry. "Thief," I gasp.

"You're the one who stole my face," she retorts. With a hand to my forearm, she roughly shoves me aside.

My skin burns at her touch. And soon, all I see, all I *feel*, are sweet-scented, smoky memories.

# 9

## Ria

My vision flashes—colorful, vibrant, lively. Then comes a flood of images: *Gold bangles. Jewels. Pearls strung about her neck. Lips shaped like a bow.*

I close my eyes as visions play in my mind, rolling and tumbling into an endless cavern of hidden truths.

The sound of a motherly voice drifts through the air like tendrils of smoke. "*Ria,*" she says, hovering over my newborn body as she caresses my cheek. "*Rani,*" she continues, her gaze roving to the other girl cupped in her hands. She caresses my cheek once more, but there's something wrong. Something off.

"*My twins,*" she says.

The vision vanishes. Was that a memory? A part of my past I never remembered?

I release the princess's arm and stumble back. "What was that—?"

A chill spreads through me as I take in the princess. The way her skin reflects mine. The blue sari she wears, choking her body like a vise.

Rani's sharp-brown eyes cut to mine. "Mother. Father . . ." She studies me again. Right now she looks nothing like the princess of Abai. She looks shocked.

"It's some sort of hallucination," I cut in, reasoning with myself more than her. "M-maybe your—your magic."

Princess Rani widens her eyes. "Is that what you think? That I was using my magic? I am just as baffled as to how that happened as you are, Ria." She shakes her head. "That memory . . . I could not have done that alone."

I tilt my head. "So, what? You think we did that . . . unlocked that memory . . ."

"Together?" Rani finishes.

My eyebrows scrunch. "But . . . *how*?"

Rani ponders my words before her eyes light up. "Each magic is connected to another in some way. Snake magic is deeply tied to thoughts and memories; it's why we can connect so well to our snake familiars and read their minds."

"That doesn't explain why we unlocked that memory."

"What if we unraveled our magic, our memories, hand in hand?" Rani explains. "I know, this—"

"Is unheard of," I finish, scoffing.

"Because no one has ever heard of twins using their magic *together*," Rani says convincingly. She purses her lips and paces, a finger on her chin. After a moment, her eyes swivel up to mine.

"We must have done something to trigger it." She blinks, an epiphany washing over her. "Emotion is deeply tied to magic. What we feel affects the way our magic works!"

My eyes bulge. No way in the raja's right mind could I believe this. *I* can't have magic. Magic doesn't exist!

But there were rumors in the orphanage; one about a kid who could start a fire with his eyes; another of a girl with nightmares, dreams that had an eerie knack of becoming reality.

"What's wrong?" Rani asks.

Cold fingers slide down my spine. "The fever children . . ."

"Fever children?" Rani echoes, intrigued.

I gulp. "When I was young, there were babies who screamed with endless fevers. Some kids thought they had magic, remnants of it, at least, from the Fire Master."

Rani's brows lift.

"We were told that magic didn't exist. Even speaking of it meant consequences. The whip. A visit from the Charts. Worse . . ."

"Father has always told me we're the only ones with magic left," Rani says, eyes wide. "To think other magics exist is blasphemous!"

"Yeah, and I wasn't expecting to meet a look-alike with weird snake powers, but here we are."

"I told you, we're *twins*," Rani counters.

"That's nonsense," I say, only half meaning the words. "We can't be twins. I have no magic! That woman"—I point to a portrait of the king and queen—"is not my mother. This is not my life. It's yours."

She shakes her head. Walks over to me and stops a breath away.

"What if it could be yours? Just for a little while?"

Our unified stares are like two burning suns.

"Wait a minute." Princess Rani's gaze trickles down to the birthmark on my inner right arm. Most days I thought it was an ordinary mark, but now I see something on Rani's left arm. Something similar.

She presses my arm to hers, and in the mirror above her dresser, the whole birthmark comes together, shaped like a snake rising from shadows.

*No.* I pull away. All my life I just wanted a family. But this? The *royals*?

Princess Rani purses her lips, casting her gaze to the jewels on her vanity. She tosses off the bangles on her arms and slides them on mine.

"Wait—what're you doing?"

"Even if you don't believe it, even if this is some odd twist of fate, it is as you said. You never had your shot. But . . ." She shakes her head like she can't believe what she's about to say. "But now you *can*. I've always wanted to escape the palace. Now I have a reason to do so. My tutor wanted me to find something." She gulps. "I need to prove myself to Father, find a stone that could change this coming war. If I leave the palace, I might just learn of its whereabouts. And you—you have the chance to know what it's like to have a family. To be the princess you were always meant to be."

"Hold on. You expect *me* to be the princess while you're off looking for a *stone*?"

"If I manage to find information on the stone, that is,"

Princess Rani corrects. She worries her lower lip. "Haven't you always wanted to live in the palace? Not worry about where or when you'll get to eat? The palace doesn't have meals. It has *feasts*."

I scoff, but her proposal isn't as absurd when I realize: Isn't this everything I ever wanted? Months' worth of food, a bed to sleep on, laps full of riches and jewels.

Safety . . .

I shake my head vehemently. "I can't. I won't leave Amir behind."

Princess Rani raises a brow. "A boy? Is he . . ."

"No!" I clear my throat. "Amir's my friend. He calls me *Princess* sometimes, and I call him *Prince*. . . ." I picture his face. I always thought he might be my family, even if we weren't bound by blood.

Princess Rani raises her chin. "What do you want most in the world, Ria?"

A few minutes ago, I would've said *To leave Abai*. But now? Even though I don't want to tell the princess any of my deepest, darkest secrets, I can't hold back.

"To meet my family," I reveal in a single breath. "To see them, Amir, and myself, safe. Always."

"I know your life hasn't been fair," Rani says. "If I lived out there—where I've never gone—I might be a thief, too. And you, a princess."

"What're you saying?" I clasp onto the bangles, trying to stop shivering despite the warm wind drifting through the open window.

"I'm saying that this is what we've been waiting for. A chance to change fate, and on Diwali night! I must leave the palace, Ria. I've been shackled here, and there's something important I must do."

I step back. Not everything is clicking together. "Do you really mean it? You want to leave the palace?"

In her face I read the truth, solemn as ever.

A voice slices the air. "Rani!" Clacking footsteps sound from afar. "Come downstairs this instant!"

Alarm fills Princess Rani's face. "Trust me," she says, "this is my chance to fulfill my destiny *and* my old tutor's wishes. To be like Queen Amrita." Her eyes light up as she speaks.

No way in the skies am I made to be a princess. My skin is taut from harsh winds and dirt; hers is scrubbed clean with silky lavender soaps, smooth and hair-free. But we've got the same face, the same voice—

"I can't," I say again. "I need to get these jewels to Amir, so we can leave—"

"You told me, Ria, that you don't have a passport. Well, the Charts will never let you pass without one, and they will never accept jewels as payment."

"Then we'll find another way," I say, sidestepping Rani and turning away. Though I say the words, I'm caught between two worlds. How can I leave Abai when the truth of my birth is hidden here?

That's when Princess Rani catches my attention. "What if I could get you out of Abai?"

I whirl toward her. "How?"

"I will make it so. You will be given safe passage from Abai with your friend, but you must do this for me first." Rani's eyes sparkle with anticipation. "We can both get what we want."

I laugh at first, but the plan settles in my head like butter on warm naan. It's ridiculous. Absurd. But I can't help but feel a bit of wonder slithering through my veins, too.

I weigh my options the way I do before a quick chase. Calculating, analyzing. Leaving now would mean turning my back on everything I've discovered, with a couple jewels in my pocket that may or may not get me out of here. Staying would mean a whole new life, a new opportunity for Amir and me.

"When would we switch back? I can't stay in this palace long—"

"Before the truce ends," Rani promises. "It shall be enough time for me to look for what I need, and for you to figure *this* all out."

I gulp. My whole life, I've only ever stolen two things: coins and food. Can I steal the princess's whole identity?

My stomach tightens. *Maybe this is all too much*, I think, though a thrilling buzz rushes through me. What if I'm not the baseborn village girl I always thought I was?

And if I'm not, how can I refuse the opportunity of finding out who I really am?

I skirt around the bed. "I'm not going to put my life in danger without some coins in the end."

"You can keep the jewels you've taken. Plus, I'll give you all the money you need. And passports for you and your friend to sneak out of here when I return," Rani promises. "I'll arrange for transportation out of Abai discreetly. The Charts will never see you, and you'll be gone before the border is closed."

I cross my arms and tap my elbow. "No games?"

"No games."

*Skies.* I could learn the truth of my birth . . . and then Amir and I could get out the way we always dreamed. Even if it takes a little longer than we'd planned, I won't get another opportunity like this.

Mama Anita's voice returns, sweet and smoky. *One day, you'll find your true family. One day, you'll feel them—in your blood.*

I send a prayer to the sky.

"Deal," I tell her firmly. No going back. "But *no one* can know about this."

Rani's face mimics my same emotions: a pinch of fear, a bolt of excitement. Just minutes ago, she was nearly sobbing. "Oh, believe me, I know. Before the truce ends, I shall return. We can meet at the fountain to switch back." She analyzes my face, then my hair, gasping at the ragged ends. "Wait here," she says, rushing off to the bathroom.

When she returns with a pair of shears, my stomach drops.

"I've done this plenty," Rani assures me. I squeeze my eyes shut at the *snip snip snip* of the shears. A comb soft as clouds brushes through my hair. I open my eyes at Rani's contented sigh.

In the mirror, my hair is trimmed straight at the ends, resting at my elbows like Rani's, and the frizz is gone—*poof,* disappeared. She takes the crown off her head and fits it snugly on mine, pinning my hair in place. I'm no longer Ria.

"Come here, quickly," Rani begins, pulling me to the bed. "Tell me about the boy. Amir."

"I've known him for eight moons. We're . . . thieves." It's weird to admit it aloud, like I might be sent to the Pit the princess had mentioned earlier. "He's waiting for me in the Moga Jungle. You won't miss him, not with his scar." I trace its location on my own face with my fingertip. "We've been ready to leave Abai for a long while." For the first time, those words taste bitter, a mixture of lies and truth all at once.

To my surprise, Rani's lips turn up at the corners. "Thieves. I've always wondered what it would be like to make my own way."

I stare at her again, still in wonderment at the exactness of her features against mine, like a mirror in plain sight. "But you have *everything.*" My words are a blend of anger and pity.

Rani only shakes her head. "I have parents who don't look my way unless I do exactly what they want." She pauses. "I have a kingdom to rule but no place to do so. And don't even get me started on Amara. My betroth—" She cuts herself off unexpectedly, her eyes straying from mine.

"Your what?"

"Never mind," Rani says quickly. "Just watch out for Shima."

"For *who*?"

"Rani!" a voice calls again. "Hurry up!"

We both bolt up from the bed.

"My maids will be here soon." The princess grabs a cloak from her closet and wraps it tight around her body, then tucks a small book from her dresser into a hidden pocket. "They'll wash and dress you until you're cleaner than the palace itself. You'll get everything you ever needed. And more than you ever wanted. That's a promise."

A bout of jitters winds through me. I want her to tell me more, tell me it's all going to be okay. All I say is, "See you soon."

Rani gives me a bittersweet smile before gathering the folds of her sari. When she rushes out the door, her scent fills the room: lavender and cilantro. I lift my armpit to my face and sniff, immediately gagging.

Without Rani, the room feels emptier, and my task looms ahead. The images in the vision we shared pull me back, tug at me like strings on a puppet.

Growing up without a family, blood and water are no different. Amir is in my veins just as much as Rani. But Rani promised us everything we'd need, all before the truce expires. I could get us out of Abai for real. And forever.

I turn to the window and pause. I could escape right now if I wanted to. But those visions—they were real. They just won't leave, and questions keep swirling in my brain. Was I given up? Considered lesser? Shame builds inside me. This isn't just a simple lock to pick, a puzzle to solve.

This is my life. And I'm going to find out who I really am.

# 10

## Rani

I'm running through the halls, my head pounding. Everyone around me swims in and out of view. *You're the one who stole my face*, she said.

I roll her name over in my mind. *Ria. Ria.* My twin. But *how?* My parents could not have kept a secret this big. Not from me. But they did. They have.

Every artery within me feels like it's about to burst with questions. Who is older? Where did she go? Where has she been her whole life? From her clothes, she looks like she's come straight from Nabh. Maybe, if I had actually been attentive, I would have known. I would have felt her in my bones, the blood thrumming through my body, missing its other half.

A part of me feels like Amran has answered my prayers. This turn of events has given me an opportunity—to escape this palace, to find what Tutor wanted me to find.

Perhaps to head off this bloody war.

To prove I can be more than a princess.

I could be like Queen Amrita. I could make change.

My veins are hot and fiery as I pull up the hood of my cloak and hurry through the palace. The last time I had need for a cloak was when I first secretly met up with Saeed after my fifteenth birthday. I once fantasized leaving the palace with him, even put a few coins in the pouch hidden in my cloak in case. Thankfully, they are still there now.

I take the narrow halls I once walked for solitude on nights when I felt Mother was ignoring me, or when Father was gone on diplomatic missions. I find the place I am looking for: a sleek, wide hall I've heard servants nickname the Hall of Eyes. For a hundred eyes are staring at me now, portraits of rulers past. Their gazes latch onto me, following as I rush down the hall.

At the very end is a portrait of Queen Amrita, one of Abai's few female rulers, who reigned over five hundred years ago. I remember the lullaby Tutor sang to me: *They called her the Gem of Abai, the queen who passed so young . . .*

She died young from an unknown disease, and her portrait depicts a youthful glow.

There must have been a reason Tutor told me all those stories, whispered her name in his last breaths. Speaking to Ria, I finally understood why.

Sitting in her curls is a silver tiara with a ruby embedded in the center. A gem.

She was called the Gem of Abai, both for her gentle nature,

and for the ruby in her crown. The Bloodstone. How could I have forgotten what Tutor taught me? Queen Amrita was rumored to be the last royal to have the stone, after it had been passed down for centuries.

People believe Amran's own blood exists in the stone—and that it could grant a single wish. I close my eyes, seeing the ruby-red stone flash behind my eyelids, dark as crimson nightmares.

It could end wars altogether, Tutor told me.

*The Bloodstone. The Bloodstone. The Bloodstone.*

Is *this* what Tutor wanted me to find? A stone to grant wishes? A stone to stop this war? Renewed energy sparks through me. "I'll find it," I say to her, though it is a promise to myself, too.

Soldiers' boots echo from afar. I rush away, finding the nearest exit. This is what I've always wanted—to abandon the palace. But not only that. This is my first true act of defiance against Father. If I fulfill my plan, might I, too, fulfill Tutor's wish? He gave me my first clue: the symbol on the ring, a stalk of leaves. Now I know that the plant refers to the Mailan Foothills, wherever that may be.

In seconds, I'm through the main entrance and outside. It is quiet out here, cool, though the heat in my body is unchecked. In the distance, stars are stitched in the night sky's fabric. The air is clement compared to the castle. I relish it.

I love it.

A gust of wind hits me as soon as I register where I'm standing: before the Fountain of Fortunes. Water laps in lazy circles. There are no Charts in sight except for two stationed far outside the main gate, backs facing me. The others must be in the Western Courtyard, acting as security for the celebration.

I step closer to the fountain as the burnt candles bob along the water. All I see is my reflection.

No—*Ria's* reflection.

Before I can turn away, the water swirls, rippling out into rings. An image blooms to life: Me, standing in the jungle next to a teenage boy with shorn hair and a slim scar cutting through his face. The boy disappears and is replaced by a girl with bright hair and a strange star-shaped birthmark on her cheek. She is standing in a bazaar.

I lean in deeper, but the images shatter like glass. A voice like burnt honey permeates my mind. Hard on the edges, curved around a mouthful of sweet riddles.

Seek the place of stone and glass
Where emptiness hides and fire flames.
A lurking magic you will find
Through the ancient guards' lost ways.

Smoke swirls around the images until they disappear into thin air. I blink rapidly, breathe protractedly. All too soon, the smoke, the scene, the voice—everything vanishes.

Like a warning bell, footsteps drum along the concrete, quick and sharp.

The march of Father's soldiers.

I nearly trip over the hem of the cloak as I rush away. I barrel forward, headed for the nearest courtyard, and hide myself in the brush with bated breath, concealing myself with the cloak. Blood rushes to my temples, and my head pounds with fear. The Charts skirt in opposite directions, shouting and securing the perimeter.

Reality seeps in. I need a plan. I peek through the hedges into the crowded Western Courtyard. A certain dead end. I gnaw at my lip until my eyes fall on Father's stables. Within seconds, everything slips into place.

I rush into Father's stables and make out the gleaming silver coats of his stallions. They each wear a royal-red headpiece to signify that they belong to the king. A memory of an old horse-riding lesson surfaces: I was nine summers old, and I'd lost control of Father's horse. Even worse, I had accidentally let all the stallions free of their stalls. Father had punished me to a week alone in my rooms but let me go four days early out of guilt. Where did that guilt—that sympathy—go? When did he become so hardened?

I reach out, feeling the horses' soft manes beneath the pads of my fingers. With quick hands, I unlock three latches and pull the gate wide open. Hooves fall, horses neigh, and with two fingers to my mouth, I let out a piercing whistle.

*Go.*

A trio of horses floods out, stirring up dust as they pummel past the Charts and through the main gate. A few of Father's soldiers run after them, but it's no use; the diversion has worked perfectly.

I suppress the mix of thrill and dread in my stomach. Thrill, from being outside, from finally *doing this*—and dread from everything else that has happened tonight.

From seeing those visions. From finding Ria.

From uncovering an unknowable past.

Could I forge a new future?

I mount the nearest steed and urge the stallion forward. Dust collects behind us, a veil between what is ahead and what lies in our wake.

I ride out of the stables and past befuddled Charts, my hood masking me. More soldiers have already rushed to close the gate, so I press my knees into the stallion and snap the reins. Before me is a gargantuan gate with menacing pointed tips, sharp as a viper's fangs. If I don't get out now, the gates will close, and Father's soldiers will catch up to me.

*Three.* The air turns thick, difficult to breathe.

*Two.* My heartbeat echoes like clanging swords.

*One.*

We leap into the jungle without a second to spare, and I nearly slide off the horse from the impact. I peer back. No red coats in sight. For the first time in ages, I laugh. It's high and joyous, a sound I almost don't recognize. I'm out. I'm finally *out.*

I let my eyes shutter closed for an infinitesimal moment, savoring every sound sharp and clear. Tigers pacing with quicksilver tails; snakes traveling along too-high branches.

Without warning, the stallion jerks to a stop just as someone rolls into view. I nearly fall as the horse raises its hooves, its neigh reverberating against the trees' thick bark.

"Down!" I shout. I catch sight of the boy: long limbs, dirt staining his cheeks. He's shrouded by the jungle and wears dirt like armor.

He coughs as the dust settles. I try to relax my heartbeat, but it only shoots up when he stays right where he is. "Out of the way," I command.

"Hello to you, too," the boy says. "I thought you'd never get back." He returns to his bout of coughs, and I dismount, clutching the stallion's reins still.

The boy examines me. "Raja's beard," he says in a husky voice, "what're you wearing? And where'd you get that thing?"

*Raja's beard?* Some sort of peasant slang. And certainly no way to speak to a princess.

"That *thing* is a stallion," I retort, unable to adjust my high royal voice to match his.

"I thought you never learned to ride."

My cheeks redden. "It's not as hard as it looks. And . . ." I touch my earrings. "I had a little time for dress-up."

The boy chuckles. "Well, you could've told me you'd be awhile! I had to knock a soldier out with a melon. I was freaked out after you left me, but now that you're back . . ."

"You did *what*?"

"There was a spare melon on the ground! I had to escape the bloodcoats after I made that diversion." He eyes my necklace.

"Bloodcoats?" I wonder.

Amir raises a brow dubiously. "Y'know. *Charts.*"

"Oh." I cannot comprehend who in the raja's right mind this peasant boy thinks I am. Then Ria's voice floods back to me. Her friend, who would be waiting for her at the edge of the Moga Jungle.

Amir.

*"Prince?"*

"Yes, *me*, Amir." He steps into the moonlight and points to his face, but my eyes are drawn to the scar across it. I hadn't seen it before, but it divides his face into two halves, diagonally down the length of his visage. "Now tell me what happened in the palace! Did you get the jewels from the queen's chamber?" His words crash into one another with excitement.

"Yes," I lie breathily, nerves tingling all over. From his relaxed stature, I know he hasn't realized I'm not who he believes me to be. My fingers settle on the necklace at my throat. "I only managed to take this."

To Amir, it is a simple thing. Sold for a pile of rupees and freedom. To me, it's the encapsulation of my life. Trapped forever, silenced by a bejeweled object that has done nothing more than choke me into submission.

"Here," I say, practically ripping the necklace from my throat. Once it is gone, my shoulders lift, as if relieved of a fate filled with unconceived fortunes and untold stories.

"*Only?* You took a whole necklace fit for a queen!" He laughs and closes his arms around my shoulders in a hug. I still at first, unsure what to do with my hands, but then relax my shoulders, letting myself be wrapped in the cocoon of this strange warmth.

He pulls away. "Think it'll be enough to get us fake passports?"

I recall Tutor's final words. "Actually, I managed to take one other thing." I show him the ring. "It has a special symbol."

Amir cocks a brow. "Looks like a bunch of crops. What d'you think that means?" He eyes it like a hawk ready to swoop down and sell it for a cool coin and, hopefully, a steady future.

"I've seen it before." I attempt to look not too knowledgeable, slouching down and tossing the ring over and over in my palm. "In some books at the orphanage. It's the symbol of some sort of territory. The Mailan Foothills."

Amir stiffens. His gaze shoots sideways.

"You've heard of it?" At his reluctance to answer, I add, "You have, haven't you?"

Amir sighs. "It's in the Hidden Lands."

"I've never heard of those," I respond. Surely a princess would know the geography of her own kingdom. Then again, I'd never known about the Foothills.

"That's because they're *hidden*. Wouldn't even know how to get there, honestly."

I can sense he's holding something back. "But you know someone who could?"

"Well . . ." He sighs. "There's this girl. I think she works at a bazaar, or nearby one. . . ."

"A girl?" Ria never told me Amir knew others out in the jungle, but he must have some kind of past, a family he left—or that left him—behind. My mind turns back to the fountain, to the girl with hair bright as the Abaian sun, standing in a bustling market. "Light-brown hair? Star-shaped birthmark?"

Amir's gaze shoots to mine. "How'd you know that?" He looks at me as if I am a stranger, a foreign entity.

"I saw her," I say carefully. "In the . . . fountain." How much does Amir know of the Fountain of Fortunes?

Ria's friend raises both brows before loosing a staccato laugh. "Yeah, the *Fountain of Lies*. Seriously, Ria, how could you know that—"

"Because it is the truth," I cut in, voice haughty. It's how I speak to my servants, to Saeed, when I want to be sure they'll listen, but I try to swallow my tone. I cannot let Amir spot the differences between Ria and me.

I say the only thing I can think of. "I overheard servants in the palace who wanted passports, too. They dropped this ring . . . I think perhaps they wished to go to the Foothills themselves. If we find the girl you know, and she can help us get to the Foothills, we might find someone who can help us escape, perhaps even make our passports." Bitterness sits on my tongue, but us snakespeakers have a way with lies. A natural affinity in our bones for spinning tales and telling stories, thanks to the Snake Master. It's helped me get what I want more than once.

My powers might not work against Father—but could they work with Amir?

The boy still looks skeptical, but I gaze deeper into his eyes and prepare to channel my words, my *mind*, against his.

"Trust me," I say. I dig into the snake magic in my veins and tug, pulling him in, closer, closer . . .

As if a cloud has lifted from his face, a hopeful look spreads over his features, and he slowly nods. Amir's eyes light up, as if this is another one of his and Ria's heists. A game.

It works. I've never used my snake magic with a commoner before. Excitement threads through me.

"Fine. We'll go to her. But once we're in the Foothills, we'll only stay as long as we need to find a passport maker."

I agree quickly. I must find information on this stone if I want to show Father I am worthy of things greater than an idle figurehead. The fountain's riddle wasn't simply a fortune, but a prophecy. This boy, that other girl . . . Something greater is at work, and only I can set it into motion.

"How'd you get into the palace, anyway?" Amir eyes the horse. "See any of those bloodcoats in there?"

"No," I lie. He speaks of them the way one says the word *rubbish*. It's a cacophony of hate, of disgust. To me, they've hardly been more than servants, carrying out orders, protecting our family.

"Hmm," Amir responds, leaning in closer. His scent rubs off on me: tree bark and melon—an interesting combination. I examine him, his slim body, his shorn hair. I curl my toes, welcoming the dirt underneath my sandals into the crevices of my feet. I feel like each of my senses have come alive after being suffocated for so long in the palace.

"We should get going if we want to get to that market," Amir says finally, pocketing the jewels, though I hear a drop of dread in his tone. Whoever we're meeting, the two of them must not have left off on good footing.

I mount the horse, and the boy gets on behind me. His lanky arms are a foreign feeling around my waist; I'm used to Saeed's— the roped strength of his muscles.

We take off, the horse's hooves beating like a drum along the forest floor. The star-flecked sky cloaks me, like a warm blanket on a chilled winter night. Amir's arms tighten around my waist, his breath warm against my back.

Fireworks light in the distance. The signal is a reminder: back home, I am a prisoner.

Here, I'm overflowing with everything I never thought I would feel. Because in this moment, I am not Rani. I am free.

## 11

### Ria

I peer over the ledge of Rani's window. It's a far drop, but nothing I can't handle. I could run out of here if I wanted to, pretend none of this happened. But I can't betray my promise.

I can't leave until I get the truth.

Something hard and deep pangs in my chest. *Want*. A desire to know who I am. To know what happened to make me—Ria, a nameless girl—turn into Rani, a girl whose name is rich with history. But wanting to know means searching for answers. And searching for answers means staying here.

"Rani!" a voice snaps.

I spin. A woman stomps into the room, heels furiously grinding into the floor. She takes in my dirty garments, picks up my chunni. "What are you doing in those *clothes*?" Her cheeks flush.

I unhook myself from the windowsill, a thousand questions locked in my throat. Behind me, the curtains flutter from the warm Abai breeze, taunting me, telling me, *Get through palace life for a few weeks, and you'll get that ticket to freedom just like Rani promised.*

The woman makes the rip bigger, pulling the threads apart. I yelp. *My chunni!*

"Tasteless," she scoffs. "What are the maids giving you?" Her expression is one of disgust. "How many times have I had to tell you to stop running to your room? We've been looking all over for you, Rani."

I let out a grunt of apology. I need to get away from this riled-up woman, whose familiar face holds nothing but disdain.

Disappointment.

It's only then that her voice comes back to me. The woman from my and Rani's vision.

*"Ria . . ."*

*"Rani . . ."*

This lady is the same one from the portrait on Rani's wall. Could she be . . .

*My mother?*

No—Mama Anita was my mother. Mama Anita cared for me when no one else had. She was the only mother I'd known, even if she didn't have my blood. But if the queen is also my mother, which one of them is my real family? The one who shares my blood or the one who shaped my life?

I should feel thrilled at the possibility that my real mother is standing *right here*. It's what I always wanted, to find my real family, yet right now, I only feel more lost.

"Jasmin! Neela!" she calls. Moments later, two girls shuffle in.

"Get Rani changed, then downstairs. Right away!"

"I—" I can't speak; my throat is tight with a sea of unspoken words. The girls rush me into the bathroom.

"Wait—no—"

My worries go unanswered. The girls do as they're told, slipping me into a sari bedecked with gold, dangling earrings I've never even dreamed of touching. The outfit is entirely impractical for a thief.

I swallow, trying desperately to stop my hyperventilation. *Play along*, I tell myself, taking deep breaths. *If you do, you'll discover everything you wish, and Rani will get you that money. . . .*

When they're done, the vanity is a mess. They've touched up my face with pots of brown paste, lightened my eyelids with powder, and glossed my lips until they're smooth and plump. The mirror does not reflect me back; it reflects Rani.

"Downstairs, miss," a maid says, prodding me forward like cattle.

The queen gives me an eerie smile when I arrive at the courtyard. I recognize the shape of her lips in my own. I want to hurl.

"We are making the announcement now, dear daughter," she whispers when I'm close. "Remember, the party is coming soon!"

What party? And what *announcement*?

A man approaches us who could only be the merciless raja himself, sporting a royal red turban and waving at onlookers as he walks near. He turns his gaze to me, his brows lifted like he's surprised I'm standing here. Like he's never seen his daughter before.

Does he know I'm not Rani?

I stare back unflinchingly. After all, a successful masquerade hinges on confidence.

When I envisioned this moment, finding my *real* parents, I always thought I'd be ecstatic. But how can that be if my father is the *raja*, Abai's cold and merciless king?

Clinking glasses call the courtyard's attention. We stand at the doorway leading into what I assume is the throne room. The courtyard is massive, holding curious strangers' faces.

"Thank you all for coming," the queen booms. She grasps my shoulder. I want to jerk my body away, but with hundreds of eyes on me, it's no longer obeying my command.

"We have been waiting a long time for this night. Tonight, we celebrate Diwali, but more so, the future leadership of our kingdom. Our daughter." She strokes my cheek, and my body turns to stone. She has a small birthmark near her left eye, mirroring mine.

"It is time we finally present to you all our daughter, Rani. Your future queen of Abai!"

Thunderous clapping from the audience. I twitch out a smile like I know what I'm doing. I survey the raja and queen. They smile. All teeth and manicured secrets.

"Tonight, we reveal some exciting news." This comes from the raja, who has moved to my other side. Internally, I cringe. Nothing could've prepared me for this. Now I know why Rani hasn't shown her face in years: her parents' gazes are like leashes, reining me in, willing me to stay put.

"Please step forward, Amara, mother of Saeed Gupta," the queen says. "We would like to formally announce our daughter's engagement, with a party to celebrate in under a half-moon's time!"

*Engagement* party?

I stiffen. The crowd roars. The queen smiles down at the crowd, and a red-haired woman—Amara—comes up. Behind her, a man strides toward me. Everything is moving too quickly, faces spin around me, and I barely take him in. Tall, curly hair, and walking like everyone else in this raja-forsaken palace, like he has a stick up his—

He lifts my hand and kisses the back of it. My cheeks turn red, red, red.

"I will honor this bond, Princess Rani. Forever."

The crowd sighs dreamily.

*Saeed Gupta.* He's the man I saw in the fountain, the cool, rippling water that showed me my supposed future. And worse—he's the man they think I'm going to marry.

"May the Masters and Amran bless you!" An auntie squashes rupees and sweets into my hands. I can't even focus on the money she's given me. Instead, Saeed's words stick to my mind like too-syrupy honey. *I will honor this bond, Princess Rani. Forever.*

Forever is too long a time to wait for Rani to get her prissy-princess self back here. Of course *this* was what Rani had almost told me—that she had a *betrothed*. Anger simmers in my veins; what other crucial details of her life has she left out?

Above us, fireworks pop in the air, signifying the light of the day, the light of Diwali. Yet right now everything feels dark. Upside down.

"Blessings upon you," says a woman. It takes me a moment to remember her name, but her mehendi-streaked hair brings it back: Amara Gupta. She kisses the top of my forehead, and I smell her breath laced with wine. Most likely imported from some rich kingdom like Retan. I know the smell of it well from nights in alleyways, the air soaked with bitters.

When she pulls back, her eyes find mine, but they don't hold the love and care I expect. They are harsh and hooded, molded into cruel marbles and vicious, glassy pupils.

I gulp.

At the end of the night, servants sweep me back into the palace just as the gold doors leading out of the throne room shut. I catch one last glimpse of the sky. Foggy trails of smoke make ribbons in the air, remnants of tonight's fireworks. I've never been close enough to the palace to see them. Now, on the evening of Diwali, how could my fate have changed so much?

A maid glances at me nervously as she ushers me through the palace. "Are you well, Princess? You seem unnerved."

I manage a nod, but her comment reminds me of how daunting this task will be.

I'm a weed in a palace of flowers, mud on a slab of marble.

Only one thought tumbles through my mind: How long can I pretend to be someone I'm not?

PART TWO

# A Kingdom Divided

# 12
## Rani

Ten miles outside Anari's city center, we bring our horse to a canter and then rest by a half-dead tree. Amir ties the horse to the trunk as I pour water into my mouth.

I nearly spit it out.

It tastes stale. Like my final kiss with Saeed, under a moon ago. My birthday.

*"Saeed, do you love me?"* I asked him. For moons, our meetings had been nothing but kisses and gifts, and while I enjoyed how he treated me—as both his future partner and queen—I wanted more. More than flitting glances and half-baked conversations and fevered meetings in the dark.

Saeed had buried his face in my neck, fingers trailing down my back. *"Love isn't the right word for this."*

He'd dodged the subject every time I brought it up to him, which had been frequently of late. At first I thought nothing of it; Saeed was handsome, intelligent, supposedly my perfect match. Then I asked Mother why Saeed and I had been promised to each other so young in the first place. Why we were supposedly destined for matrimony.

*"Marriage is a meeting of minds,"* Mother explained. But what if Saeed's and my mind *didn't* meet? Where Saeed was practical and confident, I wanted him to be bold. Where he was pristine and practiced, I wanted him to be free and unrestrained. And most of all, I wanted him to admit his love for me, the same love I thought I felt for him. Is it fair to want someone to be different from who they truly are?

So, a moon later, I finally plucked up the courage to ask Saeed the question again, that night in my bedroom. The night before Tutor was killed.

*"Of course I love you. It is my duty,"* he finally relented.

My heart shattered . . . or at least I thought it had. Love was a fulfillment of his destiny, not a yearning of his heart. And that wasn't the destiny I wanted.

Amir's voice unravels the memory. "There's not much food left. We'll need to steal some more," he says, allowing the horse to nibble some leftover bread crumbs.

Erasing every thought of Saeed, I remind myself of my mission. *Follow the prophecy, fulfill Tutor's wish.* I am quick to remember that Amir does not know how full I am—from the wide array of palace foods, when servants answered my every beck and call.

"What about morals? Altruism? I'm sure someone will offer us food if they see our situation."

*"Our situation?* Okay, now you're definitely joking." Ria's friend chuckles, and I look at him blankly. Although Ria told me she is a

thief, I don't feel quite prepared for this.

Amir must notice my confusion because he says, "Is something wrong? Ever since we left the palace you've been acting . . . weird."

Of course. I am nothing like Ria, from what I've learned. I must try harder.

"I just . . . saw things in the palace. The raja and queen," I confess. The words *Mother* and *Father* nearly slip past my lips.

"You saw the *royals*? Why didn't you tell me before?"

I think quickly. "I didn't want to talk about it."

"Well, obviously," Amir answers, nonchalant. "The royals are arrogant, bloodthirsty tyrants." At my flinch, his eyebrows frown. "Did you see their reptile faces? Did they hurt you?"

My mouth falls open. "Reptile—no!" I snap, voice cracking. "They're not—I just think they might be . . . misunderstood."

"For their taxes, their conscription, their cruelty to nearly everyone in Abai? I think we understand them just fine. And those bloodcoats, too. Bunch of cowards."

I hang my jaw in shock. Surely Charts are no cowards, not if they have the gall to look Father in the eye.

Anger pulsing through me, I look away. I must remind myself of the truth: that though Amir is Ria's friend, he is against *me*.

It doesn't matter. He is a means to an end, and that is all he will ever be.

"Enough royal talk," Amir says. "I don't think I can travel much longer without some sleep."

"Of course," I say, though my veins are still on fire. "But the girl in the fountain . . . how did you two know each other?"

Amir shifts his gaze away from mine. "You'll learn soon enough."

His very voice prickles my skin, but he is my only way to find the girl, the one who might have information on the Foothills— my only path to the stone Tutor died for. My limited knowledge of my kingdom crumples in on me, but I remain level-headed. Tutor taught me a princess never falters. They think, they act, they succeed. I must unravel the fountain's fortune—and use it to help me get to the next stop on my journey.

Amir sits and relaxes against the old tree. After a pause, he clears his throat. "Sorry about bringing the Charts up earlier. I know it's probably still a shock."

"Pardon me?" I say, then quickly amend it to, "I mean . . . shock?"

"Yeah," Amir laughs, but it's a nervous sounding chuckle. "Y'know, your name on their conscription list. But don't worry. Pretty soon, it'll be the least of our worries."

I blanch. Ria was conscripted for the war effort? I think of what Father told me, how war is necessary. But drafted? Without a choice? The thought sickens me, and the weight of my mission— searching for the stone—sinks deeper onto my shoulders.

Amir gazes dreamily at the sky. "My hands have been itching to grab some food." Finally, finally, he allows himself the smallest of smiles. "I can practically smell the naan. . . ."

"Then let us take our rest," I tell him, but at Amir's expression of puzzlement, I am quick to change my wording to that of a commoner's. "I mean, let's get some sleep. We can find food in the morning."

"I'm with you there," Amir agrees, though his gaze is still suspicious. I lie down opposite Amir, still thinking about Ria's name on that list. A snore permeates the air; Amir is already fast asleep.

My lips frown instinctively. I cannot let this news disturb me; I will play Ria with all the might I have. I practice a grin that does not falter.

One fit for a princess *and* a thief.

The beating sun shines on the trees' emerald leaves, bringing the jungle to life with gilded dawn light.

We dismount the stallion, which will be far too conspicuous to bring into the village and draw too many questions. Father's horses don't belong in villages, and they're trained to find their stables—and Charts—with ease. I give it a parting touch and join Amir at the outskirts of the jungle.

"Whoa." At the first sign of village life, Amir is muttering blessings instead of curses, even with his fiercely foul tongue.

The sight *is* a welcome one. This is the first and only village I've seen up close, and it is a flurry of activity. Merchants set up their tents in the grand bazaar, some already hawking their wares; vendors yell for foot traffic, hoping to catch a straggling customer. But what shocks me most are the abundance of villagers crowding the streets, offering their morning graces. Not far from them are the beggars, palms open, as if coins will fall from the sky.

Amir turns to me. "First things first, let's grab some food. You go left, I go right, and we meet in the middle." He says the words as if we've done this a thousand times.

It takes a moment to gather my wits. Getting caught is not an option. I head to the nearest stall, which boasts measly jewelry and silks. A squat, bulb-nosed man greets me but does not hide his gawk at the gilded sari hidden beneath my cloak. Only now do I realize how ostentatious my attire is. I clutch my cloak tighter around my frame and head to the next stall, which holds an array of fruits. Lychees, teeming with juice. Fresh mangoes, ready to be split open.

A woman dressed in a fraying salwar kameez greets me with a smile and offers me a fresh bundle of herbs silently. I shake my head and instead say, "I'm looking for a girl who may have come by here." I think back to my vision in the fountain. "She has . . . an unusual star-shaped birthmark and . . . light-brown hair. Have you seen her?"

The woman purses her lips.

"Was she here earlier?" I press.

A nod, albeit slowly. She opens her mouth, then closes it, as if unsure a voice can come out. She points to her eye, then to her open mouth, with a shaky finger.

"I don't comprehend . . ." I trail off. The woman taps her lips.

Only then do I notice she is missing a tongue.

I gasp. A few stragglers stare at me curiously. My cheeks heat with simultaneous fury and horror. Who did this to the poor woman?

Amir's words echo from last night. Could it be the work of the Charts? And if they've done something *this* cruel, what else have they done to silence Abai's citizens under my father's orders?

The woman catches my attention once more, lifting up a thick string and tying it around one finger. A perfect bow. Then she mimes a slingshot action, right over my shoulder.

I whirl. A girl, standing just paces away by another stall, catches my attention. Light hair. My heart hitches. I nod at the woman in thanks and head for the girl, stopping but steps away.

My heightened senses, thanks to the Snake Master, kick into motion. She smells like mint leaves and jungle trees, fresh earth. I scrunch my nose; already the heady perfumes of the palace are slipping away from me.

That's when I catch a glimpse of a bow and arrow in her hand. Was that what the woman was trying to tell me before?

In one swift motion, the girl turns before I can get a good look at her face. She disappears into the crowd of people.

"Wait!" I call out to her, shoving my way through village people who throw me strange looks. A hand grabs my wrist and I jolt, readying to defend myself. But how? I have no soldiers guarding me, no sword to wield.

"Ria!" I spin to find Amir holding a pair of ruby-red apples, gleaming like palace jewels. "Check these out." He grins a thief's grin. "What'd you get?"

"I . . ."

Amir takes notice of my empty hands. "Why didn't you—"

Before I can speak, a voice rings out across the market, "Thieves!" The man with the bulbous nose parts the crowd, rushing from his stall toward us. "They have taken my prize apples!"

The crowd turns to us, some mothers clutching their sons to their chests with unease, others pointedly staring, leveling at us the dirtiest looks.

My heart sinks in my chest. But Amir just laughs, and before I know it the apples are hidden, tucked beneath his vest as if they had never been there in the first place. "I think you've confused me, sir," he says. He glances at me like I'll fill in the rest.

My throat closes up.

The man only stares at us harder.

*Use your snake magic,* I think. *Get out of this.* "My . . . *friend* here is correct," I jump in. "I'm a famous marketeer from Anari." That familiar slither of serpent blood hits my veins, the twist of a lie dancing on my tongue. It thrills me now. It probably thrilled Ria, too.

"She examines the markets for any mishaps, business falsities," Amir adds. "I am her assistant. Are you accusing us of taking from our very own businesses?"

A few of the villagers mutter at that. Whispers riffle through the crowd like spilled wine.

"You're a liar!" the man shouts. He points a finger at me. "Look at her sari! Even a marketeer couldn't afford such a thing. She is a thief! They both are!"

I wrap my cloak around me before anyone can get a good look. I channel my connection to the serpents—to *Shima*—again and invoke the name of the Snake Master. But it's like the magic is flickering instead of fueling. I have never tried to use my magic more than once in one day or on an entire *crowd*. I lost my control of Shima just last night; who's to say I won't lose control of my tale-spinning affinity now?

"Really, sir, you see—" Amir begins to lift his hands in defense, and one of the apples slips from his clothing and bounces on the ground, gathering sand and dust onto its skin.

"Amir?" I say, voice cracking, unable to move my feet. *What would Ria do?* I think, but I already know the answer. *Run.*

Amir scoops up the apple in one quick swoop. We bolt through the streams of villagers, not paying attention to the people surrounding us. I need to find a way out of here—I need to find that girl with the bow and arrow.

As if the Masters are listening above, time slows, and I channel that inner snake magic in my veins. I will not let it fail me now, not when I need it most. I haven't used my heightened senses often, but I must now. It's my only chance at finding this mysterious girl.

I concentrate the way Shima does when she's sniffing out a meal, homing in on that scent of dirt and grime I could smell on the girl from a meter away.

"This way!" I call out to Amir, and we veer left, into the path at the edge of the jungle.

A nearby tavern looms two stories tall, all wooden boards and half-fallen roofing. The sign plastered to the front is illegible. Entering such an establishment would normally be far beneath me—the thought of it makes my heart race.

Voices form a riot of noise behind us, and I know we haven't much time. It's the tavern or the woods, and neither option looks very pleasant.

"In here," I tell Amir, rushing forward. We head into the tavern, pausing to collect a breath when we're through the doorway. This place stinks of wine and unpleasantries I have never before encountered. People hug their drinks to their chests and peer over their cups with beady eyes. All too aware of my palace clothing, I tuck my cloak around my body and follow Amir forward, keeping my eyes on the creaking wooden floors. I sidestep a puddle of spilled wine, wrinkling my nose at the smell. Thankfully, the grumble of the tavern starts up again, and the din of yelling from outside fades into the distance. Words float all around us, peppering the air with gossip.

*"Heard the Charts came through Kali yesterday. Wrecked half the village."*

*"Better than paying those taxes,"* another responds.

A barkeep narrows his eyes at us suspiciously.

Amir audibly gulps. "I know this place. This is where we last met. Me and . . . and the girl," he clarifies to me in a whisper. His words are sorrowful, woven with pain and loss. Who is this girl, and what could she have meant to him?

My stomach swirls, but I step toward the barkeep. "Good day, sir," I say, sure to keep my voice low.

He nods, eyebrows tucked into two dark lines. "Can I help ya?"

"Sanya," Amir says as if cursing, slapping one of the jewels from the necklace I gave him earlier onto the counter. "She here?"

The man eyes the jewel like he's never seen anything more valuable in his life. "What's it to ya?"

"We need to speak with her," I demand. "Now."

"Ha." The man presses a hand to his belly, eyes flashing with anger. "She *works* here. I told her to stop making friends on her shift breaks." He rolls his eyes. "Sanya!"

A girl—the one I saw just minutes ago at the bazaar—trudges to the front, scowling. Her skin is a shade darker than mine, unrelentingly scorched by the Abai sun. She wears a green chunni, and a few strands of light-brown hair poke out from behind it.

The girl halts midstride, the same bow and arrow clutched in her palm. Her eyes land on Amir's, and her whole body turns rigid.

"You," she whispers. Tears fill her eyes, but she blinks them back, face turning to stone. "How'd you find me? Where have you *been*?" Her head turns sharply toward me. "And who's this? Making new friends, are we? Pretending your family never existed?"

The tavern falls silent, watching the conversation unfold before their eyes. Some munch greedily on their meals as they gawk, like an audience to a show.

"Sanya," Amir calls just as the girl rushes to the back of the tavern and out into the wilderness. He drops his head into his hands. "Raja's beard."

"Who was that?" I murmur, a hundred eyes pricking my skin.

Amir slowly lifts his face. "That," he says in a whisper-soft tone, "was my sister."

# 13

## Ria

I wake to the sound of a hiss.

My eyes fly open to the sight of a three-foot-long green-blue snake uncoiling before me. "Raja's beard!" I shriek. I throw off the bedding, scrambling out of the bed and half landing on my rear. I rush over to the window. "Stay back!"

That's when I finally notice the purple-bathed room I'm standing in. This couldn't've been the bed I slept on. No, I slept on the street as usual, covered in a fine layer of Nabh's dust, tucked under the cloak of night. I don't sleep in fine silks, or a palace fit for royals—

Sharp pain cuts through my head. I press a hand against my temple to suppress the pang, but instead of helping, it only makes the ache sharper. In a snap, the pain is gone, replaced with a feeling like a stretched tightrope running through my brain. Like someone's latched onto me without invitation and *pulled*.

*Did you know identical twins come from the same egg?* a voice says.

"Skies above," I whimper. That voice is deeply rooted in my mind, yet I know it can't belong to a human.

I reach for the nearest thing on a vanity—a handheld mirror—and brandish it like a sword. The serpent appears over the bedside railing. Its scales ruffle as if annoyed by my presence. Its eyes swivel all over my body.

A flood of memories hit me: Mama Anita, telling me of the royals' affinity for snakes. How, as descendants of the Snake Master, they bond with serpents and respect them as their familiars. I think of those snakes I first saw in the terrarium when I entered the palace last night. When I was younger, I heard snakes' voices in my nightmares, thinking it was a product of my imagination.

I glance up, and it's at that moment—when the snake *smiles*—that I lose all feeling in my legs.

*You catch on pretty slowly,* the snake says, *for a girl who pickpockets for a living.*

I drop the mirror and rush out of Rani's room, leaning over the nearest banister. *Breathe, Ria*—

From the corner of my eye, I see the snake slither out of Rani's room. An icy shiver cools at the base of my spine. Fear plants my feet to the floor, but I manage to turn and grasp the banister behind me.

"Am I delusional?" It would've been nice if Rani had told me she had a pet *snake*.

*We are not pets,* the snake corrects. *We are familiars, and we are as connected to your blood as the Snake Master himself.*

Familiar. Snake Master. *Magic.* They all exist?

"W-what's a familiar?"

The snake ponders this. *Let me think . . . Ah, yes.* A Guide to Snake Magic, *chapter two: "A snake is no object but a living being. Once a snake and human form a unique companionship, they may form a blood bond through a ceremony called the Bonding Ceremony, when a royal selects a snake to be their familiar for life. The snake then injects a drop of venom into the royal's blood—"*

"I didn't ask for a history lesson." Still, I shiver at the sound of that—the Bonding Ceremony. "Did you and Rani do that?"

*Five years ago,* the snake responds. *The ceremony is more than a tradition; it is a symbol of trust between human and snake. The snake injects just enough venom into the human's wrist to form a heightened bond but not fatal. Of course, snakespeakers like yourself have a certain immunity to venoms already.*

Another piece of information Rani conveniently left out before her hasty exit.

Sharp steps echo from down the hall. The red-haired lady, Amara, comes into view. She grabs chai from a servant trailing behind her. She takes a sip and spits it out. The servant jumps.

"This is cold as ice! Get me a fresh cup—don't just gawk!" She thrusts the cup back at the servant, who's just a young girl. Stiff-backed, she rushes away. I recognize her from yesterday. Aditi, the girl with the flying braids.

*That's Amara's personal servant,* the snake says darkly. *And you can call me Shima.*

Rani's words from last night flood back to me. *Just watch out for Shima.*

Oh, yeah, thanks for the warning about the three-foot snake!

Shima slithers up my arm. Her scales are smooth as sand slipping from my fingers, and unexpectedly warm. I stumble back, wide-eyed. I want to collapse to the floor. My whole body quakes. "Don't be scared," I tell myself, "she's not talking to you, snakes don't talk, don't be scared—"

*Who do you* think *is talking to you?* Shima laughs. *We share a connection, you and me. Your twin and me. Rani has spent many years learning snake magic; yours seems as natural to you as your thieving.*

"What do you mean?" I whisper.

*That crevice in your mind. I slipped right into it. It is an opening into the magic buried deep*, the snake continues. *You and Rani are both snakespeakers—able to wield snake magic—yet you are opposites.*

I'd rather greet a tiger than talk to a serpent. Then again, if this snake is Rani's familiar, and she knows about *me*, she might know . . . other things.

The snake continues, *I have sensed it in Rani's blood. A missing half. Have you ever felt a deep connection to serpents? An affinity to spill lies? A tendency toward stories instead of truth?*

My mind whirrs. I have. Stories have always been in my blood. "So the vision was true. I'm a royal. I've got . . . snake magic."

*Yessss,* Shima hisses.

"You've known I was alive this whole time? You know what happened to me?"

*The latter I am unsure of,* the snake replies. *But if I were you, I would—*

More clacking heels in the hall. "Come, come," interrupts Amara, approaching me and taking hold of my arm with sharp nails. She pulls me down the helical staircase, and that thread between Shima and me loosens. She unwinds from my arm. I throw a desperate glance back up at the snake as we descend, but she's gone.

I turn back to the bottom of the staircase, where I see Saeed standing. He takes me by the hand and I bristle, but he doesn't seem concerned. As if my lukewarm greeting is . . . normal.

"Rani," says Amara, "there is much to be prepared in time for the engagement party. I expect you to follow Saeed to your lessons and attend your fittings tomorrow after the luncheon." She eyes my nightclothes. "And for the love of Amran, change first."

Amara sweeps away before I can say a damn thing, and I soothe the faint depressions on my skin from where she held me. I don't know what Rani thinks of Amara, but she sure seems full of it to me.

Rani's betrothed leans in and murmurs, "You played the part well," against the shell of my ear.

Played the . . . does he know?

Does he know I'm not Rani?

My heart flutters.

I shrug. Answer with not-an-answer. "In the grand scheme of things, it wasn't hard."

Saeed's brows knit together. "So you don't want to stop the engagement after all."

*Huh?*

I open and close my mouth like a fish. Rani wanted to stop the engagement?

Saeed sighs. "You're a sea of confusion, Princess."

My stomach falls. So he *doesn't* know I'm Ria.

I didn't know I had a twin. Neither did Rani. No one around here seemed to know it, either. Has it been kept from *everyone* by that skies-damned raja?

An idea slowly takes root in my mind. If Saeed can't tell the difference between Rani and me, that means I can mold him, manipulate him. Then maybe *he* can help me get answers.

I control my features and shape my lips into a soft smile. I peer up through my lashes. All the hallmarks of a princess, right? "I thought it over last night. I was wrong," I tell him.

He raises a brow. "About?"

"You know," I say softly, hating how vulnerable my voice sounds. But it doesn't matter. I'm reeling him in, and I don't even realize how quick he is to bring his thumb to my lips and lean down for a—

My stomach swoops. *Raja's beard, no! He's Rani's betrothed, not mine.* "Look—it's a perfect day to stroll around the palace. Don't you want to take your future queen for a walk?"

Saeed half grins, one brow arched. "I know you don't want lessons, Rani, but the queen would like for us to continue them before the engagement party."

The only lessons I've ever needed were Amir's—how to slide a piece of jewelry into my hands with a whisper, stuff rupees into my empty pockets. I could steal before I met him, but he turned me into a near professional. Still, if I have to get through this *lesson* to find out more about my and Rani's birth, I'll do it. I've impersonated enough girls before to get what I want. This should be no different.

After I quickly change, Saeed leads me through extravagant dining halls and past decadent tearooms. As I'm distracted keeping an eye out for any jewels, we stop abruptly by a wide set of gilded double doors. He swings them open.

"I thought you might want to take your lessons here," Saeed tells me. "The terrarium was once your favorite part of the palace, if I recall correctly."

I chance a step into the room, then stop in my tracks like I've seen a Chart. There aren't any soldiers—but there are banyan trees swirling high up to the ceiling, a glass pane separating me from the folds of nature. It's like a pocket of the Moga Jungle right here in the palace. Snakes hang lazily from the trees while lizards leap from branch to branch.

I yelp. Raja's beard, this is the terrarium I saw yesterday.

Before I can collapse, Saeed takes hold of my arm and pulls me toward him. My eyes find his, a startling gold in the sunlight filtering through the room. There's something about them that clings to me, calls to me. Is it the thief in me, drawn to their luster, like coins? No. Somehow, it feels like something else.

I erase the thought, forcing my weak knees to hold as he guides me through the terrarium. I shield my eyes from the reptiles, even as the sound of swaying branches brings me a greater sense of familiarity than the barren silence of the palace halls.

*It's just one lesson. One lesson surrounded by snakes—*

"Physics or astronomy?" he asks. Neither feels important right now.

"How about history?" I ask. At least that might give me some clue about my birth, this palace, this kingdom.

Saeed chortles. "You despise history."

"Maybe I've decided to become more informed."

Saeed's lips tilt into a pleased but surprised smile, like he hadn't expected to hear that. "History it is."

We pause under a dome-shaped ceiling on the far side of the terrarium. I find a singular chair, a desk, and a podium holding several books. Saeed approaches the podium and sifts through the books until he finds the one he wants. He cracks open the leather-bound spine.

"Shall we pick up where we last left off? Chapter three, the Rao Monarchy . . ." He clears his throat. "A few centuries after the Great Masters' Battle, Kaama's king, known reverently as the Rao Raja, was—"

He looks up and notices I haven't taken a seat. "Something wrong?"

"N-no." Except for one snake that keeps eyeing me from behind the glass. I quickly veer away and, without looking, take my seat.

I let out a piercing shriek.

"Shima!" I cry and fall flat on my butt for the second time this morning. I cast aside my panic in favor of annoyance. This snake was on my seat. And it likes to embarrass me, apparently.

*Better look before you sit, Princess*, the snake says. She slithers off my chair and waits patiently next to my desk.

"Rani!" Saeed calls, rushing over to me and taking my hands. "Are you all right?"

He checks me for bruises. I wave him away. Looks like all I bruised was my pride.

"Here." He helps me up, perching a hand on my lower back. "Better?"

Warmth overwhelms the space his fingers touch. I glance away. "Yeah. But I want that snake gone."

"I don't understand; Shima always sits in on our lessons."

Oh, perfect. "Never mind. I'm fine. *Perfectly* fine." I glare at the snake before examining the chair, and finally, I sit.

Saeed returns to the podium. "As I was saying . . ."

He tells me a story of the Rao monarch, one of Kaama's earliest rajas, who was a fierce soldier and loyal leader—if a greedy ruler.

"Rumor was, Rao wanted to invade Abai and colonize the land," Saeed says. "But Abai's raja did not reprimand the Kaaman king. Instead, Raja Arnav of Abai decided it was time to settle the dispute between Abai and Kaama."

*The same way you need to settle this dispute with Rani and Saeed*, Shima hisses. What is she talking about? Saeed *had* mentioned something earlier about Rani calling off the engagement, or at least trying to. What's happened between them?

"So Raja Arnav, diligent as ever, proposed something that would unify the lands and promote trade and travel." He turns the book to face me. Sketched in ink is a bridge, connecting the two lands. It's an interesting thought, uniting two kingdoms that despise one another with something that could help them both.

"Despite their intentions," Saeed continues, "the bridge was never fully built. There was too much suspicion by nobles and villagers alike. And since then, Abai and Kaama have never tried to restore peace until they saw the Creator's ire and proposed the Hundred-Year Truce."

"I've heard about Raja Arnav," I say. But Mama Anita taught the story to me differently.

"I would hope so, Princess." Saeed's tone is amused. "Given that we've been studying Kaama and Abai's past feuds for the last few months. Not that you've been the most attentive pupil. . . ."

"No, but you've got a part wrong. It wasn't Kaama's king who wanted to invade. It was Abai's raja who wanted to invade Kaama," I clarify.

Saeed quirks a brow. "Where did you hear this?"

"Umm . . . I . . ." I glance away, right at Shima, and something unexpected starts to happen. Her scales change color, redden like my cheeks. Flustered, I continue, "The book is wrong. Abai's king was the hateful one, and Kaama's the peacekeeper."

"Explain." Saeed closes the book with a thud, but his gaze is on mine, and a smile turns up the corners of his mouth that emboldens me to continue.

"Stories have different perspectives," I say, "depending on who's telling them."

Saeed shakes his head. "I'm . . . impressed, Rani. You've grasped today's entire lesson, far ahead of plan."

"I did?" I squeak, standing.

He nods, abandoning his post at the podium and approaching me. "History isn't all facts. It's largely written by the victorious or the powerful. It's lore, it's stories, it's moments of the present that shape our futures. Like . . ." He blushes, then shakes his head.

"Like what?"

He bites his lip. "Like the moment I privately proposed to you."

I'm speechless for a moment. "I . . . I suppose so."

Saeed smiles, like he's recalling the memory. "Mother helped me get the roses delivered to the throne room. I wanted every inch of the room to be covered in petals . . . for everything to be special."

"It *was* special," I say. With the way he's looking at me, his honey gaze clinging to mine, you'd think we were inseparable lovebirds. Maybe Rani and Saeed were, once.

"Special enough for a princess?" he quips with a half smile.

Part of me wants to playfully elbow him the way I would Amir, break up the tension. Another part of me enjoys the push and pull, the game of dice I'm rolling with my sister's betrothed.

*My sister's betrothed.*

I'm backed into a corner with no idea what to say next. Shima seems to sense this, because she says, *Echo me.*

"Huh?" I whisper.

*Tell him the proposal was a moment made for history . . .*

"Um—it was a moment made for history," I manage. Shima nods from behind Saeed. I echo the rest of Shima's words as she continues speaking in my mind. "For people to talk and write about. It wasn't *real*. It was a show."

Saeed pulls back. "Perhaps it was. But I've never heard it put so bluntly."

The moment spoils. I curse inwardly. I never should've trusted a snake, of all things.

"Well . . . maybe we should just cancel today's lesson."

Saeed's eyes harden. "I know you want our engagement to end, Rani, and I will respect your wishes if that is the case. But as your mother and father have stated, I cannot retire as your tutor. Your training to become queen must continue. They've asked that I give you a new schedule."

I huff. *More* lessons? "Fine. Is that all?"

Saeed quiets. Guess that means the lesson's over after all. I head for the exit, ready to get out of this terrarium, but Saeed's voice makes me pause.

"Wait."

I turn. Saeed exhales, staring at the ground. "It's true that I've been holding something back from you, Rani. I tried to tell you yesterday in the throne room. I—I don't know who else to turn to."

My interest piques. I step closer. "Go on."

Saeed finally looks me in the eye. "I've been having strange . . . dreams. My mother's been giving me a tonic to help rid me of them, but they still recur like nightmares."

*This* is what Saeed wanted to tell Rani? He's been having bad *dreams*? I don't see the issue, but fine, I'll bite.

"For how long?" I prod.

"Many moons now. But they're not just dreams. I see Mother, sometimes, or . . . or you." His cheeks burn, and mine flare in response despite the cool terrarium around us.

"Me?" My voice comes out as a squeak. *Rani me or Ria me?*

Saeed bites his lower lip. "Rani, this may sound bizarre, but I never stopped you from wanting to end things because . . . I foresaw it."

I snort. He's so lovesick he's been *dreaming* of Rani. I tap my fingers on my elbows, trying to appear cold, the way Rani would.

Apparently it works, because Saeed says, "I knew you'd think me delusional. Tell me, Rani, when did it start? When did your heart turn cold to me?"

I freeze. I can't answer that. Obviously. As much as I look like Rani, I can't channel whatever reasoning she had for shunning Saeed.

"I can't say," I reply honestly. I keep my voice flat and rough. I clear my throat and recite something Mama Anita told me once: "All I know is that love shouldn't be fated. It should be earned."

Saeed ponders my words. He keeps a respectable buffer between us as he says, "You once told me our love was written in the stars. That nothing, and no one, could change that."

"Things have changed." *More than you know*, I add silently.

"Even us." He says it as neither a question nor answer but something in-between. His relationship with Rani is somewhere in the air, and I'm not sure if I can grab it and bring it back down to reality.

"Even us," I echo softly. I want my words to ring flat, emotionless, but there's something in them that holds a question. A promise.

Saeed takes another measured step forward and gently lifts my hand, thumbing the spot where an engagement ring would be. "I always thought this was what you wanted. I suppose I was wrong."

I stare at our entwined hands. It's traitorous, pretending to be Rani in this moment—an intimate moment between Saeed and the girl he loves—but I ignore the guilt in my stomach. I must win my freedom. And Amir's. I've stolen, begged, bartered. I've done things worse than this for far less.

"What happened between us . . . is difficult to explain." I look for an excuse to get away from all these snakes. And this conversation. "Can we save this for later? I think I need some rest."

Saeed casts a glance downward, shaking his head and scoffing.

"What is it?" I ask, unnerved.

"*I think I need some rest*? Having been with you for three years, I can tell when you're making up excuses."

"Who said that was an excuse?"

"Who told me earlier they were wrong about our relationship?"

"Well, clearly, I *was* mistaken." The words fly out before I can shove them back in. They're cold, harsh, whipping like lashes.

Saeed's face is drawn. Anyone else would feel guilty at that pained expression, but I feel nothing. Years in the Vadi Orphanage, followed by months on the streets, have hardened me more than I wish to admit. Turned me into who I am: a girl whose place in the world is still undecided.

But I can't go making this situation worse than it already is. "Saeed, I'm sor—"

"No more apologies, Princess." I watch as Saeed makes his way to the exit. He glances over his shoulder. "I think I've become numb to them."

With that, he leaves. Shame stings my cheeks, like I've been slapped.

My aim was to make as few waves as possible till Rani returned. So much for that. I don't have time to deal with her lovesick betrothed right now. I must keep looking for clues, figure out why the king and queen kept my whole existence a secret.

I shiver and glance up, catching my reflection in the terrarium's glass walls before touching my cheek with roughened fingers. Coming to this palace wasn't a death wish but a gift in disguise. A chance for me to discover the truth.

That's when everything registers. If I want to survive in this raja-ruled palace of impenetrable stone and brick, I won't just have to look like Rani; I'll have to *become* her. I'll have to pull off my biggest heist yet.

# 14

## Rani

*Sanya.* I taste the name, each syllable, on my tongue. There's no question—she is the girl I saw in the Fountain of Fortunes. *She* is the one tied not only to my destiny but Amir's.

We've followed the girl out of the tavern, to her dismay, and now pause in a clearing. In the distance, banyan trees sway to life in the Moga Jungle. The girl halts six feet away before turning around, her bow and arrow glinting in the sunlight.

I study Amir's sister. When I was younger, Tutor taught me how to control myself. Control my innermost feelings, paint a look of calm on my face.

Sanya's face looks anything but calm.

Her mouth is twisted into a dubious scowl. Her cheeks are flushed from rushing into the hot Abai air. Unlike at the market, she now smells of sweat and alcohol from the tavern. Her hair is frazzled, as if every inch of her is trying to flee in a different direction. In the sunlight, the strands look like burnished gold.

"I told you to never come back," she spits, staring at Amir. She tightens her grip on a beaded necklace at her throat. The girl stands a little taller. "I told you I wouldn't follow you."

"A year can change a person," Amir admits, but I catch the way he's squeezing his palm against a fisted hand.

Ria's friend is related to the girl I saw in the Fountain of Fortunes. I must be doing something right if I've found her as the fountain predicted. A thrill rushes through me at the thought.

"Listen, Sanya," Amir begins when his sister remains tight-lipped, "a lot has changed recently. Ria and I left Nabh and—"

"Running away again?" Sanya scoffs. "Where to this time? I hear the southern cities are nice this time of year. The lakes in Kakur are especially beautiful if you're going for a swim. Or maybe—"

"I'm serious," Amir responds. "Yesterday Ria and I made it to the palace. We got jewels, and now we need some passports to get out of Abai."

"You shouldn't joke about that," she retorts, turning toward a tree and resting a hand on it, as if exhausted from speaking. "You know how much Ma hated your imaginary games."

Amir's gaze darkens. "Ma isn't here anymore. And I'm not kidding."

The two of them are silent. Amir's body is tense next to mine; it's like he's forgotten I'm here.

"Well, a year has changed me, too." Sanya straightens her back, newfound confidence shining from her eyes. "And Irfan."

Amir's gaze flickers to mine. "I've heard that name before. . . ." He turns to me. "Samar mentioned him the other day. We saw the Charts take Samar to the palace."

"Samar's dead," Sanya deadpans. "He died in the palace. Snakes got to him, I guess."

A pang hits my stomach. Sweat stamps my palms. "Samar?"

Tutor. They're talking about Tutor.

"Rumor is the princess choked," she continues. "She doesn't have the guts for death."

"And what's so wrong with that!" All of my practiced poise floods out of my body. Heat sweeps through me as Amir flinches, gazing at me like I am a being he's never seen before.

Cheeks flushed, I clear my throat. "I mean, I learned a lot while at the palace. The man who died, he was—he was the princess's tutor." The words come out in stutters, in bits and pieces as fractured as my new identity.

Amir's gaze volleys between mine and Sanya's. "We . . . had an interesting night," is all he says, as if to explain my strange habits. I don't glance back at him, for fear that he will see right through me.

Right through this charade.

"We can play catch-up later," Sanya says roughly, her eyes landing on Amir's. "What did you really come here for, brother?"

Amir worries his lower lip. "We want to go to the Mailan Foothills in the Hidden Lands. For passports to escape." He firmly plants one hand on my arm, pulling my gaze to his. "And it's not a joke, or a game. Not even one bit. Can you take us?"

Sanya glances away pointedly and dodges the question. "Looks like you finally found the partner you always wanted."

I pull my gaze from Amir. Something about her tone implies I'm more than just a *partner* to him, and I don't appreciate it.

"She's the best damn thief in Abai," he says. My stomach warms at the compliment before I remember he is speaking of Ria, not me.

"Whatever." Sanya shakes her head, her eyes wandering. "Oh, look who decided to join the party." She tosses the bow and arrow to someone behind me.

I haven't heard a sound, but I turn to find a hooded man wreathed in shadows, his vestments threaded the color of midnight. He catches the weapon deftly. The man looks as though he could be a shadow. My snake-magicked senses kick into gear, and I smell something like steel mingling with the jungle air. A weapons forger, perhaps. Or merely someone used to sharpening knives for his own use.

"Got it repaired for you at the market," Sanya says, pointing to the bow and arrow.

"Thanks," he says, the sunlight sweeping through the trees illuminating only a sliver of his face: a sharp, bearded chin and a half smirk. "I thought we weren't provoking strangers anymore."

"Roll out of the wrong side of the bed?" Amir quips. The man chuckles, to my surprise, and moves closer, steps agile and lithe as a tiger. My curiosity piques as he lowers his hood from his face.

The first thing I notice is the dirt claiming his features, the thick brows framing his eyes. Silver irises envelop dark pupils. Tutor's history lessons surge to mind: silver eyes are less than uncommon; they are the mark of Amratstanian heritage, the mountain people of the northwest.

But there is something eerily familiar about these eyes, like a shared secret.

The man only purses his lips, contemplating me for a moment. He raises his hands in defense. "Who's the princess?"

My breath hitches before I realize he's pointing at my sari.

"This is Ria. She's no princess," Amir cuts in, his gaze bouncing between Sanya and the silver-eyed man. "Wait—you look familiar. . . ." Amir's eyes light up. "You were on some wanted posters a while back, weren't you?" His gaze shoots with alarm to his sister.

The man lifts his brows in surprise. "Is this the famous thief brother I've been hearing all about?"

Amir's brows knit together. "What'd you say your name was again?"

"Never did."

There's a pregnant pause. Then a flash of surprise: frown lines forming around Amir's mouth, crinkles blooming by the corners of his eyes. "You're Irfan. The vigilante. You *are* the guy on the posters! You're the one the Charts were looking for!"

The man extends his hand. "That's the name. I'm a mountain man, born and bred, but I guess I'm famous around these parts." He shrugs. "Except I dropped the whole vigilante thing a while back."

"You mean, you were a hero of some sort?" I ask.

"Yeah," Sanya answers for him, "and when I found him in the

jungles, I helped, too. We stole food from the palace kitchens, stuff they would just throw out. We gave it to the ones who needed it, found orphans looking for food and water."

"*You* did that?" Amir asks.

"Did you think I'd become some beggar without you?" Sanya snaps. "I'm smart, Amir. I found a way to survive. On my own."

Amir looks affronted.

"And now we need to survive more than ever," Irfan says, arms crossed against his chest.

"Why?" Amir's tone is genuine.

"Trackers. They learned about what we were doing," Sanya reveals. "Figured out who Irfan was and plastered his face on a bunch of wanted posters."

That word sends a frisson of heat down my back. Trackers—a division of the Charts whose sole job is to find traitors against the monarchy. Those against Father. Those against *me*.

Amir's brows arch. "People called Irfan a hero."

I stare at the silver-eyed man. His build would easily get him into the barracks of Amratstan's army. He's young enough, too, a few summers older than Saeed. I imagine him draped in Amratstan's signature sapphire, speaking in their high, lilting accent. The man's hair is wild, clothes nothing more than rags, but his eyes are alight with a barely dampened fire, a rage bottled in glass.

"Sorry to disappoint," he says. "I'm just . . . this. But I'm doing what I can, and trying to avoid rotting in a pit of snakes in the end."

We all shudder. Indeed, the snakes have been getting more than their fair share of meat lately. And what Irfan and Sanya were doing was certainly noble—feeding the hungry. Should they be executed for that?

Sanya continues, "I took a job at the tavern to keep a low profile. Not surprised you knew where to find me."

At my blank stare, Amir fills in: "We used to stay here a lot as kids. The barkeep let us have a cot."

"And now I barely have any shifts," Sanya mumbles.

"What happened to wanting to be a healer?" Amir asks.

Sanya bristles. "Long story. Maybe this time you'll be around long enough to hear it . . . brother."

Amir looks as if he's been stung by a jungle crow.

Irfan gives me a once-over, as if seeing me for the first time. "Have we met before? You seem familiar."

I slump my shoulders, act the part of a lifelong peasant, though I'm afraid this sharp-eyed man will see right through it. "I'm just a villager looking for the Mailan Foothills. Amir said Sanya could help us get to the Hidden Lands where the Foothills are located."

"Yeah, and if the Trackers are after you, it's not safe to stay in one spot, anyway," Amir says. "Just hear us out. Helping us can help you, too."

Sanya sighs audibly. "Don't get your kurta in a twist, Amir. We don't need the two of you in the way. C'mon." She turns away, heading back into the tavern. Irfan follows her; Amir stays still as stone.

"That's it?" I ask him, staring at their retreating forms. "You're not going after them?"

"What's the point? You heard her. I'd just get in their way."

But that cannot be the only reason he doesn't want to follow his sister. Something happened to them, their family, that split them apart.

*What would Ria do?*

I start off at a jog, turning at the end of the trail. "Aren't you coming?" Eventually, Amir follows me with a sigh, and we catch up with Sanya and Irfan at the tavern's back entrance.

"Think you could get rid of us that easy?" I ask as Irfan slinks back inside. Sanya is about to do the same, but she halts.

"You just can't leave us alone, can you?"

Amir reddens, about to pipe up a response, but I go first. "We'd be grateful for a place to rest." I nudge Amir, who echoes my words somewhat begrudgingly.

Sanya glances at her brother. She huffs as she swings open the door wider, then brushes us inside. Without a word, she turns away from the barkeep and patrons and toward a narrow staircase. I follow close behind, shielding my face. The stairs creak under our weight as we approach the second floor.

At the end of the hall, Sanya pulls out a brass key and unlocks her room, a meager space for two with a bit of floor space. Certainly far from my four-poster bed and vanity.

"I can't afford another room," Sanya says. "I'm using all the savings Ma gave me before . . ."

"Like I said, we're grateful. Aren't we, Amir?" I need Ria's friend to play along, or I'll never learn more about the Foothills.

One night on these floors might be unseemly for a girl of my status, but at least it's not dirt.

Sanya grunts. "Only for tonight. Ma would've wanted that."

Her voice softens in a way I haven't heard before. Perhaps she hardened herself, alone on the streets, the same way Amir and Ria did.

I feel as if I'm intruding on their space, unresolved tension crackling like a winter hearth. But I won't deny this offer, not when this girl could be my ticket to the Foothills.

Though I've never picked up a broom in my life, I spend the day with Amir helping Sanya clean the tavern to repay her. I'll do anything to get further along my quest.

That night, after a small meal of papad and pickled vegetables, we take our rest on the floor, a scratchy blanket shared between Amir and me.

When Sanya enters the room, candle in hand, she doesn't say a word. Amir is already sleeping, but a question itches at my throat.

"Do you think you and Irfan would ever go back to it?" I whisper amid Amir's soft snores.

Sanya sinks onto the bed. She knows what I'm asking; would they ever return to their life of charity, of helping others for no reward.

Sanya hesitates. "Yeah. But it doesn't really matter anymore, does it?"

Her question doesn't invite an answer. Instead, her words drift like smoke in the silence. Then she blows out the candle.

## 15

### Ria

"Ow!" A thin sewing needle pokes me in the ribs.

"So bony," an auntie remarks, scrutinizing my waistline. "We'll need to tailor her a size down."

I stand in the middle of the women's room, an animal pinned under the spotlight. Rani's maids hold rivers of fabric of all weights and colors, from heavy golden blouses to light silver skirts. Behind the maids are a beehive of gossiping aunties, the commentary on their tongues ready to sting. They prod my skin, measure my torso, spin me in dizzying circles.

It's my second full day at the palace and I'm already exhausted. This morning I woke to a fresh schedule at my bedside and a cold note from Saeed, written in precise scrawl.

> *Your mother has asked that I provide you a strict schedule for lessons. We will rotate with other classes as needed. This schedule will be put into effect beginning tomorrow.*

*History of Abai—Reptile Terrarium, Ninth Bell*
*Physics—North Tower, Eleventh Bell*
*Etiquette—South Tower, Fourteenth Bell*
*Saeed*

He must've known today was dedicated to fittings and engagement party talk, and given me a day off. After waking up late, I feasted on the lunchroom's offerings: soft mattar paneer; crunchy pakoras; bright, spicy curries; steaming lentils. A bout of nausea turns the memories bitter: I've never eaten like that in my life.

Like royalty.

Another poke in the ribs, and the food is forgotten.

Ever since I spoke with Shima and Saeed, I've had my mind on one thing: finding the raja and queen and figuring out the truth. I have a little over a half-moon until Rani and I switch back, which means the clock is ticking fast.

"There's our princess." Amara appears in view, standing before me expectantly. Her stare is sharp, like she can see through me to who I really am. A thief. A fake.

Any sickness I felt seconds ago subsides, replaced by a cold slither down my spine.

"What have they been feeding you?" She lifts my right arm and taps me on the ribs, as if that'll magically make my skin grow thicker.

Amara grunts and turns, her attention on the bare counter in the center of the women's room. "I ordered a fresh batch of roses yesterday! Are the servants inept?" She shakes her head. "No matter. Well, Maneet? What do you think?"

Queen Maneet enters my view, sporting a sari bejeweled with gold and purple beading. My eyes burn into hers. *My mother.* But calling the queen *Mama* is too strange. She's not Mama Anita, and she'll never replace her.

Her smile as she looks at me is soft, yet wan. Too thin to be true but too wide to be meaningless. Maybe she sees *me*, her missing child, in front of her.

If only I could be with her alone, ask some questions—

"My daughter," she says, tilting my chin left and right as if to inspect my face for imperfections. She acts like she's more interested in Rani's appearance than her marriage, her thoughts, or the future of the kingdom. "Tell the maids to keep you from the sun. Your engagement party is coming, you know. And you must start eating properly—your cheeks are getting hollow."

Instinctively, I touch my right cheek faintly. Deep-seated shame sears my face. I pull away, not because of the way she's inspecting me, *criticizing* me, but because the queen doesn't seem to notice me, the person, one bit.

"Are you prepared for your engagement?" one woman asks.

"Your lehenga should be red," says another. "The color of tradition and true love."

"No," another interjects. "Magenta is the new trend."

Amara thankfully whisks me away from the women and behind a folding screen. A maid dresses me in a fabric that's bright yellow at the top and seeps into a ruby red. When I present myself to the aunties, they all shake their heads. Amara snaps her fingers, and another maid comes forward. The next is a lehenga that's snug at the hips and sapphire blue with a matching blouse. When the maid fastens the chunni around my neck, I imagine it's my own—the one I stole from a silk merchant in a faraway village two moons back.

"Raja's beard," I say, shocked at the silky material. From the confused expressions on the maids' faces, I quickly say, "Do you think it's . . . suitable?"

The queen's look is one of disapproval. My stomach drops, and I clear my throat to hide my disappointment. I'm not here to play dress-up, but I need to get this over with. The quicker I'm out of here, the quicker I'll get my answers.

And yet even as much as a part of me detests this, another part is astounded. Maids, following *me* around? Dressing *me* in the finest silks in Abai? I shouldn't like it, not even the thought of it, but it all makes me feel like a little girl dressing up in Mama Anita's finest clothes. I didn't care how oversize they looked on seven-year-old, bony me—I dreamed that I was a noble person, someone worthy of attention.

I try on more, and the queen looks almost bored by the options. She rises, clapping her hands twice. "These colors aren't agreeing with me. Red, on the other hand, is tried and true. Amara, let us break for a while. In the meantime, please take Rani to start looking at jewelry." The queen makes for the door, the maids close behind.

"Wait," I say, but the queen is gone, disappeared out the door, the maids right behind her. "Won't I need her approval?" What I really want to say is, *Won't I get another chance to speak with her?*

*To . . . get to know her?*

My stomach swirls with confusion. I feel light-headed.

Amara sighs. "Remember, Rani, that I am your father's adviser," she whispers darkly. "Which means that aside from his, mine is the opinion that matters most now."

I shake my head. Though the words are harsh, Amara says them with sickening sweetness, as if afraid the queen will walk back in at any minute. As we make our way out of the room and across the hall, I pass a collection of whispering Charts who straighten when I'm near. They are pillars of strength, of force. The closer they are, the more I fear them. Right now I'm the princess, but the guise feels flimsy as the soldiers' eyes settle on mine. Eyes like black, steaming coals.

I force myself to look away. Amara guides me like I'm cattle, and we end up in a smaller room holding arrays of jewelry on glass stands. I salivate at the thought of all those jewels spilling out of my pockets.

"You heard your mother," Amara snaps. "Choose." She grabs a collection of necklaces, clutching them like they're scraps of metal instead of precious jewels, and thrusts them at me. I hurry to try on a necklace, then a set of bangles Amara selects from a stand.

"Too orange," she decides flippantly, unclipping the necklace. She throws on another set and grimaces in disgust. "Certainly suitable for peasants."

"What's wrong with peasants?" I blurt.

My bangles jingle as she twists me around, inspecting me.

"The world doesn't live as you do, Rani. There are thieves out there. Rats."

My hands tighten into fists. "A thief isn't a rat. Some people aren't born rich."

Amara sticks up a brow. "I didn't realize you felt so strongly about this topic, Rani. I thought you to be a self-serving princess all these years."

My cheeks burn. "I meant you don't have to be a princess, or any kind of royal, to belong here. In the palace, in Anari, anywhere. After all, *you're* here."

Amara's silent after that. Even my own words make me quiet.

I've said too much.

"I'm only here thanks to your parents' generosity. After I set up your mother with the raja, I became like a noble myself. They accepted me to live here after Kumal's passing. Saeed's father was only twenty-four. Or have you forgotten that detail?"

"I—I'm sorry." I didn't realize how important Amara was to the king and queen. Or that Saeed's father died so young.

Amara takes my wrists in her hands. Too thin, she's probably thinking. A clear difference between Rani and me.

I stare at her hands, suntanned and marked with blisters on the palms. No . . . not blisters. Some sort of scar, faded with age. And above them, bracelets, cuffs, locked onto each forearm.

I point at them without thinking. "What are those?" They're gold-plated cuffs inscribed with a symbol. An eye.

This is the kind of jewelry that would sell in the marketplace for at least fifty silver coins. A couple moons' worth of food and shelter.

"These?" She bristles, then clasps her hands together. "A simple gift from my father. Before he passed." She says the words matter-of-factly, but her face is drawn, and she glances away.

"Would you talk to him again? If you had the chance?" I don't know where the words come from, but I'm suddenly reminded of Mama Anita. What I would do if I could just talk to her one last time. But she's gone.

"Such a magic doesn't exist," Amara snaps.

"Oh. Right." The words eke out of me, and I wish Rani had told me more about Amara—their relationship, her past. I don't know how to read her. Amara turns, putting some jewelry into a silver-laden box, and I catch a glimpse of what looks like keys dangling from a loop on the waist of her sari.

*I am your father's adviser . . .* Rani hadn't mentioned that to me. Had Rani and Amara's relationship always been taut as a stretched rope?

"That was a long time ago." She clenches her fingers into fists, then exhales. "And of no importance to your fitting."

She turns me back to the mirror and begins prodding me with more jewelry. After a few moments, I can't help but ask the next question that comes out of my mouth. "What tonic do you prescribe to your son?"

"Excuse me?" Amara looks entirely befuddled in the mirror, her expression quickly giving way to anger. "You set your damned snake on my son. Don't you think he needs something to help him rest?"

*Rani* let Shima loose on Saeed? But why? *How?*

And Saeed said he'd been having dreams for a while now. That's what the tonic is supposed to be for—not trouble sleeping. So why is Amara lying?

I need to get things back in my control. *I'm* the royal one here, and I'd better start proving I belong. "Is that any way to speak to the princess, Amara?"

Amara chuckles derisively. "I can speak in any way I please. And if you forget to call me Amara-ji again, I'll make sure your father will hear of it. Every. Last. Detail."

Her heels clack, stabbing the floor with each step as she paces the room. I attempt to hide my frustration. No wonder Rani hadn't mentioned her to me. Her mother-in-law *and* the king's adviser? Amara's very existence is nothing more than a recipe for torture.

As Amara moves, the jangling of keys echoes in the room. That sound catches my attention: with Amara as the raja's adviser, she must have keys to some pretty important places.

Maybe even places containing important records.

Records that could show me the truth of my birth.

*The whole reason I stayed in this Masters-forsaken place.*

"Amara-ji," I call out sweetly, grinding the name down with my teeth. "I apologize dearly; I should treat my father's adviser with more respect."

"As you must," Amara concurs, still pacing. "Your engagement party is less than a half-moon away. I expect only the best for my son."

"Of course," I say, careful not to stutter. I turn on my charm, the one that got me through so many nights on the streets. "Please have a seat, Amara-ji. It's only right we find *you* some jewelry for the engagement. After all, you are the mother of the groom."

Amara eyes me like she's on to the game I'm playing. Thankfully, she takes a seat at the vanity and begins to try on earrings. I eye the keys at her waist hungrily.

Now or never.

I bend over, using one hand to sort through the jewelry, while my other roams to the key ring on Amara's side, the keys splayed along the velvet chair.

I press a hand to the keys, silencing them with my fist. I try slipping them off the key ring, slow and steady, just like I'm thieving fresh naan. I'm so close, tasting victory on my tongue, when the door flies open. The keys slide out of my grasp.

"Any progress?" the queen asks, holding a cup of tea in hand.

"Not much," Amara says, scanning her nails. Meanwhile, the queen strolls to the vanity, sets her cup down, and takes another look at me. With a gentle hand, she brushes away a stray lock of hair. It feels . . . wrong. Unnatural. The act is too sentimental for the Snake Queen, for someone other than Mama Anita. I don't want her near me, but she looms so close I can't escape her without causing a scene. She has my eyes, my lips, my skin. Her hands are long and slender like mine, her hair dark and just as wiry. *My* hair. Except hers has been tamed into submission.

My heart pitter-patters. This is what I wanted—a chance to talk to my parents. A chance to discover who I really am, before Amir and I escape.

So I force a lie off my tongue. "Saeed gave me an assignment. I need to record my personal history. I need to know about my birth, my childhood—all of it."

The queen eyes me quizzically, then laughs. "Rani, dear, I am not sure where to start."

I force myself to speak. I'm *her* daughter, but right now I just feel like a fraud.

"You've told the story many times, Maneet," says Amara, as if bored.

The queen nods. "It was a simple birth, Rani. All went as planned."

She's obviously holding back. Frustration boils my blood. Why can't she tell me why I grew up in an orphanage?

"And my father's reaction?" I press.

The queen glances away. "Hmm. What did he say?"

Before I can speak, Amara stands abruptly. "Why are we discussing such trivial details? Come now. The fitting is not yet over."

The queen agrees, snapping her fingers and calling for the maids to draw me back to the women's room, where they wait with more lehengas.

Anger flares deep in my belly. It was as if the queen *didn't know* she'd birthed two daughters.

I've been starved of more than just food. I've been starved of a family.

I force a smile as the maids hold out the new outfits. They flood toward me, as if I'm some kind of magnet. Maybe I am. Rani and I lived on opposite poles, yet inched closer together, until finally, everything clicked.

And then split apart.

I play along with the fitting, knowing I'll be out soon enough. Because in the back of my mind, I'm not thinking about the color of the decor, or the assortment of bindis and bangles and everything else a princess should care about. I'm watching the halls, the servants filtering in and out, the Charts reporting to the raja.

A few soldiers march out of a hallway where I spot, farther back, a room with a sleek desk, behind which now sits the king himself. *His office.*

It's not like I can just barge in there and demand my birth papers. Could I? If I make things too obvious, the raja and queen might suspect something of me. And it's not like the queen was giving me straight answers about my birth, either.

I need to figure this out in secret. *Wait. Watch. Strike when the time is right.*

That's how I steal. And that's how I'll uncover the truth.

"Let's wrap this up now," Amara says with a clap. "I'm tiring myself with all these tasks."

The queen nods and leaves, but I'm not done yet.

A thief's work is never finished.

I make my way to Amara and lay a hand on her shoulder. "Thank you, Amara-ji," I begin, "for all your help with this engagement."

"Don't butter me up," she replies, though I can tell she's enjoying every sweet utterance from my mouth. "Be ready for another fitting soon, dear Rani."

She leaves, only her footsteps echoing behind her, not a jangle of keys to be heard.

I lift my hand up to view my slim thief fingers clutched tightly, a glint of gold peeking out from underneath. I grin, pocket the keys, and leave the room without a sound.

# 16

## Rani

"Eat."

I jolt in my spot. I rub my eyes, suppressing a yawn as watery sunlight creeps into the tavern's dining area. I spent the night poring over Tutor's book on plants, trying to decipher the strange symbols he'd written in the margins and failing. Now Amir pushes a tray toward me, holding a plate of chopped banana sprinkled with cinnamon and a cup of fresh water. We eat breakfast in our own little bubble while awaiting Irfan and Sanya. I try not to gawk at the lack of silverware, the mud-brown utensils we use in its place, the copper-rusted tray.

I imagine I am sitting in a grand hall with candlelit tables. I imagine a maid running her fingers through my tresses. But today, there is no crown on my head.

"Where is your tray?" I ask Amir.

"That's for both of us. What—not enough for you, Princess?" He licks his fingers like he wants more.

*Hardly,* I think, but refrain from speaking it aloud. I swallow the pride itching to escape me, the part of me that wakes only to finely brewed chai and freshly baked breads. How could anyone survive on such meager portions?

Meanwhile, Ria is likely gasping at the spreads at the palace. How does she feel, being locked up in the palace the way I was locked up my entire life? I've spent a day out here in the wilds of Abai, walking more than I ever have, seeing more than my eyes have ever seen. It all hit me when I fell asleep last night, and now, at nearly high noon, my body craves the palace's cool climate.

"Just a little famished is all," I manage. My stomach growls, and a pang of hunger, like an aching cramp, seizes me. I am reminded of the days when I first practiced snake magic. My gift was so weak that the nurses had to give me a daily tincture of venom to build my strength, even if it made me sick at first. The cooks laced my food with it to build my immunity, until I turned thirteen and performed my Bonding Ceremony successfully. I still take the tincture every now and then to boost my magic.

*"Famished?"* Amir laughs. "This is more than we've had in days!"

"You ate the apple," I remind him.

"So? That was hardly anything. And you were supposed—" He stops himself.

"I know. *I* didn't steal anything." My voice is sharp as a blade.

Amir huffs quietly. "I'm sorry. I didn't mean it like that. We're just usually so in sync, y'know?"

I bite my lip. Why can't I be more like Ria? This charade would be much simpler if I were.

Slowly, Amir reaches a hand across the table and covers mine. "You're still the best thief in Abai. *And* my best friend."

My heart thuds. Even though he speaks of Ria, a pleasant warmth fills me. And for a second, I understand what thieving means to them. It's not simply a performance. It's a code. And it's survival.

A voice knifes into our conversation. "Looks like you two sleepyheads woke up late. We already ate our breakfasts." *Sanya*. She tips her head at Irfan, who now sits across from me. Amir leans back.

I offer a practiced smile at her as she takes a seat. "Your spirits are up," I gibe. My gaze falls to her fist, gripping her beaded necklace with ferocity. Each bead is made from mango wood—the same wood that adorns Father's office. A faint pattern swirls over the beads, drawn in white ink.

"Your necklace," I say to Sanya. "Those markings look familiar." I know what the symbols are—but I wonder if Sanya understands them in the same way.

"They're said to be drawn inside the Glass Temple. Symbols of magic. The necklace belonged to our mother."

Sanya thumbs the heirloom. Every royal knows about those markings and the Glass Temple. Now we rarely speak of the magics those markings represented. In the Old Age, people would go to the Temple and pray to their Master. But the location of the

Temple was lost to time, and thus, the Temple itself was mostly forgotten.

"Those markings remained on the Temple's walls to remind us of a time when all magics thrived," I say. "The ones drawn on your necklace depict devotion to the Earth Master."

Sanya's gaze flicks toward mine. "Where'd you learn that? I only know about this magic stuff because of Ma."

"I . . . had a tutor at the orphanage."

"Since when do orphanages have tutors?" Amir challenges.

Thankfully, Sanya cuts in before I have the chance to speak. "You know, we wouldn't need a *reminder* of magic if we still had it. Rumors be damned."

"Rumors?"

Amir stiffens. "No one really believes magic still exists." He looks at me for confirmation. "People've been whispering in the villages. Saying some are showing rare signs of powers." He waggles his eyebrows at me for good measure.

Rare signs? I think of what Ria mentioned to me—the fever children. Kids showing an inkling of power. Could there be truth to these rumors?

Sanya, for once, agrees. "Damn the royals. It's their ancestor's fault that most magic's been wiped out. You know, I bet that the raja is the real killer, not just the snakes. He probably lures his prey into the palace's Snake Pit and kills his victims with his own fangs."

"You truly believe those stories?" I snap. "The royalty might speak to snakes, and they may share similar attributes, but they are not serpents themselves."

"I'd have to see a royal to believe it," Sanya says, wearing a cruel smile. She seems to enjoy my discomfort.

*Believe me*, I think, *you already have.*

"Enough," Amir says. "Can we eat our food in peace without any bickering?"

Sanya shuts her mouth. I stuff mine with food before I can say something out of turn. At least with the table now silent, I can ponder Irfan and Sanya's hushed conversation from early this morning. I overheard them at dawn, chattering about no longer wanting to be wanderers, and needing horses. . . .

Sanya had mentioned yesterday that the barkeep was barely giving her shifts. And after getting changed this morning into some of Sanya's spare clothes, I noticed that Irfan and Sanya had already packed their bags. Like they were prepared to leave at a moment's notice. Perhaps they were ready to look for a new place, a fresh start.

I inquire of Irfan, "Have you always been a nomad?"

"Not always," he says mysteriously. "I've been looking for others to join me. There's strength in numbers."

I've dreamed of living life with no chains or shackles. Free. It always felt like a fantasy, a dream too far out of reach.

Sanya cuts Irfan a talwar-sharp look. "Are we sharing all of our hopes and wishes with each other now? Telling each other our life stories?"

I eye Irfan, wondering about his familiarity, though his silver irises mark him as a stranger in this kingdom. "We know your story. You disobeyed the royals to help others. Now you're fugitives."

"What's it to you? It's been months since we last offered passage to—" He cuts himself short. "Those days are over."

What had he been about to say? I thought they'd only brought villagers food. Yet his eyes tell me there is more to the story: he didn't simply forget his lawless ways; he abandoned them.

"Sanya told me last night that if she had the chance, she would go back, help villagers like you used to." At my words, Sanya's eyes turn to red-hot coals, steaming into mine.

"Why—" She pauses, glancing around the tavern, and lowers her voice. "I told you, we stopped when the Charts noticed what we were doing."

"But you didn't want to stop." It's a statement, one that clearly resonates. The two exchange a long glance.

"If you help us, it'll be like old times," Amir reasons, catching on. "You'd be helping us, and we'd be helping you."

"How?" Irfan retaliates.

"I heard your conversation this morning." My voice is so quiet, the wind whistling through the tavern nearly takes it away. "You want horses for transport out of here, don't you? We could help with that."

Amir catches on. "We're thieves, and damn good ones."

Sanya harrumphs. "And how would we help you?"

"Amir said you know of the Mailan Foothills," I tell Sanya. "We don't want money. We want knowledge."

Sanya crosses her arms tightly. "I'm guessing Amir never told you? We lived there—with our parents when we were children. We left about ten years ago."

"What?" I turn to Amir. "You told me you'd only heard of the Foothills, not that you'd been there."

Ria's friend bites his lip. "I'd nearly forgotten about the place before you brought it up. After our parents . . ." His gaze flickers to Sanya's. "Well, it was more Sanya's dream than mine to go back there."

Sanya's glowering softens.

"You see?" I press. "Our goals align." I can't give up this opportunity. This is the only way I can get to the Foothills. I might be on this mission to prove something to Father, but Tutor also asked me for his help. I need to remember what Tutor told me, to come into my own the way Queen Amrita did. I'm more than just the Snake Princess. I'll prove it.

Sanya blows a breath. "Truth is, Irfan and I didn't just steal food. We—we smuggled people. We helped them escape the draft. Kept them away from a life as a soldier."

"What? You didn't mention that yesterday," Amir says.

"Well, the less you knew, the better," Sanya says spitefully. "I remembered the way, so I led people through secret routes to the Hidden Lands. It's a safe haven for people, for families who were desperate."

"It's been half a year since we last went," Irfan divulges. "When Sanya found me, she made me realize this war is big but not too big for us to stop. They expect us to die, but the best revenge is to live."

The words settle into my bones.

Amir's eyes widen. "So why are you guys staying here? In the tavern?"

"I was saving up the money for Jas Auntie," Sanya says stubbornly. "And now the barkeep is kicking me out. I barely have enough coins to keep a bed at the tavern. As for the passports . . ." She gazes at Amir. "Every time I thought of them, I remembered you. How much you wanted them for us. So I convinced Jas to start making fake passports for people we brought to the hills. So they could escape if need be."

"Jas Auntie?" Amir asks. "Making . . . fake passports?"

"Yeah, that's why we need the money—to get materials." Sanya must notice my confusion, because she clarifies, "Jas is an old family friend in the Mailan Foothills. She helped my parents out for a while." The memory offers a flicker of yearning in Sanya's eyes. "Amir and I met her as kids. Over the past year, I returned to her a few times with as much money as I could muster. But now even if I wanted to go back, we can't afford a new steed. Sold our last one."

"You don't need to pay for a horse when we can steal 'em. Maybe this is our best bet," Amir convinces. "Do you really wanna sleep on the streets like I have? Sanya, we both dreamed of more than this."

Sanya's eyes go glassy with remembrance, but she shakes her head. "We shouldn't do anything else to draw attention. Charts are on our tails as it is. And if they're looking for the stone Samar was after . . ."

The air itself freezes. My heartbeat is in my fingertips. "The Bloodstone," I say. I hadn't known villagers were knowledgeable on the subject.

"So you've heard of it, huh?"

"Just a bedtime story."

"Not all stories are make-believe," Sanya huffs. "The Bloodstone is very real, very powerful, and very hidden."

*And my first clue to finding it is in the Foothills*, I think. Tutor handed me a clue—the ring. The ring with the leaf from the plant that grows in the Foothills. I need to follow it.

"Rumor is, the raja's got the Charts out looking for the stone— he wants it before the war starts. To *win* the war," Irfan says.

I am startled by his words. Father has been preparing for this battle against Kaama for years, inspired by King Amrit's cold-blooded fervor. If he found a stone that could change the fate of Abai with just one wish . . .

Perhaps Father wants to do what his great-grandfather could not. Find a way to become the most powerful king to have ever existed.

Is this why Tutor left the palace four years ago? Did Tutor know the king and his soldiers were looking for the stone?

This situation is more dire than I thought. We need to leave, *now*.

"Look, Sanya." I add a layer of vigor to my tone. "Right now you need horses, yes?"

Dejected, Sanya nods.

"Then you'll both need a thief's hands. And two thieves would be all the better. We'll steal a few horses for transport and get to the Foothills." I reach into the pouch hidden in my cloak, offering a few shining coins. "I don't have much, but you can get all the materials you need. Do we have an agreement?" A part of me wants to keep the money—I'm running out quickly—but I need these two on my side.

It takes a moment for Sanya and Irfan to consider the offer, but with no other choice, they agree.

Now I have two strangers and a thief on my journey, and time is ticking away. I won't waste a second of it.

"So, what's the plan, Princess?"

Amir's words nearly make me jump out of my skin, but I quickly remember the nickname to be a jest.

We're standing in a village—Vadi, I remember from my lessons—and a poor one at that. It looks nothing like Anari, the capital, with glittering spires and flourishing markets; here, everything is coated with a fine layer of dust, even the air we breathe. A newsboy in a green kurta rushes by, reminding me of palace servants in their jade attire. But while the palace gleams like a diamond, the huts here are dull like aged sandstone. A deep sense of unease starts to grow in me as I take in the squalor around me, so far from the opulence I grew up with.

As I step forward, I realize the ground is cracked and uneven. "Has a drought passed through here?" Even the air feels stagnant, sticky.

"Not that long ago," Irfan says, eyeing me as if the answer should be obvious. "Hundreds of years without tidesweepers have cost us." He sighs. "The balance in our world isn't the same. Everyone's noticed, even if they don't realize the cause."

Shame burns my cheeks. How could I have never known that magic has ripped my kingdom of its resources? Cost my people their lives, their comfort? If tidesweepers still existed, water would not have to be such a limited resource. With flametalkers, heat could be restored with just a touch on a cool winter's night. All I have ever known is snake magic, and the lives it can so easily take. I've never thought of the *good* magic could do.

The good I could do.

"Follow me," Irfan says, urging us out onto the dirt-paved road. I train my gaze ahead, though I see heads turning, as if they sense something amiss with my too-perfect features, or the healthy glow of my cheeks.

Men and women plow their wheelbarrows through the dirty streets, faces lined with grime. The air is smoky, filled with fog and mist, secrets and sorrow.

The stables are in my line of sight. Irfan's plan echoes in my ears: head to the east quarter, find the stables, distract the merchant. *Simple enough*, Amir had replied. Except for the fact that I am certainly *not* the best thief in Abai. I am no thief at all.

"Ria? What's wrong?" Amir says at my silence.

"Nothing," I snap harshly. Too harshly. I glance around, watching Irfan and Sanya head to the crest of the Moga Jungle. "I'm a bit on edge is all. Maybe we could just, I don't know, tempt the horses out of the stables with food?"

"*Horse* food?" Amir laughs. "You need to relax, Ria. Stealing is like being in quicksand. If you panic, you'll drown."

Although Amir's advice is sound, nothing can stop the fear rising in my throat. "Perhaps you should do it."

Amir's brows scrunch in confusion. "You mean . . ." His eyes light. "I knew you had a plan brewing! You'll distract the merchant while I get the horses to Irfan and Sanya."

"Um, well—"

"Perfect," Amir says. Before I can utter a response, Amir spins me in the other direction. Everything blurs together; I'm a fish without water, a princess without her throne. A girl in a beautiful sari about to become a horse thief.

But I must look like I know what I'm doing. Ahead of me sits a gate to the merchant's stall, behind which stands an endless array of horses. Amir is nowhere to be found, already moving like a shadow.

*Distract the merchant. Do not get caught.* The words sizzle in my bones like one of Father's cold commands. I approach the stall as though I am the raja: confident, poised, calm. Tutor's words ring to mind. *To be royal is to act royal. Be poised, be precise, and you shall be unquestionably a leader.*

"Good day," I say, keeping my voice light and regal. The more attention I attract, the better.

The merchant stands as tall as he is wide. He's got at least a head on me, his arms bulky and roped. Fine gray hairs sprout from the crown of his head.

"Whaddaya want?" Merchant Man asks.

"I'm afraid I'm very lost," I say, turning my voice to a whimper. "I was wandering through the jungles with little food when I found Vadi. I haven't much coin to spare, you see." Exhausted as I am, I call upon the magic in my veins, praying my voice will be as luring as a snake's rattle.

"Yeah?" He narrows his eyes. "Where'd ya get those earrings?"

"I am humbler than you think, sir. A gifted jeweler from Nabh offered me this." The words taste sour, but they slip off my tongue easily.

"I am quite lost," I repeat. "Perhaps you could help me."

"I ain't a map." He juts his thumb behind him. "Scram."

I sneak a glance at the stables. One horse gone. *Keep the charade up a while longer.* But I cannot think of what else to do. I need to think like Ria—like a thief.

"You don't seem to understand," I say, drawing out the words. I reach into my pouch and fish out a coin, quiet as a whisper. I slide it to the merchant and lean in.

"I'm looking for information on an artifact," I begin, voice low, "long believed to be a fable."

"Could be anything," the man says, though his gaze sharpens

as he observes the coin, curious. Wondering what kind of game I've orchestrated. He slides the coin to his side of the table and examines it in the light. "You know the name of this object?"

I swallow, thinking carefully. "I believe it to be called . . . the Bloodstone."

The man laughs, his lips forming a mocking grin. "Yeah, that thing only exists in people's nightmares. Rumors pass around here all the time, though. A man was searching for it, thinking the bloody thing existed."

My heart skips a beat.

"The man . . . was his name Samar?" I ask, my voice more desperate than I'd like. I think back to the ring he gave me. "Was he—or the stone—connected in any way to the Mailan Foothills?"

Merchant Man huffs. "If you want to know more"—he glares pointedly at the pouch—"I'll need another coin."

One less coin. If that's what it takes to find more information on Tutor and the stone, then I shall offer him so.

I pluck the shiniest coin from the pouch and hold it before his eyes. He licks his lips greedily, and before he can swipe for it, I pull back.

The man narrows his eyes. "I didn't know the man's name. All I knew was he had a wife living in the Foothills, her home. Now gimme."

My eyes widen, and I withhold a breath as I offer the coin.

If Merchant Man is discussing Tutor, then could this man be

telling me about Tutor's wife? What if Tutor didn't give me the ring just to lead me to the stone? What if he gave it to me to find not only some*thing* but some*one*.

*His wife.* Tutor had told me she has a matching ring. Perhaps he wanted me to find the stone . . . by finding her first.

While the man inspects the money, my gaze shoots back to the stables. Two horses gone. Almost there—

"If I didn't know any better," the man says, "I wouldn't think a wealthy girl like you, with those earrings and so many coins to spare, would be interested in an old man chasing fairy tales."

My cheeks burn. "I told you, I am a humble girl."

Three horses gone. I turn to leave, but the man grabs my wrist, shackling me to him. His grip is like iron. That quicksand pools beneath me, and Amir's words flash through my head. *If you panic, you'll drown.*

A sea of fears eclipses the confidence I once felt. That sand inches higher, threatening to swallow me whole.

"Hey!" Merchant Man spins, noticing something amiss, his two beady eyes drilled to the open stables. "My horses are gone! Thief!"

I snatch the coin back from his grimy fingers. "I prefer the term *purloiner.*" Without a moment to spare, I break for the jungle, where Amir is waiting.

I glance left and right, legs still pumping, and just as my eyes lock on Amir, two roughened hands clamp onto my leg.

"Give it back, girl!" the man says, and I tumble into the dirt face-first. Merchant Man wears a hungry grin as he grapples for the pouch in my cloak. On instinct, I kick up between his legs and he curls inward with a pained yell. I scramble upward and sprint in the opposite direction, stopping once to look back only when I'm a few paces away from my destination.

Merchant Man is still doubled over. Something makes me pause. I might be pretending to be Ria, but I'm no thief. I brush off my sari, reminding myself of the poise I have always known, and step toward him.

"Here," I say, pulling off my earrings and letting them fall to the ground next to the merchant. "Payment for the horses." In my head, I chant the words Tutor instilled in me: *My voice is power, my voice is strength.*

"You shall not speak of this to anyone. Forget me," I say.

The man only stares at the earrings, perplexed. "What—" He gathers his thoughts. "What was your name again, girl?"

I gather air into my lungs. Feel my power running through my veins. I shake my head. "I'm no one."

Without a second to spare, I run as fast as my legs will carry me, into the nearest brush. I rest against a tree, praying Merchant Man hasn't come to look for me again. I loosen a breath just as a hand grips my arm.

It is Amir: eyes lit, scar pronounced against his flushed skin. The look on his face nearly makes me sigh in relief.

"You got the horses?"

"Yeah, thanks to you," Amir says. He leads me farther into

the trees to where Irfan and Sanya are waiting. "Those horses are damn hard to tie down," he continues, "but three will be enough."

Irfan brings his gaze to mine. "You really are the best thieves in Abai."

"But still strangers," Sanya finishes, gaze flinty. Her voice is rough, unflinching, but I pay no mind.

"A deal is a deal," I reply. "We've got the horses, now you need to get us to the Foothills." *Where Tutor's wife might still live.*

Irfan nods, looking to the group for confirmation. Though Sanya's face looks cut from stone, he and Amir seem content with the plan.

"Let's move our tails, then," Sanya says. "I'll lead the way to our material supplier, then we'll head to the Foothills."

Sanya spins and mounts her horse, Irfan just steps behind her, heading for another steed. I mount the third horse, and reluctantly, Amir follows. The feeling of his hands on my waist—so unlike Saeed's—unsettles me. They are warm, too warm. I like the feeling of cold in the air, ice against my skin. I like knowing no one, nothing, can break through that.

The horses spur, then kick off. Amir grips onto me tightly. "How'd you do that?" he asks.

"Do what?"

"Stop that merchant from chasing after you," Amir replies. "I heard you. You didn't run like usual—you spoke to him, stood your ground. What'd you say?"

I stiffen, but despite myself I enjoy the spark of admiration in

SISTERS OF THE SNAKE

his voice. I keep my eyes focused on the trail ahead, adjusting the reins as needed. "Nothing of import. Besides, you can't run from everything." The words burn my tongue. How hypocritical of me; here I am, running—from Father, from the palace, from destiny.

Still, Amir looks at me like I'm the sun and he's a planet locked in my orbit, steadfast and true. In the palace, I am simply moon dust: cold, untouched. Out here, I am not bound to the fate of a princess. And, for at least a little while, I'd like to keep it that way.

# 17

## Ria

The dining room is stifling hot, and it doesn't help that it's full
to the brim for tonight's dinner. I brush my braid away from my
sweaty neck and touch a finger to the threads of gold that snake
through my hair. They look like a trail of tiny, radiant stars. Jasmin, one of the maids, dressed me in a plum lehenga for tonight
with matching jewelry. I make a mental note to pocket the gems
I'm wearing; who knows how much it's all worth?

But right now I'm not here to be a thief. *Quit fantasizing. Look
like you're in command.* I repeat the words in my head, and to my
surprise, they feel as natural as my heartbeat.

A servant pulls out a seat for me, the second-nearest chair to
the raja. He sits at the head of the table and chats over something
with an adviser. A few of their words stick to the air, reaching me:
"*Weapon . . . searching . . . Irfan . . .*"

My brows arch in interest. That name—*Irfan*—is so familiar . . . yes! It was the name Samar had said back in Nabh, moments

before he was taken away. *"You won't find Irfan."* So why is the raja talking about an old naan merchant?

The back of my neck prickles, like someone's watching me. It's a thief thing, a sixth sense, feeling someone's gaze on you. I know I'm right when I spot Amara's eyes on mine, her lips painted a shade so bright red, I'm afraid it's blood. She's busy at the table making fruitless gossip with aunties from the women's room and some other nobles I don't recognize—but her eyes are fastened on mine.

"Princess," Amara says, interjecting my thoughts. "Please sit. Everyone has been patiently waiting for you!"

*I'm sure they have*, I think, but grin tightly instead and sit, pretending I didn't just steal a bunch of keys from her in the women's room. I need to stay quiet, smile and nod. Play my cards right. Wait for my moment to slip into the king's study.

What feels like a hundred gazes ruffle my demeanor, but I smile through it. I notice an empty seat across from me. Saeed isn't here tonight. Clinking sounds fill the air. Servants bustle in, handing out bowls of red onion steeped in vinegar and sprinkled with pepper. Minutes later, a tray of fish pakoras is laid out before us. My stomach rumbles. Fish isn't common for villagers to eat in Abai, with the kingdom's few bodies of water. Must be something the royals don't think about twice. I devour my food, almost moaning at the taste. I won't be able to figure everything out on an empty stomach, I reason.

By the third course, the table has settled into rhythmic

conversation. When Rani said the palace has feasts instead of meals, she wasn't kidding. I cool my palate with spiced dahi. The yogurt was one of my favorite foods from back in the orphanage.

Abruptly, someone arrives in the dining room, dressed in a crisp ivory shirt paired with silver bands on either arm. Saeed quietly shuffles toward an empty seat across from me, eyes downcast. I notice how tired he looks. For some reason, I thought he wouldn't show up to tonight's dinner, that maybe he was avoiding me. But then his warm eyes find mine, and I can't help the blush rising to my cheeks. He glances away.

I can tell there's something bothering him. He clenches his fingers around his fork, the creases between his brows deepening.

He's *definitely* not over yesterday's conversation.

Servants come around with mango lassi to wash down the meal. Hastily, I take two cups, placing them in front of me. Saeed's voice resonates in my mind. *No more apologies, Princess.* What went wrong? And what about those weird dreams he was talking about? And Amara's obvious lie about his tonic?

I sneak a glance at him, his golden eyes honey-drenched. Honey—food—*right*. I reroute my focus, turn back to my plate, but I suddenly feel the need to down this cold lassi to soothe the heat in my cheeks.

I eye the unused golden fork next to my plate, thinking on instinct of how I can slip my hand around the utensil and tuck it away. Just as I'm reaching for the fork, keeping my hand out of plain sight like Amir taught me, Saeed clears his throat. My fingers freeze. I stiffen for a moment before returning my hand to my side, his eyes settling on mine.

"Good evening," he says, jaw clenched.

"Evening," I reply lightly, wondering why he's suddenly making conversation with me.

"Enjoying your food?" He gestures at my plate, practically licked clean, then eyes my dirty silk napkins. *Definitely* not proper etiquette.

I stuff the napkin in my palm and press it to my lehenga. Just a second ago the raja was eyeing me with approval. Now, after I've gulped down my food, he looks at me warily, like he's confused to see his daughter so unrefined.

"Rani, dear," he laughs, and his voice booms so loud the entire room quiets. "Playing villager, are we?"

I glance down. The dirty napkin has left a trail of haldi on my clothes. The turmeric stain means nothing to me but everything to a royal.

My eyes snap up to the raja's, and I can't stop the irritation that sparks through me. "Villagers aren't dirty, if that's what you're insinuating."

A trio of gasps. Had Rani ever spoken back like that to her parents? I've been beaten and scarred before and never been able to use my voice. Now that I'm a princess, how can I be silent?

The raja is quiet before he forces out a good-natured chuckle. "That's enough, Rani."

"It's not," I say before I can stop myself. Whispers grip the table. "Those so-called peasants work themselves to the bone. If they're covered in dirt, it's because you made it so." I stare right at the raja.

He forces a smile. "Yes, everyone must do their part in our great kingdom. How about we enjoy the next course?" He claps, and servants warily bring teapots and desserts. A nervous chatter resumes.

"I think I'll pass." I shoot up and push the chair back with my legs, flinging the haldi-stained napkin on the table before I turn on my heel and stride out. The queen looks like she wants to call after me but doesn't want to cause a scene.

*Serves the raja right.* He should be listening to his people, not berating them. He'll have to listen once he knows who I really am. I finger Amara's keys in the band of my lehenga, letting that anger simmer into my familiar thief instincts. The raja will know better than to come after me, prissy princess that I am. Which means now's the perfect time to find his office.

But I still don't know my way around these halls. And it's not like I've got some handy map to help me. I scour the corridors, looking for the familiar shape of the raja's office door, and end up stumbling into a foreign part of the palace. The smell of simmering onions draws me in, and I walk in a sort of trance until I'm at the kitchens.

Inside, steam rises as the cook works on her meal. Servants, all merely children, carry trays of chai and fennel seeds. Aha! Maybe one of *them* can lead me to the raja's office. An older servant passes on orders and requests from the nobles, while a different girl is staring so deeply at the tray in her hands, she seems hypnotized.

She looks familiar. Of course—it's Aditi, Amara's servant, with two braids hanging from either side of her head.

She's still looking down as she clasps the tray, laden with a pot of tea, empty cups, and a fresh rose, heading for the exit.

"Excuse me?" I say at the door.

"Oh!" she cries, wobbling, just as I say, "Sorry, er, Aditi," steadying her.

"That's the first time you've apologized to me," Aditi mumbles, awestruck.

How little did my sister apologize for her actions? It's clear the servants don't dislike her—they *fear* her. Which means they fear me, too.

"I'm sorry, miss. I should have been paying attention. Is something the matter?" She doesn't quite look me in the eye, instead focusing on the odd smear of turmeric on my outfit. "You don't normally enter the servants' quarters."

How would Rani respond to the girl? Aditi looks nervous, like I'm about to dole out some punishment.

"I was just a bit lost, I'm afraid." I keep my voice low but rigid, like Rani's. "Could you escort me to the raja's office? I have business there."

"O-of course." Aditi, tray in hand, scuttles off into the corridor. The halls are like a maze as we make our way out of the cramped servant quarters and into the polished, marbled halls. "Here we are," she says when we're ten feet away from the room I saw earlier. I was right, this is his office.

"Thank you, Aditi. I can take it from here."

Aditi nods fast, then scurries away. Finally alone, I reach into the band of my skirt, finding the keys I stole from Amara. Last night I tried picking a few locks in different palace doors, but they were all duds. Thank the skies I was able to get Amara's keys today.

With these, I can crack open the truth of my birth.

At the doorknob, I wiggle one of Amara's keys a touch to the left, then the right, feeling for the latch. I pretend I'm just a girl back in Nabh stealing naan. A thief in princess's clothing is no less of a thief. A girl in disguise is no different from one blending into the shadows.

But the key isn't listening. I move on to the next key on the ring, then the next. I turn the key once more, and when I hear the telltale click, I hide a smile. *I'm in.*

The raja's office unfurls before me. Inside sits a velvet chair and a wooden table covered in parchment. Velvet drapes line the room from floor to ceiling, and the whole room stinks of royalty.

My gaze roams around until I catch sight of a piece of parchment lying on the ground, covered in hooked lettering and fancy scribbles. With furrowed brows, I lean down and pick up the top sheet carefully. Words leap off the page, capturing my attention.

*This weapon will be the finale of peace, the bringer of war. It shall change the tide of Abai's future. The fate of our world . . .*

I freeze. What weapon could this be about? My stomach turns when I see the word *war*. I'm supposed to be a soldier, a bloodcoat, as Amir would say. I drop the sheet quickly, as if these war plans will stain my fingers with ink. Mark me as a thief.

Something else on the page catches my attention.

*Kaamans want to break the truce . . . more soldiers are necessary.*

I shake my head. The handwriting is odd, loopy and spaced out, and way different from the caption at the top of the page. Who wrote this? And why would the Kaamans want to break the truce early? It makes no sense.

I move on from the sheet and head for a different corner of the room filled with drawers and bins, each holding papers with official wax seals. I begin to ruffle through the raja's cabinets, careful to keep quiet. Most of the files are unreadable legal documents and the like, war and taxes and crop productions. Any other time, I would pick through them and learn more about this damned Hundred-Year Truce, about the future of this kingdom, but I'm not here for that. I have one mission, and I need to fulfill it while I've still got the chance.

The cabinets turn out to be a bust. Of course there wouldn't be important information about a princess's birth just lying around in unlocked wooden cabinets. There's barely anything on Rani here at all.

I push myself away from the cabinets and spot something ahead of me, tucked into the corner of the office. A glass case enveloping a long, golden staff—a scepter with a carved snake head.

When I'm just a breath away, its eyes flash like rubies.

I leap back, but I can't pull my eyes away from the serpent's. Because they're no longer stone; they're flashing, inviting. In them are moving images: tears streaming down bruised faces; snakes' jaws gaping; faces blanching in horror. I feel their terror, feel the snakes' thirst for blood. I reel back.

I don't know much about snake magic—don't even know how to use it—but I know the rumors Amir told me about snakes feasting on villagers . . . it isn't a lie. The Snake Pit's real.

My skin crawls.

Overwhelmed by everything I've seen in the snake scepter's eyes, I tear away from the glass case. I spin and tumble past the raja's desk, past the door, and shut it closed with a thud. I'm done here.

"Find anything interesting?"

I jump. Behind me, Saeed looks like he's hiding a laugh, hands clasped behind his back. Strange to see him wearing a genuine smile instead of his recent scowl.

"Saeed! How'd you find me?" I whisper, though no one's around.

But I'm wrong. Aditi pokes out behind a pillar, still carrying her tray and looking small.

"Aditi brought me to you. I figured that if you weren't going to endure our engagement party details at dinner, neither should I have to. That speech was . . . bold of you."

"It's not wrong for a princess to speak up," I say. "Or a villager, for that matter."

"True, but it isn't like you to do so."

I bite my lip. I should be more careful. "It's not like I ditched dinner because of you. I thought you weren't even coming."

"I . . . got sidetracked. What were you doing in the raja's study?"

"I just needed some air."

"In your father's office, with the door closed," Saeed supplies. "Yes, I'm sure the air is much better in there."

The atmosphere between us turns thick as ghee. "Your point?" I don't break eye contact as I cross my arms.

Aditi's voice shakes as she steps between us. "M-Master Saeed, your tonic." She holds up the tray to Saeed, who finally rips his gaze from mine and pours himself a steaming cupful of liquid. He takes a sip before grimacing and setting it down. The liquid in the cup ripples and something inside my blood surges in kind. I sense . . . something.

Beads of sweat break out on Saeed's forehead, and his normally bright eyes darken. "Something wrong?" I ask.

"It's nothing. Just a little bitter." But I detect the lie easily. "Good night to you both." He bows, maybe out of spite, before he disappears down the hall.

I ignore my heated cheeks and turn to Aditi, inspecting the teacup on her tray. "May I?"

Aditi nods, offering me the cup, but she hunches her shoulders like she's afraid of stepping closer. I hold the steaming liquid up to my nose.

*Skies be good.* There's something familiar about the scent. Something that makes my blood stir.

I pour myself a fresh cup and hesitatingly take a sip. There's something coppery about it, something strange. "What's in this?"

"Mistress Amara asks that I not speak of it."

"And the rose?"

"She always asks for a fresh rose with the nightly tea. The brew is for Master Saeed, but I was headed to her room next." The girl trembles the way she did on Diwali night. Raja's beard, was that only two days ago?

"You can tell me." I pray she hears my honesty.

Aditi's voice is thin as a blade of grass. "I make it every night for Master Saeed, at Mistress Amara's request. It's a sleeping draft with song beetle juice—"

"Song beetle?" When I was seven summers old, the orphanage had an infestation. Turned out to be song beetles, which had flown from their native kingdom of Pania. I can still hear Mama Anita sweeping them away with a broom.

I snap back to the present. It's not beetles I'm worried about. It's that I sensed something *else* in that tonic. The coppery taste in my throat . . . I'd felt that before. When I first spoke to Shima. When I stared into that scepter in the raja's office.

Everything clicks into place. What I tasted wasn't song beetle juice.

It was snake venom.

# 18

## Rani

Sunset crests over the edge of the Moga Jungle when we dismount our horses and enter a steep path, mares in tow. Mine, a rough-maned horse with gentle eyes, has taken to nibbling at my pack, filled with ribbons of dried mango—hardly enough to snack on over a day and a half's travel. Yesterday, we stopped to get the materials we would need for Sanya's passport, and then we passed through grassy plains, which were enough to settle the horses' stomachs but certainly not mine.

The whole way here, Amir and I exchanged stories like keepsakes. Mine, my first lesson with Tutor, albeit a bit refined to leave out the palace. Amir, tales of his mother—she was sharp, unerringly kind, and with a wicked sense of humor that he apparently inherited. Sanya, within earshot the entire time, was silent. Or perhaps silently brooding.

"Here," Sanya says now, rolling up her map. She points ahead at an array of foliage indistinguishable from the surrounding fauna—until she pulls the branches and leaves back. This is no ordinary part of the jungle. In fact, there stands a wall before us, formed of sand and stone, with markings matching the ones on Sanya's necklace.

Marks of magic.

"Where are we?" I approach the wall. When I touch the sand, it reacts to my snake magic, and a frisson runs through my fingertips. Granules of dirt snake along the indented markings. The circular shapes bend to my will as I drag my finger down the wall just in front of me. Magic has always called to other magics . . . I just hadn't realized the Earth Master's magic had survived. Yet here it is, in this very wall.

Father was wrong. Other magics *do* still exist! But why is there earth magic here? I pull my hand away before the others can see.

"This," Sanya says, "is the entrance to the Mailan Foothills."

"I remember this." Amir joins me at the wall. "Ma and Papa held us on their shoulders so we could see over the wall, but we still weren't tall enough."

"These are ancient marks of the Old Age," I say.

"The same ones on my necklace." Sanya grasps the beads out of habit. "Ma got it from the Foothills a long time ago. She told me this place was forged by the stonebringers . . . you know, when magic thrived."

"The Foothills are a place of magic? Of the stonebringers?" I wonder. Stonebringers are descendants of the Earth Master. People who could manipulate rock and stone, or grow trees from the driest soil.

Sanya says, "Hundreds of years ago it was. The stonebringers mostly lived in Amratstan." She juts her chin over at Irfan.

"Amratstanians grow up with the legends," he says. "Stonebringers found refuge in their own magic-made mountains in Amratstan, after the Great Masters' Battle that ended in the Masters' disappearance and caused magic to fade away. But some stonebringers chose to stay here, in Abai."

"In the Hidden Lands," I say. "Why?"

Sanya sucks her cheeks in, and she looks a few years younger than her nineteen summers. "Ma and her friend Jas told me the story privately. Many of the stonebringers chose to stay and created the Foothills, a place to keep themselves secret from the snake-speaking royals. There are two parts to the Lands: the Mailan Foothills and the Forest of Hearts. The Foothills was their own settlement, named after their leader, Maila."

"The stonebringers could form dirt into rock," Irfan says. "They could make the sand levitate in the air like snowflakes."

I gasp in a breath, thinking of the sand dunes of Retan, the snowcapped mountains of Amratstan.

"Imagine what life would be like if we still had that," Sanya says, as if in a faraway dream. "The stonebringers could plow through fields and pick crops with just one thought. They were powerful people, more powerful, some thought, than the raja of Abai himself. But magic, Jas taught me, is like an elixir. If we drink too much, we're drunk on it. Our minds aren't as clear as they might be otherwise."

Has Father been drunk on magic? It would explain his sudden

fervor to acquire the stone and use it against the Kaamans. . . .

I paste on that thief's smile I practiced my first night in the jungles, but now it's too stiff, fake. This whole charade should mean nothing, but the deeper I play this role, the more I uncover the truth of my father's kingdom, and the more difficult it is to stay impartial.

I press a hand against the wall again. "How do we get past this?"

Sanya unfurls her map, pointing to one corner. "There's a password I wrote down," she informs us. "Our mother gave it to us when we were kids. It was something she and Papa recited every time we came to the Hidden Lands."

I turn to Amir. "Do you remember this?"

Amir sucks in his cheeks, an embarrassed frown on his lips. "I . . . think it always stayed in the back of my mind. A mantra."

Sanya smiles sheepishly. "Ma played a game with us to help us, remember?"

Suddenly Amir looks down. "We were kids. We aren't any-more."

A cloud passes over Sanya's face. "Guess I didn't realize becoming adults meant forgetting our childhoods."

Amir looks as if he is about to retaliate, but I interrupt. "Weren't you the one telling us to stop bickering?" I turn to Amir.

Amir grunts.

"What if . . . ," I begin. "What if you both say the password together?"

Amir and his sister look at me as though I've claimed something preposterous. Anger still lingering in her gaze, Sanya finally says, "Fine."

She offers Amir one side of the map, and together, their voices are like the sound of sharpening blades, almost entrancing: "*Freedom runs within us, deep inside the veins of rock making up our earth. Freedom cannot be taken from us. Freedom is immovable as mountains.*"

Their voices curl into the air like smoke, resting for a moment before the ground itself reacts.

The wall begins to shake, the sandstone cracking and forming fissures that look like tributaries of a river. The granules cascade to the ground, and Irfan pulls me back before the wall itself crumbles down, creating a massive thud as the stone hits the floor. Dust and debris fill the air, and I cough and wave away the haziness.

Before us is nothing but sandy plains, as though we've crossed from jungle to desert inexplicably.

"But . . . where is it?" I wonder.

"Just wait." Sanya takes hold of her horse and steps forward. She closes her eyes, and then her body begins to fade, as though swallowed into the air—until she is gone.

I gasp. What magic is this? Certainly Tutor never told me of people who could disappear into nothing.

"She's not gone. C'mere." Amir holds out his hand. At first I refuse, but eventually, Amir convinces me. I feel the warmth of his hands, the grooves and rough lines of just-healed cuts. He leads me forward. In one step, his body disappears, and in the next, a strange ripple bubbles in the air. I step inside, and it is as though a wave washes over me. For an instant all is dark. I feel, see, hear nothing. Then the wave recedes. My senses kick into motion, immediately overtaken by what is before me.

The Mailan Foothills.

The world here is a spiral of color. Where once the plains were empty, now I see an entirely different picture, as though a painter's brush has added color and vibrancy to the land. The plateau up ahead is cloaked with a sea of bodies, which cover the hills rolling as far as the eye can see. There are tents instead of huts to mark each hill, and a tree as tall as it is wide grows in the center of the Foothills. Music lilts on the wind, light and inviting, and people dance on the rocky plateau, resplendent in fabrics as bright as lemons. The evening air smells of Father's festive feasts.

To the right of the hills are trees—the Forest of Hearts that Sanya mentioned. Some of the trees hold fresh mango blossoms.

"Amir," I breathe, "this is amazing." It's like a whole world of its own, hidden away by some surviving magic. Another of Tutor's secrets. Perhaps he wanted to show me someday.

"It is," Amir replies, as if he cannot quite believe it himself. "There're so many people."

"But how did they simply appear?" I wonder.

"They didn't just appear—they were hidden." Sanya points behind us, where Irfan stands with the remaining two horses. The wall has reemerged. A magical entryway.

"This land was created by people, stonebringers, who wanted to ensure no one could enter without first speaking their maxim."

*"Freedom is immovable as mountains,"* I echo.

Sanya nods. "This was a place of refuge for many stonebringers. A hideout, if you will."

"And the raja never knew. . . ." I turn back to the scene, the people milling about with such . . . happiness.

Sanya urges us onward, spurring her horse forth, and we make our way through the Foothills, past the smells of simmering daal and crackling fire. We pause and dismount, surveying our surroundings. I think back to the fountain's prophecy. *Seek the place of stone and glass, where emptiness hides and fire flames . . .*

Emptiness is hiding something right in front of our eyes. Our maps have always deemed this area an unclaimed land, unoccupied, a vestige from a past life. And yet, all of this is here. Could this be the place of the fountain's fortune?

Amir takes my hand with a featherlight touch. "Over here." We pass by crimson tents, children playing a game with sticks and rocks.

"You see that?" Amir points. "Sanya and I used to play that when I was little. I think I can just remember the rules—"

I eye Amir, realizing we're still holding hands. Even though I barely know the boy, his touch is warm, and he speaks with a kindness I haven't heard in the palace in years.

"You helped me," I whisper. He believes I'm speaking of Ria, but in truth, he's helped the real me—Rani—more than he knows. Without him, I would have never made it past the market-place where we found Sanya. His boyish grin turns bright, and his profile is strong and soft all at once. A boy of dirt, a boy of hope.

A tap on my shoulder makes me jump. Irfan. His silver eyes are dim.

"We're unpacking our things." He juts his thumb toward two sapphire tents billowing in the distance. "Sanya and I will be staying here to keep low."

"And the passports?" Amir asks. I, too, have not forgotten my promise to Ria.

"Sanya will take you in the morning to find the passport maker," Irfan replies.

I nod. I think back to my own mission, to find Tutor's wife, and thus the stone. I must find her quickly; my pulse thrums at the thought of seeking her out now, in a place like this. There's so much color, excitement, wonder.

"I think I'll take a look around," I say, and Irfan nods. A few days here will not be a hitch in my timeline with Ria, but it's already taken nearly two days to simply reach the Foothills. I cannot waste a second more.

I never imagined such a group of people outside the palace. They seem genuinely content, smiles on their faces despite their lack of wealth, their rags of clothing. A smile sneaks onto my lips. This is the world I want to live in. A world that determines its own worth. A world defined not by titles but actions.

Amir leaves with Irfan. I take the opportunity to sneak away and begin my search for Tutor's wife. I clutch Tutor's ring in my fingers, feeling it burn a hole through me.

I weave through the crowd of people, eyeing their fingers for the matching ring, offering sweet smiles but feeling my faith diminish every minute with the magnitude of the crowd. Abai's sun, why did I ever think this would be so simple?

"You look lost," a voice says from behind me.

I swirl, clutching the ring on instinct. It's a man, bearded and tall, standing at least a head above mine. He has tiny oval glasses perched upon his nose and his brown skin is sun-darkened, wrinkled from age. He seems to be a man as wise as his years, like Tutor.

"I—I'm looking for someone," I say, unable to keep my words to myself any longer. "A widowed woman. I was told she might live here. I thought this ring might mean something to her. . . ."

When the man catches sight of the ring, he narrows his eyes. "Where'd you get that?"

"You recognize it?" My heart fills with hope.

The man's hawk eyes scrutinize me. "I know who'll be able to help you." He turns, throws his head over a shoulder, and says, "Follow me."

Curiosity overtaking any sense left within me, I trail the man's footsteps, keeping my breath locked in my chest. My mind whirls as we head up the nearest plateau. The humid air grips me like a vise one minute, and the next, a cool wind circles past us. A dense cluster of trees look like shadows in the arriving moonlight.

When we reach a scarlet tent, the nameless man pulls back the folds, revealing a world awash with more color. Linens of red and gold drape the walls. The tent looks more like a library, with tattered books forming precarious stacks.

"Jas," the man calls, "you have a visitor."

My stomach coils. Jas . . . the name of the woman Sanya mentioned. Her parents' friend. The passport maker.

A woman with graying hair is sitting at a wooden desk. She flips the page before her, ignoring us, clear in her stance. She looks like she could be an older mother, perhaps a wizened auntie from the women's room.

She replies in a husky voice, "You know I don't allow visitors, Karan."

"I think you might want to reconsider." Karan pulls the tent flap open wider and prompts me forward, until I'm standing before the table. He juts his chin toward the hand that holds Tutor's ring.

I glance between the two of them before unfurling my fist before the passport maker. Jas finally looks up, face impassive, before lowering her glasses in disbelief.

"How did you come by my husband's ring?"

# 19

## Ria

Saeed's hands are warm in mine as we spin through the ballroom. *Spin*, because this dance lesson is spinning out of control, and I can't seem to stop stepping on his toes every two seconds.

At the ninth bell, I came to the reptile terrarium with Shima, thinking I'd be getting another history lesson, but instead Saeed surprised me and led us to the ballroom. Turns out today's lesson isn't for the mind.

"Mother asked that I allow us time to practice our dance for the engagement party," he explained. I just know that if I keep my head low and do what I am asked, I'll be out of these lessons soon enough.

After I step on his toes again, Saeed says with a tilted smile, "And you told me you were a dance prodigy?"

*Only when she feels like it*, Shima snickers. She's coiled up far away. My "chaperone." Apparently Shima trails Rani wherever she goes, especially to her lessons, which makes being undercover that much more—

*Interesting? Exciting?* Shima supplies. I spin away from her and focus.

Step, twirl, arms out, arms in. I suppose thieving is a sort of dance, a tap of your toes and wiggle of your fingers. But it's a secret kind of dance—*not* the one you share with a guy you're supposed to be in love with.

"Light steps," he reminds me. "Angle yourself like this," Saeed shows me. We resume the steps: forward, side, back. I'm dizzy by the time Saeed finally calls for a break.

"Thank the skies," I huff. Saeed lets go of my hand like it's as hot as iron sitting in the sun.

"Forgot your steps?" he asks me. I can't tell if I hear sarcasm or genuine care in his voice.

"Why do you care?" I snap. I wish I could clamp those words back into my mouth; I should be *helping* Saeed after what I discovered last night, not berating him like Rani once might've.

At the flash of hurt in his eyes, I say, "I'm sorry. I shouldn't've said that."

"That's all right, Princess." He stares out the jalis, but there's the faintest twitch in his jaw.

I puff my chest. "No, it's not," I tell him, "and it isn't fair for me to treat you this way." If I want Saeed to listen to me, I need him to trust me. Which means burying all this stuff with Rani into the dirt. "It's like the bridge between Abai and Kaama. Just because they failed to finish building it doesn't mean it was meaningless. If they tried to build toward peace, why can't we?"

"You mean . . . we should start over?" Once it's out in the air, that concern on his face blossoms into hope. A hope I could never fulfill as an orphan-thief. A fake princess.

I nod. Stuffing down my guilt. It's not like I *mean* to toy with his emotions.

"You know, there was more to that story," Saeed says. "If you're willing to continue our history lesson."

"Yes," I say a little too eagerly. History was always my favorite subject with Mama Anita; it made me feel like I was part of something bigger than just the orphanage. More than a nameless girl with no past and no future.

Saeed smiles. "Despite the fact that the bridge was not fully built, two lovers, one Abaian and one Kaaman, would try to meet halfway across the bridge. They would see each other in the distance but could never come close enough to reunite. Legend says they never stopped trying, until finally, in their old age, they leaped toward each other, and clasped onto one another so that they could at last be together in death."

His gaze holds mine. It's a tragic, romantic story, but it's more. "Their bond shows that there truly isn't a good kingdom or an evil one; just two kings with opposing beliefs, and their people, caught in the middle."

Saeed gazes at me intently, a spark of something in his eyes. It's like he's excited to see me—Rani—this way. Maybe Rani would've scoffed cynically at the story and missed the deeper meaning; maybe I would've too, once. But something about

Saeed's teachings enraptures me the way Mama Anita's stories once did.

"You're a good tutor, you know," I tell him softly. I don't realize how close we're standing until I notice the dark circles ringing the underside of his eyes. Curling in front of his eyes is a dark lock of hair, lush and soft. I'm tempted to sweep it back, and before I can stop myself, my fingers brush the strand instinctively.

A dark residue comes off on my hand. The curl, once black, now looks . . . white.

"Y-your hair—" I begin.

Saeed quickly sweeps back the curl and grimaces. "Stress," he answers, too quickly. "I've been covering the strands with Mother's special powder."

He's right; it was black powder that came off on my hand, revealing the white underneath. But stress? I touch the side of his face, a thumb gently pressing to the deep purple bloom under his eyes. He winces, like he's not sure if he should give in to my touch or step back. "You look tired. Is it the dreams again?"

Saeed sucks his cheeks in. "I'm taking the tonic." It's not a question, though his tone lilts, and I can sense the lie sitting on his tongue.

"Every night?"

He nods after a beat. "My dreams aren't going away, just becoming less clear. Like something's clouding them."

*The tonic.* It must be affecting Saeed's mind somehow, the snake venom. He has to know the truth. "Saeed, what your mother is giving you—it isn't a sleep tonic. Unless sleep tonics use venom these days." I grumble the last part.

"What do you mean?" he asks innocently. "Mother consulted a physician in Anari. Song beetle juice, valerian, lavender . . ."

How do I put this gently? Skies take it, maybe the best way is to rip off the bandage. "I meant she's giving you something else. It's snake venom."

"I don't understand." Saeed steps back. But I'm dead serious, and he can read it on my face.

"It's hardly noticeable to someone without snake magic," I say. These powers might be new to me, but I feel them simmering in my blood, ringing true. "Saeed, I think she's poisoning you."

Saeed starts, a bit of anger in his eyes, the first time I've seen such from him. "Rani, this is my *mother* we're speaking of. How can you make such an accusation?"

Maybe I shouldn't've been so up front about it, but Saeed deserves to hear the truth. "If you don't believe me, give me a chance to prove it."

He shakes his head, still in disbelief.

"Trust me. I'll explain everything. I can show you I'm telling the truth. Will you meet me tomorrow after our lessons?" I ask.

"You've told me enough," Saeed says, though his voice is one of curiosity.

"Just give me a chance."

Saeed's hazel eyes touch mine, and out of nowhere, he takes me by the hand and resumes our dance, spinning me out. I loop back to him in twirls until he catches me in his arms and lowers me back toward the floor, his face inches away from mine.

"A chance?" he asks, but his gaze isn't on me. It's on my lips, so dangerously close to his.

"I . . ." I'm dizzy from all the spinning, the blood rushing to my head. "I think there's more going on here than you know."

Saeed eyes me. For a second, it's like he *knows* I'm different. The facade begins to slip away just as Shima shouts in my mind, *Time!*

I shoot up, nearly knocking into Saeed's forehead. "Thanks a lot, snake," I grumble. I almost forgot she was there.

Shima smirks. Saeed glances over at her and shivers, probably still afraid of her after whatever incident happened between them.

"So?" I ask Saeed.

"Your lessons come first. But . . ." He sighs. "Meet me at sunset tomorrow. The Stone Terrace."

By late evening, after I've finished the rest of my lessons, the palace is still bustling. It's like I'm back in the jungles, except instead of birdcalls, all I hear is gossip. Nobles filter through the front doors, followed by maidservants with trays of almond-shaped sweets. The servants remind me of the girl, Aditi. I scan the servants until I find her, but she's rushing off so fast all I see is her chunni and braids as she whips around the corner. I hurry to find her until she swims back into view. Her eyes dart around with suspicion as she heads out of a separate corridor and toward a set of large double doors.

Curious, I sneak behind Aditi, hiding behind pillars until she's standing before the doors. Adjusting her jade chunni with one hand, she rushes into the room, and with quiet footsteps, I follow. Once I pass the gilded doors, I step in—and gasp.

It's miraculous. Rows upon rows of shelves hold books and journals. A musty scent perfumes the air, one that could only belong to the smell of old parchment.

The library.

I peer through the shelves, spotting Aditi. I inhale the tomes' dust, my nose tingling.

And I sneeze.

*Oops.*

Aditi's braids whip through the air as she turns. "Who's there?"

My heart thuds in my chest. No more hiding now.

I step out from the shadows, a weak smile painted on my face. When Aditi spots me, she looks scared out of her wits, eyes wide and chunni hanging lopsided from her tiny frame.

"P-Princess, what are you doing here?"

I think on my feet. "I just came to the library for some light reading," I squeak.

Aditi isn't convinced. Maybe Rani isn't the type for some *light reading.*

"Do you know your way around the library? I'm looking for a book that could teach me more about snake venom."

"Of course, miss," Aditi says. "Right this way."

The girl scurries to a far shelf, retrieves a book, and returns to me. The tattered cover reads *The Complete History of Magic* by Suneel Nanda. Even in the low light, I can tell the spine is creased, pages yellowed and weathered. I can probably count on my hand how many times I've held a book in my life. The orphanage wasn't so fortunate to have many resources. It's not like the raja cared much for struggling students.

"I'll go back to work straightaway if you wish, Princess." Aditi's so still, she looks like a statue among the other books. But her eyes betray her—alive, and scared.

"No, don't." The words surprise her. "Do you mind staying? I'd . . . like your help with this book." Something about her presence is comforting, familiar.

Aditi nods slowly, flips through the book, and offers it to me spread-eagled. On the pages are an intricate diagram of a snake jaw and fangs. My brains swims, and I feel my serpent power emerging. There's something to detect here. I catch a whiff of a scent emanating from the book. Very specifically, and most strongly, from these two pages—roses and chai. I think of the first moment I saw Amara, shoving her cup of tea back at Aditi—and of Amara's constant demand for fresh rose blossoms.

I run a finger over the page. There's a droplet on one side of it. My breath catches. The tonic.

My mind reels back to the moment Shima and I first met, what she told me. *Snakespeakers like yourself have a certain immunity to venoms. . . .*

On the next page there are instructions for making a tincture of snake venom, and something below it:

WARNING: This tincture is designed to be administered to snakespeakers only, as it helps fully develop a royal's powers. Ingestion by non-snakespeakers will have a price.

A price? I quickly read off the rest of the page. "Side effects include memory alteration, brain fog, and sleep disorders. Physical symptoms include whitening hair . . ."

Wait. White hair? Hadn't I just seen Saeed's hair earlier, one of the curls white? Stress, he'd thought. Or maybe something else.

Saeed's tired eyes, the nightmares, the white hair. It's all because of *this*. Instead of helping Saeed sleep, his mother is doing something else. She's making things worse.

On purpose.

I have to tell Saeed—this is exactly the proof I needed—but we arranged to meet tomorrow. And I'm sure he wouldn't be thrilled at the sight of me.

"Could I borrow this book from you? I promise I'll put it back here when I'm done."

The girl eyes me strangely. "It's your library, Princess."

I manage a nervous chuckle. "Of course." The moon is high now, and Aditi's eyes droop as she stifles a yawn.

"If you're tired, you can—"

"My apologies, miss." She stiffens, alert. "I shouldn't have yawned. I'll begin double cleaning duties tomorrow—"

"Wait," I interrupt. "You think I'm going to punish you? For a yawn?"

"That's what you said to the servants last week," she squeaks. "You said if any of us stepped out of line again, our new home would be with the snakes."

*Rani* said that? I shiver at the prospect of my sister threatening her own servants. When we speak again, I'm going to make sure she appreciates the people who work tirelessly to enable her fancy life.

"No need for cleaning duties." I try to keep my voice as princess-like as possible. "Instead I want your honesty."

Aditi looks up her nose at me. "Of course, Princess."

"Has Amara told you anything about that tonic? The ingredients? Where she gets them from?"

Aditi is quick to press her trembling lips tight. I lower myself so we're at eye level and she fumbles back, hitting the nearest shelf.

"I'm not going to hurt you," I say. "I just need your help."

She gulps. Fright ebbing away, she opens her mouth to speak. "Mistress Amara doesn't like me to speak of this, or any of her business." She lifts her hands shakily. Scars ribbon her palms. I can tell where those scars came from. Whips. I have a few of them myself.

All the same, horror dawns on me, and I hold Aditi's hands, disgusted by Amara's actions. What Aditi and I have both gone through.

"Amara," I curse. "What has she done?"

Aditi worries her lower lip. "If I don't comply, she has . . . methods. She's only just become the raja's adviser, but she's been using us servants for a long time. Keeping us silent with the help of a Chart." Her voice turns to a whisper. "She requests books from the library. I ask her, sometimes, if I can read something from here. Not research. But she forbids it. Servants aren't supposed to read."

"But you do?"

She shrugs stiffly. "I started reading this after Mistress Amara was finished with it. But I used to read other things, too. Books about faraway worlds and fantasies, something I could . . . escape into."

Aditi's voice grows small. I stayed at the palace for one reason, and one reason only: to learn more about my birth. But it seems like during my time here, I've been unraveling other secrets. Saeed's dreams, the raja's war plans. Amara's cruelty.

My stomach knots. What have I gotten myself into?

Outside, the bells chime. Aditi quivers at the sound. "I'm sorry, miss, but I must go deliver something for Mistress Amara."

Before I can reply, Aditi turns to leave. Her braids fly behind her as she scurries out of the library, quiet as a mouse.

# 20

## Rani

Shock. Confusion. Guilt. With everything I feel, I cannot seem to place the right words on my tongue.

"That is all, Karan," Jas says, and the man takes his leave. The woman pushes away from her desk and stands, an obelisk among ruins. Jewels, fake to the trained eye, lie haphazard around the room, an audience to her show.

Is Tutor's wife truly none other than Jas, the passport maker Sanya spoke of?

In the faint light from a nearby oil lamp, I take in Tutor's wife. Weathered lines snake out from the creases of her eyes, and dimples mark her cheeks. Her kohl-rimmed eyes are the color of still-brewing chai. A ragged quilt is draped over her shoulders, almost entirely concealing a ring hanging off a plain necklace.

It matches Tutor's perfectly.

"What is your name, child?"

Bile rises up my throat. "Ria," I force out.

"And how did you know my husband, may I ask?" With the few torches and firelight scattered around the tent, her eyes look like golden-brown orbs. Only now do I take in the wrinkles on her forehead and above her lips, the widow's peak crowning the top of her head.

"It's a long story," I confess. "But he gave this to me for a reason. I believe he wanted me to come here—to the Foothills, and to you. He wished for me to find a stone . . . the Bloodstone."

Vexation flashes in Jas's eyes, followed by utter confusion. "How did you— Your search for the stone is foolish. You'd be better off forgetting about it."

"I need your help," I tell her. "Please—"

"Ria?" a familiar voice interjects.

I whip my head to the voice. A figure rustles through the tent entrance. Sanya appears, dressed in new garb: a simple shirt and loose trousers. "How'd you get here?" she asks me. Her voice is strained, accusatory. But her eyes soften when she finds Tutor's wife. "Jas Auntie," she says, rushing into the tent. She embraces Jas in a fierce hug, one riddled with familiarity and history.

Jas pulls away and tucks a stray lock of hair behind Sanya's ear. "My dear Sanya, what are you doing back here?"

"It's a lot to explain. I'm sorry we ever left." Sanya's mouth pulls into a frown.

Jas looks at Sanya with the reverence and love of a mother to a child. My heart spikes when I remember Mother, the queen of Abai. I've never been away from her this long. And it's been even longer since she's held me close like that.

"How do you know Jas?" Sanya asks me.

"I—I don't," I stutter, cheeks aflame. "How do you know each other?"

"I told you," Sanya says. "My parents were family friends with Jas." Sanya turns back to Tutor's wife. "I'm so sorry. I heard about Samar."

"It seems we have both lost the ones we loved," Jas says tenderly. Her face hardens with memories. "Does Amir know?"

She nods. "He knows about Samar's death . . . just not who he is to you."

At the tent entrance, Irfan and Amir appear.

Irfan steps forward and folds Jas into a hug. "I'm sorry about him."

Jas's eyes darken as she pulls away. She wraps her hands around his. "Samar told me many things about you that you have yet to admit to me, Irfan."

Irfan swallows, throat bobbing. I don't miss his shifting eyes, nor the way he looks like he didn't want me and Amir to overhear those words. "I'm truly sorry, Jas," he repeats. "I did everything I could before he was taken."

The two share a look, one filled with heartbreak and melancholy.

Two people who were connected to the man I always considered a father. There was so much I never knew about him. My heart thumps with grief.

SISTERS OF THE SNAKE

"Jas? Is that really you?" Amir says.

"Amir," she whispers. "You still have that boyish twinkle in your eyes." She gathers him in a hug.

His voice cracks as he says, "It's been so long, I barely remembered this place."

"Nearly ten years," Sanya supplies. "I thought you'd remember, little brother."

Amir pulls away from Jas. The air crackles with tension until Sanya finally speaks. "Amir . . . you need to know something."

Amir's brows knit. "Go on."

Sanya huffs. "You know how Ma and Papa were close to Jas? They were close to her husband, too. To . . . Samar."

"The man who was taken by the Charts?" Amir shakes his head, a terrible realization dawning in his eyes. "Wait, that's your husband?"

Jas lowers her head. *"Was."* She straightens her posture, looking to the skies. "Samar was always gone on those trips I would tell you about as children. I never wanted you to know his true occupation. He took the job at great risk. He was a great asset to our people. He gathered secrets. He knew things that kept us safe. He was the princess's tutor."

My skin ices over.

"What?" Amir tries to process the information. "Sanya, how'd you know all this?"

"I didn't until I met Irfan. He introduced me to Samar. That's how I found out that he was looking for the Bloodstone, and how he used to live in the palace. Until he had to leave."

Amir stares. "But . . . the Bloodstone. Did he ever—"

"It doesn't matter anymore." Jas turns away. "His mission died with him."

"But it didn't!" All eyes swivel to me. "He wanted to find the stone," I say, turning to Sanya. "And now the Charts and the raja are after it."

Jas's hard stare is replaced by curiosity. "The raja?"

I nod. "He means to use the stone for the war. Samar's mission isn't over. It's more important than ever before."

"A mission that's only resulted in death," Sanya adds bitterly. Even Amir stiffens. Irfan glances at Sanya, as if perturbed she would bring up such fresh wounds. Unspoken words fill the space between them.

"Is that why he was taken?" Tears well in my eyes, but I force them back. I am the reason Tutor is gone, and only I can amend this.

Jas sighs. "I'd been planning routes, tracking Charts' movements from the plateau . . . I wanted the Bloodstone as badly as my husband did. When he left to work in Nabh, I thought perhaps he would come back. That we could complete this mission together." She turns to me, her eyes now fastened to mine. "It has been of no use. Samar is gone."

Sanya bites her lip. "Jas, we actually didn't come for a reunion. Amir and his friend, they're looking for passage out of Abai," she says carefully.

"You wish to leave?" Jas eyes Amir and Sanya, who stand breaths apart but look like two frozen statues.

"Before the war. She's been conscripted. We need passports," Amir explains. "Can you help?"

Without answering, Jas takes another hard look at me, at the ring still clutched in my palm. As if she can sense who I am: the girl responsible for the death of her beloved husband, even partially. I itch at my skin, wishing I could scratch away the truth, but it would only leave a raw, red lie.

"I met your husband once," I say, the lie creeping onto my tongue. "Not long after, he gave me his ring, and something else, too." I reach for an inner pocket of my cloak and find the pocket-sized book of Tutor's. I offer it to Jas perfunctorily. "He told me to look for the stone. It was his dying wish."

"You never told me that," Amir says, glancing at me quizzically. "I thought we were here to get passports."

"We are," I amend, though my speech is too quick. "I never thought the stone to be of much importance. A story," I lie. "But then Sanya mentioned the Bloodstone, and now I know of the Charts' mission. Perhaps there is more at stake than we realize." *Like the fate of my future queendom. One I had never considered I might share with a long-lost twin sister.*

"And where do you think this Bloodstone could be?" Amir asks me, though Jas seems to ponder the question as well, glancing down at the book in her hands with wonder.

"Doesn't matter," Sanya says stubbornly. "We shouldn't've

brought this up. It's dangerous, searching for the stone again—"

"Again?" I echo. "You've searched for it before?"

Sanya stops herself and marches to the tent flap in frustration. "Keep talking about your precious stone. I'll be out of here faster than you can say *Raja's beard*."

I arch a brow once Sanya's gone. Irfan offers a gesture of apology.

"She doesn't like to think of the past," Irfan explains.

"Why so?" I ask myself.

"Because," Amir pipes up, "our parents were the ones who went after the stone, years ago." His gaze, dark as burned-out embers, crashes into mine. "That's how they died."

Everyone is still.

"I'm so sorry, Amir," I whisper. My first true apology. It seems we have all lost someone, all experienced grief in some form. Why did I ever think these feelings were exclusive to me? That no one could ever have experienced a worse pain?

With a goodbye salute, Irfan raises a hand in good night to Jas, and leaves the tent with stealthy quickness, Amir following right behind.

Jas tucks the pocket-sized book of Tutor's close to her chest. "Thank you for this," she says, her voice shaking, "but I must ask you to leave."

I nod. Silence, vast as the Satluj Sea, hangs over me as I move to exit the tent.

"And Ria," Jas calls.

I turn, stomach flipping.

"I know you want to continue my husband's legacy," she says, "but looking for the stone is not something to be taken lightly."

Normally I would fume at such a tone, but she is correct. I cannot take this lightly. I am more than a peasant girl on a mission; I have the weight of a kingdom on my shoulders.

## 21

### Ria

At sunset the next day, I find the Stone Terrace. It's located in the north end of the palace and takes ten agonizing flights of stairs to get there. Am I already out of shape from just a few days of palace life? I huff and continue onto the terrace, where Saeed sports a fresh kurta and matching gold shoes. I spot that bit of white hair, and I realize instantly he must also be wearing facial powder to cover up his purple eye bags.

"Am I late?" I ask, tucking the book from the library behind me.

"For the princess, I'm early." He bows, but the movement is stiff, like he's not sure how he feels about submitting himself to me. I'm not sure how *I* feel about it. It's not like we're on friendly terms at the moment, despite our lessons.

"You wanted to speak to me about my mother?" He gestures at the wooden swing set with two cushions behind him and we sit, taking in the blushing roses and flowers that fill the gardens below.

"I know I dropped a lot on you yesterday," I begin. "It wasn't fair of me to surprise you. *But* . . . I've brought you proof." I show him the book from the library, open to the page describing snake venom, and point a finger to the list of side effects. Saeed's eyes flicker over the symptoms.

"What are you implying?" Saeed asks. "I told you, it's a simple sleep tonic." He's trying to deflect; I know what denial looks like. Skies, after Mama Anita died, I wouldn't say her name for months.

But we don't have the luxury of denial right now. Time to let it all out. "I mean that your mother's lying to you. There's no song beetle juice in your sleeping brew. The tea has a diluted dosage of snake venom, something that alters your mind, your memories, maybe even your dreams and sleep patterns."

My voice quiets. "Saeed. You have every single one of the side effects listed here. And the physical symptom . . . white hair."

Everything stills, save for the *clip, clip, clip* as the gardeners trim the hedges.

"You don't believe me," I realize.

"You haven't always been honest with me, Rani," he says. It's true; Rani didn't even mention her betrothed to me before she left, which would seem to indicate she's not exactly enthusiastic about their relationship. Inconvenient when you're about to be engaged.

"However," he continues, facing me now, "I haven't been entirely honest with you, either."

I grip the cushioned seat. "About what?"

"I've grown up with nightmares. Mother called it a phase. But they always came and went, and mostly I could ignore them." His shoulders tighten. "Lately, the dreams have returned, but they're cloudy. Still . . . I noticed a weird pattern. Sometimes my dreams become reality a day or even hours after I see them. The other night, when you were in the raja's study . . . I didn't need Aditi to lead me there. I already knew."

My breath hitches. "How?"

"Remember how I arrived late to dinner? Well, I had told you I was sidetracked when, in truth, I had accidentally fallen asleep beforehand and had a dream. A dream of you in the raja's study."

I gulp.

"I've thought about it over and over. And the meaning of it seems . . ." He weighs his next words. "Impossible."

*Impossible.* I think back to Mama Anita, her reassuring words when she brushed my hair as I fell asleep. "Nothing's impossible," I recite. Mama Anita's courage fills me now, being here at the palace, finding the magic I never knew existed inside me, yet always had a connection with.

Saeed glances down, a cluster of curls covering his eyes. "You think they're not just dreams? That they might be . . . something more?" His voice is hesitant.

My mind whirls. Can it be true? Could Saeed . . . ?

"Do you remember our lesson, Rani, when I taught you about paired magics? Each magic has a connection to another magic. A kind of bond, a pair. They're like two sides of the same coin."

*Like Rani and me,* I think. "And?"

"Fire calls to Tide. Earth calls to Sky."

I think of all the Masters. That leaves two: "Snake calls to Memory."

A shiver runs through me. The night I met Rani, she told me of how each distinct magic was connected to another in some way. *Snake magic is deeply tied to thoughts and memories,* she'd said.

"Exactly. I think there's a reason we're so drawn to each other . . . that we feel something inexplicable when we're near."

We stare at one another until Saeed leaps up from the swing and paces the terrace before gripping the railing.

*"Memory magic.* I didn't believe it. I *couldn't* believe it. . . ."

"A few days ago, I wouldn't've believed it either," I say, meeting him at the balcony's edge. I think of the moment I touched Rani, the memories we unleashed. The hushed rumors peppering the villages, that magic wasn't really as lost as we thought. The children at the orphanage with odd gifts, who vanished in the night.

I can no longer deny my own magic—how can I deny his?

His gaze reaches mine, alight with realization. "Mother doesn't have magic, but . . . maybe someone else in her family did. Someone in my bloodline may have been a mindwielder. That would explain my . . . *visions.*"

I'm quiet after that. But his words ring true; what if Saeed has a connection to the Memory Master?

"Saeed, maybe we're not the only ones who know this."

"My mother?" he asks. I nod, and he shuts his eyes. Curses. "Mother came from Kaama with nothing but rags, a few spare coins, and me. She tells me all the time, I am everything she has. She wouldn't hurt me."

"Maybe she knows your dreams are more than that," I reveal. "She knows what you can see. Memories. Visions. The Memory Master was powerful, almost as all-seeing as Amran."

I recite the stories Mama Anita taught me. She knew magic existed, deep in the earth, rare as a polished diamond. Maybe she even knew magic existed in *me*.

I straighten myself the way a princess would. Even if it's against every thief instinct in me, it feels good. "My snake magic allows me to sense venoms; I know it was in your tonic. Saeed, I don't mean to be harsh, but this is the truth. She's doing this on purpose. She's stopping you from discovering your . . . magic. But the question is, why?"

Saeed's knuckles whiten. "Even if she did want to stop my magic—and I don't know *why* she would—Mother would never intentionally poison me. Never."

"I'm sorry." I don't know what else to say.

His breaths come faster. "When the visions got bad a few moons back, I had adverse reactions to the tea. Mother promised they were natural side effects, that I would grow used to it after time. She said it would heal me." His voice breaks with anger.

"We don't know her true intentions just yet. Maybe she didn't know any better." Even as I say the words, I know he can tell I'm lying. Trying to soothe him.

"The strangest thing is, I've dreamed about Mother. But in

my dreams, she was different. Cruel. Her eyes were red and her voice harsh. What if I saw her in the future, saw her changing?" Anguish fills his features. "What if she has something planned, and she's keeping me from finding out about it and stopping her?"

I need to be delicate about this. "We've got to work together if we want to figure out what your mother's doing."

"Then what do you propose?" Saeed asks. "I *spy* on my own mother? I know you dislike her—"

I grasp his palm in mine, and I'm surprised to find it's warm and smooth, unlike Amir's worn and roughened hands. "Just keep an eye out. And stop taking the tonic for a few nights. Promise?"

Saeed's eyes trail down to our intertwined hands. "What will you do?"

"I'm working on it."

Midnight strikes the moment I step into the Western Courtyard. The wind is tame tonight, like it wants to wrap me in its warmth. The perfect hiding spot for a thief—and a servant.

I'm hiding behind a large, ancient tree, its trunk wide and full of strange markings, some of which look fresh, others crossed out or faded. Are those numbers? I peer closer, letting my fingers trail over the marks. What do they mean?

Just then, Shima slips over my legs, and I shiver at the slick scales, nearly forgetting I invited her along. Damned snake. It's not like I can get rid of her, or people will realize something's up.

Aditi peers out the palace doors and spots me. She shuffles across the grass until she's an arm's length away.

"You got my message?" I called for Aditi after meeting with Saeed. Despite his reluctance to spy on his mother, he promised he would do his part to figure out the truth. Now it's time for me to do mine.

Aditi glances around nervously, like she can't look the snake in the eyes. She doesn't step any closer until I pull out the book, *The Complete History of Magic*, and her face lights up.

"Miss," she says in disbelief. "Is this why you called me here?"

I nod, then gesture for Aditi to have a seat. It takes her a moment, but she finally lowers herself. A bunch of mauve flowers sway ahead, shivering in the gardens. Aditi, too, shivers with excitement as she races through the book again.

"The book is yours to keep if you want. If anyone asks, tell them it was Princess Rani's orders."

"B-but—" Aditi's jaw drops. "That's very kind of you."

"It's nothing," I say, settling a hand on Shima's head. I knew I'd need the snake tonight, in tandem with the book and Aditi's assistance, to help me understand more about snake venom and what Amara's up to. Luckily Aditi doesn't look too bothered. She smiles a real smile, and it makes me feel as warm as fresh ghee. Truthfully, I knew because of the way Aditi looked at the book, like she was starving and only words could stave off the pain. I used to be like that, too, in the orphanage. Books were rare, but

Mama Anita always had a story to tell.

"I brought Shima here tonight for a reason. I need to learn more about snake magic, from her and this book."

*You can't begin to understand snake magic until you first learn its properties*, Shima says. With her head, she prods open the book. I flip through it, noticing a page has been ripped out, and then find the one I'm looking for. *Subsets of snake magic.*

Aditi shivers. "I've never been so close to a snake before."

"Think of her as . . . a tutor of sorts." I nod at Shima, even if sitting next to a snake still makes me nervous. Aditi nods.

I read the page aloud. "Subsets of snake magic. There are four levels at its heart: communication; verbal manipulation; heightened senses; and increased immunity to venoms." I skim the page until something hooks me. "Look at this."

It's a page on the Snake Pit, with a haunting illustration of the Pit's walls, snakes writhing at the bottom.

*Keep reading*, Shima encourages.

I do. "The Snake Pit was created by the Snake Master, and his descendants built the Abaian palace around the Pit. His scepter, passed down to the kings and queens of Abai, could unlock the Pit itself, revealing the snakes within." I think of the raja's scepter in his office, the flashing eyes, memories of death, and shiver. "Its walls are embedded with gems, which naturally form from the magic imbued in the Pit. Each gem is said to . . ." I pause.

"Yes?" Aditi wonders.

"Each gem is said to hold the spirits of the dead," I finish. "Of those who died in the Pit. Skies be good."

"What's wrong, miss?"

"Nothing." My mind scrambles. Could Mama Anita's soul be in one of those gems? I once dreamed, *ached*, to hear her voice again, to see her one last time before she was chained and dragged to the Pit.

Maybe now I can.

Aditi can clearly see the sorrow on my face, because she closes the book and holds it tight to her chest. "We could continue this another night, miss."

I carefully hold Aditi's shoulder. "Call me by my name. It's all right."

"R-Rani, of course. Queen," Aditi states.

"No, not like queen. I want to be free of titles."

"Then what shall I call you?" Aditi wonders.

*Ria*, Shima tells me. But I can't give away my identity, not if I want to stay safe.

"You might've heard frightening things about me, but I'm not the Snake Princess. I'm different."

"How can I trust that?"

"Shima," I tell the snake, "I need to speak with Aditi alone for a minute." *Please*, I add, unsure if she'll hear it.

*As you wish.* The snake slithers off.

I turn back to Aditi. "You can't. But you can do this—don't treat me like a princess. I'm no one special. I'm just me, and you're just you."

Aditi presses a fingertip to her small, pointed nose. "I gave everyone nicknames back at the orphanage."

My eyes snap up at those words. "You lived in an orphanage?"

She nods. "There, I had friends. But here—"

"When did you leave?" I ask curtly.

"I was no more than a few summers old," she says. "I can hardly remember anyone. Just a few of my friends. I nicknamed one Fox and knew a boy called Tiger. They called me Mouse."

I smile sadly. At the orphanage, I didn't have enough friends to warrant a nickname. I only had Mama Anita.

"Well, Mouse," I begin. "What should be my nickname?"

Aditi thinks. Grins. "Lynx."

A lynx and a mouse. The most unlikely of pairs but then again, so is a servant and a princess.

Aditi peers up at me. Part of her is still afraid of me.

"I'll make sure you have your servant duties cut down over the next couple days, so I can come look at the book with you."

"Th-thank you." Aditi finds my gaze. "But Mistress Amara wouldn't like me being away from her for very long. She needs Master Saeed's tonic, and her roses—"

"Roses?" I say. "But she doesn't really *need* a rose."

Aditi shakes her head. "She does, miss. She requires them every night. I serve them on my tray. It's why I had to leave the other night for my delivery."

She *had* left in a rush. I didn't question it at the time.

"Aditi, do you think you could look into where those roses

come from? Maybe do a little more research in the library, just in case?"

Aditi nods firmly, sure and steadfast. "I'd do anything to repay your help. When should we meet next . . . Lynx?"

# 22

## Rani

*"You can be more than what the stars wish for."*

Tutor stands before me, eyes soft blue, forehead wrinkled. I reach out for him, wishing to feel his fatherly touch, the warmth of his hand on my head. Is this a dream? He looks alive, his dimpled cheeks plump and rosy.

"You must keep going," Tutor says, "for I cannot. You must find the stone."

"I will," I say, lips wobbling.

Tutor's hands grasp mine. But they're cool as ice. I see him falling, falling, falling. Into a pool of ashes and nightmares.

I gasp awake. The tent is empty, and Amir's cot is cold beside mine. There is a dent in the mat from where he was sleeping softly; he likely woke up a while ago. A soft quilt that wasn't there when I fell asleep covers my body. Had Amir left this for me? It still feels warm from his touch.

I shake away the dream and reach for the clothes at the foot of my bed: a tunic, matching leggings, and a chunni. When I've changed, I scratch at the rough fabric, so unlike the palace's silks. Thankfully, the clothes smell fresh, like the palace gardens' potted turmeric plants.

Outside, the Foothills are alive with smell and sound. Men pass by, carrying hefty bags of grain on their backs. From the nearest firepit, a line stretches for breakfast.

"Ria." Sanya swims into view, resting on a log near a firepit. She holds out a cup of tea.

I approach her and take it. The taste of the chai is sweet, and too strong for my taste. If my maids had given me this, I would have spit it out in a heartbeat. Yet now I take another gulp, and another—the very act a sort of rebellion against my past.

The spices, familiar to me as the palace throne room, invigorate me. Cinnamon, clove, cardamom. Shima once taught me that spices help reset the magic levels in my blood; now I feel my magic swim through me, alive and ready.

"They fit." She nods at the clothes.

"They do." What was the polite thing to do? Whenever someone spoke to me, they bowed, but that felt wrong with Sanya. I settle for a simple nod of thanks.

"Come," Sanya says. "Jas has been waiting for you."

"For me?" I wonder. She didn't seem to want to be near me last night.

"Yeah." Is that resentment I hear? But Sanya simply guides me away.

The morning light washes everything with gold. The sandy plateau ahead looks dipped in honey, the rocky pathway steeped in a gilded elixir. We crest over the steps and climb until we reach the plateau.

When I look down, my stomach churns. It's dizzying, the swarm of bodies, the low-hanging clouds. The familiar smells of paneer and daal cooking in a patila waft up to me. Far out from the Mailan Foothills, I spot a glittering lake and the caps of the jungle trees swaying in the wind.

"In here," Sanya says, gesturing to a grand scarlet tent, the same one I'd visited yesterday. Inside, I overhear a voice speaking, "I don't even know what I want anymore."

It's strange how easily I can recognize his tone. I peel back the rough canvas and step in. Amir quiets, turning. He almost looks princely in his white kurta. I can't quite place what about it is so regal. Is this the first time I've seen him in new clothes?

Jas sits at her wooden desk, working carefully with a feather pen and sporting slender glasses. Her hair is woven in an intricate bun at the top of her head, and her clothes are simple: a suit the color of a ripened plum, bangles that clink melodiously as she moves. In the sunshine streaming through the tent's opening, I can make out the details of her features better than I could last night. Her face tells a story: a partially cleft lip; eyes both warm and cool; a slender, upturned nose.

"The passports are nearly ready," Jas says without looking up. She refills the ink of her pen and finds me standing before her at the threshold. "You came."

"Why wouldn't I?" I approach the desk, strewn with passports. "Your handwork is marvelous."

Jas lowers her pen and stands, both hands flat on the table. "I was trained professionally at the Academy a long, long time ago."

"Academy?" Amir asks. "Never heard of one."

"Not in Abai," I clarify. "Retan. They're known for their calligraphers and scholars alike."

"Very smart." Jas looks surprised when I speak but nods approvingly. "Knowledge is a bridge to all things, you know." Her eyes twinkle as she massages her wrists. "I know much of the Foothills, too. Samar was a very smart man, and we shared our knowledge."

A low pang hits my stomach. Jas is not wrong about Tutor. He taught me nearly everything I know. But I'm learning every day that there is still so much more I have yet to discover.

"They're nearly done, free of charge." Jas smiles.

"But—" Amir begins.

"The passports aren't the only reason I called you here." She turns to me. I briefly wonder: What was Amir talking about before with Jas?

"You, dear Ria, are the first person to mention the Bloodstone to me in a long, long time."

"But—you thought me a fool," I start, utterly caught off guard. "You thought—"

"I thought I was right," Jas says. "I've been waiting here in these tents, having forgotten the importance of everything my husband loved. Then you gave me his book, where we used to write each other notes. . . ." Her eyes turn misty.

"The notes in the margins were written in code," I tell her.

"Indeed. Samar and I used to write messages in our own sort of language. The symbols ensured that if our notes were intercepted while he was away working, no one would know of our true intentions with the Bloodstone."

"That's . . . kind of brilliant," Amir remarks. "Making up a whole language."

"It was simplistic but held up." Jas pulls out the book and offers me a glance. There are symbols of the sun, a gem, a small hut, and a strange square with lines drawn through it diagonally.

"What do those mean?"

"I believe . . ." Jas pauses. "He was writing down the location of the Bloodstone. The gem represents the stone, the square a piece of glass. The sun, a symbol of Amran."

"And the hut . . . a house. A home." The pieces click together. "Do you mean to say Samar believed the stone was in the home of Amran?"

Jas nods. "The Glass Temple. He even wrote a possible route of how to find it."

She points at more symbols, explaining the strange code further. "He left instructions, details about the Temple. Perhaps for himself . . . perhaps for me." She shutters the book closed.

"He knew?" All this time? A painful memory of his death resurges. The words on his lips. What if he died before he could tell me more?

"He had a hunch," Jas confirms. "Even I had my doubts, but

he once told me of the Temple and its forgotten importance to our world. This journal reminded me that the search for the stone should never have ended. My husband wanted more than adventure—he wanted freedom. For a while, I forgot what it was like to see that commitment. That courage."

I hold my breath. Commitment? Courage? It certainly took some of that to run from Father and speak my mind. But my intentions were selfish. They still are. I seek to show my father the truth. To prove to him my worth.

But Tutor, Amir's parents—they struggled for something far greater. Something that was not just for them. It was for Amir, with his scars and stories. For the woman with the missing tongue. Even Sanya helped others find the Foothills and escape a worse fate.

The realization settles heavily on my shoulders.

Jas takes my hands into hers. "If my husband entrusted you with his ring, that could only mean one thing. The Charts are close to finding the stone, and we must stop them."

"You truly mean it?" I ask her, hope bubbling inside me.

She lists her head to one side. "I know what I said last night, and I know what I'm saying now."

"You want to go after it?" Amir peers at her quizzically. "My parents died on this quest! Your husband died! How will this time be any different?"

Jas purses her lips. "Because this time, we'll have new blood in our search." She smiles an elderly smile, one that's seen both love and hardship. "Thieves."

Amir laughs, as though he cannot quite believe our conversation. "I'm not special. There're hundreds of thieves out there."

"Don't you wish," Jas says, "that for once, you could live a life where you could be handed what you desire instead of taking it?"

Amir grows silent, but the answer is plain on his face. *Yes.*

Jas squares her shoulders and looks at each of us intently. "With just one wish, the Bloodstone could create vast destruction—or be used for peace. It is not difficult to see which one the raja prefers. If we were to retrieve the stone before the Charts, *we* would get a chance to have what *we* wish. There might not have to be a war at all. No fighting about the Masters, no waiting for destruction after a hundred years of peace.

"All I ask is your agreement." Jas's steady gaze finds mine. "I've spoken with Sanya and Irfan. They agree this mission should not be left unfulfilled. And I believe this journey will grant you more than just the passage you desire. It is up to you."

She holds out the passports. Pages that represent nothing but freedom. Amir takes hold of his, eyes hungry. Everything he ever wanted.

He slumps onto the nearest seat. "And let's say we *do* go looking for this stone. How long would that take?"

I think back to the fountain's fortune, how it led us to Sanya—with Amir's help, thank Amran. Its prophecy is still clear as day.

*"Seek the place of stone and glass, where emptiness hides and fire flames . . ."* I recite the start of the prophecy.

"What're you saying?" Amir's brows dip.

I bite my lower lip. "Remember how I told you I saw a girl in the fountain? The girl who turned out to be Sanya? Well . . ." I inhale deeply. "I think maybe the fountain told me something else. A prophecy."

"What did it say?" Amir prods. Even Jas looks at me with great interest, as if she cannot believe I have peered into the Fountain of Fortunes itself.

"It mentioned something about magic and a lost ancient guard. *A lurking magic you will find, through the ancient guards' lost ways,*" I recite, turning to Jas. "Do you have any idea what such a prophecy could mean?" It's clear I cannot learn all the answers myself; Jas will be my looking glass, my flame in the darkness, to help me decipher the mysterious code.

"The guard," Jas says, nodding. It is as if something has flicked on in her mind. She paces toward her desk and shovels through piles of parchment until she lands on the right one. "Of course. This is it."

"What is it?" My words are impatient, too high-pitched to sound like Ria's voice, but right now that is not my care. My pulse pounds in my ears.

"Samar always told me stories—fiction, I had once thought— of a group of ancient warriors," she begins. "He said they protected the Glass Temple. What they protected inside, however, I wasn't certain . . . until now."

"You think they are protecting the Bloodstone?" I supply.

"Perhaps." She turns to Amir. "Which means retrieving this

stone will not be easy. Our minds must be sharp, our bodies prepared."

"There'll be Charts everywhere," Amir reminds us. "They're desperate to find draft deserters *and* the Bloodstone. How will we be safe?"

He's thinking of his parents again. Instinctively, I take his hand, squeezing slightly. "We can't know for certain. But . . ." An idea springs to mind. "There won't be as many Charts around in the coming days. Not with the princess's engagement party coming up. They'll be pulled back to the palace."

I count the days in my head. My own engagement, and I will not be there to celebrate.

Jas nods, and even Amir looks a bit relieved.

"I will have to continue decoding Samar's notes—there are directions here, but they're unclear. I will determine the route he found to the Glass Temple." She stares at the both of us with stern eyes. "The only question now is, are you two up for the task?"

Amir works his jaw. He glances over at me, as if this is all one grand jest.

That could not be further from the truth.

"It'll be just like stealing naan," I tell him. "Except . . . bigger."

Amir stares deeper into my eyes, over my face, as if memorizing my features. He seems to be mulling over the prospect of finding the stone, but I can't help but wonder if he, too, wants to somehow fulfill his parents' dying act. The same way I am enacting Tutor's dying wish.

Perhaps we are more alike than I had originally thought.

"I never thought you'd be the savior type," Amir jokes at me, but I know I've won this round when his smile tips up, and I catch myself staring. His eyes linger on mine for a beat longer, then he shakes his head as if to clear it, turning toward Jas. "Yeah. We'll help."

Jas nods resolutely and takes both of our hands into hers. Amir's warmth mingles with Jas's motherly touch. I barely remember a time my own mother touched me with this kind of warmth.

"Before you go," Jas says, "I have something for you, Amir."

"Me?"

Jas fishes for an object in her belongings. She produces a cloth wrapped with twine. It must be fragile by the way she holds it—or sentimental in some way.

Amir carefully takes the cloth and unwraps the package. He gapes at the sight of it: a gold timepiece with the initials *A.B.* on the back.

"Amir Bhatt," he says. "Who did this?"

"Your father." A twinkle lights up Jas's eyes. "He meant to give it to you for your birthday, but he—"

"Couldn't," Amir answers, voice strangled. He turns to me. "My family was descended from goldsmiths. Papa knew the tricks of the trade . . . even wanted me to learn, eventually. But life doesn't always go according to plan."

"I hope you know how much you meant to him," Jas says. Her fingers graze the timepiece. Amir wraps up the chain and tucks the object into the cloth. I wonder if I see tears welling in his eyes.

But he smiles all the same. "I do."


Outside, Sanya paces vigorously, like a tiger with a swaying tail. Her belt is lined with daggers. "Did she tell you?"

"Yes. The Glass Temple," I whisper, even though no one else is within hearing distance. Stories of the Glass Temple are nearly fables. Could the fountain have been pointing me there this entire time?

Memories of Tutor weave back into existence: the lessons where he told me of the famed Glass Temple, forged where the Masters first touched the earthen grounds.

Not even my father, nor any of the past kings and queens, knew of the exact location of the Temple. Some believe it to be a place royalty of neither Abai nor Kaama wanted to visit until the truce had finished. But Tutor had been in the palace a long time. I wonder just how much he learned from the palace books; about the history of our world, of the Temple. Of the Bloodstone.

Enough to fill a book's worth in code.

"You're really doing this?" Sanya asks Amir. "You don't have to. Ma—"

"Didn't die for nothing," Amir finishes. I haven't heard this tone before. He gulps. "You and I've been running away for so long. But now I wanna run toward something.

"You've always been there for me, Sanya. Even when I wasn't here for you." His final words are rushed, whispered, but I catch them on the wind. I think of Sanya and Amir, having lost their parents too soon. The comfort she must have found in Jas and Tutor.

"I suppose you're right." Sanya maintains a cool distance from her brother. Something about her has softened, but Amir's sentiment is not enough to wholly defrost the iciness between them. "Then I guess it's time."

"For what?"

"Training. Last time we came to the Foothills, Irfan forged weapons and taught people self-defense." She pats her belt of daggers. "C'mon, he's already waiting."

Sanya heads back down the cliff. For a moment, Amir and I pause and survey the world around us.

"We should go," Amir says, but I stop him.

"Wait. I wanted to thank you. For the quilt." I muster as much gratitude as I can. I certainly lacked as much in the palace.

"Oh." Amir's eyes widen, then he shrugs, hiding a shy smile. "Sanya kept it; it was our mother's." He goes silent. "You looked cold."

I want to thank him again, but the words feel paltry in comparison to the action. My thanks have never meant much in the palace, if I offered any at all.

Amir's smile, slow and lopsided, makes my heart leap. Something compels me to lean forward and I do, trusting my instincts and pressing my lips to his cheek. I linger longer than I should before pulling back.

Amir lifts a hand to the cheek I kissed him on, now a bright red. "It was no big deal."

"It was to me." I bite my lip and find the courage to ask him, "You were telling Jas about how you didn't know what you wanted anymore. What did you mean?"

Amir lowers his hand. "Well . . . look at this." He gestures at the Foothills, from the tallest tree to the children playing with rags. "I kinda forgot the world could be like this. Peaceful. Caring. My dad's gift, it reminded me that time is precious. It moves forward, and so do we. My parents' death wasn't for nothing." He clutches the cloth holding the timepiece.

Amir is right. It is clear how much he admired his father, the same way I once admired Tutor. But it wasn't simply admiration. It was love.

As Amir loved his father, I loved Tutor. His death cannot be for nothing. Everything becomes clear. Tutor was more than my teacher or a father figure. He led people to believe in freedom. He taught me to how to be a leader because he was one.

I can be more than what the stars wish for. And I am just getting started.

# 23

## Ria

Shima's scales are a curious, buttery yellow as she leads me to the throne room. After last night's research with Aditi and the snake, I knew two things: I needed to open the Snake Pit, the place that holds those special gems—and maybe the answers I seek—and I would need Shima's help to do it.

Now I remain a long distance behind her as she slithers through the halls. I shiver from the sound of her hiss. Her scales ruffle, changing color as my emotions flicker: a deep maroon for anger; yellow for curiosity; soft pink when I recall Mama Anita. Maybe it's Rani's connection with Shima as her familiar that's granted me such a strong connection with the snake. Or maybe my gift is stronger than I realized.

*You spend much time thinking about your magic, for someone so afraid of snakes,* Shima says in that snarky tone of hers. *You also often muse on that young man, Saeed.*

"No I don't! And keep your thoughts to yourself," I bite out. "If you don't step on my toes, I won't step on yours. Got it?"

*Snakes don't have toes, Princess. But yes, I understand the senti-ment. And I'm sorry you're so afraid of me.*

"I never said I was."

*Everyone fears me, Princess Ria. Even Rani did, once. But love proves stronger than fear—wouldn't you agree?*

"I . . . guess." I shake my head. Doesn't really matter how I feel—I'll be out of here eventually, far, far away.

I struggle to keep up, and the way she guides herself smoothly over the tile directly in front of me almost looks like I'm con-trolling, puppeteering her actions. But Rani told me that snakes are familiars. *Friends.* Not pets.

Whatever Shima and I have, it's definitely not friendship.

We pass by a hall filled with royal portraits. I recognize one of them: Queen Amrita, her crown shining like the sun. One of the first ranis of Abai, she fought for equal education and passed when she was young. Another story of Mama Anita's.

We continue on. I shiver at what I'll find inside the throne room. It's the most talked-about place in Abai, the room where snakes kill, and those who catch the ire of the royal family are their prey. *Rumors,* of course. I never wanted to believe that the royals used their *magic* to kill. Now I know better.

When I step inside the room, it's like the air withholds a gasping breath. I expect to see a writhing sea of snakes, but there's nothing but a couple of throne chairs and the shining marble floors.

"Where's the Pit?" I wonder aloud.

*It's not something that simply exists,* Shima says. *It appears by magic and was forged from it with the help of a powerful ancient talisman.*

"The raja's scepter," I whisper, remembering the book. My eyes flicker to Shima's. "The scepter opens the Pit."

*Indeed. But that was not the only talisman to exist. The scepter is one of many relics from Amran,* Shima explains, forming a circle around me.

"What do you mean, one of many?"

*There is more than one talisman,* Shima says. *Each Master had their own, an extension of their magic, if you will, with their own unique powers. Many of these talismans have disappeared over the years.*

"Where've the other talismans gone?"

*Most have been lost, hidden, or buried.*

"Great." I turn to Shima and whisper, "I don't have the scepter. How am I supposed to open the Pit?"

*The book didn't tell you one thing. There are more ways than one to open the Pit. You can use your magic. It's already inside your bones,* Shima says. *You need only awaken it. Pull it from your marrow and empty it from within.*

Of course. I roll my eyes.

*Think of this as your first lesson in magic,* Shima says. *Many magic users, especially novices, invoke the name of their Master to help them connect more deeply to their power. Rani did that a lot as a child, and still has a habit of doing so.*

"I'm not invoking any *Master*. Plus, the Snake Master was deceptive," I add. "And no one knows where he went after the Great Masters' Battle."

*Deceptive?* Shima wonders. *So the story goes. You said yourself that stories change depending on who's telling them. Perhaps there is more you do not know.*

"What's that supposed to mean?"

*That though he is your ancestor, you can control your choices. You can make your own magic.*

I ponder that.

*Lesson two: Snakespeaking isn't only about communicating with snakes. Snake language has a different alphabet of sorts, that's all instinctive feelings instead of letters.* Shima must notice the lost look on my face, because she rolls her eyes and huffs. *Rani had trouble understanding it at first. It helped her to see the magic in her mind as drawers, each filled with power she could funnel at her will. Your gift, however, feels quite different. Like thieving, it appears by instinct.*

I think of all the times I've stolen simple foods, jewels. It *is* an instinct. I relax the way I would before a steal, and the air seems to shift. I gaze around. And then I hear it beneath the floor: the snakes, a hundred whispers that sound like an endless rattle of hisses.

I press a palm to the ground and shut my eyes. "What do I do now?"

*It's simple*, Shima says. I stand as she forms a ring, as if outlining the Pit itself. *Focus on the life beneath your feet . . . and let it open.*

With one hand still on the ground, I do as Shima says, letting those hums drive deeper into my brain. But suddenly, all I can think about is the sound of snakes piercing flesh—all the deaths that've taken place here.

Including Mama Anita's.

Repulsed, I push away. "I—I can't."

*You can*, Shima says. *The Pit is not a death place; it is a life force.*

"For you, maybe," I retort, though I can't stop thinking about Mama Anita. She died, right here, and for what reason?

*Think not of the deaths that have occurred but the spirits that remain. Go to them.*

I think of her. The one who took care of me when the rest of the world forgot I existed. Tears fill my eyes, and my heart angrily snaps in two.

Beneath my feet, the marble cracks. Shima nods, like she's been waiting for this to happen.

*Oh.*

She did that on purpose, letting my emotion lead me. Rani said something about magic being buried deep within us but coming out when we touched. When our emotions heightened. Maybe Shima knew that getting me to feel that yearning was the only way to open the Pit.

A hole yawns open like a monster's mouth, a dark cavern expanding right in the middle of the throne room floor. I shrink away from it, but a morbid curiosity blooms, forcing me to peer over the edge.

Darkness, save the glint of scales, gleaming like black diamonds. The Pit walls sparkle, carrying the faintest glow of gems embedded in its walls.

The snakes writhe with hunger as I say, "Don't tell me I need to go down there."

Shima shakes her head. *Wouldn't want to get that lehenga dirty, now would we? The Pit carries deep magic; you seek one of these gems, carrying the souls of the dead. You need only reach in, grab one, and focus on the life you wish to see.*

"Even better," I mutter. I try to shake off my nerves, but my body's shivering all over, and not just because of the cool palace air.

I reach a hand into the Pit, inch by inch, touching the cold, damp walls. I listen as Shima tells me to feel for a gem I can dislodge. The coppery smell of the Pit overtakes me, and I press my fist to my mouth. *This is just another steal,* I remind myself. I've stolen plenty of jewels. This should be no different.

Except for the sea of scales beneath me, glimmering like sunlight reflecting off water.

I move quickly, reaching deeper for one of the gems, an emerald as green as the lush Moga Jungle. I grunt as I stretch farther, inches away from my goal. But something rises from the Pit—steam, followed by a voice that makes me physically scramble back.

*"Return to my hiding place, the gift in the cobra's mouth . . ."*

The voice makes my teeth rattle, like it's right inside my head and I can't shake it out. It's all around me, like a voice of the skies, but that's impossible.

In seconds, the steam disappears, and the voice with it, like it never even existed. I shake my head furiously as if to rid myself of it further. Must be hearing things, honestly. My mind is getting soft. Maybe from the too-rich food. Or oversleeping on Rani's too-cushioned bed.

I reach down again, and finally, the jewel shifts in place. I collect it in my palm, watching as the gem glistens up at me. When I hold it to my face, I hear something faintly from below: a scream, maybe a sob. Then the sound of hissing snakes. I know what they're saying; their language is my own now. *Feed. Feed us.*

I scramble away from the Pit's walls as it stitches itself back together like a sewn wound. The floor crackles until the Pit disappears altogether.

Raja's beard, I'm never doing that again. The hisses and screams rattle in my head. *The sounds of people who died in the Pit.*

But I don't have time to waste thinking about this monstrous place. "Now?" I ask, staring at the precious jewel. "How do I use it?"

*Lesson number three,* Shima says. *The Pit is the home of darkness. To find the soul you seek, you must look into the light.*

"What's with all the vague riddles?" I wonder. But Shima's already twisting out of the throne room, and right now I've got no option but to take her advice.

"Bye, I guess," I grumble after her.

I bundle up my chunni and hide the gem in there. It glints

emerald-green and fits snugly in my palm, exuding energy. The kind I don't want to hold on to for long. This isn't some random gem I'd steal from the palace riches, like I once yearned to. *This* is a gem that holds the spirits of the dead. A soul I can call upon.

While the courtiers are busy with breakfast, I rush into the courtyards where I met Aditi last night. A gardener passes by, giving a low bow. I almost respond, then stop. *I'm* not the one who's supposed to be bowing, but it's strange to just take it in stride.

When I'm alone by a tamarind tree, sunlight filtering through the leaves, I look into the light and clutch the jewel to my chest. I know who I have to summon. I just don't know if I have the strength to do it.

But I have to. How else will I prove I belong here?

"Mama, do you hear me? I need you." When nothing happens, I clutch the gem harder and shut my eyes, surprised at how easily I summon the snake magic in my veins and fuse it with the gem. I think of her holding me, clutching me tight like she'd never let me go. "Please, Mama. Come back to me."

When I open my eyes, there's nothing but sunlight marring my vision and a few birds eyeing me quizzically. I think of Shima's words again. That snake had given me a riddle, and I thought I decoded it. Wasn't she saying to look into the light? Or maybe . . .

Maybe she meant something else.

*The Pit is the home of darkness. To find the soul you seek, you must look into the light.*

I hold the gem up to the sunlight, watching the rays refract and form a rainbow of color. "Mama, I'm calling you," I say, voice wavering.

A few seconds pass. Nothing. *I've failed again*, I think, but after a moment the air seems to shift. The sun filters through the gem until a mirage appears like a hazy, wavering vision on a scorching summer's day. I step back, lowering the gem until the strange light takes shape. Then, a voice I've heard a thousand times.

"Mama Anita," I cry. The voice seems to come from within me and without, forming a bubble of warmth. In the light, I make out the faint shape of Mama Anita's round cheeks, her thin lips and gentle eyes. It's really *her*. Her soul, her spirit. Maybe this is why I came to the palace . . . maybe this is my last shot at ever saying goodbye to my mama. Even if this is all I achieve, it would be worth it.

"Ria." She smiles.

"Mama, is that really you?" I say, blinking the tears away. "I need you."

"I know, dear child," she whispers. "I have felt your spirit near."

"You have?" I sniff. "Mama, did you know—"

"I sensed your magic the moment we met." Mama Anita nods. "You have always been special." Her voice sounds like it's raining from the skies.

I press a hand to my lips. Mama Anita knew, all this time?

"Did you know why I was given up?"

Mama Anita's face goes serious. "Ria, do not harbor resentment. You have been protected."

"Protected?" I blurt. On the contrary. I was abandoned like garbage. "Mama, you're the one who always protected me. Then I ran. I ran away from everything, right into this whole mess. And I don't know how to get out."

My heart stutters, trips. "Tell me, Mama. Please." I glance left and right, afraid someone might see us out in the open, but the gardens are luckily empty at this hour. "Tell me about the night we met. The night I came to you."

Mama Anita nods. "There was a prophecy."

I gasp.

"The raja entrusted me to care for you because of a prophecy about twins."

"What?" I shake my head. The raja knew Mama Anita? Then why would he execute her, the woman he entrusted to take care of his daughter, if he knew Mama personally? "I don't understand. What did the prophecy say?" My heartbeat lodges in my throat.

"That was never known to me." Mama Anita says. "But Ria, listen: This prophecy does not matter. Your life is yours to choose. Your fate is yours to hold. You have always been my family."

Mama Anita's form begins to ripple.

"Don't go, Mama," I cry. "I have so much more I need to know. I need to find my birth papers. I need to find proof of who I am."

"Retrace your steps; go back to the start; and follow your heart. Remember who you once were, and find who you can become."

Tears clog my throat. "I will. I promise."

The stone is growing dark. "I'll always be with you, my

daughter," Mama Anita says. "From morning to night. Dawn till dusk."

"Don't leave me!" I whisper fiercely. *Not yet.*

But I know, as I clutch the stone to my chest, that she won't be gone completely. Not really. She'll be in my heart; she always has been.

"I'll never forget you, Mama," I tell her. "I love you."

The dust and smoke all fade away. I fall to the ground, breathing heavily. Tears prickle my eyes before I spot a glimmer of scales. Shima, here, her eyes dark, as if she can feel my sadness.

Despite my instincts, I hold out a hand and let her curl onto me. She twists, letting her head sit on my lap. I stroke her scales as I look out at the gardens.

For the first time in a while, I don't feel so alone.

# 24

## Rani

Pain, hot and flashing, lances through my skull as I slam against the rough stone beneath me, vision blurring. I groan.

*Another point to Irfan.*

Fresh, purpling bruises mark my body from the spar; I have yet to determine if those marks are badges of courage or foolishness.

"Up," Irfan calls again. The world is dizzying as I rise and spot Amir on the side, face tight at the sight of my fall. Tonight's training session is far from formal; we spar on empty grounds on the outskirts of the Foothills with Irfan's strange assortment of weaponry. Last night's practice involved a bow and arrow, a princess's game I was familiar with. I'd grown up with archery lessons from Father's noblemen, but physical combat appears to be Irfan's specialty.

Never has a fencing session at the palace ended up with me like *this*.

I rub a sore spot on my back as Irfan's instructions knife

through me: *fighting is about instinct, not knowledge.* In the palace, I was taught that to spar is a dance: a choreographed movement of your foot and parry of your sword. Fencing was never about survival, merely intellect and grace.

No matter. I lunge again, aiming my practice sword at Irfan's leg. I've trained in fencing for over four years; I know how to attack.

Yet with a nimble movement Irfan dodges my attack and hooks a leg under mine. I fall face-first this time, the world canting sideways.

"Irfan, is this really necessary?" Amir asks again. Irfan ignores the comment.

"I said to keep your mind clear. Only get up if you're ready to fall back down again."

I spit dirt from my mouth, rise to my knees, and find my footing. When Sanya said we would begin training, she certainly meant it.

"Let's try again." Irfan cracks his knuckles and then leans down to retrieve his sword. Before he can stand, I charge. Irfan ducks and I tumble over his back and catch myself on my elbows and knees. *Abai's sun*, I think, *get up.* I spring for him just as Irfan sidesteps me, and my arms whirl, circling for balance.

"Ria!" Amir rushes over and steadies my arms, his hands oddly warm, but there's a smirk on his face. "I've seen you jump onto the roof of a hut. Lost your balance?"

Though his voice is teasing, I reply, "I know how to stand my ground."

"Well, maybe you forgot one of my thieving lessons: always keep an eye on your enemy."

But my memory holds no nights of thieving lessons, of bruised knuckles or alleyway run-ins. Who I am has nothing to do with scraping out an existence on Abai's streets.

"I'm training you so that you're prepared. The Charts will take one look at you, and they'll snap you in half," Irfan says.

A Chart wouldn't dare hurt a princess. Still, I glance down at my commoner's clothing; perhaps Irfan's trouncing is justified. That doesn't mean I like hearing myself dismissed so easily.

Another match, then. A lifetime's worth of survival instinct siphoned into one afternoon. Tomorrow is our departure; I must be ready. Ready with supplies, ready to blend in with the villagers, ready to find the Temple that harbors the ancient guard. I push Amir gently aside, feeling every ache come alive as I move.

We resume, but our sparring leaves me sore and dizzy, and I'm getting nowhere. I admit defeat. "Enough."

Irfan lowers his sword. "You wait too long to strike, Ria. This isn't a fencing match; it's real life."

"Then what would you have me do?" I ask him, tone biting.

"Watch your opponents' feet; it'll tell you where they're headed. Dodge, then strike. It's how I learned to fight: with instinct."

I bite my cheeks.

"We won't be prepared if we don't practice, Ria. I'm trying to help you."

"You might enjoy fighting," I state, "but to me, weapons are not an expression of power."

"Then what is?"

"Words, thoughts. Our actions. The Charts aren't powerful because of their swords. They are powerful because of their leader."

Irfan smirks. His irises are startling, two silver coins pressed flat and polished to a shine.

"The Charts won't stop their fighting because of words. I've been training my whole life, running drills since I was enrolled in Amratstan's child-soldier practice camps. Facing off with bandits who stole from my family." He heaves a breath. "Who took my parents' lives."

A stifling silence. "I . . ." The apology won't reach my throat.

"I've learned my lesson." Irfan laughs without mirth. "Bad things happen to good people. The world isn't fair; it's like this training ground—a little uneven. While the Charts and the raja are on top, we're at the bottom. And the only way to get to the top is to fight back."

I find Amir's gaze. He gulps, then offers: "We *do* want to fight back. We . . ." He steels himself. "We want our freedom back. From the raja. From the soldiers."

"Me too." From Father. Mother. Amara. They have always held my freedom in their palms. *But not any longer.*

"You have to decide who you want to be in this world. A fighter, or a bystander. Which are you?" Irfan asks.

He says the question as though I should know the answer. But I have left my old identity behind, shedding her like a snakeskin. And I don't know who I will be when all of this is over. Perhaps,

I will be worthy of being named Queen. Names and power are dangerous things, and in some ways synonymous, like two halves of one stone. Twins.

"A fighter," Amir and I answer simultaneously.

"Then we'll fight." Irfan passes a sword to Amir and gestures us to face each other.

We hold our swords up, circling each other slowly, like fencers in Father's court. Though our movements are more like those of a doll's: clumsy and stiff. I dart forward with my sword, nearly knocking aside Amir's and pressing the blade to his throat. But Amir stumbles back and as I shift closer—

We both fall to the ground, blades and limbs tangled. We're nose to nose for an infinitesimal moment, but it feels like a life-time. I don't know if I've ever seen his features like this before: his brows thick yet framing the rest of his face just right; his deep-brown gaze, an ocean wide; his lips slightly parted. His breath is laced with a hint of clove lingering from this morning's chai.

*Why can't I look away?*

I shift off him. "Amir?"

His eyes flit closed.

Panic grips my chest. I jump up, shaking Amir's body.

A moment passes before he exhales and laughs, eyes crinkling. "Gotcha."

"That's not funny!" But something breaks loose in me as I laugh, and flutters low in my stomach. Perhaps adrenaline from the spar, though Amir's gaze makes me think of something else.

A thrill runs through me that I haven't felt in ages. Not since I believed in my love for Saeed.

*Stop it, Rani,* I berate myself. I help Amir stand and regain my composure.

Irfan claps twice, jolting me back to reality. "No time to waste. Remember, fight with instinct. Get ready for second position."

I inhale deeply as we ready our next spar. This time it's Amir who moves first, catching me in the side with a dull blade. I stumble back.

*Do not show weakness. You are a princess.* I may be a lie parading around as a thief girl, but my blood is more precious than any copper pot or iron coin—a fact that I have almost forgotten.

I recall Irfan's advice and watch Amir's feet intently. I feel wind against my skin, smell the faint scent of rice that perfumes the air, taste a future of freedom, sweeter than nectar.

And I charge.

My blade hits Amir's sword and I swipe left. Amir blocks my last move easily, but it doesn't feel like defeat. It feels like a step forward into the unknown, thrilling and dangerous. I stop thinking. I fight with instinct.

Nightfall arrives when we finish our last spar. "We leave at dawn," Irfan tells us.

As Amir exits and I'm ready to step away, I catch sight of Irfan packing up. I approach him, watching as nearby torchlight illuminates his rugged features.

"Thank you for this. For training us," I clarify.

"I hope you didn't take too hard of a fall." When he's finished packing, he slings his sheath over his shoulder and grunts. He clutches it and finds me eyeing him. "Just a little sore. You may not hit your target nine times out of ten, Ria, but when you do . . ."

Irfan's gaze flickers down. Silver eyes, silver secrets.

Something niggles at the corner of my mind. The reason why Irfan seems so familiar . . .

"We've met," I say boldly, "haven't we?"

Irfan sucks his cheeks in. "Our pasts haunt us. Always."

I step closer. It's on the tip of my tongue, his secret.

"Didn't you wonder why Samar died?" Irfan whispers. His eyes turn hollow. Saddened.

Burdened.

"He was a traitor to the king," I reply, voice shaking.

"He was hiding a secret," Irfan amends. "My secret. And secrets are dangerous things. Best you'd stay away from them."

Before I can reply, the silver-eyed man salutes his farewell, heading downhill. His retreating form disappears into the folds of the autumn night.

One thing is certain: Irfan is hiding something. And I must find out what.

With Sanya and Jas decoding Tutor's route to the Temple, Amir and I relax our tired muscles by sitting under a mango tree in the Forest of Hearts.

Under the stars we lie side by side at the trunk, peering up between the leaves.

"They say one bite of a mango in this forest will make you fall in love. At least, that's what Ma said," Amir adds quietly. "We used to sit here and look up at the stars."

He points up at the outline of a circlet. The crown constellation.

"Ma said she named me for it," Amir chuckles. "Big joke, right? Me, a prince?"

I'm quiet as Amir takes my hand in his and traces the faint string of stars beneath the crown. The outline comes into being: a face, eyes, lips. Have those always been there? Or are the stars trying to tell me something?

"Ma said a prince should always care for his people." Amir lowers my hand. "But I've realized . . . it's not the royals who care. It's us. Our friends, our family."

Amir might have a reasonable distaste for royalty, but still, I sit up. "Perhaps the royals have changed. Perhaps they've learned from the past and want a brighter future."

And while I no longer truly believe that of my father and mother, I want Amir to believe in *me*. I want him to see me here, and what I'm trying to accomplish.

Amir leans up on his forearm, gazing at me. "Did you hurt yourself during training? What happened to the Ria I met eight moons ago? She would fume at a mention of the raja, or his family."

"That Ria doesn't exist anymore," I say fiercely. "And I'm not hurt. Except perhaps for my pride, and a few bruises."

He scrutinizes me. "You know, I don't think I've so much as

heard you say *Raja's beard* since we left the palace."

"Raja's beard?" I say weakly.

"C'mon, Ria. I know when something's different about you." Gently, he tilts his head and examines my face.

He means the way I've been acting. Standing my ground when I should have run. How I kissed his cheek in thanks. Suddenly I feel foolish; Ria would've never done that.

"I don't remember this," he says, eyes trailing down to where a small nick sits at the base of my chin. A souvenir from a game Saeed and I once played as children on the rooftop of the servants' quarters. The cut never quite healed.

I need him to look away, stop him from seeing the minute differences between Ria and me. "Perhaps it was from today's training. Which reminds me . . . I never knew Irfan trained as a soldier before. Did you?" I'd heard of Amratstan's rigorous training program for children, having them practice to become soldiers before they're even of age. Father would never allow such a thing in Abai. A small comfort.

"I haven't spoken to him much since we met by the tavern. Honestly, at first, I kind of despised the guy for hanging out with my sister. Like . . ." He looks away.

I don't need to be a mindwielder to read his thoughts. "Like he was taking your place."

Amir's gaze swivels up. "I know, it's stupid. But everything's just been so sudden. After our parents died, we only had each other. And I wanted that to work, but I couldn't stay in our village any longer, couldn't deal with life without them. I left her, and I forgot I ever even had a family. Now I look at Jas and Irfan and Sanya, and . . . they almost look like one."

More than he and Sanya ever did, he means. I place my hand on his for comfort. "You never meant to hurt your sister, Amir. But she doesn't know that. You need to tell her why you left. You need to end this rift between you two."

"I don't even know how to find the words," Amir admits.

"Any words will be enough. They don't have to be the perfect ones. They just have to be from you. All she wants to know is how you really feel."

Moonlight washes through the branches, landing on Amir's cheeks, his brow, the crown of his head. My gaze locks on his; his lingers on mine. He looks like he's battling something, his body pushing forward and pulling back. As if he's caught in that fragment of time when day becomes night.

"Here," he says after a moment. With haste, he fishes for two identical bands of twine. "Jas told me everyone in the Foothills wears one. The strings symbolize how everyone here is a family. They work together to make the community stronger."

I take the twine and, without hesitation, bring my hands to Amir's bare wrist. His skin is visibly callused, a pattern of strength, of loyalty.

"This place could be home," Amir says wonderingly. "You're safe here. From conscription. From the raja's army. If we forgot about the Bloodstone, the passports . . ." He leans in closer, and

I'm startled by how handsome he looks up close, his rugged grace. For a second, I consider it. Living without care, staying in the Foothills forever.

I tie the twine and look away. "That's not possible, Amir," I say. *Home.* What does that word mean anymore?

"Why not?" His voice comes out rough. The heat between us is stifling.

"Because," I reason. *We don't belong together.* Amir and I, we're opposite ends of everything. Heat and ice. But here we are, threads unspooling until we are one being under the stars.

"It's a fantasy, staying here," I continue. "This could never be our home. This is the land the raja rules. If we don't get the Bloodstone and stop the king, we'll be powerless." Though the words sting me, I cannot indulge in Amir's illusions of a better life right now, not until I have the Bloodstone in my hands. And if I achieve my goals, I need to remember where I'll be at the end of all of this: back in the palace. Not in the Mailan Foothills. Not with Amir.

Amir pulls back. "Ever since we got here, all you've been talking about is that Bloodstone and the Ruthless Raja. All you do is defend the royals! I thought you cared about freedom, not power. I thought . . . I thought you cared about us." He gulps. "I don't get it, Ria. Whose side are you on?"

I flinch. His words aren't harsh—no, they're almost gentle in a way I hate, confusion simmering beneath the surface. The heat, palpable just a second ago, has dissipated for an iciness that feels too familiar for comfort. I push myself to my feet. I want to tell

Amir our worlds could collide, that I am changing and shifting more than I ever thought I would. But what of my end goal? What happens after the stone? He is not in my future.

"Perhaps our thoughts are more different than we expected."

Hurt flashes in Amir's eyes. "Or maybe I just never saw the real you."

My stomach coils. I haven't a clue why I care what he thinks, but I do. I storm off.

*Whose side are you on?* Amir's words echo in my ears. I came here for myself, to prove something to Father. But what of my people? Shouldn't I have been thinking of them, too?

It seems the world has split into two: rebels and royals. A line has been drawn in the sand, but I am not sure which side I belong to anymore.

# 25

## Ria

"Swing your leg over, like this." Saeed demonstrates mounting a black mare with ease, like it isn't a living, breathing beast beneath him. I attempt to climb onto my horse, *again*, but slide right off with a grunt.

"Something wrong?" He eyes me as I struggle to position my feet.

*Yeah*, I want to huff, *I barely got a wink of sleep and I've never ridden a horse in my life*. The mare lets out a loud snort, and I jump. Saeed looks like he's biting back a grin. He's both humored and confused by me, probably still wondering what exactly I've been up to these past few days. With all of the engagement preparations, our lessons have been postponed more often than not.

I spent all of the last two nights in the library, even fell asleep in there trying to learn more about this mysterious prophecy Mama Anita mentioned. *That's* what holds the answers to my birth, the answers to why I ended up in the orphanage. Not to mention

Aditi still hasn't gotten back to me about those roses Amara's so attached to. Despite all my looking, I found nothing.

Now it's late afternoon, and I'm still bone-tired and chilled from this morning's downpour. The cool air calms me when I finally, *finally* mount this blasted beast, and we leave the stables to head down a trail within the palace gates.

I've never been so close to a mare. Why ride a horse when you can run? And can't horses smell fear or something? I surreptitiously smell my arm, then lower it once we're in the thick of a copse of trees, a lonely plain of land far enough from the palace to feel alone but close enough to remember I haven't escaped.

"How'd you get the raja's permission to get me out of there?"

"Took some convincing," Saeed admits, "but with Mother as the raja's adviser, your father allowed it, so long as I stay close to you. He seemed to think a horseback riding lesson would do us some good, especially since we're . . . how did you put it? *Starting over.*"

"You told the raja that?" I thought after my accusation of his mother, he wouldn't want to spend another second near me.

"Have you changed your mind?"

"No . . ."

"I know when you're lying, Rani."

"*I'm* the snake sniffer! I mean, the snakespeaker." Saeed softly snorts. My cheeks burn. Why are my words getting all tangled up? Must be from the lack of sleep. I'm supposed to be a cool-headed thief whose hands work faster than her heart, not some lovestruck princess.

"All right, *snake sniffer*," Saeed teases. His eyes flicker to mine. I don't give him the satisfaction of returning his half glance, nor can I wonder what that glance means.

"In truth, I wanted to take you on this ride to apologize for my behavior. I've been acting out of turn, been overprotective of my mother, who needs no protecting. I hope you'll allow me the chance to explain."

"O-of course," I eke out.

Saeed clears his throat. "My mother wasn't always harsh. She told me stories of her and the queen, how they became friends. Mother was kind. She felt love more than hatred. In Kaama, before my father's death, she was . . ." He laughs. "She was *normal*. And then in recent years . . . it was like all she wanted was for me to sit on the throne."

My gaze flits downward. "What changed?"

Saeed toys with a loose thread hanging from his trousers, lost in thought as the horses carry us onward. "I've never told you this, but back in Kaama, my mother hoped that someday I would grow up to become a Kaaman Warrior and join their army like Father. Then he died on a routine mission. There was an accident. I was only two summers old."

A seam rips open in my chest. What can I say? Sorry isn't enough. *Sorry* never filled the aching in my heart when I missed Mama Anita.

"Since Mother was born in Abai," Saeed continues, "all our ties to Kaama were lost. My mother was ridiculed. That's when we came to live in the palace, since our mothers were already friends. Mother thought I'd become an instructor once I finished my education, since I'd be safe from the army in that position. After Father was gone, she never wanted me near the Kaaman Warriors.

"And so I grew up in the palace." His gaze softens with remembrance. "Do you remember when we played together as children? We would hide out in the servant staircases and watch the Charts, pretending to be on secret missions."

"*Rani* did—?" I start. "I mean, *we* did that?"

He gives me a once-over, as if confused by my outburst. "For a time, yes. Then your studies took over. And then we were grown, and thrust at each other as suitors. I must admit . . . I miss how we were, in the beginning. But your wishes are most important to me now. Our parents wanted us married for a long time, but . . ." He shakes his head. "I just want you to know that you were truly the only companion I ever had. And you were more than that. I admired you, Rani. I admire you still. I wish things had been . . . different."

His stare becomes all too hot, like it's warming me from the inside out. Silence thickens the space between us.

"I haven't really treated you well," I tell him, looking away. "I'm sorry. I want to change that."

I peer at him. A corner of his lips lift, like a flower gently unfurling. "You've seemed different lately, Rani. The way you walk about the palace, the way you speak up. You're less rigid. More . . . *you*."

My cheeks redden.

"You know," he begins as we round a corner on the trail and enter a thick row of trees, "Mother has always protected me. She's often been the only one. But since our engagement was announced, she has been acting strangely. I began to think that your words were truthful. So I listened to your request."

My grip tightens on the horse's reins. "You didn't take the tonic?"

He turns to me as our horses pause at the end of the trail. "I pretended to drink it so Mother would seem satisfied. And then last night . . . I had another vision. But it wasn't clouded. This one was stronger than the others, and so clear I knew it couldn't be a dream."

I hold my breath. "What did you see?"

A beat passes. "Mother," he finally reveals. "She was speaking to the raja during a council meeting, pushing him to conscript one able-bodied person from every household for the war." He gulps. "She spoke without reverence, without fear. She seemed . . . controlling."

So *this* is what Amara wanted to stop her son from seeing? Her role in agitating the war?

"That's tens of *thousands* of people—sent to die in a pointless war! Did the councillors agree to the measure?"

"I woke up before the vision was complete," he admits. "But everyone seemed so approving of Amara as the raja's new adviser. It was . . . strange. Mother's always been interested in politics, but even I was surprised she got the position."

"Strange," I agree. But even stranger is what Amara is *doing* as the king's adviser.

"I need to see the rest of that vision." He pauses. "You were right about the tonic affecting my mind. I'm sorry I didn't believe you at first. I had little faith when all you wanted was for me to learn the truth."

"Oh." I'm surprised by his candor.

"Really, Rani. You helped me. And now I think that together, we can figure out what my mother's hiding. Maybe we can even restore normalcy to this place. To this country. To both our lives. Together." The horses pick up again as we turn around, back toward the palace.

I consider his words. *Together.* A thought bubbles to mind so ridiculous I wonder if it'll even work. But it might be worth a shot.

"Can you ever . . . call up a vision?"

Saeed shakes his head. "I only have visions when I sleep."

"What if there was a way for you to have visions on command? Like dreaming while you're awake? Have you ever tried?"

"No." Saeed ponders this.

I think of the memories that blasted to the surface when Rani and I were together. "Memory magic is deeply connected to snake magic, right? They're two sides of the same—"

"Coin," he finishes, breathless. His smile tips up.

"Maybe together, we could help you conjure a vision."

Saeed raises his brows. "Do you really think we could do it?"

"It's worth a try." I dismount my horse, and Saeed follows more gracefully. We stand face-to-face on the trail, only breaths apart.

"Maybe if we, um, touch . . . ?" I'm guessing, fumbling for a way. Saeed squeezes my hands tight. "All right," he says, and we close our eyes. I think of Rani, the moment we made contact, what I felt in that instant. Confusion, strangeness; hope, understanding.

Questions answered; questions left unfulfilled.

"I see her," he says finally. "But it's fuzzy. . . ." His eyes fly open, and so do mine. "We need our connection to be stronger." His breath hitches. "Do you remember what I told you about how your snakespeaker magic is more powerful when you're closer to Shima?"

I nod, trying to understand what he's getting at.

"Perhaps we need to be closer, somehow," he murmurs. Then his gaze flutters to my lips. He seems embarrassed by the words, even though I don't get what he's—

*Oh.*

My skin freezes. "I—" I begin, but what is there to say? Rani and Saeed have done this plenty of times. But that doesn't mean *I* have.

Saeed looks sheepish. "Perhaps there's another way—"

It would be over in a second, I reason. I shake my head, a mixture of dread and something *else* twisting in my belly.

When I came to the palace, my wants were my basest desires. A ticket out of Abai, freedom on my lips, answers about my past.

Then Amara came into the picture, and now everything is a jumble of knots.

I always thought the best I could do was make myself invisible and escape Abai. But maybe I belong here. And if I belong here . . . well, then I can do something bigger than I ever thought. Maybe, by making myself seen, I can help this kingdom, and the people in it, the way the raja never did.

"We need to see the rest of this vision." *The future might depend on it.*

"You're sure?" he asks.

I squeeze his hands tighter in response. I brace myself, even though Saeed's brows dip into a gentle knot, like he, too, is nervous.

When he leans in, he lightly brushes his fingers against my cheek. It's my last chance to pull away, and he's giving me an opportunity to stop, but I don't. I grab his neck and pull him closer. His mindwielder's aura presses against me, calling to my own magic. I tip my head up and his lips brush against my cheek, the corner of my lips—

The vision startles me when it arrives, swimming under my eyelids like a moving image, blocking out the world around me: Amara, standing in what looks to be a council room. Behind her reads today's date, written in ink on parchment. Councillors sit around her as she announces the conscription, the raja nodding in agreement. Then comes the sound of bells ringing. Once, twice . . . seventeen chimes total. The words muffle and shift in the vision—and it's over too soon. The vision turns to smoke. I plummet back into the present when Saeed pulls away, the almost-kiss broken to dust.

"Did you see that?" he asks, breathless.

I nod. No words escape my throat.

"Your father's council room," he supplies. "We need to go there now."

The palace bells ring ahead. I count up to sixteen and shiver. Saeed's vision is about to come true at the end of the hour.

We hurry back onto our horses. I hold on for dear life and gallop straight for the palace.


"*This* is where we used to play?" I half whisper, staring up at the rafters. Saeed has already climbed onto the beams, leading straight from the servants' quarters and into the ceiling of the raja's council chambers.

"Too scared to climb now that you're grown?" Saeed asks as he hauls me up. I've climbed trees plenty of times but palace walls? Not so much.

We shuffle side by side through the rafters on elbows and knees, and after a moment, Saeed grumbles a laugh. I prickle.

"What? So I'm not the *daintiest*. I can't help it."

Saeed shakes his head. "No. It's just . . . I never thought we'd be like this again."

I gaze at Saeed questioningly, aware of our pressed bodies, before finally shaking him off. We continue on our path until we're right above the room. A small slit gives us air to breathe and a view directly into the raja's chambers. I'm like a ghost, silent and nearly invisible, just like during a steal.

Amara's fire-red hair drapes over her shoulders as she stands at the front of the council room. Next to her is the raja and Samvir, who Shima taught me is the raja's snake familiar. The snake's scales are deathly black, flickering with red, and I can almost smell the magic in the air as the raja pats the cobra's head. I hold my breath as we listen.

"As I mentioned earlier, my last topic for today will be conscription. The raja needs soldiers; this war won't win itself."

The council members give a murmur of agreement. Chatting about war so leisurely makes me sick.

"I've already discussed this with the raja, who has given me full support in bringing up this next suggestion: the conscription age at the moment remains eighteen, as it has been for all of Abai's history. This is no longer enough. We must lower the age and have Charts collect the new soldiers for recruitment as soon as possible. Henceforth, one able-bodied member of each family from the age of fourteen will be drafted into the soldiers' ranks. Families will be awarded a small sum for each child they admit for recruitment, for their willing generosity," Amara says sweetly.

Raja's beard. It's worse than we thought. Not just a person from each family but *children*.

I dig my nails into the rafters. I'm so furious I could explode. How could Amara force *children* to fight in this war? The raja nods, confirming to his council members the severity of the situation.

*We must have more soldiers . . . Kaama's army is growing . . .*

I can't listen to this any longer, and Saeed can see it on my face. He holds me back, even as horror dawns equally on him.

At the seventeenth bell, the council members disperse. They've agreed to Amara's claim, and she looks pleased.

Only the raja remains in the room, standing now face-to-face with Saeed's mother. I lean forward, careful to keep my breaths quiet.

"The stone will soon be in our grasp," Amara says to the raja. "And we will tear down the Kaamans one by one. The blood of Amran will grant us the greatest power in existence."

The raja nods, though his gaze is far away, as if caught in a daydream. It's not until then that everything clicks into place. A stone that's a weapon of war. Made from the blood of Amran . . .

*The Bloodstone!* It's the famed jewel Mama Anita told me stories about. The one that caused the fight between the Masters, that made the Snake Master powerful above all others.

I whisper to myself, "The stone Rani's looking for is the Bloodstone."

"Bloodstone?" Saeed whispers next to me, confused. I don't respond, because my attention is caught by Amara. No—Amara's bracelets, those cuffs she'd been gifted from her father. Carved onto them is a symbol of a single eye.

I squint, peering closer at them. They're . . . *glowing.*

"Did you see that? Her cuffs?" I ask Saeed, offering him a gap through the beams. He peers through, then shakes his head.

Shimmers wink off Amara's cuffs, a reflection from the candlelight, before disappearing. Was I seeing things? A flicker of the light?

The raja speaks louder now. "We will recruit a fresh set of Charts immediately after Rani's engagement party. With greater numbers, the Bloodstone *will* be found."

They finish their conversation, Amara bowing with reverence. Samvir's scales shimmer oddly as he and the king steal out of the room. Amara remains rooted to her spot, the room eerily quiet.

Then Amara looks up.

Stunned, I fall back, and the rafters echo from my sudden movements. Saeed's eyes grow wide. Neither of us can hide from this.

"Spying on me now, are we?"

I freeze. *Caught.* Saeed's eyes hold a mountain of fear.

We descend from the rafters and drop into the council room, the tasseled red rug beneath us a symbol of the oh-so-rich royals. But it's Amara's own venomous gaze that does me in.

We might've been caught, but Amara's been caught, too.

"We know what you're up to, Amara," I say.

Amara ignores me as she examines her son with curiosity. "Saeed, I thought you were supposed to take our dear princess on a ride?"

"I did," Saeed clips. The fear melts away, replaced by bold courage. "Mother, this isn't right. Lowering the conscription age isn't only wrong—it's a rejection of Abai's morals. Do you want villagers thinking their only worth is to fight? That we'd rather their children die than remain protected?"

"Their *duty* is to protect themselves," Amara spits. I've never seen her talk this way to Saeed, and even he seems stunned. But I only feel emboldened by Amara's indignance.

"Saeed's right. As a royal, my father isn't supposed to be forcing commoners into the war. He's supposed to be helping them. And as princess of this kingdom, I won't stand for this."

Amara's demeanor changes, flickering from anger to intrigue.

"Son, tell my servant to prepare my chambers. I think I'll get an early rest tonight—after I speak to Rani."

"But—"

"Privately," Amara interjects.

Saeed glances at me. He almost looks like he's waiting for me to say something. Maybe he wants me to ask him to stay, but I can't bring myself to. He opens his mouth again before turning on his heel and marching out of the room like the dutiful son he's supposed to be.

Amara walks around the table, eyeing me like a tiger would its prey. She drags her nails across the wood, leaving streaks in the grain. With her confident stance, she looks like an otherworldly being, a Master above all others, but underneath she's nothing more than a snake.

Amara glares daggers at me. "It seems as though you and I need to chat, *Rani.*"

"Obviously," I say. I can't help but speak fluent sarcasm to her—Shima's favorite language. The snake would be proud.

Amara saunters toward me. "Oh, Rani. Did you forget all those years of training?"

I put on my best impression of Rani. "I don't follow."

Her hair drapes down her back like an inferno. "It's not polite to listen in on private conversations. You know, a princess doesn't *sneak* about the palace. Tell me, Rani . . ." She steps closer. "What are you so curious about?"

I bring my fingertips to my elbows and dig into my flesh, reminding myself to play the part. "What do you want, Amara-*ji*?"

She exhales and straightens herself. "I think you know what I want, Rani." A saccharine smile lifts her lips. "The truth."

My heart stutters as Amara moves so close I can practically smell her breath. Wine, *again*. So predictable.

What's not predictable are the words she utters next.

"If I were you, I wouldn't get servant girls who work for me to do your bidding."

My stomach drops.

"Books belong in the library," she continues in that low voice. "Especially ones about magic."

My gut hollows. *No, she couldn't know that, too, she couldn't've seen it*—

"It's a pity that my own servant seems to have forgotten her place. I don't abide disloyalty. Don't think that little girl is getting out of this without any punishment," she threatens. "Or that I won't be watching you and *Aditi* closely from here on out."

Just hearing her name makes me want to crumple. I imagine Aditi in the Pit—dead. Just like Samar, and Mama Anita before him.

"Don't you dare say her name." I speak before I even think, anger thrumming through me.

"Why not? She's *my* servant, after all. But I think there's a more pressing matter here." She taps her chin, stepping closer. "What name shall I call *you*?"

I freeze. "You—you've had too much to drink."

"My mind is clear. What I wonder now is how to bring you to confess the truth to the raja. Or perhaps I'll leave that all up to you . . . *Rani*."

I'm breathing hard now, and my voice comes out roughened with rage. "You're feeding venom to your own son. And—and you were talking to the raja about a weapon. The Bloodst—"

Before I can continue, the sound of whooshing air splits my speech. I barely register what Amara's doing before I feel her bejeweled hand strike me across the cheek.

At first—nothing. No pain.

Then I'm reeling. Heat spikes through me, coloring my tear-filled vision crimson, mirroring Amara's own smiling lips.

"Feel lucky I didn't use a stick against you like they do in Kaama," Amara spits. She offers me her hands, palms up, and through the tears I see what look like permanent scars. "I know pain better than you ever will."

I can't even respond. My skin stings. My teeth sing. My skull rattles.

I touch a hand to my cheek and spot the blood dotting my fingers. The familiar taste of metal fills my mouth.

"The raja will hear about this. I promise," I grit out.

"Hear what? That his dearest Rani has been replaced by an impostor?" She smiles. "I need only reveal that mole that doesn't belong. But don't you worry. You've got an engagement to get ready for, and I'll make sure you play the perfect bride." Her grin widens. "It'll be our little secret . . . for now."

Amara saunters away, but her poisonous words rattle my brain. I rush up to Rani's bathing room, slam the door behind me, undress, and sink into the bath. The truth of our conversation finally hits me.

Amara knew. She was watching me. I can't even tell the raja what Amara's done, or she'll reveal my secret. It's my word against hers. And I am the liar.

I'm overtaken by fury, by grief. For the first time since I've been in this palace, I heave a sob. A catalyst. The sobs rack my body, and shame and foolishness burn the wound on my cheek. My head pounds.

Thief. Princess. Thief. Princess.

I sit in the bath, losing track of time, letting the water warm the stinging bruise on my face. I'm unsure of where Amir is, if he's safe. I'm unsure of what I'm doing, trying to be Rani and always failing. And I'm not sure where my tears end and the water in my bath begins.

# 26

## Rani

The morning air is crisp and sings of tales whispered on the wind. Tales of girls whose stories shall be told forevermore.

Tales of girls like me.

"Grab your things," Irfan tells me. "We're loading the horses."

I nod firmly. My passport—no, *Ria's* passport—burns a hole in my pocket. We're leaving the Foothills now, headed toward the Glass Temple. A place I never thought I would see with my own eyes. But any excitement is drowned by the fact that this journey is a race: the Charts are looking for the stone, too. We have little time to waste.

At the entrance of the Foothills, Amir pauses and turns back to admire the world we've come to know, a land of people who believe in freedom and truth and equality. But last night's conversation comes flooding back: about whose side I'm on, about where my loyalties lie. He won't quite look me in the eye, and I have yet to find my answer for him.

I step out of the Foothills first, the air shifting before me as I escape the strange bubble. Behind us there appears only desert plains and warm winds. Sanya, Amir, Irfan, and Jas emerge seemingly out of nothingness as they exit, and the Foothills magically seals itself away from us. Jas holds Tutor's book close to her, the route to the Temple sketched out next to Tutor's pristine code. I help her onto the horse, then mount mine.

Traveling with Amir while we are on rocky terms is harder than I thought. His hands on my waist feel different now, his grip looser, as if he cannot stand to be so close to me. *Whose side are you on?* The words pound through my skull.

Three days of travel through the jungle later, we reach a clearing. Exhaustion settles in my bones like a heavy blanket.

"Let's set up a fire for dinner here and refuel," Irfan says. "We're not far from the next village. We'll sleep here and leave at first light."

I dismount and untie the packs strapped to the mare. Across from me, Amir does the same for the other horses, eyes flickering up to me as he undoes the ropes. Our conversation has been short, businesslike. Nothing more than what we must communicate to complete our tasks.

I glance away and focus on my steed, getting her tied up and watered down. But all I can think of is Amir. I yearn to speak with him, but I'm not about to blurt an apology so easily. Was it so wrong to express a different viewpoint?

After my horse drinks the water, I brush her mane and tail.

The movements are so instinctual to me I nearly grow sleepy from the rhythm. Father always used to let me into the royal stables as a child.

"May I?" Amir appears next to me.

I start. "May you what?"

He points at the brush I have for the horses.

"Oh." I hand over the comb, hiding my rouged cheeks, and his fingers gently touch mine as he retrieves it. He brushes another horse in silence. All I can think of is my fingertips, burning from where he touched me.

*You're supposed to be mad at him.*

I turn away. Jas sets up a hearth of flames with ease, and soon enough, she's offering us bowls of chole. She canned chickpeas before we left, prepared for the journey and the hunger it would bring. It's clear Jas is skilled with herbs—both for healing and for cooking. The chole warms my stomach, my chest, in a way the Abai sun never could.

"Stories are sacred things in Abai," Jas says once we're settled. "We used to host campfire nights all the time in the Foothills. I have many stories that Sanya used to love to hear." She glances at Sanya with the loving care of a mother, placing a hand over top hers. "The first step to healing our wounds is to speak of them. That's what stories do. They teach us to remember, and to overcome."

"I don't have a story." Sanya kicks at the ground. Silence falls over the camp.

"I'll volunteer, I guess," Amir says. He fidgets as he rubs knuckle against knuckle. His eyes flick up to mine, as if by accident, but he holds my gaze. My cheeks heat.

Amir breathes deeply. "I've never told anyone the story of how I got my scar. It happened years ago, but I remember it fresh as yesterday."

Why does it sound like he's speaking only to me? My gaze flutters up to the scar. He thumbs his lips, staring at the ground. Stubble forms a prickly veil on his chin, and his visage is half shadowed.

"I was in one of those fabric shops. It isn't hard to steal jewels off chunnis The jewels don't sell for much, but they're something. Before I could get away, I saw a child hiding a couple of chunnis behind their back. They were so thin—hunched over like a dog someone forgot to feed. They didn't know I'd seen them, but when the owner turned back, I—I knocked over a display of goods. It was enough time for the kid to get away. They left with the chunnis and a few other things—earrings, necklaces, the works. When the owner figured out what was missing, he thought the kid and I were working together. . . ." Amir fiddles with the hem of his shirt. "I took the blame."

He doesn't have to say the rest for me to fill in the blanks. He steals a look at me, and I don't glance away. I can practically feel the tender raised flesh where his wound sits.

"I don't even think the owner wanted to hurt me this bad," Amir adds softly. "But I guess I deserved the whipping."

"You didn't. You never did." It doesn't matter that I'm not supposed to be talking. The words slip out of me, steely and harsh. I imagine the swaths of fabric, oranges and hot pinks and fire reds, saris and suits peppered with luscious jewels. Amir, a boy who only wanted to pluck them like ripe fruit, his only chance at food, at something to sell for spare change.

The whole camp is silent. I'm aware of every eye on me and Amir.

"I guess it's proof," Amir says. He glances around the fire. "If I ever loved someone, it would feel like that."

"Like what?" I say, though the words come out in a whisper.

"I dunno," he says, with a laugh meant to deflect. "Like sacrifice."

*Sacrifice.* That was not what I imagined with Saeed. Love was stolen kisses, silken lips. I thought I loved Saeed once. Could I love him again? If I tried? If I went back?

I'm not sure I want to.

Irfan, silent as stone as he sits across from me, cuts into my thoughts. "Who's next?"

I turn away from Amir, who's still staring at me, and my stomach twists. Inconspicuously, I cover my face with a few strands of hair, praying for my too-hot cheeks to cool down.

Across from me, Jas shifts in her spot. "There was a story my husband always told. A story of two people from opposite sides of life, a stonebringer and a currentspinner, and their impossible task."

I know this story. Under Tutor's tutelage, I learned stories aimed at teaching about all kinds of magic. Currentspinners, descendants of the Master of Sky. Stonebringers, who could move the earth with their fingertips.

I don't listen as Jas finishes the story. I already know how it ends. With the characters forever at odds. Never finding a way to make peace. I begged Tutor to tell me another ending, to tell me there was hope.

I tug my chunni closer to me, despite the stifling air and the fire billowing right in front of me. Next to Jas, Irfan fidgets with his hands.

"And what's your story?" I ask him.

His silver eyes pin mine. "I've got nothing to tell."

"You said you trained in child-soldier camps?"

This spikes Irfan right where it hurts. "I don't like to talk about the past. What's done can't be undone."

"That's not always true. The past—"

"Will haunt you," he says, just like he told me days ago, eyes alight. I catch his fingers tightening at his sides. "We all hide something."

My heart thuds as I speak my next words. "And what are you hiding?"

Irfan's eyes burn. "Most people know I come from Amratstan. What they don't know is how one day, I went home and found our house empty, wrecked, in shambles. My parents were dead because of bandits. They raided my village and spared only the children."

The group is silent.

"I came to Abai, tried to make a home for myself." Irfan hesitates here, as though he has to force the next words out—but when he speaks, it's a shorter story than I expect. "I worked for a while, but I didn't love my post, so I left, started stealing food for those who needed it. I only took for the good of others."

Irfan, perhaps subconsciously, touches his shoulder. He glances at me, and I can barely see an old wound under his collarbone peeking out from his shirt. After our training, he'd been clutching his shoulder in pain—was the wound flaring up?

With that, Irfan is standing up. "We should get some sleep. I'll take first watch, just in case."

With the whoosh of a match striking, Irfan changes. He's no longer Irfan-with-the-deep-secret, Irfan-with-no-family. Just the Irfan I've come to know: a rebel who wants more for his kingdom.

*Does that make him any different from me?*

I know I cannot sleep tonight. During my watch, I sit on the outer edge of the encampment, observing the swaying trees. When I look back, Sanya is snoring softly, Irfan sleeping a few paces away. Not far from me is his pack.

I narrow my eyes. An idea comes to mind—I might not get secrets out of Irfan himself, but I can find out something about what he is hiding.

Like a true thief, I crouch near Irfan's pack and tug it toward me. I breathe shallowly as I move the pack closer, closer, and pull it open. Besides a few stray arrows and a notebook with barely decipherable handwriting, I find nothing.

Then I notice something glinting deep inside, burnished a reddish gold. I loosen it from the bottom of his pack.

And suppress a gasp.

It's Abai's crest, stamped on a burnished coin. Only one kind of person has that sort of coin—official palace employees.

How can this be? Did he steal this coin? No—he said he only takes for the good of others.

Which means Irfan is—or was—employed by my father.

Irfan rustles. I put the coin back and quietly smooth his pack closed. Whatever Irfan's hiding, I don't like it. I can't sit here any longer.

I step back, watching the group return to a soft slumber. When I turn away, I find myself at the precipice of the woods, the jungle air thick and cloying. I enter.

Through the trees I can make out the nearby village, smokestacks leaning into the skies. My mind is ablaze with questions. *Irfan and Father.* Never would I have thought the two could be connected.

I step deeper into the jungle, newly aware of how tired my limbs are. Of how they ache for sweet relief . . .

Ten steps later, something feels wrong. The jungle fades away into blotches of inky black. I pinch myself—not a dream.

An ominous snap resounds in the distance, and I whirl just as a dark shape rushes toward me.

# 27

## Ria

The throne room is alight and full of color: curtains of royal red swath every corner; pillars are wrapped in silks and matching fabrics. Servants dress in shades of cerulean and mauve instead of green, and each carries a pillow with nuts and dried fruit, like nests holding eggs.

It's Rani's engagement party. Probably one of the most important nights of her life.

I can't screw this up.

Luckily I've already made my entrance, sporting a red lehenga dusted in stars.

The maids Jasmin and Neela stay at my back as aunties from the women's room come to me in floods, fawning over my outfit. Saeed is due to arrive any moment with his mother, so all the attention's on me. But all I can think of is Saeed's mother. I press my fingers to my faintly aching cheek, Amara's slap still jarring me days later. Her words flash through me: *What name shall I call you?*

One wrong move and all of this is over.

Gold-painted elephant statues, three of them, lead up to two pillows where Saeed and I will sit. Scarlet drapes and bright lamps hang from all corners, bathing the room in light. Two of the aunties rush me over to the pillows, and I sit reluctantly. Beads from my lehenga dig into my flesh. Skies, who designed this? I adjust the skirt and examine my hands, covered in a deep-red mehendi design that the aunties applied yesterday. The last time I had mehendi on, I was ten summers old. I'd stolen some of Mama Anita's stash and piped a flower on my palm, though it turned into a misshapen blob. It didn't come off for days.

A dhol provides the background music, rhythmic and entrancing as people mingle. When Saeed walks in, his mother at his side, his eyes find mine, and something about them makes my heart skip. My gaze flits to his lips, and it's like the music and even the sight of Amara fall away. He eases onto the pillow next to me and smiles. "Evening, Princess."

Sensations bloom in my head. *Lips touching; the feeling of his soft skin on the corner of my mouth.* Skies, get a hold of yourself, Ria. This is your sister's betrothed. I try to smile, but my mouth tugs to the side awkwardly, and I twist away before I can embarrass myself further.

A servant approaches and offers us sweets—whole laddoos (gross), jalebis (too sticky), and chum chums (just right). I stuff my face before realizing Saeed is watching me curiously. *So much for being ladylike.*

I chew, swallow, and pluck up the courage to say hello properly. But he cuts to the chase, placing a finger beneath my chin and tipping my face to greet his.

"Do you want to . . . talk?"

"Now?" I pitch my voice to a whisper. I watch as the guests form a line and the official greetings and money offerings commence. It's custom to offer gifts, money, to the couple, or at least that's what Mama Anita said when I was young. I've never actually *been* to an engagement party. "Is this about the dreams?"

He frowns slightly. "I left you alone with my mother. You are still alive, which is an excellent sign, but, Rani, what did she say?"

Before I can speak, the line begins to move, and a silvery voice claims, "Here they are!"

A chill dances down my back. I stiffen, but from the sweet tone I know it can't be Amara. It's one of the gossiping aunties from the women's room—Parvati.

Internally, I groan. Externally, I smile.

"You look positively gorgeous, Rani. Just like your mother on her engagement night!" she croons, offering a pile of rupees into the fabric on our laps.

More women approach, each one as curious as the last, and with no regard for my personal space. One of them comes up to me and squeezes my cheeks. "Unhhh," I say, though what I really want to say is, *Get your hands off me.*

"Amara, come here!" Parvati says to Saeed's mother, who's making idle chatter with a few nobles. A few breaths pass before she stalks over, her mouth painted into a crimson smile. "What did you want, Parvati?" Condescension slips from Amara's lips like spiced wine. "The line is growing—"

"It's Saeed and Rani. Their engagement announcement on Diwali night was so . . . pure! Don't you think it's time we saw a kiss?"

"Now, now, Parvati," Amara says. "You know Kumal . . ." She chokes on her words. "You know my husband and I were never ones to show signs of affection in public. Why should Saeed and *Rani* be any different?"

I glare at Amara. She doesn't want a stranger's lips on her son's, that's for sure.

"Kiss!" the aunties encourage us. "Kiss, kiss!"

I avoid Saeed's crisp stare. Ignore the heat blooming up my neck.

Before we can succumb to the women's wishes, more nobles shove forward and the aunties lose their chance. I bite my cheek to stop myself from grinning at their enraged looks. Nobles flood forth, praying for a prosperous engagement.

All I'm praying for is that the rest of this night goes smoothly.

Finally the raja and queen approach, and the line abruptly ends. The queen gives me a gold band—a ring—and tells me, "It's time."

My stomach knots.

Saeed takes me by the hand, and we rise. The crowd holds a collective gasp. I want to be sick. The country is preparing for war and death and this family is having a lavish party over a sham of a marriage. It's all too much to bear.

I slip the ring onto his finger, and then he slips one onto mine. The studded diamond on my ring gleams up at me. A rock of this size doesn't belong on my hand—it belongs in my pocket, like everything else I've ever taken.

Applause sounds from every corner of the room. As the crowd disperses, the queen steps before me, eclipsing my view of Saeed. "I wanted to speak to you tonight, Rani, to discuss how you've been behaving of late."

My tongue goes numb. "F-for what?"

"I've been watching you and your snake familiar closely," the queen begins. My mind races. Did Shima rat me out about my sneaking around?

"It seems you have taken a greater hand in your magic lately. Shima's newfound obedience has not gone unnoticed. You've been spending more time together." Her smile beams.

My tongue is limp. Something else swells inside me. The queen, my mother, *proud*? It's true, Shima and I have been spending time together since the moment she helped me open the Pit. But Rani had been studying her snake magic for *years*, hadn't she? I thought my own abilities would be pitiful compared to hers.

Skies, I'd better thank that snake.

"Your father and I believe you should be allowed more freedom outside the palace. I expect you agree?"

I nod, my tongue too numb to respond.

When the queen is gone, Jasmin and Neela keep at my side, fixing my chunni and lehenga. They stand there stiffly when they're done. I don't know if I should be ashamed of the happiness I feel at the queen's words. I never thought I'd see my mother look at me like that. Only Mama Anita looked at me fondly, telling me I had a face as bright as the moon. Her words ring through my mind, something she told me nearly every night. *I'll always be with you. From morning to night. Dusk till dawn.*

Dusk and dawn. Moon and sun. Ria and Rani.

I find Saeed's gaze; not taunting, the way he first looked at me. Just . . . Saeed.

He takes my hand and pulls me into the center of the room. The crowd turns into an audience. It's time to show off the dance we practiced together.

We move in sync, starting with a bow to the audience, then raise ourselves at the beat of the drum. My hands twist back and forth as we spin around each other in dizzying circles. My skirts swish, a blur of red, as we meet each other again and take hold of each other's hands. Our legs move faster now, and I stick out my hip the way we practiced. Saeed dances around me while I cock my head. Left, right . . .

I lose myself in the dance. I forget all about Amara. Then I'm spinning so fast I trip over my feet. My breath stops. I fall back, landing on—

Saeed. He twirls me back up, and I press my hands to his chest. This wasn't part of the routine, but I hear a roar from the crowd.

They're loving it.

We end our dance in sync, stomping our feet on the final beat. Claps echo throughout the throne room. We did it. I smile at Saeed. His is so wide, it's like he's never been this happy before.

But the moment shatters when I remember what I'm doing, dancing above the Snake Pit. Pretending to be the very person Amir and I would make fun of.

The crowd parts. Saeed's smile slips as he notices my expression. "What happened?"

"N-nothing." I step away from him. "I just need some space."

I rush away from the crowd, past the bustles of servants and the bored stares of the Charts, until I find the nearest empty corridor.

Saeed must know something's up, because he trails behind me. "Rani!" He takes me by the elbow and spins me toward him until we're chest to chest. His features, alert and worried, bring me back to reality.

"Saeed," I breathe. "The crowd was overwhelming."

Heat spreads through me as his gaze lands on mine. "I felt the same way."

I blink. "You do?"

Saeed nods. We round the corner for privacy. "I wanted to celebrate our engagement, but knowing your stance on our relationship, I was worried. . . ." He blows out a breath, cheeks pink. Is he blushing? "I need to tell you something, Rani, before the night is over."

My lips part. I can't keep my thoughts straight. Remembering Amir, I had felt like Ria again; dancing with Saeed, I was Rani. How can I be two different people at once?

"The other day, in the rafters," he begins, "I realized something."
My breath hitches. "Yes?"

"We've known each other for a long time, and I always thought
I was doing my duty, courting you the way I did. But, Rani . . .
you're beautiful. It was so easy to try and love you. It was so easy
for duty to be enough. We've always been promised to each other.
But what I felt then wasn't love."

My heart stutters. I keep my fists at my sides, even though
what I really want is to take his hands in mine.

"Ever since Diwali, it's like I've seen a whole new side of you,"
he says, lips quirking into a smile. "You reminded me of the fun
we used to have as children. You opened my mind more than I
ever thought. The night we ended things between us . . . what I
said was true. Loving you was my duty; it always had been. I know
you were not content with the answer. But over these past several
days, you've helped me understand that I can feel more than that.
You've helped me realize that love doesn't have to be about duty;
it can be an adventure."

*Adventure.* That's exactly the right word. Being on the streets
was survival. Thieving was instinct. But this . . . this is a new
surprise every day. A constant thrill. My heart forever leaping in
my chest.

"I've felt something, too," I whisper.

He raises my left hand and thumbs my engagement ring.
"I've realized . . . I do love you. And you were right to be angry
with me."

"I'm not angry," I tell him before I fully take in his statement. Saeed loves me? *Ria* me?

*Kiss him*, half of me says.

*He's your sister's betrothed*, the other half thinks.

I'm a storm of opposites: raging fires and frozen seas.

Saeed plants his palm on my cheek, thumb brushing my lips as he leans in.

I suck in a breath as his lips reach mine.

And when they do, they're soft as silk. Smooth as honey. He tastes sweeter than ripened mangoes.

This is nothing like days ago, on our horseback ride when we tried to call up Saeed's magic; that was nervousness, heated lips and magic-warmed skin. Now? I pull back gently. Saeed looks at me like he can see past the frilly clothes and find the real me: the small birthmark beside my eye; the sallowness of my cheeks; the fine hairs at the crown of my scalp, dipping like an arrowhead. The thief. Everything that defines me as Ria, not Rani.

He grazes a hand across my jaw, inching me closer, and our lips meet again. This time, it's insistent, like a fire lighting in my belly. Like I'm truly in a princess's skin. A girl whose fate isn't written in the stars but forged with a sword.

I'm lost for words, for thought, for anything but his touch. For a moment, this act as Rani, this charade . . . it's not a performance.

"Praise the seven Masters," Amara huffs. "*There's* your kiss."

We jump apart. Amara stands at the end of the corridor, a few buzzing aunties close behind. Her mouth twists in a sardonic grin.

"What a cute boy!" one says.

"Sweet kisser," adds another. "Lucky girl."

I press my fingers to my lips. Shame burns my cheeks. It's a line I never should've crossed. How much had Amara seen?

"Mother, what are you—" Saeed begins, but Amara's stare is quick to silence him. Her eyes snare onto mine now, like a hunter to a rabbit. The corner of her mouth flicks up, red as blood.

"I—I should go," I tell Saeed, catching his gaze. His lips are spread apart slightly, and he blinks, lost. I slip past the women, all of whom are now laughing amid the music.

Tears rise as I rush as far away from the laughter as I can. My head and heart tangle in knots. The way Saeed looked at me, like he could see through me . . .

No. I'm not some show for the women to fawn over. Saeed and I kissed because it felt right, not because it was a performance. Right?

I coil my hands into fists, spinning to find an alcove where a pink-scaled snake sits.

"Oh!" I cry. "Shima, you scared me." I wipe away my tears as fast as I can, but the snake is smarter than that.

*Emotions aren't as easy to define as we thought, are they?* she tells me. *I felt your confusion, your . . . desire. I knew I'd find you here.*

"I thought snakes weren't supposed to slither around during parties."

*Contrary to popular belief, snakes are often the life of the party, so showing up where we're least invited only makes things more interesting.*

I harrumph. I'm lost in a place of in-between, caught between two worlds I can't decipher.

"I shouldn't even be part of this engagement," I blurt, voice low in the emptiness of the palace corridors. "Rani doesn't love Saeed anymore."

Where is Rani when I need her? When all I want to do is spill my real feelings to her? Saeed, Amara, Aditi, this whole mess . . . Is that what sisters do—chat, give each other advice? I never knew I wanted that so much.

I wish there was some way I could talk to her, tell her Amara knows I'm not Rani. It's not like there're some kind of messenger snakes to get mail around in Abai.

*Wait . . .*

Shima's gaze locks with mine. *Concocting another plan, are we, Princess?*

I glance left and right, but the halls are empty. I wipe my tears with a quick brush of my finger and sweep into the alcove. "Shima, I need your help."

*Again?* the snake prods, moving lazily upward, as if stretching in the tight space.

"It sounds impossible," I begin, "but . . . Rani. I want to speak with her. And you can speak to both of us, can't you? You even knew Rani had a twin without ever meeting me."

*There is a large distance between Rani and me,* Shima explains. *There is no way for me to reach her thoughts alone.*

My hope fizzles. But I think over her words again. When I bring my gaze to hers, I swear she's almost grinning. "You said you can't do it *alone.*"

*Ah,* Shima says, that smile reaching her eyes. *Now you're understanding, Princess.*

"But how can we speak to each other? Is there something that could bridge our thoughts?"

*Such as?* the snake inquires.

"Our minds," I whisper, a light flickering on. "Connected through yours. You're the only person who can speak to us mentally, and who's already made a blood bond with Rani. That should give you a stronger connection, right?"

Shima ponders this. *Snakespeaking is most powerful with proximity,* she finally answers. *Rani is far from us. But you . . .*

"Are right here," I finish. "Us being twins—doesn't that mean we have an innate bond, a link, stronger than any other two people?"

*That is an interesting theory,* Shima says, coiling her tail. *Though I must admit, I've never bridged two human minds before.*

"But it could be done?"

Shima rocks her head from side to side. *In a manner of speaking.*

"Which means yes." I wipe away all thoughts of the engagement, of Amara, of Saeed. I pull all my anger and sadness and frustration and channel them into my words.

"Help me speak to her in some way."

*Your earrings,* Shima replies.

My mind goes blank. "Huh?" Shima doesn't elaborate but waits expectantly.

After a silent moment, I pull off the extravagant pair of

diamond earrings. Less than two weeks ago, I was stuffing these into my pockets, gawking at the shape of the jewels. Now I barely feel their weight on my ears.

*As a possession of Rani's, the earrings will make the mind link stronger*, Shima says, like it's common knowledge.

"Good idea." I squeeze the earrings in my hands and go quiet. In my mind there's only a hum, and something like a band beginning to squeeze around my head. I focus on the pulse in my throat, beating like a mallet. I flinch when Shima wraps around my wrist, forming a reptilian armlet.

Shima's heartbeat flows in time with mine. My hand shakes as I clutch the earring harder.

*It is not ssstrong enough*, Shima admits, uncoiling herself.

Disappointment floods through me. I don't just want this to work; I *need* this to work.

"My first day at the palace," I tell Shima, "you told me about a . . . ceremony? Something that connects you with Rani?"

*Yesss*, Shima says, as if unsure what I'm getting at. *The Bonding. It creates the blood bond I spoke of. It is a special thing, having a familiar to bind with for life.*

I imagine the snake biting into my skin, the venom pouring out of her into my veins. Would it kill me, a girl who just discovered her powers? Or would it bring Shima and I closer together? Close enough to connect me with Rani?

*Do you fear me?* Shima asks.

I can't lie to a snake who can read my thoughts. "Yes."

*You have to decide now, Princess. Do you want to keep living in fear, or find your future?*

I gulp, steeling myself. "I won't stop fearing snakes," I say. "I want to, but I can't. Not yet. And that's the truth."

Shima looks at me with solemn eyes.

"But my fear doesn't erase what I have to do," I continue. "I have to be brave. I have to speak with Rani. This is the only way."

Shima ponders this, gaze slitted. *What are you proposing, Princess?*

I shut my eyes, gulping at the thought of what I'm about to do.

I hold my wrist out. "Do it."

Shima hisses, peering down at my wrist. *This is a delicate process. Do you trust me?*

I hold back the fears burning in my throat. I remember her curling at my feet after seeing Mama Anita. A strange, warm comfort. "Yes," I whisper, the truth blossoming from my lips. "I must."

Shima doesn't hesitate. The puncture feels like a knife, and heat fills my veins—and then darkness rushes up to greet me.

I gasp at the pain.

But then I spot her in the distance. Covered in dust and jungle earth, cloaked in secrets and suspicion.

Rani.

# 28

## Rani

I'm in a dream. Or perhaps a nightmare. Either way, the forest, the campfire—all of it is gone, as if extinguished by a sudden rainfall.

There is only darkness.

And a figure heading toward me.

Like an unearthed diamond, she winks into existence. *Me.* An illusion, perhaps, for I am wearing an extravagant outfit, a traditional yet modern ensemble fit for a bride.

*"Rani,"* her voice calls, a rougher version of my own. I stare at the girl ahead.

Could it be?

I press a hand to the floor, now a polished obsidian slate. It feels real, as real as the floor of the Snake Pit, but the girl before me flickers. Her cheeks are fuller now, her eyes sparkling in a way they hadn't when we first met.

Ria. My sister.

She is a portrait of a true rani, wearing a lehenga that hugs her body the same way it would mine. Her face is molded with sharp cheekbones and pouted lips, a slightly hooked nose and eyes framed by long lashes.

It takes all of two seconds for her to say, "Raja's beard."

"Abai's sun," I reply at the same moment.

For a second I think neither of us will move. A heartbeat passes before she rushes over to me. She stops breaths away, as if afraid to come too close.

"Ria—how are you doing this?" My voice echoes off of nothingness, and around me, the blackness and the jungle begin to chip away. Faintly, the marbled palace halls appear, familiar and warm as a mother's hug. A pang deep in my belly. Homesickness, perhaps. Haven't I always dreamed of escape?

"It's Shima. We found a way to bridge our minds. With the Bonding Ceremony and our twin connection. Shima says she can help guide the mind link, but it won't last long."

"You did the Bonding Ceremony with Shima?" I ask, incredulous. I didn't bond with Shima until five years after my official magical training began.

Ria's gift must be strong . . . stronger than I ever could have imagined. The thought overwhelms me, sending a shudder through my body.

"We don't have much time. Rani? Are you listening?"

"Yes, of course. It's the night of my engagement party, isn't it?" It seems I'm already forgetting palace life, so quickly, so . . . easily.

Ria nods, looking solemn. "Yeah. And I know you didn't want

to go through with it. But the queen and Amara have been planning everything, making me go to fittings and—"

"It's fine," I say truthfully. We might be engaged formally, but
Saeed knows my true feelings. "Does anyone know about us?"

"Shima, of course." Ria pauses, cold creeping in her voice
like a sudden Amratstanian snowfall. "And Amara." Her voice is
pinched with pain.

"No." I shudder at the thought of Amara's bloodred lips and
harsh gaze. "And as Father's adviser . . ."

"She's been speaking with the raja," Ria reveals, "about something called the Bloodstone. That's what you're searching for,
aren't you? Amara knows about it—she's *looking* for it. I think
Amara is more involved in all this than we thought. She wants war
as bad as the raja does, I just don't know why."

First, Amara somehow knows Ria is lying. Now she's seeking
the Bloodstone? For what purpose?

My voice chills. "Does she know we're twins?"

"I'm not sure," Ria says, voice small. Suddenly her eyes pierce
mine. "Are you with Amir?"

"Yes. We're . . . fine. With his sister's help, we've pinned down
the location of the Bloodstone. But the Charts are scouring the
streets and villages. I fear they might locate it first."

"H-his sister?" Ria's pallor lightens. "I never knew . . ."

I frown but continue. "We're safe, and on track to find the
Bloodstone. Amir doesn't suspect a thing about me. Mostly . . ."

Ria raises a brow.

"He's seen a few differences in our attitudes," I reveal. I don't want to tell her about my and Amir's fight. "Nothing major. How's Shima?"

It takes a moment for her response. "A real help, actually," she says, though a hint of fear crosses her face. Her makeup is smudged on her cheek. Is that a bruise underneath?

"Ria, what happened?"

"It's no big deal. Just Amara—"

"That witch!" I cry. "Ria, you mustn't let her get to you. Father and Mother will be outraged."

"If I say anything, Amara will reveal our secret to them." Her voice shakes. What has Amara done to her? She glances around furtively. "I've gotta stay low."

"Amara is only one person," I say. "*You* are a princess."

"It doesn't matter what I am. I haven't found my birth papers," she says, voice thick. "Until I do, I don't even exist in this palace."

"You do," I reply. "You belong here."

"I know I belong," she says with resolve. "But I can't prove who I am to the raja or queen without the papers. Rani . . ." She bites her lip. "I don't know if I'm meant to escape Abai anymore. There's so much I need, *want*, to do."

In her eyes, I see her visions align with mine. My sister wants more for her kingdom—*our* kingdom—than both of us could have ever realized.

Gently, I raise a palm and offer her my hand. "The truth is, I'm not done, either." An idea springs to mind. "We showed each other our memories before. What if we can do it again?"

Ria's body trembles. "I'm scared—"

"But we can do it," I insist. "We did it before through our most vulnerable emotions." I think of the shock we both felt when we met, the way the memories burst forth at our first touch, as if releasing from a locked cage. "Show me, and I'll show you. All we need to do is feel. Like that first time we met."

"I can't," Ria says.

"Just try," I tell her. I take her hand in mine. "Close your eyes."

After a moment, Ria follows suit, and I sense that power thrumming through our veins, beating hungrily, unchecked. Orange bursts flash behind my eyes. I'm seeing everything. A servant girl with braids flying behind her. Ria riding on a mare next to Saeed. Ria reaching into the Snake Pit. Amara telling the raja and his council of her conscription plans. A woman with a soft smile and round cheeks, taking care of Ria before being dragged away by Charts.

Then, a voice, rising like steam from the Pit. *"Return to my hiding place, the gift in the cobra's mouth . . ."*

I rip my hand from hers, unable to take another second. We're both gasping for air, processing each other's memories with lightning speed.

"What did you see?" I ask her.

"You," she breathes. "Amir. And another man . . ."

She reaches for my hand again, and clenches it in hers. Her heartbeat races through her fingertips, matching my own. Then we're hit with another flood of memories. Mother and Father, peering deep into the Fountain of Fortunes. In the rippling waters are a younger me and Ria, nose to nose. Eyes hardened. I watch us growing up, training to become queen, but instead of the sisterly bond I expect, we battle against one another. We disappear from the water just as I hear something: the Memory Master's voice tied to the fountain, speaking to our parents.

Sisters of the snake shall be born from Abai's royalty,
Twins of opposing forces, one of light and one of dark.
While they train to become queen, a long-held battle
    will spring anew
Their kingdom shall fall, destroyed by one.
The girl of light will perish at the other's hand, while the
    victor survives.
Only one can reign.

My blood is cold as the voice fades. How can this be true? Shock and incredulity are written on Mother's and Father's faces.

"This cannot be," Father says. "One of them will destroy the other. Destroy . . . the kingdom."

The vision changes, lurching into a new scene. Now Mother and Father are pacing his office. Mother holds back a sob, cradling her stomach. I have never seen her this way. Not for me, the daughter she never wanted. No—this is for the daughter she never knew.

Mother stumbles, falling to her knees. *They're coming.*

The vision dissolves. Words fall from Mother's lips, but they perish into nothingness. The visions fade, and I lurch back to the present. Ria shivers in front of me, stumbling back.

"W-what did you see?"

"Our parents," I say gravely. "They found out the prophecy from the fountain. . . ." I glance at my birthmark. Next to Ria's, the full image makes a snake rising from shadows. *Sisters of the snake*, just like the prophecy said.

"It said we would harm each other. That we'd destroy this kingdom. I knew it, I knew they got rid of me because there was something wrong with me—"

"No." I shake my head. "This can't be right. We aren't meant to destroy the kingdom; we're meant to save it." Saying the words aloud feels like sending a wish into the skies.

My stomach coils as Ria says, "Our parents never loved me. They gave me up because of a stupid prophecy. And for what? For my *safety*?"

If my blood was cold before, it has turned into ice.

"We're not going to harm each other. I promise you," I tell Ria. She looks at me through glassy tears.

"Now I know why I was given up. That I *was* given up," she says with resentment.

I place my hand on hers again. "No matter what this prophecy says, I don't believe it. We're stronger together."

"How would you know?" That cynical Ria voice I first heard on Diwali night in the palace returns. She wipes off the tears. "They gave me up because one of us would be too powerful. Maybe we

were supposed to be apart. Maybe I never should've done this."
Ria paces, frazzling her hair as she speaks. "Could've been past the
border by now if I'd stuck to who I really am. A thief."

"You're wrong," I tell her. I push on, determined. "You're far
more than that. You're my blood, Ria. I don't want to forget you."

Ria hesitates before she says, "I don't want to forget you, either.
But sometimes I feel like I'm not the old Ria anymore. Like I've
lost myself."

"You've changed," I tell her. "So have I. And what you've
learned on the streets will help you handle Amara better than I
ever could have. Don't underestimate yourself."

It takes a moment, but she nods in agreement. Her gaze travels
behind me, and I wonder what she discerns, for I have seen her
world and I am sure she is seeing mine. Does she see the jungles
I've stepped into? The campfire where her friend sleeps soundly?

"Amir?" she asks. I spin around.

Sound erupts behind me. The dreamscape world melts away.
Ria's body disappears before me, and the mind link shatters like
broken glass.

A hand takes hold of my shoulder and I whirl, grabbing it
in the darkness and jerking it away, those fighter instincts Irfan
taught me kicking in. Reality is painted anew. The darkness of the
jungle is so different from the dreamworld.

"Ria, it's me!" Hands spin my waist. "We were calling to you!
Didn't you hear us? What're you doing alone in the jungle?"

I sigh with relief. It *is* only Amir; Ria had seen him, too. "What is it?" I cannot help the ire in my voice. I might have had a few more minutes with Ria if he hadn't broken our link.

Yet Amir does not look furious with me; in fact, he seems afraid.

"What happened?"

In the distance, a hundred sounds come to life. I think again of the palace I saw in the dreamscape: a prison holding stiff walls, thin smiles, cold commands.

It all comes rushing back to me when I hear the marching boots.

"Amir, what's happening? Where are Jas and Sanya and Irfan?"

"They ran to the nearest tavern for safety. We need to hide. They"—he catches his breath—"they're here."

"*Who* is here?" I ask carefully.

"*Them.*" His body is still as glass except for one finger, raised to the jungles before us. "The Charts."

# 29

## Ria

Rani fades away, and the world comes back in splotches—and pain with it, shooting up my wrist and down my back. It feels like my body's splitting apart. I yelp from the agony, but that fiery feeling begins to cool. Another sensation begins to take hold: light, snaking through my chest and around my heart.

"Enough," I gasp out. I grip my wrist. Two faint puncture marks slowly fade to nothing. The pain ebbs away, leaving behind a cool, crisp feeling. Then, there's only warmth. I feel what Shima feels. Past pain, future anticipation. And in the present: peace. Maybe even a bit of smugness.

Shima's slitted, curious eyes come into focus. She slithers back, and it's clear the connection—the mind link—has worn her out, in both mind and body.

*What happened?* she asks.

"I saw Rani. We heard a prophecy, but the connection broke too soon. And Amir . . ."

My voice fades as I recall what Rani told me. *Amir's sister.*

Amir never told me anything about a sister. He never told me anything about his family, except that his parents died.

Why would Amir have lied to me? I guess it wasn't a lie so much as an omission. It's not like I told him much about Mama Anita. And I didn't tell Rani I kissed her betrothed, either.

"Rani," a chilling voice says. "A word?"

I slowly turn to find the raja himself, dressed primly, eyeing me and Shima. Nearby, his snake, Samvir, lurks. His scales are striped red and black, like he can't decide one color to settle on.

"My adviser has told me that you abandoned the party. This is the second time you've left improperly."

I gulp. The first time was the dinner when I stomped off.

The raja looks at me with disdain.

*My father. The one who gave me up.*

"I'm sorry . . . *Father.*" I can hardly get the word out. Tears threaten to return, and the prophecy haunts my mind. My next words rush out of me without care. "Why do we give so much trust to the fountain? Would you give up your whole world—your whole life—for some vision? Something that's supposed to seal your fate for good?"

"What? Where is this coming from?" he scoffs. "Rani, don't try to change the subject—"

Angry words rise to my lips. "Don't you remember? You got rid of me like a scrap of unwanted silk. And you won't even admit it!"

Something like fury flames in the king's eyes, then sizzles away.

He turns and signals for me to follow, leaving his snake behind. A Chart appears at my back, as if making sure I won't run away again. Her golden sash winks in the light. Rows of golden buttons and tassels cover her left breast pocket, symbolizing years of work. Years of hatred.

The raja's office looms ahead. He pauses at the doorway, one hand on the knob. The office I broke into.

He sweeps in and takes a seat before his desk, gesturing for me to sit. The Chart bows and leaves.

The raja slides on a pair of eyeglasses attached to a beaded chain. The beads clink together harmoniously. "I understand your frustrations," he begins as I take a seat.

I gape. Is he going to admit it?

"I have let you down," he continues. "When I let Saeed take over as your tutor, I never checked on you or acted as a father does. I was always busy. But I promise," he says, leaning in, "that I will become more involved in your training to become queen. It is as your mother told you: we've noticed a great change. We are proud of your efforts, Rani. But these childish flights of fancy must end—when you are queen, you will be expected to see these functions through to the end, no matter how distasteful you find them."

He speaks to me without pretense. Is this the Ruthless Raja? The bloodthirsty king Amir and I have always feared?

"Now," he continues at my silence, pulling out an envelope with a broken purple wax seal. It's a crest depicting an eye, beholding the viewer with strange intensity. Haven't I seen this symbol before? It hits me: My second full day at the palace, I'd seen the eye on Amara's cuffs. Then again, the day Saeed and I snuck into the rafters.

"I did not want to ruin tonight's festivities, but a few days prior I received this note from a Kaaman messenger hawk. I'd like you to read it."

My hands shake as I take the note. The handwriting looks familiar, but I can't place it.

*Meet where the kings' truce came to be, the waters imbued with magic . . .*

It's an invitation of sorts. Not the kind to a party, but the kind inviting a fellow raja to war. To battle.

*On the eve of the truce's end when the sun has set . . . our Warriors will be ready.*

Signed by none other than King Jeevan, a name whispered across every town and village of late. We all know the name of the man Abai's meant to go to war against. If this envelope came from the Kaamans, then the eye must be part of their kingdom's crest, a symbol of the Memory Master whose descendants built Kaama from the ground up. An eye makes sense as their seal, something to show visions of past and future. But if that's the case, why does Amara have the enemy kingdom's crest on her jewelry? And why does she wear it so freely around the raja?

I look up at the king. Bone-deep exhaustion lines his eyes. I've never seen my father up close before, never thought about his own thoughts, feelings. He's always been the Ruthless Raja. How could he be anything else?

"We will need fresh blood in our ranks. An induction ceremony," he tells me.

I hold my breath. I think of my name on those conscription lists. Did he know his own daughter was drafted? Or did he leave conscription for the Charts to sort out?

It doesn't matter. The raja's drafting more people. *This time, children.*

"But fresh blood in our ranks will not be enough. I will have to provide Amara another trip to Anari Square to get the supplies. We'll need snake venom to tip our Charts' swords with, if we are to win this war."

*Anari Square.* Is that the place where Amara gets her venom for Saeed's tonic?

"We must focus on the future of our kingdom, acha? The Kaamans, they will not hold back."

"But . . ." I find my voice. "There must've been a time when you didn't want war."

The raja peers at me, and his eyes flicker like a cloud has lifted, before they become stern again. "Certainly, when I was a boy. But these past few years, things have . . . changed. The war is greater than you might realize, Rani. When the time comes, we will have a weapon on our side that will change the course of history. And we must, if we are to survive."

*The Bloodstone.* Something that could create chaos in the wrong hands.

"You want to destroy Kaama."

"No. I want to obliterate the entire memory of it."

My head spins. Kaama has always been the king's enemy, but it's full of people. Men and women. Children. Flesh and bone. Hearts that beat.

I'm a princess, and with that, I have a power greater than magic. I have a voice. I must find a way to prove to the world who I am. Who I *really* am.

Without second-guessing myself, I say the words that have been taunting me since the moment I discovered my and Rani's secret. "Do you remember the day I was born?"

This time, the hopeful glint in his gaze is gone, and he drills his eyes into mine. He licks his lips slowly, then says, "I do."

"W-was there anything special about it?"

"Of course. Your mother loves to tell everyone." He smiles, the first I've seen on his face. "You were born on Diwali."

The date of Diwali changes every year, usually in late autumn. That's the time of my birthday, according to the orphanage papers.

"I know," I say. "But was there . . . something else? Anything unusual? Did I scream a lot?"

"Quite." He tilts his head to one side, scanning my face. "You screamed enough for . . ."

My breath catches in my throat. If anyone knew the difference between twin daughters, it would be their parents. Can the raja tell I'm not Rani?

But he blinks and the moment is over. "Now that your engagement celebration is over, you have other things to focus on. As I have said, I expect you to fulfill your role as future queen, not run away from your tasks as you have before."

"But—" At the raja's look, I find the strength to nod. If following in Rani's footsteps will make the raja trust me more, maybe I'll be able to get him to open up to me. Tell me what's really going on with the Bloodstone—and with my birth.

When I'm back in Rani's room, I'm shaking. Tonight, I saw my father—my *real* father—for the first time. In his presence, I was struck with a fact more chilling than Amara's revelations in the council room. The raja, my own father, couldn't acknowledge my existence. Almost like something was preventing him from remembering . . .

But that couldn't be true. Still, this whole engagement night has taught me nothing is as it seems, and there's still a whole lot for me to uncover.

The day after the engagement is alarmingly quiet, and so is the one after. Servants dust away the remnants of the party, and Amara and Saeed are nowhere to be found. So I spend my time with Shima, quite literally mapping the boundaries of our magic. I nearly make it thirty feet through the palace before our connection breaks. After what we pulled off with the mind link, I know my magic is strong. Each time I use it, I feel it come more naturally to me, like a muscle gaining strength.

A crackling fills my bones now, like the snake magic is trying to free itself from my skin.

I remember what Shima told me the first morning here. *Rani has spent many years learning snake magic; yours seems as natural to you as thieving.*

What if the prophecy was right—what if I would've grown too strong, too powerful? Would I have killed my own sister?

Is my magic a curse? The reason I grew up in filth and spent nights shivering in alleyways?

*No.* My sister's words float back, settling my thoughts. I would never hurt her. I'm never letting that damned prophecy come true.

Last night, I found Aditi in the library. We pored over books until midnight, keeping a paranoid eye on the door. Thankfully, Shima was our lookout. Amara's threat toward Aditi lingers in the air, and I refuse to give her more ammunition. Though Aditi's been doing research on Amara's roses, so far we haven't found anything fruitful.

Now, on the second evening after the engagement party, the throne room is bustling. "Charts' induction ceremony," says a feminine voice. It's the queen, sporting a magenta sari. Her hair has been pulled into a tight bun. Freshly dyed, from the looks of it.

The raja hasn't spoken more with me since Rani's engagement, either, too busy in meetings about the upcoming battle.

It's like our chat never happened.

I face the king and queen. We exit the throne room and pause at the entrance to the Western Courtyard. I spot the ancient-looking tree I sat under the night I met up with Aditi to give her the book. In front of the tree, the courtyard is filled with silk-curtained chairs. The seats face three large thrones, covered in scarlet drapes. As if this is a *celebration*. More like a funeral. The death of those whose lives might have been different, had they never become Charts.

The air grows cold with discomfort. The queen heads for the raja just as a warm gasp of air comes from my right. Shima slithers up toward me and settles at my feet.

*Evening, Princess*, she tells me.

"Evening," I tell her, though my voice is washed away by the bustling courtyard as nobles take their seats. My eyes scan the crowd, looking for Saeed. A flutter fills my stomach, but I ignore it. I've tried not to think about him ever since the-thing-that-must-not-be-named.

*Let me spell it out for you, Princess. K-I-S-S. And you liked it.*

I burn holes into Shima's eyes with my stare. She's more smug than is warranted. Though it *does* help that I haven't seen Saeed since *that* moment.

I take my seat by the queen and raja, facing out toward the crowd as the sun sets.

The induction ceremony is legendary—mainly for its brutality. No one knows much about it other than that. This ceremony is the very reason Amir and I came to the palace. We wanted to escape this. I never wanted to be a part of it. And now here I am.

The raja stands. His presence is stifling, and the heat of the air turns thick, reminding me of nights in Nabh.

"King Amrit," the raja begins, "was a man who set Abai on its path to greatness. Creator of Abai's army, the Charts, over a hundred years ago, when our wars with Kaama would not relent, King Amrit even forged them a home: Anari's Charts' Sector." A thin-lipped smile, fingers tightening around his golden serpent staff.

"Over the decades of his reign, King Amrit divided the Charts in two: the Veterans, experienced Charts to stay at the king's side"—the raja points to a Chart near him, wearing a gold sash—"and Trackers, soldiers who journey into Abai's villages and streets. Every year, we welcome over a dozen new Charts into our home. Tonight we mark the largest induction of new recruits into our ranks in our history—a celebration of Abai's forces strengthening, readying for battle."

The audience of nobles looks like a group of vultures ready to pick through the flesh of Abai's enemies. I've felt it, the shift, the fissures in the ground widening at the thought of the Kaamans readying their weapons. Of the truce's inevitable end.

"And now it is time I hand over the reins to my daughter, the future rani of Abai." The raja turns to me. "Present the recruits!"

I don't know what to say. My lips are stitched together, bound tight. They expect this of me, the raja and queen. They know Rani will one day have to lead a kingdom, maybe they've even been training her for it. But the raja has never led us to any victory, so how could I?

With a gentle prod from the queen, I stand, looking out over the crowd. Nobles swim in and out of view.

"Y-yes," I say after what feels like an eon. I turn to the audience with no idea what to say or do next. *Do what Rani would do. Say what she would say.*

"Let's all welcome our recruits." I look out at the crowd. "The newest Charts who will protect Abai and help us grow in numbers . . . against the Kaamans."

Each word feels like death, like dust against my tongue.

The raja grandly extends an arm, gesturing in the newest line of Charts like he's inviting guests to a party.

A portion of the new recruits enter like a river of blood. They have thin garments and forlorn faces. Some look younger than me, as young as fourteen, according to Amara's new demand. Some shiver, and my eyes prickle. I would be one of them, if the Charts had found me. Maybe I would've been standing there tonight, if I'd never met Rani.

They each kneel, eyes dampened. Hollow. The raja steps down from his throne and pauses by each of them, scrutinizing the recruits under his piercing gaze. I see one flinch, a boy. I wonder if his family tried to escape this fate the way I did.

"We will begin with the oath," the raja orders, ripping me from my thoughts. The crowd before us holds its breath, as if awed. "Repeat after me. I am a Chart. I am a leader. I am a fighter."

As if on cue, the soldiers all stand and speak in synchronous harmony.

"I am a Chart. I am a leader. I am a fighter." Their voices reverberate, as if the trees are instruments playing a tune.

"I promise to fight. I promise to defend."

The soldiers' lips open and close. I don't even realize the soldiers have finished their oaths and are now being taken to the center of the courtyard, where a bed of hot coals and an oddly shaped iron poker await. My heart rate spikes. Are they about to be . . . branded?

*The Charts each have their own number,* Amir told me when we once came close enough to escape Abai. I'd never considered how they got those numbers. That escape attempt was just two moons ago, but it might as well have been a thousand moons now, my life looks so unfamiliar.

"This tree we stand under is legendary," the raja says. "The Mitti Tree is where the first Chart was branded, and each Chart thereafter. The tree was planted centuries ago by a stonebringer, and its roots were first intended to be the grounds of many marriages, tying the lovers to the tree, ensuring their bond would last as long as the tree stood.

"Now we use the tree's magical properties to bind soldiers to their oaths. The Charts' numbers, as they are branded onto their skin, appear in the bark of the tree."

I gasp. *That's* what I saw in the tree bark that night. The Charts' numbers.

"My adviser, Amara Gupta, will perform the official branding."

"Thank you, Raja Natesh," Amara says, appearing from the crowds. She smiles sharply as she takes a poker from the Head Chart, the iron glowing and smoking at the tip. "With the magic fibers of the Mitti Tree imbued into the steel of the poker, I now bind the Charts to their rightful place as the king's soldiers."

The soon-to-be Charts, many of them children, stare at Amara fearfully. I shiver; Amara's been missing these past few days, and her disappearance didn't escape me. Aditi says she was on an errand, but it's strange to me how she completely deserted the palace.

Has *Amara* been pulling these children from their homes?

She approaches one soon-to-be Chart, her steps steadfast, and leans forward. The boy's eyes are wide with fear, and I can tell he's trying to hide it from the way his fists are clenched at his sides. Amara, on the other hand, looks unbothered. Like someone else's pain doesn't matter to her, which it probably doesn't, not after that slap she gave me. When the iron reaches the boy's skin, right under his collarbone, he bites down on his own lips hard but cannot fully stifle his scream. My fingers tighten around the arms of the throne seat, as if *I* can feel the pain on my own flesh.

The number *234* glows on the tree.

Again and again, the poker sizzles against skin, and one by one, numbers turn into scars. The skin beneath the poker turns raw, puckered. Too suddenly, I remember the scar on Amir's face. The one running down my leg. We're all victims of what the raja's made this kingdom to be.

It's not only the branding that scares me. It's the look on Amara's face, like there's a smile simmering just beneath the surface. She *enjoys* this.

A set of Veterans with golden sashes approach with the

traditional Chart vestments, dressing the new soldiers in their signature red coats.

"You are now loyal members of the Charts," Amara says, "The soldiers behind you will train you until your souls sing of Abai. Until your flesh is hardened into stone. Until we are one people, and no other kingdom can betray us."

The raja nods. "Stand together, and Abai will be undefeatable. But disloyalty will not be tolerated, and a consequence awaits those who turn traitor to their brother and sister Charts." He points at a few of the numbers on the tree, crossed out. Are those meant to represent the traitors?

The ceremony ends, and the crowd before me claps. It takes Queen Maneet's glare for me to join them, though it feels like betrayal.

"Never put a name to a face," she warns me. She's smiling, yet her eyes are dark, foreboding, something sad in their depths. "It is the only way we can win this war."

She means the Charts. Those whose lives have been lost, like mine. Her words are a threat coated in silk and jewels. Nonchalant, but a threat all the same.

"And the villagers thrown in the Pit?" I retort, thinking of Mama Anita. Her senseless death. "Do we ever bother learning their names?" I'm shaking, and my voice matches.

The queen's nose flares at the question, like it's preposterous. "Everyone who dies in the Pit has been brought there for a reason. A tradition that began with the Snake Master, and a tradition we do not forget today."

The queen stalks off. The courtyard is near-empty now, the new recruits gone and the bloodthirsty audience with them. I turn away from the scene, rush back to the front staircase of the palace, and rip the whole ceremony from my mind. But the world becomes dizzy, and fast.

My tongue is dry, and suddenly, it's like I'm young Ria again. Curled up next to Mama Anita, dreaming up some fantasy I never thought would come true. I'm reminded of her stories—of the Masters' magic, of the impending war.

But she's gone now, murdered in a ceremony not far from the one I just witnessed. Though her life ended, her story is unfinished.

Why did Mama Anita die in the Pit? Is there something I'm missing here?

Mama's words float back to me. *Retrace your steps; go back to the start; and follow your heart.*

She was telling me something.

To figure out all the palace's mysteries, I need to start from scratch. Refresh my search. Go back to the beginning.

The orphanage.

# 30

## Rani

"We have to go, now," Amir repeats.

Everything still feels out of touch, as though I'm waking from a dream. Ria had just *been here*, so close it was like she was here in the jungle. But the harsh, rhythmic thud of the Charts' boots grows louder. It's enough to snap me back to reality.

A shiver crawls up my spine. Father's soldiers are traveling through the Moga Jungle, on the night of his daughter's engagement party? Why?

Amir takes hold of me by the elbow, spins me, and points at the mostly empty encampment, save our packs. The once-billowing fire is now a plume of smoke. Two of the horses are gone; Irfan, Sanya, and Jas must have already left.

"W-where—?" I stutter. I'm still thinking of Ria, everything she told me about Amara, the strange dreamscape we were both in.

"I was looking all over for you," Amir says, out of breath. "You were just standing out here in the open. I thought . . . I thought they took you." His voice breaks on the last word.

My brows raise. Amir was . . . searching for me? Of course, he wouldn't leave Ria behind, I remind myself. A stuck-up princess, on the other hand, he'd be happy to forget.

Clip-clopping hooves sound in the distance. I'm surprised to feel Amir's hand wrap around mine as he pulls me behind the nearest tree in one swift motion, out of sight from the arriving threat. My back jerks against the tree trunk, and an ache spreads through me just as Amir moves forward to cover me. The sounds grow louder, louder, like a painful drumbeat in my ear. One glance at the clearing shows a growing pool of red. The soldiers are here, their noses tilted into the air like Amratstanian icewolves on a hunt.

Jas, Sanya, or Irfan might've put out the fire, but smoke clings to the air, a sure sign that travelers were just in the area. Not to mention my and Amir's packs are still lying in the middle of the clearing.

"Do you have your knife?" I whisper to him. Sweat beads on Amir's brow, and he shakes his head.

Amir's chest presses against mine, so close I can feel the beat of his heart. My own heart races. Danger is near. Darkness shrouds my vision, and my breath hitches as his chin accidentally brushes my cheek. My eyes flick up to his. Part of me wants to erase the worry I find there, while the other seethes at the way my body heats at our close proximity.

Traitorous, double-crossing feelings.

"Smell that?" one of the soldiers calls, her voice a clap of thunder.

"It was just put out," another says, observing the smoke. "They left their packs. Can't have gone far."

"Search for them," the first soldier says. "We've still got villagers missing from our conscription list."

I peer through the branches and find three Charts, two side by side, the third roaming the clearing. He's younger-looking than the others, peering around nervously, and I see he is barely older than I am. The two together are a man and woman, the man wearing a suit of fine decoration.

I hunch back down. "Three of them."

"Who has their weapon out?" Amir asks. He inches his head past the tree trunk, squinting.

I grab Amir by the shirt and yank him back. "Don't you dare move any farther."

"They'll find us hiding here," he argues, then gulps. "The timepiece my dad gave me . . . it's in my pack. I can't leave it behind." I never thought I'd hear it, but Amir's voice breaks.

My fingers bunch in his shirt. "So what's our plan, then?"

His eyes fix on mine. "I've got something in mind. And it involves you."

My hold slips. After the days of silence, this is unexpected. I'd thought he wanted little to do with me.

"And how do you think I can help?"

"Take a talwar from under their noses," Amir responds. "I'll keep 'em busy until I get our packs. Just don't forget to slice my bindings if I'm caught, 'kay?"

"W-what?" I begin, just as Amir steps out from our safe spot.

"Oy!" he calls, waving his arms up and down. "Looking for me?"

Masters above, he's going to get us both killed!

"Ha," the first Chart laughs stiffly. I hear her footsteps crunch closer toward the tree I hide behind. "You know, we don't normally find villagers so . . . accommodating. How'd you like to become part of our ranks?"

"Eh, I thought about it," Amir says, shrugging. "But I decided red isn't really my color. To be honest, it isn't yours either."

A growl escapes the woman's lips. Amir glances sideways at me, offering me a covert wink before continuing his speech. "You know, you'd be better off searching for villagers deeper south. No one likes being near the palace."

As he speaks, I ready myself for what I'm about to do. If Amir trusts me, I cannot falter. I take a deep breath, adjust my chunni over my head, and crawl away until I'm behind the other two Charts. They stand in the clearing, not far from the woman, alert with their backs facing me. My eyes land on the younger soldier's talwar, sheathed in the scabbard across his back. I step with light toes into the clearing, eyes trained on the sword. I hear Amir's voice in the background, raucous and loud, but it's muffled as all my focus homes in on the weapon so close to my grasp. The closer I get, the farther I reach out, fingers just inches away from the hilt.

I've only just got the hilt in my hand when the soldier turns.

"A girl!" the man next to him says. The woman Amir was speaking to spins, braid whipping out as she aims her sword at my throat. As I wheel back, Amir springs into action, rushing forth and grabbing the soldier I was about to steal from. The Chart buckles, a clear sign he's still new to Father's rankings. In one smooth motion, Amir clutches the soldier's sword and launches it in the air.

*At me.*

I barely catch the sword by the hilt, and it's so heavy in my palms that I almost drop it to the ground. This is no training sword. Amir wants me to fight. He *believes* I can fight.

The soldier closest to me, the one dressed in finer decoration than the other two recruits, lunges forward. I block the blow and return his attack, but the Chart is quick on his feet. Blow by blow, we spin in dizzying circles. I keep my head low and defend myself against the soldier, but the Chart strikes downward, and I lose my balance. I fall back into the trees.

Irfan's words echo in my ears: *fight with instinct.* I have no fighting instincts inside me, but I do have knowledge. I know how Charts operate. I've seen them train in the practice fields.

A Chart's weak spot is simple: how vastly they underestimate their opponents. He'll expect me to remain defensive, so I need to attack. I watch the Chart's feet, the way Irfan taught me, anticipating his next move. He veers left and I leap forward with a grunt. I swing my sword wide, forcing the guard off-balance. The decorated Chart falls to the ground, disoriented.

But I have no time to celebrate knocking down the soldier. The young Chart is back on his feet, a blur lunging at me. Amir attempts to punch the Chart but the soldier blocks him and aims a blow of his own.

"Duck!" I cry. Amir follows but takes a punch to his side. The next thing I know, the woman is after me. I panic and block attacks from the soldier, her braid flinging through the air. My mind clouds. *Is Amir all right? What if he's—*

By the next hit, I fall on my back, my chunni flying off. Moonlight illuminates my features, leaving me bare.

"Is that . . . ," the woman begins, her face blanching as she takes in my features.

"It can't be. *Princess?*" The younger Chart leans in. If they know who I am, they must be from the palace grounds. A few of the younger trainee Charts spend time inside the palace before working in the villages. Either this is poor luck, or I should have been more careful disguising myself.

For one sweltering second, I let fear in. The Charts know who I am. But I have more than one weapon.

I clench my fists and open the drawer in my mind, calling on the threads of my snake magic. "It's Ria, actually," I tell her, feeling that bite of coppery magic. "An orphan. But names don't mean much right now."

Confusion settles on their features as the magic seeps into their minds. A rush of wind hits them, and I know instantly that the magic is working.

It feels good to use my snake magic again. Like a horse's reins in my mind, it is something I can tug on and control at my will.

"An orphan named Ria," the younger Chart says, blinking.

"The missing girl . . . from the conscription list?" the woman asks.

Abai's sun. Why had I brought up my sister's name?

The Chart raises her talwar. I scramble back with the little strength I have, searching for Amir. He was on the ground a second ago, but now I don't find him in the clearing. He's gone.

*He left*, a voice amends. No. Amir wouldn't leave me. Out of the corner of my eye, I see a shape scaling the nearest tree. Someone steps out on the branch, now hovering over the Charts. The branch cracks.

Arms out, Amir leaps from the tree and at the Chart with the long braid, taking her down with him. I scramble to my feet, but the scrawny Chart has his sword trained on me, wobbly and unsure.

I dodge his first blow, ducking and rolling around his legs. I shoot back to my feet, woozy, while he's still turned, using my elbow to jab him in the neck. He gasps for air, and I kick the back of his knees. As he falls, I reach around and grab ahold of his talwar and press it to the back of his neck. Adrenaline sings in my veins, a strange thrill in the dark night.

But the moment collapses when I see what's happened to Amir. He's no longer knocked down; the other two Charts have taken Amir hostage. The decorated Chart ties rope around his wrists, keeping them bound behind his back, while the other draws a knife, holding the blade so close to Amir's lips that I see his breath fogging the steel.

"Drop the sword." The Chart's voice is as sharp as the knife she holds. She dips the point into Amir's cheek, drawing blood.

"Stop!" I shout, but the Chart continues.

"Don't listen to them. Get out of here, Ria," Amir manages, but he lets out a cry of pain.

The Chart jeers as she pulls back the blade. She clucks her tongue. "Look at the boy. He's smitten."

Amir's eyes never leave mine. "Love isn't a crime."

My cheeks heat. Is he distracting Father's soldiers again? Hatching a new plan? Or does he truly mean what he says?

I think of his words from earlier. The trust he placed in my hands to get us out of this situation. That unshakable faith. Now when I glance at his eyes, they are not taunting or teasing. There is no humor laced in his voice. This is an Amir I have rarely seen: a prince in a pauper's clothing, unafraid of his words and unflinching in his actions.

I will not leave him. I drop my weapon.

The soldier on the ground recoups his blade. I need to act fast. As the man's eyes find the woman's, an idea sparks in my mind. My snake senses sharpen, and I smell a whiff of perfume coming off the decorated Chart.

Not his own.

I dig into what little snake magic I can harvest, wringing every last drop until I feel it fill my veins. Every smell sharpens, every sound heightens. I recall the way the decorated Chart walked side by side with the braided Chart, their fingertips brushing. . . .

"Yes, love is not a crime. But Charts are forbidden from palace romance," I say, twisting my head so my eyes meet the soldier on the ground. "Your fellow Charts are involved, aren't they?"

The Chart's eyes grow wide. "Y-you're wrong," he quivers. But I can tell he's scared, unlike the other Charts. I must distract them.

"Actually, I'm far from it." I slowly step forward. The scrawny Chart's sword quivers, and I step farther away from him, headed for the pair of Charts holding Amir. "I'm no orphan. You're look-ing upon the face of the Snake Princess. And my father wouldn't be pleased to know of romance in his ranks."

Amir's mouth falls open. *What are you doing?* he mouths.

I nod at Amir. *Trust me.*

With the two Charts baffled, I take action. I leap over to the woman holding Amir hostage and sweep a foot behind her leg, jerking her off-balance. Her grip loosens, and I steal the knife from her hands. I spin and knock the hilt of the blade against both Charts' heads, and they sink to the ground, unconscious.

"Ria," Amir breathes as I slice off his bindings. "What were you thinking? *Snake Princess?*"

"I've used this trick before," I say, trying to play it off, drained from the magic I just used. The bloodied knife makes my stomach twirl, so I drop it to the ground, ready to forget this entire scene. But the young Chart in the clearing gives me pause. He rises and begins to approach us.

Amir sees me tense up and turns. He leaps forward and knocks the younger Chart with a punch to the face. His aim leaves a welt on the soldier's lip, and the Chart reels back, dropping his sword. He raises his hands as if in surrender.

"Please," he begs. His teeth are stained with blood. "I don't want to hurt you. I don't want any of this. I was pulled from my mother's home when I was eighteen. I never wanted to be a Chart. Let me come with you."

His sentiment is so far from the hardened words of Father's guard. Charts aren't supposed to have feelings . . . they're not supposed to have these thoughts.

The other Charts lie on the ground, bleeding and bruised.

"Why should we believe you?" Amir asks. He pulls back his fist, ready to land another punch, but I hold him back and pull him aside.

Out of the Chart's earshot, I say, "Don't you think we could use him? Get him to help us find the stone?"

"But he's a—"

I glare at Ria's friend, and he relents. We head back to the Chart.

"Tell you what," Amir says. "We know you're looking for the Bloodstone. We won't hurt you if you tell us what you know."

The soldier spits out blood. "Fine, I'll help you," he says. "But I could use some gauze first." Then he collapses to the ground.

We have taken a Chart hostage.

Still unconscious, the man lies before us, his face sharp as a sword cut on a whetstone. Amir and I met Irfan, Sanya, and Jas in a tavern in town. The tavern looks like it's been overturned: chairs in disarray, arrows scattered on the ground, boot prints trapped in the floor's dust, drinks abandoned on countertops. As if people were just here.

"What's happened?" I ask them.

"A raid," Irfan informs me. "We had to fight off a few Charts. They wanted to collect coin."

Sanya leans in and, tilting the Chart's face back slightly, examines the damage. She unravels a roll of gauze from Jas's pack, using her teeth to cut a piece loose.

"You've learned healing practices?" I query. Sanya looks methodical in her work, hands steady and eyes narrowed.

"Jas Auntie started my interest in medicine when I was young, before we left the Foothills." As she speaks, Jas applies an herb ointment to the skin surrounding the wound.

"You saved Ma's life more than once," Amir says as Sanya applies the bandages.

"It wasn't enough the last time," she cuts in, heat glossing her cheeks. Their eyes lock, and for the first time, there's a warmth instead of cold.

*The first step to healing our wounds is to speak of them*, Jas had said. I square my shoulders without hesitation. "If you don't mind my asking . . . what happened?"

Sanya gnaws at her lip as she finishes the wrappings. "Our parents were out for months at a time, looking for the stone. I kept up appearances in our village, pretending our parents were gone working. I worked for the local healer while—"

"While I was out stealing food," Amir admits. He rubs his worn knuckles, like he's trying to scratch away the memory. "I should've stayed with you once we realized they were never coming back."

Sanya inhales an unsteady breath. "Why'd you go? You left me alone."

"I had to get away from the memories, Sanya," Amir says. "I asked you to come with me."

"You knew I couldn't just leave for a life of crime, Amir."

Amir finds me in the darkness. It doesn't matter that we've barely spoken in days. I urge him on with my gaze.

Steeling himself, Amir says, "Sanya, I'm sorry. I was wrong to abandon you like that. If I could go back, I never would've left you alone. And I know we can't go back, but . . . we could stop this fight."

Sanya lowers the gauze, and for a moment, her guard. "Look. The moment you found me in the tavern, it only reminded me of what we lost. I didn't know if I could trust you."

"Do you trust me now?" Amir asks, his features earnest.

Her eyes soften. "I didn't know until that moment in the jungle when you stayed back to help Ria. You've grown up. You've handled so much on your own. Ma and Pa would be proud of us."

Amir's voice is thick with remembrance as he says, "I won't leave you again."

He embraces Sanya before she can turn away. *"Oof,"* she says as her brother hugs her. Slowly, she lowers her arms and hugs Amir back.

A cough fills the room as the Chart comes to. Sanya and Amir part. At the sight of the Chart awakening, we crowd around him like bees swarming honey.

"Abai's sun," the man groans. Sanya checks his pupils and pulls a vial from her pack. With Jas's approval, she forces the liquid down the Chart's throat.

The soldier sputters. "What was that?"

"It'll numb the pain," Sanya explains.

The young Chart takes in the room around us; boxes litter the space, and lit candle sconces create ominous shadows lengthening on the walls. The room is no bigger than a servant's closet space. If they even have one.

His eyes halt on Irfan. "What's going on here? H-how did you find *him*?"

"Irfan?" Amir's gaze flicks to the silver-eyed man.

"You mean One Sixty-Two? His number is whispered everywhere in our ranks."

My mind races. I think back to the burnished coin I found in Irfan's pack. The proof he worked for my father.

I jump up. Even Amir leaps to my side, though Sanya and Jas only frown, as if they knew all along.

I look at Irfan with strange clarity. For I have seen these silver eyes on countless occasions, when I was younger. Have seen him in the palace. Only now, watching him with another Chart, do I remember, as if a sudden Abaian downpour has washed away the fog between Irfan and me.

The realization unfurls like a poisonous flower.

"You. You were the first deserter."

I think of the wound beneath his collarbone, where Charts are traditionally branded upon their induction.

I remember first meeting him days ago, thinking his build would get him into the barracks of Amratstan's Sentinels.

I remember.

And a chill sweeps over me.

"What?" Amir shakes his head. Irfan gulps audibly as he takes hold of the collar of his shirt and peels it away from his skin, as if in slow motion. The world freezes. Breath crawls from my throat in a shallow stream.

A burn covers a portion of his chest, right over his heart. The brand on his chest reads *162*.

"No way," Amir coughs out. "You're one of them? Are you all going to betray us now?" He stares pointedly at Sanya. "Are you working with the raja?"

His sister shoots up. "Amir, he isn't a Chart anymore. He's one of us—"

Just then, the other deserter's eyes fall on mine. His face withers into a look of confusion.

"Ria?" he recalls. My heart catches. Is he remembering the conversation we had in the jungle? When I used the magic on him? "But—you're—"

My veins, still singing with adrenaline from the discovery of Irfan's secret, ignite. It seems my magic on him is wearing off, based on his confusion. "It was a ruse," I say. "I am a commoner; we are villagers who simply want a better life." My gaze shoots to Irfan's. "I hide no secrets."

*Liar*, a voice echoes within me, but I shove it down.

"We aren't loyal to the raja," Irfan clarifies to me. "I broke the magical oath and suffered the consequences. It's why I feel pain in my shoulder every day. But Sanya's medicines have helped me."

Irfan turns to the deserter Chart. "There was a raid on this village. What's the raja's motive?"

"Ask the raja and his adviser," the man says, again glancing at me curiously, though it is as if he is looking through smoke. "They plan these raids. They cause uproar in the inner villages. First, they ask for ungodly amounts of tax money. Then they take what they want in blood."

My mind darts back, back, back. For a moment, I forget about Irfan, forget about this revelation, and remember: Father's adviser is Amara. Ria had told me that Amara was looking for the stone. Did she have the Charts raid the villages in her search?

In this moment, I am unsure of everything.

"So," Amir says with a gulp. "What happens when the truce does end?"

"I already told you," the man begins. "The raja and his adviser made the plans. That's all I know. I overheard them speaking . . . something about water, and a gem. I don't know."

A gem. Surely the Bloodstone. But what of the water? What could Father and Amara have been discussing?

"You're a deserter, like me," Irfan says plainly. "What is your name?"

"Two Twe—"

"Your real name," Irfan clarifies.

The man looks at him steadily for a moment. "My name is . . . Aman. I am loyal to my country. Not my king."

Something about those words breeds unkempt thoughts. "Are there others?" I ask Aman and Irfan. "Others, besides the two of you, who wish to desert their stations?"

Aman grimaces. "Irfan might've been the first deserter, but he wasn't the last by any means. Nor the first one who wanted to leave."

Irfan works his jaw, glancing over at the group of us. "I have an idea. Can you give us a moment?"

Several minutes pass as we wait outside the back of the tavern in the warm autumn night. "How can we trust any of them?" Amir asks me, though I know his real question.

*How can we trust anyone from the palace?*

He crosses his arms across his chest, accidentally brushing my arm as he does so. I stiffen. We've kept our distance while traveling from the hills, only touching when absolutely necessary. I think again to his hands spinning my hips, to his arm against mine now. The warmth is startlingly comforting.

"Perhaps trust can be earned back," I tell Amir. He gazes at me deeply. I know what his look means. *Whose side are you on?*

Until now I have been on no one's. Except my own.

"Trust doesn't come easy," a voice proclaims from behind us. "No one deserves the life of a Chart. I've let Aman go, but not without gaining an advantage."

I turn and gape in a most un-princess-like manner. I almost do not recognize Irfan—dressed in a Chart's uniform from head to toe, silver eyes demanding attention.

"Is that . . . Aman's?" I whisper.

Irfan glances down at the red coat. "I burned mine a long time ago. But at my request, Aman gave me his. Now I think I'm finally ready to wear it again." He nods, as if assuring himself. "With me in this uniform, no Chart will give us a second glance."

Sanya catches on. "We can go where we want, when we want, without hiding. It's genius."

It is dangerous. A mockery of Father's court. But I should know all about pretending. And despite myself, I begin to grin.

Irfan continues, "If we encounter the king's army, you are my prisoners, and we continue on our quest. We find the ancient guard, and then the stone." He breathes deeply, his eyes locking on mine. "In the words of the raja: We move like a king cobra."

I finish my father's mantra. "We strike first."

# 31

## Ria

The carriage rolls smoothly through the village streets, quiet as a jungle cat.

"We're nearly there." Saeed glances over at me. He nearly swallowed his own tongue when I suggested visiting the Vadi Orphanage as part of my preparation for becoming queen. I told him it'd be good for royals to see the villagers firsthand. The raja and queen approved, citing this as the first of my new freedoms outside the palace.

Two hours away from the palace. And my first time returning to the orphanage I grew up in.

Saeed is my escort for the trip. The ghost of his fingertips still trails up and down my jaw days later. I haven't seen him since the engagement. Since . . .

I think of the mango-sweet taste of his lips. His sculpted figure—muscled arms, sharp jaw, broad shoulders—enough to catch anyone's attention. *Raja's beard, stop thinking about him!*

As if Saeed can sense my thoughts, he glances over at me.

"You've been silent this whole trip," he notices. "I apologize for my mother's . . . tactless interruption, if that's what this is about."

But he doesn't know that Amara's done worse. He hasn't seen the fear, the agony, on the face of a child as Amara seared their flesh, branding them with a number as though they were no more than livestock.

The carriage jerks to a stop. Saeed unloads himself from the back seat. I take his hand and follow him out, letting the driver know we won't take much longer than a half hour's time. I wear a modest suit today, something that won't draw villagers' eyes, with a chunni pinned in my hair so it won't slip. I'm as disguised as the raja's daughter can be.

I freeze at the sight of the orphanage, just beyond the massive, open gates. My old home. Still crumbling, still brown as the muddied dirt I stand on. I recall playing games in the yard, feeling free without understanding that I never was.

Until now.

I chance a step forward and, beckoning Saeed to follow, find the hidden back door I used to sneak out through nightly, when I'd first practiced my pickpocketing. Saeed glances at me in confusion, but I only grip his hand tighter, and his shoulders relieve themselves from their tense hold. He takes hold of the knocker—a brass clawed bird's foot—and taps three times.

The door swings open. It's only a child, maybe eleven summers old, wearing plain rags. They look the same as the ones I used to wear.

I gulp.

"May we come in?"

The kid only stares at us, but someone appears behind him. Eyes sallow and hard, with endless wrinkles and eye bags.

Memories swing into my mind like a punch: the headmaster dragging me for a whipping when I didn't finish my dinner on time. The crack of the stick on the backs of my knees. The flesh splitting on my leg, blood trailing out. Blood that never left the rug.

Mama Anita would warn us there was nothing she could do to stop him.

This is not the same man.

"Is Headmaster Patil in?" My words are merely a formality; the headmaster only visited once a moon, and never this early in the morning.

The man shakes his head. "You looking to pick someone up?"

"Oh—no." I'm not sure, but I think I see the kid's face fall. Wouldn't be the first time. "There's something I'd like to see."

Saeed begins, "Sir, this is the Pr—"

"Priya," I say. "My name is Priya. I'm requesting to see the back room privately."

"Why?"

"Important checkup from the capital. Palace business."

Saeed is stiff next to me, as if he can't believe the slew of lies from my tongue. I unveil the coin pouch I put together this morning, one of Rani's velvet satchels she won't miss, filled with jewels and a few sparkling coins.

The man greedily grabs the bag and dumps the contents in his other hand. He tosses the pouch back at me. "Got anything else?"

I huff, pull off my bangles, and hand them over, letting him believe that he got a good deal. I'd give much more to get the information I need.

The man nods with approval. "Come in."

I avoid Saeed's stare as we enter the orphanage. The smell is the first thing that hits me: like slowly simmering daal mixed with perfumes of dust and debris. I step around a creaky floorboard, still dented and stained.

Past the kitchen, memories start surfacing: Mama Anita, mopping the tiled floors. Mama Anita, telling me stories of myth and magic.

"Princess," Saeed says in a low voice, "what is this about?"

"Trust me," I tell Saeed. Even though it's early, most of the children still asleep, I step onto the stairs with care. At the top, I squirrel around the wooden beams supporting the roof and find the largest room on the floor.

Mama Anita's.

I carefully nudge the door open. A fluffy cat lazily pads out of the room, stopping to sniff my feet. She purrs.

I curse. *Barfi*. I should've known the orphanage pet would still be here. From the look of the cat, her fur hasn't been shorn since I last saw her.

"She likes you," Saeed comments, leaning down to scratch Barfi behind her ears.

Likes me? She likes anyone who gives her attention, not to

mention she always tried to steal my scraps of food. *As if she didn't have enough.* The cat is more spoiled than Rani!

I shake her off and find the room is empty, and nearly exactly as I remember it. White bed, lined with clean linens. A desk holding messy stacks of papers. Sunlight filters into the room, lighting dust motes in the air.

A year, and nothing and everything has changed.

"Is there something you're looking for, Princess?" Saeed enters the room, leaving Barfi by the open door. "You gave that man your bangles. It isn't like you to barter."

"Do you frown upon it?" I ask him.

Saeed thinks. "No," he says eventually. "I kind of enjoyed it, actually. Seeing you pretend to be anyone except yourself. *Priya.*"

I turn away to hide my blush. Does that mean he likes *me*? The way *I* act? Or seeing Rani play pretend?

I rid my mind of the thought. What Saeed thinks shouldn't matter; right now I'm here for answers. I scope out the room, looking for anything Mama Anita might've left behind. Anything that might help me. The underside of the bed is empty. I grunt, turning to inspect the wardrobe. I fling open the doors. A hidden set of wooden drawers sits inside. *Jackpot.*

I scour the drawers and come up with some jewelry, but nothing Mama Anita wore. Saeed pulls open the final drawer a touch, but it doesn't give. "It's stuck," he says.

"Let me help," I tell him. We look for what's making the drawer catch. A spare salwar kameez is hooked on one of the wheels. I raise the outfit carefully, bringing it to eye level. The beadwork is exactly as I remember it.

It's hers.

"Mama," I murmur. I hold the outfit to my nose, almost believing I can smell her fragrance. Cilantro, sweet almond oil, and cane sugar from the besan barfi she would make for me. Maybe Mama Anita spoiled me, made me feel royal when I was anything but.

I can't help the tears that burst into my eyes. I bat them away quickly, but Saeed notices as soon as I drop the clothes.

"Rani, what's the matter?" Concern pulls down his mouth. "You can tell me."

"I'm looking for something. Clues that might help me figure out . . . what your mother is doing," I lie.

"You think my mother has something to do with this orphanage?"

"I'm not sure. But the royals might." The truth this time.

There must be something else hidden in this room, something Mama Anita wanted me to see. *She's* the one who told me to go back to the start, which means there's something here she wants me to find.

"Keep checking the wardrobe for anything out of place," I tell Saeed. As I move, the floor squeaks beneath me, and I rock my heel back and forth on the wood. Back when I lived here, the other orphans would always hide notes, games, even extra food under the floorboards, where the headmaster wouldn't think twice to check. That's where I'd hide my stash from petty steals, when I was only twelve summers old.

I take a few steps backward, testing the floorboards once more, until I feel it: a weak spot beneath my heel. It's almost impossible to notice, but to a thief's senses it's clear as day. I lean down and find the edge of the carpet, lift it, and spot a rusty nail in the floorboard that looks out of place. I reach down and at my touch, the floorboard gives a little pop and squeaks out. I hide a smile, remove the board, and find a tiny envelope.

There's only one thing inside. A birth certificate.

I grip the paper, turn away from Saeed while he's busy looking in the wardrobe, and stare at the parchment with such intensity I could light it on fire.

But the paper itself is already half burned, my last name seared away. Only a few lines remain legible:

*RIA—*

*Born Diwali night, on the 82nd year post-truce.*

*Second child of the successor King Natesh and Queen Man—*

*Second in line to the throne after completion of the Bonding Ceremony.*

My fingers curl into the paper, and I withhold a gasp. *Second child?* That means whoever wrote this knew the truth; the raja and queen had twins. We existed to them, both of us together, once.

My eyes burn with unshed tears.

*I'm one of them.* Why did my parents give me up to Mama Anita specifically? Why would they give her this certificate? Did they want a piece of me to still live on somehow, even as they pushed me out of their minds—out of their lives—forever?

I run a finger over the burn marks. It's like they tried to erase the proof that I existed but couldn't go through with it.

This makes no sense. But I'm not even mad anymore. With this in my hands, I can show the raja who I really am before Amara can unveil my secret—not an impostor but his daughter. And then I can tell the raja how she hurt me, and what she's been doing to her son. He'll finally see Amara for who she is.

Saeed turns toward me, and I hide the certificate behind my back. "Anything?" he asks, noticing the floorboard. I shake my head. But Saeed is too curious.

"Are you sure—?"

A meow sounds from outside the door.

"Shh, Barfi," I tell the cat. The furry feline won't let up.

Saeed abandons the wardrobe. "I think she's trying to tell us something."

He's right. Footsteps echo from the staircase. Someone's coming.

My mind is back on alert. "Put this back," I tell Saeed hurriedly. He replaces the floorboard while I carefully roll the certificate into the pouch I brought. I don't want anyone to know what we found here. Bribing a greedy man only works until someone else with money comes along.

"This way." I slip aside the window curtains, revealing the open air. From the second story of the orphanage, the ground looks far away, but nothing I can't handle.

It's Saeed I'm worried about.

"Let's go," I tell him.

"Uh, shouldn't we take the stairs?" Saeed's voice cracks.

"Change of plans. We jump while no one's looking."

"*What?*" Saeed shakes his head. "But why? You told that man you were from the palace. You—you gave him an alias. I think we can just—" The footsteps grow louder, like the clank of Charts' boots. I imagine the iron-fisted soldiers here, in the orphanage, the way they were that day they took her away.

*You're in a whole mess of trouble*, Amir would say. He would most definitely be right.

"No one can recognize us. We don't have another choice," I insist.

"Are you sure this will work?" Saeed gulps.

*Not at all*, I think. "Positive."

My assurance must work, because Saeed glances over the edge of the window and says, "Your father asked that I protect you today, not lead you into harm. So I must insist that I—"

Before Saeed can finish, I swing myself over the ledge and leap out onto the nearest surface: An old, locked-up storage bin that hasn't been used for years. I used to escape the orphanage on lonely nights after Mama Anita tucked me to sleep, when I asked if I could lie on her bedroom floor. She'd always give me the bed while she took an old patchwork quilt and used it as a mattress.

I land with a thud on both feet, use the momentum to roll to the edge of the bin, and flip around. My hands are secure on the lid, and I slide down feetfirst.

On the ground, I stare up at Saeed, whose jaw hangs open.

"Hurry!" I tell him. Thankfully, Saeed quickly hauls himself over and lands—pretty clumsily—on the old bin. I help him to the ground, and he huffs on the solid earth. "Where'd you get the nerve to do something like that?"

I shrug. "It's like climbing into the rafters."

He's still gaping when we hear voices coming from the room above.

"The carriage!" I spin away. We swerve around the gardens and find the perimeter of the orphanage. Where the gates were once open, they're now closed, locked.

Like they know an intruder's in their midst.

"We'll climb over." I latch onto the fence, feeling its weight beneath my fingers. I scale it quick as a mouse, my movements practiced and sure, and vault over the top, landing on my two feet back on the ground. I turn around and find Saeed staring up at the gargantuan gate, face pale.

"You can do this." I link my hands on the gate, and, hesitantly, he places his on mine. I secure his hands on the gaps in the fence.

Saeed doesn't wait this time. He heaves himself up onto the fence with a grunt, his shoulders tight as he hoists himself over the top. He clutches my hand before he falls into a heap on the ground, grabbing at me for balance. Air whooshes around me as I fall on top of him. I don't realize how close we are, entangled in each other's arms, until his lips are hot against my ear.

Then I hear his grumble of laughter, familiar and heady. "Rani," he begins, pulling my face toward his, "you truly are something."

I can't help it; I smile, bright and beaming, as Saeed takes in my features. Shouting from the orphanage reminds me of our haste, and I pull myself up and offer to help him to his feet. He takes my hand and we both race off the orphanage grounds. I leap into the carriage headfirst, Saeed on my tail, and he slams the door shut.

It's like one of those heists Amir and I used to do. Except now we've got a royal getaway.

"Go!" I order the driver.

With the snap of a whip, the carriage surges forward. We peel away, kicking up dirt behind the wheels.

When we're in the clear, I realize I'm still gripping his hand. "Nice work," I say, still out of breath.

Saeed doesn't let go. Instead, he laughs. Not politely, like before. A real, throaty belly laugh. He throws his head back from the force of it, and I grin, because it suits him, this laugh. "Nice work? When did *you* learn how to do all that?"

"A princess has her resources," I say mysteriously. He only laughs again, and this time, I join him.

Saeed and I catch our breath when we're alone in his chambers. He can't stop laughing, and I can't stop thinking about what I found at the orphanage.

*My birth certificate. Proof that I exist.*

Now all I have to do is show this to my parents. Soon, Amara won't have any hold over me.

Saeed takes a seat on his bed, sighing with relief. His features, which I once thought looked too perfect, too tight, now seem . . .

familiar. Relaxed. Warm. This palace has changed me in more ways than one. I've found connection, belonging. Something I never thought I'd find here.

I'd always thought of the world split in two, with the royals on top. But when I discovered I have royal blood running through me, my world blurred.

The prophecy stated that one of us, Ria or Rani, would destroy the other. But maybe I'm not meant to destroy the kingdom. Maybe, like Rani said, I'm meant to destroy what it has become. Maybe I'm meant to redeem it. Maybe . . . I'm meant to save it.

I take a seat next to Saeed, struggling to meet his all-encompassing gaze. Heat blooms roses on my cheeks.

"I think we outran those aunties," he jokes.

Entering the palace wasn't easy. People, including *many* aunties, were swarming me and Saeed, asking us how things've been since the engagement, asking where we had been, just the two of us alone. Saeed's not a bad runner for a noble.

And now, after that little detour at the orphanage, Saeed's looking at me with a newborn curiosity. If his eyes are an indication of anything, he seems more impressed than confused at what we did.

"There were tears in your eyes at the orphanage," he says, his eyes a question.

"I was thinking of someone long gone."

Memories flash of Mama Anita, the night when she braided my hair into thin plaits and dressed me in my finest salwar. The night she was taken away.

I relive that memory over and over:

*She moves with purpose, complying as the Charts push her forward. Her chunni falls to the ground at their roughness, melting into a pothole filled with mud. Her bun slowly unspools, rings of curls that sway in the warm wind.*

"No!" *I shout, rushing onto the street. I grab onto Mama Anita's leg, the only part of her I can reach with the Charts all around. She kneels down, caressing my face.*

"I won't truly be gone." *She places a kiss on my cheek.* "I love you, Ria."

*The Charts yank her up and bind her hands with frayed rope. Someone wraps their arms around my stomach and pulls me away. Screams rake my throat.*

*Mama Anita turns. She nods only once. Someone shields my eyes.*

"Sometimes it's easier to not speak about the dead at all," Saeed says. "But it would be tarnishing their memory to forget."

Grief marks his face so openly, it's like I've pulled away a bandage from old wounds. He's bleeding before me.

"Do you remember your father at all?"

Saeed's throat bobs. "All I know is he loved my mother with all his heart, despite all those who told him not to. Mother told me that he gave her a bundle of roses when they married. That the rose symbolized how their love would grow, thorns and all."

I think of his words, mind whirling, remembering those roses Amara loves so deeply. Just as I'm thinking, Saeed brings his fingers to my cheek, trailing the healing mark. "Has this . . . always been here?"

I know exactly what he's thinking before he can process it himself. Realization flares in his eyes. He leans in dangerously close, his brows pinched with fear.

Before I can open my mouth to reply, a nearby scream cuts through the air. Sharp. High-pitched. Frantic. I jump up.

"Who—Mother?" he says, his words barely audible under his breath. But we both know that wasn't Amara. The voice sounded much too youthful.

*Don't think that little girl is getting out of this without any punishment.*

My stomach drops. In seconds, I'm throwing open the door, running toward the voice. Air whips around me. I know exactly who the sound is coming from without seeing her face.

The little servant girl. My newfound friend. *Aditi.*

# 32
## Rani

Darkness descends upon us like an ever-quickening beat, thundering its own tune. A clearing by a nearby stream is our camp for the night. Our route to the Glass Temple has seemed endless over the past few days' travel: The trees have become our guide, each a star on the map of our journey, the forest our galaxy. So vast and immense and infinite. But the end result will be worth it.

After we set up, I leave camp to bathe. I know by now that the stream will be nothing like my perfumed baths at the palace, but after almost two weeks of villager life, it strangely is not a bother. I'm eager to be free of the dirt sitting in my nail beds, the grime coating my arms and legs, no matter how cold the water.

Close to the stream, I see Amir. He's sitting at the mouth of the river, shirt in hands as he kneads it through the water. My cheeks heat as I gaze at him. I must make a noise, because Amir turns his head to look at me, cocking an eyebrow.

"Come to join me?" he says, as if it's a joke, but his voice is still as cold as it's been these past few days. It seems I cannot avoid him any longer, so I take a seat next to him and stare at the waters below.

In the rippling reflection, I see Rani. But I am different. My gaze has hardened, my skin is weathered. Dark circles rim my eyes. I feel like a false princess. Playing pretend at a game too important to lose.

I work up the courage to look Amir in the eyes.

"You're still angry with me," I say, more an answer than a question.

He tucks his knees to his chest. "I was angry when I left home to live on the streets. I was angry when I saw your name on those conscription lists. I have always been angry . . . always *am* angry. Except when it's just me and you."

I count my pulse. *One, two, three.* "So then why haven't you spoken to me? Our stalemate—"

"Can only last so long." He bites his lip, and I catch myself staring. "We've just never fought like that, y'know? And not talking to you for days . . . it's not like us, Ria."

Dread coils in my stomach. Of course things aren't the same. Ria and Amir are easy together, two thieves on the run. Amir and I, we're from different worlds.

My heart aches at the truth of it.

"What I said was wrong," I admit. "The truth is, I'm not afraid of the raja anymore. I'm afraid that I'm going to fail. I'm afraid we'll never find the Bloodstone, that I've put you all in danger for nothing. I'll have let you, Jas, Sanya, and Irfan down."

Amir ponders this for a moment. "You're not the one putting

us in danger. We all agreed to this," he tells me. "We're not gonna stop fighting for our future."

I laugh weakly, looking down. "Our futures. Do you think it's all predestined, set out for us—or do you think we can be more?"

Amir quirks a brow. "When exactly did you become a philosopher?"

My stomach warms, and I chuckle. Abai's sun, why is he making me laugh? I thought we were supposed to be mad at each other.

Quick as a flash of rain, Amir's smile falls. "But I know what you mean. In the jungle . . . I was so scared. Ma taught me that to die is not the end of the story but a break in the page. I wondered, is this our fate? Is this where it ends? I was scared."

"Me too," I whisper.

He shakes his head. "I wasn't scared for *my* life. I was scared for yours."

My heart hitches. Amir continues, "Ria, I could've lost you to those soldiers. I could've lost everything."

He closes the paltry distance between us, tipping up my chin. His eyes become fire and light, flame and smoke. His breath is perfumed with cilantro, his stubble too scratchy, unlike Saeed's clean beard. But I like this. The unwieldy sense that not everything has to be perfect. It simply has to *be*.

I imagine his lips smoothing over my own, drinking him in like rose water. A noose of betrayal forms a ring around my neck, bruising me, telling me what I already know.

"You used to tell me life is fixed. That we were trapped. Now you're saying we can choose to be more. . . ." He trails off, heat creeping across his cheeks. His gaze falls to my lips, the shape of them. He's seeing me up close now; there's nowhere to hide.

"Maybe I've changed," I tell him. "*We've* changed."

Amir releases my chin and runs a hand through his shorn hair. "You've sounded different ever since we left the palace," he tells me, though his voice is not one of anger but curiosity. "At first, I couldn't understand why. Even now . . . I still don't know." He exhales shakily. "You and I—we're friends. And this person you are—this is new. I feel . . ." His cheeks redden as he trips over his words. His breath is so close, I can feel it brushing my cheeks like a mynah bird's feather.

"You feel what?" My words come out in a whisper.

Amir's lips part. "This new you . . . I think I feel something else for her."

The air burns hot as a candle, stifling with every unspoken word. He feels what's been growing between us? I cannot deny he's challenged me, argued with me, like no one before. A trait I was never able to find in Saeed, no matter how sharp my words were. When I pushed, Saeed fell back. I don't think falling back even exists in Amir's vocabulary.

Something has shifted between us since the Foothills—and within myself, too. I've known Amir for less than a half-moon, and yet it feels like there is a history written between us.

Amir glances down. "After seeing the Charts in the forest, I realized time is short. Any one of us could've been taken. . . ." He trails off. "I used to blame myself for my parents' deaths. What if it was supposed to be me gone, not them? And then . . ." He lets out a frustrated sigh. "I hated to think of it, but I even blamed Sanya." He raises his eyes to mine again. "But blaming you, blaming Sanya—blaming *anyone* for something beyond our control is wrong. I don't ever want to fight with you again. I don't want to waste what time we have. I want us to always tell each other the truth."

*The truth.* I inhale protractedly. Right now I wish I was named Ria instead of Rani. I wish I could stop pretending to be a girl whose life was forged from everything and nothing.

Amir glances at the place where Ria's birthmark sits next to her left eye. The one I do not have.

"I could've sworn . . ." His finger brushes my skin lightly. I picture what he sees: Ria's face, hardened, the birthmark next to her eye. "What happened to your birthmark?"

*Think, Rani. Stop him from discovering the truth.*

I do the only thing I can. I lean in and take his face into my hands.

My lips crash into his. The world beneath my lids flashes, vibrant as a kaleidoscope of colors. Amir, at first still, leans in, deepening the kiss. My fingers reach for his hair as he runs a hand down my back, pulling me closer. This is so different from every careful, precise embrace I shared with Saeed. This kiss is untamed, fierce.

I don't realize how fast I'm moving until we tip over from my weight, threatening to topple over the edge of the bank and into the stream.

"Oh!" I call out, just as Amir grabs onto my leg to keep us from rolling any farther. He cradles my face close to his.

We're both damp. Strands of my hair stick to my face, my thin shirt. I catch my breath as Amir runs a hand down my leg, then pauses.

"Your scar." His eyes pierce mine. "It's gone."

In the tangle of our kiss, I hadn't realized my leggings had ridden up. He stares down at the soft, supple flesh. No marks, no scars.

No Ria.

Amir lifts me up until we're both standing, still entangled with one another, before he steps back. "I saw that scar just a few weeks ago."

"It . . . must have faded," I begin, but the lie is weak on my tongue. Shame burns through me. I don't dare call upon my snake magic now. Not on this boy who I've come to know and understand.

Amir gazes at me with confusion, his eyes still glazed with lust. Wanting. Desire. I blink, feeling tears rise. Once, when I was six, I plucked an unripe mango from the palace courtyards and sank my teeth right into it, unwilling to wait until it had sweetened. It tasted sour and unpleasant and, worst of all, like a bitter, bitter lie. The taste lingers on my tongue now.

I won't lie any longer.

"You deserve the truth. You always have." My voice breaks, and a tear slips down my cheek. I wipe it away fast. I need to let the dam break, let the words flood from me. I need to speak the truth, right now.

So I say, "I'm not who you think I am."

His eyes are wide. "What're you saying?"

"My name isn't Ria," I reveal, cheeks hot. "It's Rani. Princess Rani."

Amir is still, and for a moment I wonder if he heard me. Then his face slackens. "*Princess* Rani?"

I fake a curtsy, but my legs feel like they might give way.

Amir laughs. "No," he says. "You're joking."

My expression tells him different.

A few seconds pass before his own face turns serious. He gulps. "I know you've been acting strangely, but you don't have to make up excuses—"

"It's not an excuse!" The words fly from my mouth. "It's the truth. And before you say anything more, I know you must hate me—"

"Hate?" Amir's bark of a laugh startles me. "This can't be possible. You aren't Rani. You would have to be—"

"Twins," I finish. "Yes, we are. Ria's in the palace, and I am here. When we go back—"

"Back? There can't be two of you—I *know* you, Ria, you never knew your parents—"

"That part is true," I say. "Because she never learned her true parentage."

Amir's eyes glaze over again, like the moment he'd cradled me against him after our kiss. My lips burn.

"This whole time—while we've been traveling together and fighting side by side . . . You're saying you lied to me?"

Shame fills my chest. "When you put it like that—"

"Put it like what? The truth?" Amir looks over at me again, like he can't quite believe his own eyes.

"You're Ria's friend," I whisper. "I had to." *I wanted to.*

"You *had* to? Had to do what? Pose as your twin? Deceive all your friends?" He turns away from me for a moment. "I really must've hit my head on a melon. . . ."

I'm stripped, naked before him. No masks, no pretenses, no charades. Just me. Rani. A princess and a girl all at once.

"How long has this been going on?"

"Since Diwali," I reveal. "We swapped places in the palace."

Amir is still save for the arch of his brow, the slight parting of his lips, the incredulity in his features. *Don't be true*, that mouth says, the mouth that kissed mine.

Silence cascades over us. I stare at the forest floor, drowning in my thoughts. In the moonlight, we're simply two glowing bodies, sharing secrets under a blanket of stars.

"I'm telling the truth," I say. "But revealing this to anyone else . . . it would put Ria in danger."

Amir shakes his head. "You're telling me my *best friend* is parading around as the princess in the castle?"

I nod.

Amir mutters strings of words under his breath. He pauses, stepping toward me and tentatively raising a hand to my cheek. Warm against my icy skin. "Why?"

"Because I needed to escape. To follow a path someone set me on. To prove myself. It was an accident, finding you, but I wouldn't change it for the world. Do you know that I haven't stepped out of that castle in years? Do you know what it's like to be robbed of the sky? To breathe only air that is manicured to my father's tastes?"

Amir says nothing.

"I swear, Amir, when I go back, I will set things right," I promise. "And I promise we will find the stone and stop my father from committing irrevocable harm. It is what I want as much as you. But you must trust me first."

Amir's scrutiny is agonizing. He studies my face, my lips, my eyes, as though he can find Ria in me again.

"I'm sorry." A weak apology, but I say it nonetheless.

Amir shakes his head. "I need to clear my head." He gives me one last glance before retreating.

"Amir," I whisper harshly, tears falling. My lips wobble. But he's gone.

I rush away and spot Jas sitting near the empty campfire; Irfan and Sanya are Amran-knows-where. Breathing deeply, I head toward her and plunk down on the dirt. I lean my head on her shoulder without thinking, relishing her warmth, like a mother's. Like my mother might have been—*should* have been. A shoulder to cry on. Someone to confide in, when I realized Saeed had never truly loved me. I remember my own horror when I realized I had stopped loving him. I let in the cold to protect me, and now I'm afraid it's thawing.

"Hush, girl," Jas says smoothly, like a lullaby. She turns to me and wipes a tear from my cheek. "You don't have to tell me anything."

"You heard?" I glance up at Jas.

"No. But I've watched you and that boy over our time together. And I know what you're feeling." She grasps my hands with hers. What *am* I feeling? If Shima were here, her scales would be flashing every color, every emotion.

"Was it like that with Samar?"

"Every day. Like I was falling. You and your friend have been through great dangers," Jas continues. "Love is one such obstacle, but more lie ahead. Are you ready for that?"

I'm not sure I am, but I nod all the same.

"Come now. The Temple awaits." Jas helps me stand, then places a gentle kiss on my forehead. Her touch is as healing and warm as ginger root. I linger beside her for a moment, because I do not want this to end.

But it will. Soon, my charade will be over for the rest of this crew, too. I will find the stone.

If I must go against my own blood, I will.

# 33

## Ria

The palace is quiet, hushed, but my mind is ablaze. Within seconds, I come to a screeching halt. I spot Aditi frozen on the ground, arms pinned behind her by two Veteran Charts. My body grows cold.

And then even colder when I spot Amara, her lips two bright-red slashes. She stands next to Aditi patiently, her mouth curled, like she can't hold back her sinister sneer.

Aditi lets out another yelp, this time more like a whimper. I rush toward her, but Saeed holds me back. I didn't realize he'd followed me here. He wraps his fingers around my wrist, his eyes telling me what I already know. *Don't cross Amara's line. You don't know what she's capable of.*

Except I do.

I yank my wrist from his grasp, unable to follow anyone's orders except my own. She holds no power over me. *I'm* the princess now. And that means my voice matters here, more than Amara's.

"Remove her from your grip," I order the Charts. "She hasn't done anything wrong."

"On the contrary," Amara snarls, stalking toward me, "the girl has not been following my orders. Which means *I* get to choose what punishment comes next."

My fingers sizzle, heat coursing through them and up my back. "What *orders*, exactly?"

Amara only smirks, jutting her chin toward the Charts, who tighten Aditi's wrists behind her. Aditi lets out the smallest of sobs, and at that sound, my heart lurches. I will myself to stand my ground.

"Tell her, girl," Amara says, keeping her sharp eyes on me the whole time. "Tell her what you told me."

"Mother," Saeed snaps, but Amara only silences her son with a hand. My eyes widen with fear. I glance at Aditi, step closer to her, my body crawling with anticipation at what she'll say next.

When Aditi doesn't comply, a Chart grabs a fistful of her hair and shoves her face to the floor. A cry escapes her lips, just as it does mine.

"Stop!" I yell, but it's as if Amara has some kind of silent control over the raja's soldiers.

Aditi finally opens her mouth, letting out a sigh instead of a sob. "I—I was eating," she stutters. "And I started to feel sick. I thought maybe there was something in my food—"

"*Exact* words, dear," Amara says, her voice sickly sweet, as if she were talking to her own child. Beside me, Saeed stiffens. I wonder if he's used to this voice, to Amara's commands. To listening to his mother's coldness, in the absence of his father.

"I thought it was p—" She swallows. "P—"

"Poisoned," Amara finishes for her. My stomach tumbles. Aditi's food, *poisoned*? The vile woman stares deeply at me, into my soul, like she's got all my secrets and tucked them away into her overly frilly sari.

Did Amara use venom on Aditi? Give her a near lethal dose, unlike the diluted ones she gives her son?

"Three lashings," says Amara. An order. A command.

"Mother, please!" Saeed says, just as I shout, "No!"

I soar forward. The air in my throat tightens. Rage heats my cheeks.

But Amara steps in front of me, takes hold of my shoulders, and yanks me aside. Her eyes bore into mine. She moves behind me but never loosens her death grip, and I freeze like I used to under the orphanage headmaster's lashings.

*Move, Ria. Help her.* Terror fills my chest as a Veteran pulls his whip out and slams it down on Aditi's now-open palms. Once. Twice. My ears are ringing by the third strike. She knows better than to shriek, than to do anything that would cost her another.

Amara's death grip loosens. The Charts behind Aditi tug her up by the arms, and I swear her bony shoulders loosen from their sockets. Blood spills on the marbled tiles, ivory and ebony spider-webbed with pink.

"Double kitchen duties," barks Amara. "And I want every

bathroom spotless. If I see even a speck of dirt the lash will be the least of your worries."

"Yes, Mistress Amara," Aditi says. A tear rolls off her chin. Falling away from her fear-stricken face. She looks like she's about to puke.

*I'm* about to puke. My throat is locked. My fingers curl into fists, tingling. I feel smaller than a common street rat.

"Take her to the servants' infirmary," Amara orders the Charts. "I don't need her insides all over the floor. And bring someone to clean up this mess."

My feet are glued to the ground, my body limp. It takes under a minute for everyone to clear the area, including Amara.

But I'm not alone. I still feel him next to me, Rani's betrothed.

And here I am, a shadow of the princess.

I turn to him. "No," I say, and at the confusion written on his face, I continue, "it wasn't always there." I point to my fading bruise.

Saeed goes still. "I should have known."

"But you didn't—"

"I *should* have," he cuts in, cupping my face and tilting it up to him. I don't have time to speak before those fingers race down my cheek. He's probably used to this, to seeing his mother hurt innocent servants. To having Rani just *stand* there, do nothing about it.

Either way, *I'm* not Rani. I never will be. Even if things've changed here, even if I've learned things, *felt* things I never thought

I would. I step out of Saeed's grasp, shake my head, and from that simple movement he knows exactly my command.

*Go.*

I shut my eyes. The hall feels cool, empty, drained.

When I open them, he's walking away, leaving me like a cup of chai that's slowly turning cold.

I visit Aditi in the servants' infirmary later that night. The infirmary is in the servants' quarters, tucked deep into the bowels of the palace. When I find it, I check that no one is watching, and slip through the curtains that part the servants from the rest of the world.

I expected four-poster beds, windows refracting sunlight across the whole quarter. Instead, what I find is even worse than the orphanage.

Mattresses litter the floor. They're firm to the touch, coiled springs squeaking like mice. The servants have few tables and lamps to share, and their closet is cramped with green—salwars and suits, leggings and pointed shoes, all in the same shade. Designating them. Labeling them.

Lower. Lesser.

How could I have been so foolish, thinking the servants well cared for? No wonder Aditi keeps her back arched whenever the raja is near, head tilted in reverence. This isn't a monarchy. It's a dictatorship.

The infirmary isn't far. When I spot Aditi, soundly asleep, I'm sure to keep quiet. She looks like she's found peace, for once.

But the moment I settle on the edge of her cot, Aditi shoots up, tilting her head toward me. "I thought you were her," she says, shuddering. She sighs in relief.

*Her.* Amara.

"It's only me."

Aditi flings herself into my arms, and I clutch her close, letting her tears fall onto my shoulder. Her hands are wrapped up, bandaged tight, red from all the blood she's lost. I shut my eyes, willing myself not to think of the scars marring me. Scars from years of hardship. It seems like being in the palace doesn't stop them.

"What are you doing here?" Aditi asks, pulling away. She tucks her arms tight at her sides, as if bound to keep a rigid posture. With beady eyes, she looks over me, clearly stunned the princess would ever set foot in the servants' quarters.

"I wanted to check on you," I say truthfully. *"Mouse."*

Aditi doesn't smile at the nickname. "What if Amara sees us?"

"I highly doubt Amara is going to walk in here." I give her a confident smile.

Aditi nods, albeit slowly, like she doesn't fully believe me.

I straighten a bit and continue more boldly, "I don't care if Amara comes at me with her fingernails. She won't touch you again." Every wound on my body tells a story, and the ones she's given me won't erase my past. I've seen worse than her.

Aditi blinks, eyes widening. "Amara poisoned my food," she reveals. "I know she did. She told me, you know. About the moment she found you spying on her in the rafters, and how every day after, I'd have to watch my back." She blinks rapidly, as if to stave off tears.

My voice fills with conviction. With rage. "A true mother, a woman of strength, would never do that."

Aditi twiddles her thumbs and yanks her green sleeves down over her fists.

"What's wrong?" I ask.

The silence is all I need to hear to know there's a gap to be filled. Not everything about the girl's story is clicking together, not with those flitting eyes and rosy cheeks.

"You can tell me anything." I wanted to tell Amir that, not long after we first met. He was building a fire—not for heat, just for food—after we scored some meat from a nearby shack. I was staring at his scar, unable to look away, as I always did not long after I first met him. My first mistake. Looking too deeply at appearances removed all the more important things that rested in one's soul.

Aditi's body wilts. She lets out a frustrated sob, and I take her by the elbow. "I—it's hard to explain." Her words are nothing more than a nervous jumble of things, strung together with a low voice.

My heart thuds against my rib cage. "Tell me," I plead, unsure of what's about to unfold. "If it's about Amara—"

"It's not," she interrupts. "I was just thinking about how you left for the Vadi Orphanage this morning. Why did you go?"

"I had an important task. You see . . ." I spill a labored breath.

"There was someone very important to me who used to live there. Her name was Mama Anita."

Aditi freezes.

"What is it?"

She gulps, lifts her sleeve. There, bound to her wrist, is a band made of twine.

It takes me less than a moment to recognize it, and I'm sucked back into that memory of Mama Anita and me sharing stories when I was a child. The twine bracelet she wore as she illustrated the Masters' magics in the air. Then, I think back to when Aditi told me she'd lived in an orphanage.

But not just any. Aditi looks at me curiously. Black hair braided tightly, posture rigid. Signs that she's labored in the palace longer than she's been anywhere else.

"How did you get that bracelet?" I breathe.

Aditi's lips wobble. She's solemn. All quiet. All unassuming.

"Because I once lived at that orphanage. And I knew Mama Anita."

# 34

## Rani

The famed Glass Temple rises into the sunset like the palace itself. Clear, domed arches cut through the clouds, marked with gold and silver patterns, drawn with a fine ink. Below us, the horses kick up piles of sand, which crest and fall in miniature dunes.

It seems impossible that such a grand temple could remain so hidden. Yet the scratches along my arms and legs tell another story—we've ducked through brambles, led the horses through narrow jungle passages, all to get to our destination.

Amir's hands stiffen on my waist at the sight of it. It's been just two days since our kiss, and yet I continue to feel like a fool. A fool for lying to Amir, a fool for keeping up this charade of pretending to be my sister, a fool for telling him the truth and thinking he would understand. Shame burns my cheeks. I am back in the palace, following Mother's orders. *Twirl, bow; twirl, bow.*

I am a doll. *Twirl, bow; twirl, bow.* I am a liar. *Twirl, bow; twirl, bow.* I am no one.

We dismount our horses. No one else seems to know my secret, which means Amir hasn't told anyone. Or perhaps, even though he knows I'm not Ria, he doesn't want to believe my true identity.

I stare at his clothes, a dark shade of hunter green that, a lifetime ago, meant subservience. An ode to Father and Mother, a marker of the rich against poor. Now green means no such thing. Now green is more than a servant's color. Green is a marker of those who fight for this kingdom, for its people, more than I ever have.

Smoke drifts my way, and I sniff the air, my snake-magicked senses heightening. It smells like the heat of high summer, punctured by the funereal scent of ash. As if we're in a place of Death instead of life.

The smoke wreaths our ankles, making my feet disappear from sight, and the sky darkens. As if it is angry at Father's wrath. His hunger to destroy.

His hunger for war.

"Let's keep moving," says Jas, sweeping her way next to me. I smile when her gaze finds mine, her very presence calming and healing me. She is the inverse of Sanya right now, who looks like a bundle of nerves. It reminds me of Ria, how unalike we both are, yet no different skin-deep. We are sisters. We are branches from one tree, and though we've grown in opposing directions, we will always share the same roots.

It takes mere minutes to reach the gated entrance to the Glass Temple. The gate is made of shimmering gold, with distinctive patterns making up the barrier. I find six unique symbols inscribed in the gate: a snake, an eye, a flame, a swirl, a mountain, and a wave.

The symbols of the six Masters of Magic.

But there is something else—a gaping hole in the ground before the gate.

"Look." Amir points to the hole. That's when I spot a flash of red underneath the heavy fog. At first I believe it to be blood. Instead, as I lean closer, I make out a flurry of gold fringes, sashes, buttons that declare noble status.

Jackets. Ones belonging to the Charts. And below that, a gruesome mass of flesh and bone.

I fall back and pray I won't retch.

"Their bodies are already decomposing," Jas says. "These have been here a while."

Irfan frowns when he peers down, his eyes flashing with recognition. "They're torn limb from limb."

The smoke curls around our calves, as if inching higher. It tickles softly, like lapping waves, lulling me into a false sense of assurance. But I won't be fooled.

Something is stopping people from entering the Temple.

Without warning, a sharp object whizzes past me. Lightning fast, Amir shoves me away from the next projectile. Then come the sounds, like a hundred birdcalls, sharp and insistent, and wings flapping overhead. I duck, arms covering my head, until a moment later, the sounds halt. I gaze upward.

A few beady-eyed birds stare back from their perch on the gate. Shivering, I take in their midnight-black feathers, their knife-sharp beaks.

*Jungle crows.*

Mother told me enough stories about these birds when I was a child for them to seep into my nightmares. Their feathers are like fine needles, almost razor-like, sharp enough to pierce one's soul. And the birds are rare, hardly ever seen in the skies.

They're believed to be an omen of war.

Irfan pulls out his bow and arrow, nocking it without releasing. Before he can let one of his arrows fly, the birds shift their necks, and in one swoop, soar over us, their movements precise. My gaze follows their ascent behind the darkened clouds. What are they flying toward? Or worse . . . flying from?

"I—I think I might know what killed those Charts," Amir says, adding a muffled curse, eyes fastened on something behind me. At his words, the back of my neck prickles.

I begin to turn my head toward the gate when I hear it.

A tiger's growl.

"Raja's beard," Sanya curses under her breath.

The creature paws the ground. Eyes like dark pearls. Fur white and rough, streaks of obsidian striping its body with fearful symmetry. Its eyes lock onto mine as it paces back and forth before the gate of the Temple, blocking any of us from entering.

Fiery needles fill my lungs, and I can barely breathe at the sight in front of me. The tiger looks impossibly formed, moving like a wisp of smoke—no, a swirl of sand.

"The sandtiger," Jas whispers.

I nearly forgot about the creature, first taught to me from one of Mother's bedtime stories. Some say the tiger was born in Retan and forged from the kingdom's sands, with the ability to shoot scorching flames from its maw. A companion to the Fire Master during the Great Masters' Battle.

The sandtiger guarded the Glass Temple, at least in the legend.

Irfan prepares to fire his arrow, but I block him. "Wait!"

"What're you doing?" Irfan retorts.

"Saving your life," I tell him. "The tiger will only attack if we do."

Slowly, Irfan lowers his bow, but beside him, Sanya is far from happy. Amir looks too afraid to form a sentence.

"The sandtiger protects the Temple from those without true and good intentions. . . ." I recite Mother's words—the story of the legend she told me. "We just need to prove to the tiger that we're here for selfless reasons. Good reasons."

"And how exactly will we communicate that to a *tiger*?" Sanya asks me, her voice sharp as the daggers at her belt. Her eyes widen as the tiger growls, low and insistent. The beast is fearsome, its eyes glittering with promise.

The promise of death.

If I don't figure out what to do, we'll end up in this tiger's version of the Pit. In this chasm of death.

*Think, Rani. How can I show the tiger our true intentions?*

*You have magic*, a voice tells me. *Channel it.*

The tiger growls again. I clutch my hands to stop them from shaking. *Fear only breaks your connection to the world around you*, Father once told me. The last time I was allowed to show fear was the first time I saw the Pit open. The day I met Shima.

I take Father's advice and shove my fear aside, staring into the sandtiger's eyes. I force myself to imagine them as Shima's. Though I cannot hear her, I channel my mind into hers, gripping that snake bond we created during the Bonding Ceremony. I pull out the compartment holding my connection to her. I take one step closer, then another, until I stand nearly at the rim of the chasm. My magic calls to the tiger, forming a link between our minds, and I tell the creature I am the future rani of Abai, a girl who wants more for her people.

*For people like Ria. For people who don't have a chance.*

I feel myself growing closer to the sandtiger. I inch nearer, focus on our connection. But the next instant, my foot slips at the hole's edge and I stumble back. One glance down at the gaping hole and I remember the Pit, the snakes, the death. Too quickly, the bond snaps. The tiger turns to Irfan, growling as flames spark out of its mouth and turn to smoke.

It's angry now. Ready to leap.

I rush to cover Irfan. "Wait!" I turn to him. "Take off your coat. The tiger's afraid. It thinks you're a Chart. Don't you see? The sandtiger will only let those with good intentions pass the gates—not the king's soldiers."

My voice is steady, the way a princess's should be. The way I've been taught all my life.

I won't let those lessons fail me now.

"How do you—" Irfan starts, but he halts at the tiger's look. He tears off the coat and waits.

I turn to face the tiger, and I can practically feel the beast being put at ease. I close my eyes and fuse my mind with the tiger's until we are one—one being, one purpose. I think of every moment I spent with Tutor, every wish he ever told me, the last words that hung on his lips. I think of how badly he wanted the Bloodstone. How badly he *needed* it.

A sudden wind blows through, and dust particles float before my eyes. No—sand. It's the *sandtiger*, changing form before me. But its eyes remain on mine until the last moment, sharp and golden and unrelenting, even as the tiger begins to fade, tiny grains of sands shifting into the wind.

I am watching a myth come to life before my eyes. The sand disperses until the particles reach the sky and disappear.

We all watch in shock as the hole disappears and the gate clicks open.

Something heavy forms in my palm. I turn my wrist and find a shimmering golden object resting there. I turn it in the waning light.

"That must be a gift from the sandtiger," Jas remarks.

"It could be dangerous," Irfan warns. He examines it, Sanya joining in tandem.

"Let me look," Amir finally says, recklessly picking up the object with his slim fingers. He turns it left, then right.

"It looks like an amulet," Jas says.

"Or a compass," replies Sanya.

"Or the Fire Master's talisman," a voice says. My head whips around.

The voice comes from the entrance to the Temple. I turn. Several sets of curious eyes peer out from the door.

"Are those . . ." Shadows multiply until there is a whole horde of people in front of us, lit by the waxing moonlight.

*Children.* Clothed in loose crimson robes and wearing curious expressions. A man dressed in fine red vestments exits the front entrance of the Temple and heads down the steps, past the cluster of children, until he is just before us. He holds a spear deftly in hand, red-tipped and as tall as the man himself. I know just by looking at him—he knows how to use it.

"You have opened the gates and received the compass—the talisman." Both a statement and an inquiry.

More children appear, though they cluster together, the mehendi drawn on their hands swirling in the shape of flames.

"The mehendi," I say, eyes widening. "It's moving."

A magic I've never seen before. A magic I thought to be gone.

Jas and the rest of the group take notice. Then she turns her attention back to the man. "You are the leader of the ancient guard?"

The man purses his lips. "You are very wise to know such things. And yet you travel with a Chart. No soldier has ever gotten past the sandtiger." The man eyes Irfan's coat, lying in the dirt.

"*Ex*-Chart," Irfan clarifies. He tells his story, and behind him the children's eyes widen, whispers breaking out among them.

The man only grunts, apparently unsatisfied with the answer. He works his jaw. "How did you learn of this place, and our people?" His gaze pins on Irfan's again. "Did the raja send you?"

"No," Irfan says. "If I were truly a Chart, I wouldn't have made it this close to the Temple." He points at the bodies, skeletons decomposing ways behind us.

"Only those with true and good intentions make it to our dwelling," the man confirms. "The Temple warned us of your arrival. Amran sends a sign when people near. But . . ." He hesitates. "I know a group of impostors when I see one."

*Impostors!* I nearly shout. How dare someone speak to a princess like that? Then I remember. I am pretending to be someone I'm not. I *am* a charlatan. And outrage will not solve anything.

"We are simple voyagers who followed the fountain's prophecy," Jas begins. "'*Seek the place of stone and glass . . .*'"

She recites the prophecy word for word. The man cannot contain his surprise; I see it in the twitch of his jaw.

Jas doesn't look at me, and steps ever closer to the red-clad leader. "My husband knew of you, the ancient guard. But he hadn't realized—*we* hadn't realized—that you might be . . ."

Whispers swirl through the air. "Flametalkers," I gasp. I glance at those markings again, at the red-tipped spear the man holds, their crimson clothes. Descendants of the Fire Master were thought to live in Retan, and yet here they are. "We mean no harm," Jas repeats. "We wish to find the Bloodstone and use it for good, and we believe it to be here. Protected by an ancient guard . . . the Fire Master's descendants."

The man straightens his stance, staring at each one of us in turn with great intensity. "We are indeed of the Fire Master's blood. But we do not speak of the Bloodstone."

"Why not?" Sanya questions.

"We do not wish to be involved with the bloodshed that caused the Masters' very disappearance."

I exchange a rigid glance with Irfan. "But we thought—" I begin.

"You thought incorrectly," the man says. "Some might believe the stone is here, but they are wrong. We guard the spiritual, not the material."

"I see," Jas responds, crestfallen. I mirror her gaze. This entire time, we were led astray, following the prophecy in hopes that the ancient guard had been protecting the Bloodstone. Had we falsely interpreted the prophecy all along?

Despite the hope crumbling inside me, I step forward. "What, exactly, do you guard?"

The man narrows his eyes. "This is not information we give away freely."

"The sandtiger trusted us, and so can you." I reach out. The gold chain unspools in the emerging moonlight, and in my palm, the compass glints. The one the sandtiger offered us, the tiger known to be an ally of the Fire Master.

The man narrows his eyes. He turns back toward the Glass Temple itself, where something like smoke escapes from the top-most spiral.

"Will you help us?" I ask. "This compass is, as you said, the Fire Master's. There must be a reason the tiger gave it to us."

"Indeed. The sandtiger possesses the talisman, but to offer it to someone means something much greater." The man speaks quietly, looking to the sky. Behind him, the children whisper. Their voices become a chorus. *The compass. The compass.*

The man lowers his spear. "Follow me."

PART THREE

# A Change
# of Fortune

## 35

### Ria

*Aditi lived at the same orphanage as me.*

No words leave my mouth. I'm stunned into silence.

"You mean you knew Mama Anita?" I'm sure I heard her wrong, but she nods.

"When did you leave the orphanage?" I ask, wondering if our paths might've ever crossed. But it's not like I spent much time with other kids there.

Aditi looks down. She's on the verge of tears, cheeks swelling and jaw clenched. She wipes her eyes and trembles. I tilt her chin up so she can see me—the real me.

But I think she might already know.

"It's a long story," she begins. "I was part of a lottery for the raja's new batch of servants; he would select kids from the Vadi Orphanage. It was considered a great honor, a chance for a better . . . more purposeful life. They took me when I was just five, raised me in the servants' quarters, and trained me to be a servant.

It's the only job I've ever known."

Even though her words are full of sorrow, she sits tall.

"Why would they take children from the orphanage?" I whisper in disbelief.

Aditi only shakes her head. "When I was older, they said I was lucky, the nobles. I didn't agree. I wanted to be with Mama. We exchanged letters sometimes. Before I became Amara's personal servant, I helped organize the outgoing palace mail. I snuck in my letters to Mama and helped other servants send notes to their families, too. Now Amara's in charge of the mail system. . . ."

"Since when?" I wonder.

"Ever since she became the king's adviser, Amara's been watching the mail chariots carefully. They're under her command. But, miss, how do *you* know Mama?"

I gulp. "The truth is, Aditi . . . I've been holding a secret, too. About how I know Mama Anita." The words form a melody in the air. The first time I've ever told anyone the truth in this place.

Aditi stares at me. "Lynx?" She touches the edge of my own elbow this time. She's steadying me; maybe she sees how off-balance I feel. If Aditi had enough trust in me, maybe I need to have enough trust in her.

"I'm not . . . ," I begin. My lips are dry as sand. "I'm not Rani." The words tumble, fall off my tongue.

Aditi lets out a weak laugh and contemplates my face. It's only then that I realize she doesn't only act like a mouse—she looks like one, too. Short stature, wide eyes, a nibbling nose.

"Pardon me," she says after a moment, "but . . . not Rani?"

I check that there's no one at the doorway, that I'm not being spied on when I least expect it. I spin back to her and say, "I need you to trust me. But in exchange for telling you my secret, I want to know more about Mama Anita. About her death. She was like a mother to me, too."

*And I'm dying to tell someone*, I add in my head, *other than a snake*.

"Anything, miss," Aditi answers. She trusts me. Somehow, we've both been in the orphanage. And somehow, we've both wound up in the palace, in roles we never thought we'd play. From girl to servant, orphan-thief to princess.

We're each rebels in our own right.

And for that reason, I tell her everything.

"Ria." Aditi tastes the name when I'm done with my story. "I . . . I *knew* there was something different!"

"Aditi, this has to remain our secret," I tell her, though a smile begins to quirk my lips up at her excitement.

"I won't tell a soul." Aditi leans forward. Her bandaged hands slip into mine, and I hold them gingerly. "You asked to know more about Mama Anita. Well, I got to see her one last time, before she died."

I gasp. "How?"

"I asked the Charts to let me speak to her, but they wouldn't allow it. During their guard rotations, I saw a snake hovering near the servant staircase leading to the dungeons. I followed it down and found Mama Anita. She told me her secret before she died. She wanted someone to carry on her story."

"What secret?" I breathe, heart stomping.

"Mama Anita was a Kaaman spy."

"A spy?" I'd heard stories about Kaamans spying on Abai, some kind of precaution that began decades ago to prepare for the war. But Mama Anita?

She nods. "It was only supposed to be a monthlong mission. Mama Anita was placed as a midwife in the Abai palace, but the raja soon figured out that she was Kaaman. Mama Anita told me that she begged the raja not to hurt her—insisted that she wasn't there to spy but to start a new life."

I hold my breath. So that was how he knew Mama. But did that mean Mama Anita was my mother's midwife?

"The raja must've forgiven her, because he let her go. But he gave her an important task—she was to join the Vadi Orphanage as a caregiver. The orphanage was special—it was under the raja's watch. Mama told me that she had to take a girl born at the palace and hide her in the orphanage for safety and watch over her as she grew. Mama never knew why this girl was being given up, only that some prophecy would doom her to a terrible life."

*A terrible life.*

*A terrible fate.*

"It was me. The prophecy would doom *me*," I whisper. I'm shaking so hard that Aditi's breath hitches as I squeeze her hands.

"Sorry, Aditi. I just . . . Mama Anita took me to the orphanage. She became a caregiver because of *me*." I quickly tell Aditi the prophecy, about Rani and me, and her eyes grow large, lashes fluttering against her skin.

"There's more." But before Aditi speaks, she points at a jug. I help her sip her medicine and wash it down with water. Aditi grips her cup as she asks, "Have you heard of the fever children?"

I nod. "There were rumors—"

"Not just rumors," Aditi says. "Remember that book you wanted from the library? The one about magic?"

I nod.

"I was reading it in the library before you asked for it. Because . . . the Vadi Orphanage isn't ordinary. It was under the raja's watch because *he* picked the orphans to go there. Charts would go to people's houses, inspect children who were rumored to show signs of magic. And the raja, with the help of his soldiers, only picked these special children to attend the orphanage."

The realization hits me, sharp as a needle. *Magic.* "That means . . ."

The raja had known magic was returning to the world. *Known.* And tried to hide it. Aditi nods, and she, too, is shivering. We remain silent for many minutes as we process the truth. I can't even cry, too deep in shock to feel anything.

"I haven't figured out *my* magic yet," Aditi says. "Sometimes I wonder if I even have it. I wonder if what they told me about my parents dying was true, or if . . ."

"If someone discovered you had magic and gave you away," I finish.

"Mama Anita told me the truth. She said she never wanted to stop us from learning our true inner magic, while the headmaster wanted us to suppress it. Mama believed we should be free, be who we are. But the headmaster of the orphanage found out what Mama was doing. That was why she was taken away to be killed," Aditi croaks. "The Charts must have found out from the headmaster, and she was taken away for execution."

"That . . . that . . ." I can't even find the words.

"But—" I begin. "Mama Anita *wanted* us to find our magic. She shouldn't have been punished for taking care of us." No wonder Mama always told me stories about magic. She was preparing me, *telling me*, without truly saying the words.

A long moment of quiet. Aditi asks, "Does the king or queen know you've switched places with the real Rani?"

I shake my head. "No. But Amara's figured out I'm not who I say I am. I got my birth certificate at the orphanage earlier. I can finally prove who I am to the raja. Amara won't be able to hurt me."

"Hurt you?" Aditi's eyes land on the nearly healed bruise on my cheek. "Amara did that to you?"

I nod, trailing a finger over her hands. "She hurt us both."

Aditi slowly shakes her head. "Your birth certificate won't be enough to stop her."

"Why not?" I raise myself from Aditi's bed.

Aditi looks down meekly. "I think—I think we might be in danger."

I glance around haphazardly. "Right now?"

Aditi shakes her head, taking me by the elbow and drawing me back down to her, looking me square in the eye. "Please listen carefully, miss. I've worked for Amara a long time. She is cunning. And if she knows you're not who you say you are, she probably already has a plan to silence you or discredit you. If we want the raja to believe you, we need to find something on *her*, and be ready to use it."

My mind whirls. "Like what?"

"I don't know. But whenever I clean Mistress Amara's chambers, she never lets me into her closet. She said if I did, I'd be in the Pit next." She shudders. "We don't have a choice, miss. I think we should sneak into her chambers and see what we can find. The truce ends in just a few days."

Aditi begins to shift off the bed, but I hold her back. "You're in no condition to put yourself in danger," I warn. "Aditi, you're only a child. You shouldn't be involved in this."

"I'm a child with magic," she presses. "And even if I don't know how to use it, I want to do something. I want to help you, Lynx."

I shake my head. "You won't be in any shape to help for a few days."

"Then we strike the night before the truce ends. It's the perfect time. Amara will be too busy with the raja to be in her chambers. We'll sneak in then; the Charts will let us through if I'm there. Please."

It must be the look on Aditi's face, because I give in. "Fine. But only if I can wait that long. And only if you're better."

Aditi grasps me in a hug, and I carefully hold her small body against my chest.

"I'll never tell anyone your secret," Aditi murmurs into my hair. "Mouse's honor."

"And I won't tell yours. Lynx's honor," I reply. My soul flutters with truth, knowing finally what Aditi's been hiding, and why Mama Anita was taken from me. But we're far from finished; there's still the matter of Amara to worry about. And even if Mama Anita's story is complete, the rest of mine has yet to be written.

Aditi and I plan our little heist over the next few days while we're alone in the infirmary. The night before the truce's end, we're ready to put my thieving skills to the test.

Now we're standing before Amara's chambers—me, Aditi, and an unexpected addition: Saeed. Shima sits patiently at my side, joining the group. I didn't need to call her here; it was like she knew I wanted her as a safeguard next to me, without me having to tell her. Maybe, ever since the bonding between Shima and me, we've been closer than I thought.

Saeed, on the other hand, had no clue what Aditi and I were up to.

I'd knocked on his door and told him everything—how Aditi and I concocted a plan to steal into Amara's chambers, how we're planning on looking for something Amara might be hiding. If we find something important, maybe it'll help the raja realize Amara's not the right adviser for this war. Saeed was reluctant at first, but I knew he'd agree, after what he'd seen his mother do to Aditi.

Tonight, Amara's busy with war preparations with the raja, just like Aditi said. Now that Amara's personal servant is healed, we pass the Charts with ease. Their thoughts are elsewhere. After all, tomorrow is the night the truce is ending.

"I'm still not quite sure what we're looking for," Saeed informs me and Aditi once we're inside, gazing at us curiously.

"Neither are we." Aditi offers a smile, holding up a pair of keys. I grin back at her. Stealing the keys was easy. Discovering Amara's secrets . . . *that's* the hard part.

As I gaze around Amara's chambers, I take in the crimson walls. They look as if they're bathed in blood.

I shiver as Shima curls by my feet. *I smell magic coming from that spare room*, she tells me.

"What's in there?" I ask Aditi and Saeed, pointing to the spare room Shima eyes with curiosity. No—with fear.

"Her closet," Aditi replies promptly. "She's told me no one is allowed inside . . . not even Master Saeed."

Saeed gazes down at his feet. "It's true. However, snooping inside my mother's rooms feels like a step too far. What will we even find?"

"I give Mistress Amara a rose every night," Aditi says. "Where do they go? Why do they disappear? I've had a hunch about what's in that closet. I just didn't think I'd get the chance to steal Mistress Amara's keys. If she found out . . ."

"It's just for tonight," I explain. "And I promise, she won't know a thing." My thief instincts kick in, even as I feel Shima's suspicions heighten.

I can sense the questions that riddle Saeed's tongue as we head toward Amara's spare room in the corner. Aditi sticks the keys inside until we find the right one.

The door creaks open.

Darkness, at first. Then a rickety-looking staircase reveals itself, along with a window on the bricked wall. This must be one of the palace's turrets. The stairs are littered with what look like blackened rose petals.

I gulp. "Who wants to go up first?"

To my surprise, Saeed takes a step forward. He faces me. "You were right about my mother, Rani. She's changed. She's hurt me, even if . . . even if I don't want to believe it." A pause. "If you say my mother is up to something beyond what we can see, then I believe you."

I nod, and my chest swells. My heart absorbs his words of confidence.

I let him take the first step, Aditi next, and me on the end. As Aditi and Saeed reach the top, Shima slithers in front of me, uncoiling herself until she's nearly at my waist.

"What is it, Shima?" I say, trying to sidestep her as the others disappear into a cylindrical room.

*I sense something dark*, she says.

"What is it? What do you sense?"

She shakes her head. *I am . . . unsure. But it isn't good.*

I worry my lip. "Maybe if we find something on Amara, we can show the raja."

She frowns. *Don't say I didn't warn you, Princess.*

I enter the room when Shima lets me, arriving at what looks to be the spare closet Aditi was speaking of.

This looks nothing like a closet.

It looks . . . like a shrine.

A slither of horror fills my veins, echoing the fear in Shima's bones. Raja's beard, maybe the snake was right.

I take in the room. Candlelight and black rose petals spill across the floor, forming a circle around a pile of letters. Each one is addressed to the same person—a man named Kumal.

"Those are my father's." Saeed points at a few objects in the circle. The Kaaman crest. A ring. A sword . . . and those letters.

*Kumal.* I remember Amara mentioning his name once. He passed long ago, and I can't help but wonder if this room, this *shrine*, is her way of remembering him.

"The letters are addressed to Father." Saeed turns to the pile. "I need to read them."

"But he's—"

"Dead," Saeed finishes. "I know."

I hold my breath as Saeed reaches in. I wait for something to happen, maybe a phantom wind, a strange bite of magic, but nothing happens as he reaches into the circle of candlelight and plucks a letter off the top.

He reads the letter aloud:

"'It has been years,'" Saeed begins, "'and you look no different from the day we met when you plucked a rose for me from Kaama's Conservatory Gardens.'" Saeed's voice shakes, and I plant a hand on his shoulder to steady him. Shima slithers closer, intrigued.

"'You called me ' "my sweet rose," '" he continues. " 'Years pass, and that has not changed. When I see you, it's like the moon has disappeared. When I see you, I remember why we fell in love.'"

Aditi's eyes widen. "Is this written by . . . Mistress Amara?"

I shudder a breath. "If it's addressed to her husband, Kumal, how is that possible? It looks as though it was just written."

Saeed gulps. "I . . . don't know." I can see his mind racing, a monsoon of questions swirling about. I remember him telling me about his father's death. The father he never knew.

"How does it end?"

Saeed's fingers tremble as he reads the final line. " 'When we are reunited, nothing will touch us. When we are together, the world will spin only for us.'"

"W-what does she mean, together?" Aditi's voice quivers.

Saeed takes another letter and continues reading. " 'Last night was Saeed's engagement party. I so wish you could have been there. But I fear our son is beginning to see the truth.'" He skims the letter. "'All I want is for us to be together again.'"

Saeed lets the letter float back to the ground.

"That's . . . impossible," I croak. *He's dead.*

My gaze catches on another letter in the pile. No—not a letter. It looks like a page from a book. "What's that?"

As soon as I say the words, I know Aditi's seen the page, too. She lifts it from the pile and shows it to me. It has a border that looks eerily familiar, geometric patterns lining the edges. One side looks ripped, as if torn from a book.

Hadn't I seen a page had been ripped out of *The Complete History of Magic*?

"D'you think . . . ," I begin. Aditi gulps.

I shakily read the page aloud:

The Myth of the Soul Master

Many believe that Amran, the Creator, originally intended to make a seventh Master. This, some thought, would be a Master that could control the realm of the dead. Thus came the myth of the Master of Souls, yet others refuted this theory, attesting that only Amran could control who lived and who died.

The believers of the Soul Master concluded that Amran had begun the process of creating such a being, bestowing part of his own power to control life and death into the Master. Only learned scholars of the Retanian Academy understand the secrets of the Masters and their powers.

"A Soul Master?" Saeed gapes. "I've studied history and magics for a long time—never have I heard of this."

"Me neither," I whisper. But something rings in the back of my mind. Amara's voice during the engagement party, after my kiss with Saeed.

*Praise the seven Masters.*

First Amara's strange letters to her husband, now this? Why would she keep a page on some mythical Soul Master all to herself? What does she really want?

"I'm scared, miss," Aditi says. I take her hand and squeeze gently.

"Look," Saeed says, pointing down into the middle of the shrine. "My father's sword. It's glowing."

I squint, but the blade looks dull. "Saeed, what're you talking about?"

Before he can reply, he steps into the shrine and then . . .

Vanishes.

"Master Saeed!" Aditi gasps. My breath is caught in my throat. There is only dust where Saeed once stood.

"Where did he go?" I ask, voice cracking. I blink. There one second, gone the next. It's impossible.

Or is it?

I glance down, lift my skirts, and carefully step into the shrine. Aditi tries to hold me back, as if the fire will catch onto my lehenga, but I move forward anyway, planting both feet firmly inside.

"Stay here," I tell Aditi and Shima.

The room disappears.

Muted colors surround me, like I've stepped into the scene of a painting. I'm standing in a village I don't recognize. Mountains jut in the distance from afar, and a voice calls out from beside me—

"Rani?"

I spin. There's Saeed, looking as shocked as I probably do.

"W-what's going on?" I ask him. He shakes his head and gulps. This isn't normal, that much is clear.

A man appears, likely only a few summers older than me, crouching behind an abandoned hut. He's got curly hair and hazel eyes, and wears a black-and-purple uniform.

"Is that . . . you?" I ask Saeed. But it couldn't be him . . . it could only be . . .

"No," Saeed whispers, tears filling his eyes. "That's my father."

The man turns and looks directly at us. No—he's looking in the distance. It's like we don't even exist to him.

"We're not really here," I realize. It's like we've stepped into a portal of his father's memory. Now Saeed isn't just *seeing* a vision of the past . . . he's living in one.

Saeed's father, Kumal, stands from his crouched position, his eyes widening. Shouts come from afar, but instead of running, his father stands his ground. Could this be . . . ?

*The moment his father died.*

"Run, Father!" Saeed rushes up to Kumal and tries to place his hands on his father's shoulders. But his fingers fall right through his body.

"Saeed, he can't hear you." My voice breaks.

The realization hits Saeed, and he stumbles back. His father stands tall, thumbing the Kaaman crest on his coat. As if reminding himself of his devotion to his people. To his Warriors.

And he charges. He swings his talwar with grace and ferocity, striking the attackers. But too soon, someone's sword finds Kumal's throat.

The scene changes. Splotches of the world—the *real* world—come back to me.

Candles, notes, Kumal's sword.

We're back in the shrine room.

"Masters above." Saeed looks sickly in the candlelight, like he isn't sure how any of this is real. He sinks to the ground.

"What happened?" Aditi asks, eyes wide. "Was that your magic, miss?" She's still clutching onto that page on the Soul Master, crinkled in her frail hands.

"Not my magic," I tell her. I look at Saeed. Was this *Saeed's* magic or something greater?

"Mother always told me he'd passed from an accident," he says shakily, "while on a routine mission. But he was fighting. He . . . fought bravely." His gaze flicks up to mine. "His death was never an accident. Do you think Mother saw this, too?"

"This is her closet," I say. "She must have set up this shrine. But how did she do this? She doesn't have magic."

*No*, Shima agrees from Aditi's side. *But she has power.*

Power. It always comes down to that. Is that what Amara wants—power over others? I digest everything I've seen in this strange shrine. Letters to the dead; text on a mythical Master; Saeed's father fighting to the death. Everything pieces together when I remember Amara that day in the rafters, seeing her talking to the raja about the Bloodstone.

What if she wants it for herself? She could use the stone for anything—except revive a loved one. Unless . . .

"Can I see that page again, Aditi?" I ask her. She hands me the information on the strange Soul Master, and chills sweep through me as I reread the passage.

*A Master that could control the realm of the dead.*

I shiver. "What if Amara didn't make this shrine just to remember your father?" I ask Saeed. "What if she wants to do something else?"

"Like what?"

"Find the mythical Soul Master," I say to the group. "And bring her husband back from the dead."

# 36

## Rani

The inside of the Glass Temple is painted in brilliant streaks of gold and amber. Carved glass ornaments pepper the space, blown from the first currentspinners' very breaths. Forged in the flame-talkers' fire.

I suck in a gasp as I observe the ceiling, adorned with hand-carved architecture and symbols to represent each Master, the same ones on the gate. The Temple was made during a time of peace, a time before the Masters disappeared after the Great Masters' Battle. How fitting that a descendant of the Snake Master should be the one to stop the battle to come.

*I must be that person. I must change the course of history—the shape of all that is known.*

Portraits line the walls: women and men of old, the Masters themselves, their bodies ghostly-looking in the frames. Their eyes catch on mine as we pass. Amir visibly shivers next to me despite the heat. But there's an extra, seventh portrait. It's empty.

"How long have you been living here?" Sanya asks the man

curiously. Her eyes are locked on a portrait at the end of the hall, one of the Snake Master, whose eyes are red as blood. I shiver at the intensity in his eyes, and the small quirk of his lips that suggests cunning. Despite myself, I recognize the expression—I've seen it on my face. On Ria's.

"After the Snake Master usurped power, and the Masters disappeared, there was little hope for their return. Eventually the rest of the world stopped visiting the Temple and forgot the ways of the Old Age. After magic began to disappear, many flametalkers used the Temple as a place of refuge, and we have lived here for generations."

But that's . . . hundreds of years. How has no one known? I suppose it's been a long time since anyone got past the sandtiger.

Amir gulps, glancing back at the portraits. "Are the Masters . . ."

"I'm sure you've heard the stories," the man says as we turn the corner. "The Masters' souls were banished, their heavenly bodies disappearing into the skies. . . ."

"Your tone insinuates something else," Jas infers.

The man sighs. "Their spirits are not truly gone. It is still possible to communicate with the Masters. The royals . . . they have wanted us to believe one thing, and one thing only: that they are the sole possessors of magic. They are wrong."

The man's eyes settle on mine. It is as if he can see through to the real me. The princess within. The one who's taken all her life and never given a pretty golden coin.

"If we were to come out with the truth, the royals would call it blasphemy. But signs of magic have been appearing all over Abai," the man continues, sweeping across the floor. We follow him, step by step, until we are standing before a line of carved statues.

The Masters themselves.

They look ethereal. Life-size. Even life*like*.

"Our fire powers are rare," the man says, "and certainly they cannot match those of the flametalkers of the Old Age. But the Snake Master was wrong to think he could erase all of Amran's other magics altogether. For many, they stayed . . ."

"Diminished but alive," I finish. The discovery of this magic makes me dizzy with shock.

He only nods. "I am Taran, leader of the Temple's flametalkers. It has been a long time since a group with true intentions has arrived at the Temple and passed the sandtiger's test. The others . . ."

I know what he is saying. We all do. We saw the bodies, decomposed, flies abuzz.

Taran leans down to the feet of the Fire Master's statue. "We have learned that the Masters' spirits can be called down from the heavens and enter these statues themselves."

The man's eyes flash, fire reflected inside them from the hearth just paces away.

"*This* is what we protect. The Masters' spirits. Their holiness."

It all makes sense now. We pause at the lip of the heap of ashes, perhaps offerings to their Master.

"Have *you* called upon the Masters?" I ask Taran.

"We have attempted to summon the Fire Master, but we only hear his voice in passing after offerings. But it often dissipates, like smoke. If you wish to speak to him, you will need a strong offering. The sandtiger has granted you one."

I hold out the compass talisman once more, and this time, the elder man nods, as if readying himself.

"Where are the others?" Sanya asks.

Taran leads us to a room lit with flames, which looks like a cave of sorts, an open sky cut above. Curly-haired children rush past, and the sight of them fills me with warmth. Everything here fills me with warmth: from the beautiful night sky to the hearths planted around the area. To the old women conversing the way gossiping aunties would at the palace; the boys playing games that involve throwing torn-up shoes. It's a sight that reminds me of the freeness of the people of the Foothills.

A young boy runs up to me, clasping onto my leg as another runs around in search for him. I shrug him off gently, lowering myself to eye level. His eyes are a deep brown, innocent and wide. Without realizing, I take his small, pudgy hands in mine, feeling how warm they are. The mehendi swirls in patterns of flames. The boy giggles and runs off, weaving between smoldering hearths.

Ria's voice leaps to mind. *The fever children.*

Children with buried fire magic, hidden from Father and his Charts. Taran is right—Father would consider it blasphemy. *I* did, once.

"The children connect to their magic differently," Taran offers.

I stand and face him. "They do not yet understand the deep connection within, in our blood, so they use the mehendi to visualize their magic."

My eyebrows raise, though the statement rings true. When I was young and only just connecting to my magic, calling it from my marrow was more than difficult. I would have to hold on to a serpent just to feel any ringing of magic in my bones. Now I have to compartmentalize every aspect of magic, each like a drawer in an armoire. If I want to access one subset of snakespeaking, I must reach in my mind and tug open the drawer I need, letting its magic out until I close it.

"We must speak to the Fire Master as soon as possible," Irfan says. Taran nods and calls the other warriors into the chamber. The sun has nearly set, and soon, the chamber is full.

Jas, Irfan, and Amir wait behind me while Sanya stands opposite me, watching as Taran lights the hearth. It crackles around us, and the flametalkers form a line, holding their offerings in hand.

They arrive to the hearth one by one, some children at their parents' feet, while they drop their offerings. With each offering, the hearth seems to burn brighter, ash sweeping up from the flames. The fire leaps higher, higher. A coin dropped in the rubble, a bird's feather descending into the debris. Eventually, it comes time for our offering, and the flametalkers watch us with the intensity of a hundred lit diyas.

Across from me, Sanya nods. Even Taran watches with a curious eye, and Jas rubs my shoulder as I hesitate.

The statues are like gods, watching us, warning us. The Snake Master's eyes seem to follow me.

I step into the ring of statues, finding the foot of the fire and the already melting offerings. I glance up at the Fire Master, whose marbled statue seems to teem with life, smoke from the hearth wreathing the statue's feet.

I slip the compass from my hand, the chain coiling across the compass face and falling into the flames. The fire bursts, doubling in size and licking the air as it leaps nearly to the ceiling before simmering back to the ground. Amir takes my hand, pulling me away from the hypnotizing flames, close enough to singe my lashes.

At first, all is still. Then the Fire Master's statue begins to shake, and the ground with it, making the mothers leap back, guarding their children. Taran, entranced, steps closer to the fire. I spot the talisman in the middle of the blue flames.

Swiftly, the fire quenches, as if a tide has slipped into the chamber. The smoke left behind is dark and ghostly, moving like a wisp through the air, until it takes the shape of a face. Golden eyes look down on us.

The whole chamber bows. Children falling to their knees, parents pressing their hands to the floor. I do the same, but my eyes move in awe, unable to look away.

The Fire Master.

His voice penetrates the air, thick and hoarse. *"The Glass Temple opens its doors for all who love without fear, live without lies, and learn without reluctance."*

His face is like fog, moving in and out of shape. The flametalkers watch in shock, for certainly a Master has never been called down from the heavens; or rather, from his place of banishment.

"We thank you, Master of Fire, for the magic you offer and safety you provide." Taran's voice booms through the room, and people nod their assent. But many of the children's gazes are on mine, much like the Master's, whose eyes are chilling.

*"You offered my talisman,"* the Fire Master notes. *"You have liberated me from my slumber."*

I shiver at the power rolling off his voice. "We require your help. Our kingdom is in a time of great danger," I begin. "The Hundred-Year Truce is coming to an end."

His eyes roam about the room before they settle back on mine, ember-bright and piercing. *"Did you wake me with good intentions?"*

"Yes," I breathe, looking down, unable to look the Master in the eyes. "We are desperate. We require information on the Bloodstone."

Beside me, Jas nods and clutches my hand, giving me the strength to look at the Master once more. We tread closer to the pit of smoke, watching the talisman continue to glow.

Faintly, the world around me and the Master appears to fall away, as if smoke shrouds the room. I chance a step forward, finding myself in what seems to be a formless, strange bubble for just me and the Fire Master.

The Master peers down, as if evaluating the truths within me.

"Where—"

*"I sense the Snake Master's blood within you, Princess Rani."*

"You know," I whisper.

*"Yes. You see, the seeker who will find the stone must have royal blood,"* he informs me. *"Yes . . . The Snake Master was cunning. Should the stone be lost or hidden, only someone of his descent, of his magic, could find the stone."*

My blood runs cold. I dig for my snake magic, feeling it unfurl inside me. "If you tell us the location of the stone, we can stop the raja from using it against Kaama and starting a new war."

*"And why should I believe you, snakespeaker? Lies come easily to your line."*

I shudder a deep breath. "You're right. I started this journey for selfish reasons. I lied to people I grew close to. I used them to get what I wanted. But now I'm here to stop the stone from getting into the wrong hands. I *can* do this, and I *will* save my people. I will change things for the better, like Queen Amrita. Not for myself but for the people who deserve it."

The Fire Master ponders my words. *"You remind me of the Snake Master. He had goodness inside him once."*

"What do you mean?" My eyes find the Snake Master's statue. I've never been one to speak of the so-called deception from the Snake Master. But I also know little of his life.

*"The feud between the Masters was not what people think. It wasn't all the Snake Master's fault. There was bad blood between a few of the Masters, and the stone only caused the rift to grow."*

Rift? I haven't been taught this. Is there more to the Snake Master's story that even his descendants don't understand?

*"Not to mention the stone's ill effects,"* the Fire Master continues. *"There is a reason why Queen Amrita hid it in the first place."*

Wait, what? As I open my mouth to speak, that bubble seems to pop, revealing the chamber once more. Chatter returns in waves. At my side, Jas looks on. No one seems to have noticed our private conversation.

*"And what would you use this stone for?"* the Master asks, as if the bubble hadn't existed in the first place. His face looms closer. Others cower back, but I stand firm, focusing on my mission and not the strange riddles the Fire Master uttered.

In truth, one wish wouldn't grant me anything. It wouldn't give me freedom, stop me from being princess; it wouldn't undo Ria's being given up, or the prophecy that said we would cause harm to each other. *I* wouldn't stop it, because I won't make it come true.

I won't harm Ria. I won't harm my people.

I raise my head resiliently and face the Fire Master. "We don't want the stone for ourselves. We hope to find the stone and stop the raja from using it for destruction and war."

*"A noble cause. In the wrong hands, this stone could spell destruction. Abai's king will not relent nor show mercy; his mission has been hammered into his mind for too long."*

"I will stop him," I promise. "We need only the location for me to find it."

It is difficult to decode the Master's face through the smoke now, slowly fogging up the room, but I believe he smiles.

The Fire Master begins, *"As a Master in the sky, I saw where Queen Amrita hid the stone, deep in the narrowest point of the waters between kingdoms. For a cobra does not lie in plain sight."*

"Cobra? What does that mean?" But there's something unfurling in the back of my mind, like a snake shedding its skin. I think back to seeing Ria in that mindscape, the strength of our powers fusing together. I heard a voice, one so strong and deadly it could not be human.

*"Return to my hiding place,"* I recite under my breath, *"the gift in the cobra's mouth . . ."*

The gift—of course. It must be the stone. But who has been speaking this strange riddle?

The Fire Master's shape begins to change, and the fog is pulling apart.

*"That is all I can say,"* the Fire Master finishes. *"Your truths will help you unmask the location of the stone . . . you must look to your magic."*

The last word is so low, so ingrained in my mind, I am certain only I could hear it. And then the Fire Master disappears, leaving a smoking heap of ash and charred offerings before us. The compass alone is unharmed.

At first, silence. Then the children begin to run around again in a cacophony of cheers and excited babble, and parents, attempting to be strict, pull them out of the chamber. Some stay and give their prayers before they leave.

"That's it?" Sanya says when most of the people have cleared out. "All I learned was that there's a cobra sitting in water that doesn't want to be seen."

There's that mention of water again. The deserter Chart had said Amara and the raja were discussing water while speaking of the stone. The body of water must be where this mysterious cobra sits, the stone hiding with it. That can only be one place.

"The Var River is where the two kings met, Amrit and Rahul, to make the Hundred-Year Truce. Perhaps—"

"That's where it ends," Amir finishes. His eyes find mine, burning as intensely as the fire once roared with offerings.

Sanya's voice cuts through the tension. "Where is the Var River?"

"It forms a natural border between part of Kaama and Abai, before the kingdoms' official entrance points," Taran says. "It is a hard trek. We have never visited ourselves, but our studies of the stars have taught us much." He turns to Jas now. "Follow the North Star, straight through the jungles and villages. If you are up for the task, you will find the river there. But please, stay overnight. Your journey ahead is a difficult one."

"That would be wonderful," Jas replies.

As night falls, we take our much-needed rest, filling our stomachs and our hearts. The entire time, Amir remains far from me, certainly processing our last conversation. I relive the details every moment. Will we ever be the way we once were?

It sharpens me from the inside out, knowing that might have been our last conversation, ever.

Because I will not be staying the night.

As the crew and I settle into makeshift cots down the once-abandoned halls of the Glass Temple, I keep my pack close. When they're asleep, it'll be time to put my plan into action. It will be time to leave for the Var River.

Children's chatter withers away. An hour ticks past as I wait for everyone to fall asleep. I sneak out and exit the Temple, sending off one last prayer. The sky, like blue silk stitched with stars by a palatial seamstress, spreads out before me. I take my first step, then my next. *Follow the North Star.*

"Wait."

I turn and find Amir a few paces behind me, pack slung over his shoulder. "What're you doing?"

My voice turns cold. "Leaving. Isn't it obvious?"

I turn away, but Amir is quick to take my hand and pull me back.

"You're really risking a lot here," Amir says. "Looking for the Bloodstone when the raja . . . your *father* . . . is out there."

"I don't need your concern," I tell him. I don't know what's overcome me, but that icy Princess Rani voice returns, and I hate the way it sounds on my tongue. *Forced. Unsure. Unloved.*

"Well, you're not leaving alone," Amir says.

"The Fire Master told me something secretly," I say. "Only someone with snake magic can find the stone. Which means *I* must pursue this mission myself. Please, let me go. I've hurt you, all of you, enough."

"You haven't hurt us—you helped us. And you can't do this

alone. Rani . . ." The name on his lips feels like a ray of sun on the darkest night. "Taran was talking to me over dinner. He said *thank you* wasn't enough for what you did, getting that talisman. He said you gave them hope. And you gave me hope, too. You gave me something to believe in."

At those words, figures appear from the Temple. Irfan, Jas, and Sanya wait with their things.

"Thought we'd let you go so easy? How very predictable for a thief." Sanya smirks, but I see a genuine smile beneath. I didn't know I could feel my heart crushed and then whole once more. But I feel it now. I feel it as Jas approaches, wrapping me in a hug. As Irfan nods in salute.

Friendship, trust, and love.

All I manage is a simple "Thank you," though my heart beams.

Amir squeezes my hand in his. "Let's go." Ria's friend leads the way, pointing at the North Star. My feet move of their own accord as I think of where we are headed. The Var River, our final destination, where kings made pacts and promises. In two nights, the truce will end, and I shall be back at the palace.

When I am with Ria again, nothing will be the same.

# 37

## Ria

Three knocks sound at my door the following night. But it isn't Aditi. It's Saeed, hair tousled and eyes wide, like he just woke up from a bad dream.

Or a bad vision.

"What'd you see?" I press, pulling him in and shutting my door.

Saeed shivers. "It was a different sort of vision," he begins. "I saw Mother speaking to a man. They exchanged cross words, and . . ." He gulps. "Her guard stabbed the man."

Cold seeps into my bones. "She . . . ordered this guy to be killed?"

Pain fills Saeed's gaze. "She was outside, right by Anari Square. Something about the truce ending tonight . . ."

Neither of us have spoken about what we found in Amara's chambers yesterday—strange articles that once belonged to Saeed's father, not to mention the letters. And now a vision of

Amara ordering someone's death?

She might as well be a murderer.

I barely slept last night, too aware of each hour passing, of the eerie candlelight and black rose petals. An hour earlier, I watched the raja and his Charts leaving for battle. Swords being sharpened, horses' hooves stomping the ground. How many hours are left before midnight? It's already dark outside, the sky studded with stars.

A battle will be under way soon.

"We have to find her." I hurry through Rani's things and find two cloaks. I toss one at Saeed, then swing one over my shoulders.

"She might already be gone. I'm not sure if the vision was of the present or future."

"Then we'll have to take a chance. How long will it take to get to Anari Square?" I ask him.

Saeed peers at me, like he can't quite believe what I'm saying. "Not long if we run."

I grab Saeed's hand. "Then we run."

We reach Anari Square in a quarter of an hour, thanks to my nights on the run with Amir and Saeed's fit muscles. Even still, our breaths run hot and short as we take hairpin turns through the city, through a place I never thought I'd get the chance to see.

*My* city.

Anari lights up like a star in the night. The Square is busier than I thought it would be at this time, and it takes a moment for me to realize why. The Square is filled with nobles, people with money burning through their pouches. They're grinning.

This is a final celebration before the war begins.

While the nobles, like the raja, are eagerly anticipating the war, I know the villagers are just the opposite. They're afraid of what's coming. It disgusts me seeing people *celebrating* when tonight, there will only be death.

All around us are raja-picked musicians, marking the entrance of the Square's patrons with a hundred sounds: the drum of the dhol, the beat of a tabla. The workers look like a beehive, swarming around in attempts to get their last-minute bargains in.

If Amara's here, we have to catch her.

We rush through the stalls until we're caught in the throng of people, all jostling their way past us. I keep my head shielded with my chunni, face covered by the shadows of night. Saeed hides under the hood of his cloak.

We make it all the way to the back of the square, where wooded foliage surrounds us and nobles' voices ring in the distance. Where is Amara?

I glance around and find her just outside the square, partly hidden in a copse of trees, her waving red hair giving her away.

"I see her," I say grimly, facing Saeed.

"Do you think the man was already . . ." *Stabbed,* I think, but Saeed won't admit it.

"Maybe." I can only pray we aren't too late.

We approach Amara until we're within hearing distance. She's facing away from us, speaking low . . . to someone in a red coat. A soldier, but I thought most of them were gone for the front lines. A man lies below him. I gulp. Skies be good—that must be the man from the vision. He lies wounded on the ground, his chest shuddering, and I fumble back.

A twig snaps under my foot.

Amara whirls.

"Just as I thought," she says, looking ghostly in her noble clothes, her face a picture of calm. The Chart stands a few breaths away, looking stern.

Amara strokes the petals of a rose with her fingertips. "Another trip outside the palace, I presume?"

*Another?* Right, my visit to the orphanage. "Just a late-night walk," I say with a squeaky, unconvincing tone, my gaze flying to the man on the ground.

Amara smothers a laugh. "He'll be fine, dear. Just a little injury, we'll call it."

All confidence flees my body as she saunters closer, tucking the rose behind her ear.

*Blackened roses. Letters to a dead husband.*

"My dear Saeed . . . what has the darling princess of Abai asked you for now?"

"Nothing, Mother. We were just visiting."

It startles me how easily he lies, especially in the face of his mother. But Amara doesn't take the bait.

"Have you had your tonic tonight?"

"Yes." Saeed doesn't waver.

"I think not," Amara says sharply. "My servant never made the brew. I was just out to collect more song beetle juice from my *gracious* supplier."

"You mean snake venom," I snap.

Her smile slips. "You're too smart for your own good." She glances down at the wounded man. "Apparently you ask for too much snake venom and your supplier starts blabbing."

I shudder. "You're trying to block Saeed's magic. Why?"

"I didn't want to block it, merely help him. His visions are strong. Do you know what the raja would think if he found out a boy in the palace had magic? A magic other than the only one supposedly left? People have been executed in the Pit for less."

I gulp, thinking of the Pit. Of the Vadi Orphanage, where kids were supposed to forget their magic, have it leeched from them.

"And," continues Amara, "the less Saeed saw of my plans, the better."

"Tell us what you've been doing. Tell us about the letters!" I shout. "We saw Kumal's memory in your shrine."

"You had no business being there," Amara snaps.

"Mother, we saw the moment before Father's death. He didn't die by accident. Why did you lie to me?"

Amara's face darkens. "I wanted to protect you from the truth. Do you know why I love roses so? In beauty there is always a thorn. No love is without flaw. I love you, son. I only want to help you. Help *us*."

She places her hands on those golden cuffs, which are now glowing. Behind her, the Chart's eyes look glazed.

Everything begins to click together. "Those cuffs," I say. "They're magical, aren't they?"

"Took you long enough to figure it out." Amara grips her cuffs harder, and the Chart's eyes flash with obedience. "One Twenty-Two, move the body so no one sees."

The Chart immediately drags the supplier into the forest.

I gasp. "You're . . . controlling him?"

"This isn't merely jewelry," she scoffs. "The Memory Master's talisman has served me well."

Saeed's breath hitches. *A talisman?* I think back to the scepter the Snake Master used to make the Pit. There were more talismans, Shima told me. Lost to time, buried away.

Or hidden in plain sight.

I'd seen the royal crest of Kaama—a single eye—on the letter from King Jeevan. It was the same symbol on Amara's cuffs. I'd figured out that the Kaaman crest was the symbol of the Memory Master; what I hadn't realized was that Amara's cuffs might've been the Memory Master's talisman all along.

She reveals her hands, riddled with scars, and stares at us with an intensity I have not seen in her eyes before. "Like I said, I am only doing this—*using* this magical object—to protect my son. For a mother or father should protect their children, not abuse them."

*Father.* The word pulls up a memory. I remember my second

full day at the palace, when Amara had told me about the cuffs, a gift from her father. And the night she slapped me—the whip marks on her palms.

*I know pain better than you ever will.*

"Your father," I say. The dark revelation sweeps over me like a cold tide. I point at her scarred hands. "He did that to you, didn't he?"

Saeed gapes at Amara's palms. "Mother, you told me that was from a childhood accident."

Amara grimaces. "You wonder where you got your magic from, son? It was from my father. He revered magic and despised me when he saw I was magicless. But I am not anymore. After his death when I was merely eighteen, I took the cuffs and ran. I was finally free . . . after all he'd done to me."

Saeed shivers. "What did he do?"

Amara's lips twist. "He turned me into his puppet. Controlled me with his talisman, forced me into the streets of Kaama, used me to steal and barter, and punished me when I failed." A tear escapes Amara's eye. She smooths a finger over it in remembrance. "That is not a love a father should show his children. You must see now, son, why I've done all that I have. I am *protecting* you," she repeats, her throat raw.

"You aren't protecting him," I spit, drawing my gaze away from the cuffs. "You're hurting him."

"How would you know, thief girl?" she snipes at me. All signs of tears are gone, replaced by a scowl.

"Thief?" Saeed's mouth parts gently. His brows scrunch together.

"Oh, dear boy. Haven't you noticed something different about your betrothed since Diwali? You must realize, from that night forward, she has not been the same. Because she is not who she says she is."

Saeed gazes at me with curiosity. My identity is fracturing right before his eyes.

Amara wears an oily smile. "Look at the girl you thought you knew. Look at the traitor."

Something hits him deep. In his eyes, in his heart.

"Rani?" he whispers, but the name rings false. He's uncovered the truth, like he's peeled back every layer before me and I'm bare for the first time.

My true self.

"Saeed, please," I begin, tears forming in my eyes. "I never wanted to hurt you." I turn and point at Amara. "She does."

Amara laughs. "If you didn't meddle, I wouldn't have had to expose you!" She ponders her words, tapping her chin. "Let me revoke that. If you hadn't meddled in the palace—found that book—in the first place . . . I would not have *known* the truth." She lifts a brow. "Rani was never the kind to go looking."

"What are you talking about?" Saeed's lips tremble. "Mother, tell me the truth."

"Fine. The truth is . . . your beloved has a twin sister. And she is standing right next to you."

*Raja's beard.* She knew I wasn't Rani, yes, but . . . how'd she know I was her twin?

Saeed releases a choked noise. "Twin?"

Amara looks at the sky. "Time is nearly up." She turns to the Chart, who waits at the edge of the forest. "One Twenty-Two, take them to the dungeons."

"Yes, Amara," he answers monotonously.

Within seconds the Chart is tying ropes around my and Saeed's wrists, binding us together. I'm struck by palpable fear, slithering through my veins. *Shima!* I call out, but I know she's too far away to hear me. *Rani!*

I know that won't work, either. But as tears slip down my face, Saeed's hard back behind mine, I'm more helpless than ever.

"Don't fight," Amara instructs. "One Twenty-Two, the sleep serum, please."

The Chart nods and pushes us toward a carriage waiting in the forest. We have no more than a second before the Chart throws us inside, grabs my chin, and tips my head up. He forces my mouth open and drains the briny liquid down my throat. My body grows limp, and seconds later, Saeed's body slackens behind me.

The last thing I see is Amara's face before the world becomes a blur.

# 38

## Rani

We follow the path of the North Star. We've taken shorter breaks than usual, scraps of sleep, these past two nights. Far from the jungles, the terrain spills into something like sand. Dirt hills and sand dunes appear around us. My body buzzes; something in my bones tells me we're close.

Then we see it. The waters before us look like a mirage, a sparkling dream of cascading ocean.

*The Var River.*

And beyond it, mountains looming into Kaaman territory. Far out are the Veterans in their red coats, like splotches of blood, guarding the entrance checkpoints.

I move with purpose. Closer, closer, until I'm so close to the water my reflection stares back.

I press a finger to the water, watching it ripple down the stream. The river expands endlessly on either side of us, and the desert envelops everything else.

The land where King Amrit and King Rahul made their pact, a pact that could not be broken for a hundred years.

The Fire Master told us that the stone is hidden in the narrowest part of the river. A map Jas possesses shows what must be the spot.

I am so close to the stone; I feel it in my marrow.

Amir is already knee-deep in the brook. I join him, wading carefully into the sparkling waters, hands outstretched. Jas, Sanya, and Irfan tackle the left side, while Amir and I head right. I must unlock the snake magic within me to find the stone.

I reach down for it, spring open the drawer where I've boxed it away.

It roars forth stronger than ever, flooding my senses.

A voice floats toward me, much like the voice of the Fire Master, echoing deep in my mind.

*In the cobra's mouth . . .*

Some instinct tugs at me. *There*, it seems to say. *There. It is yours for the taking.*

I get on my knees, crawling deep into the river. I plunge down, eyes burning beneath the water, but somehow, my lungs feel stronger than ever.

*There.* A ways down, something emits a glowing red light. I swim forth, using my arms to propel me closer. The light looks so close and so far at the same time, as if taunting me.

My arms burn by the time I'm near. I press a hand against the rocky edges of the river, then claw my way down, past stinging leaves wrapping around my ankles. I shove the leaves away, inching closer to the light.

It is but a pinprick when I reach it, blocked by some kind of stone wall. I shove my hands against it, but the wall will not budge.

Tutor's calm voice enters my mind, reminding me of a time when I first learned to ride a horse. Frustrated by my lack of progress, I threw down the reins and nearly caused the horse to buck.

"Show no fear, no anger, and you will get what you wish," he'd said. He demonstrated how to gently hold the reins; how to pat the horse's gleaming coat; how to feel the horse as one with me.

I rush up, gasping for breath, then duck back down into the water, both hands pressed against the stone wall.

I do not push. I think; I believe.

The same way I believe in Ria. The way I believe in Amir. The way I have seen them both believe in me.

The way I have come to believe in myself.

My magic rises up.

A voice echoes in my mind, eerily familiar. *Return to me . . .*

And then the voice disappears. A grinding sound reverberates through the water as the rock wall begins to shake. Hairline cracks form, racing through the stone. I pull back as the wall crumbles, and behind it, a shape appears, dark as obsidian: a cobra with ivory fangs. Lodged in its mouth is the ruby-red stone, pulsing like a heartbeat.

*The gift in the cobra's mouth.*

I wrap my hands around the Bloodstone, triumph singing through my veins. Below me, something flashes. I spot a shimmering crown split in two. Queen Amrita's tiara!

My magic bursts through me like water through a broken dam.

I've discovered what Queen Amrita had hidden. And it seems she hid it herself! For the first time, I feel like a true royal.

A voice seeps out of the stone, echoing in my mind.

*"Your one wish this shall fulfill, for Amran's lifeblood is its will."*

Crimson light washes over me. I pull myself out of the river, watching as the Bloodstone's light grows more powerful. I hold the stone above my head for Amir, for the others to see. But there's no one here except hulking shapes in the darkness. Animals? No—

*Charts.*

All I see is red—the sight of a summer sunset. Red—the color of Amara's lips. Red—the smell of blossoming death.

Father's army, hulking and deadly, approaches the river on horseback. I rush out of the water, finding Amir and the crew already on land. He points at the soldiers.

"We need to go. *Now*," Sanya says. She shivers in the cool night air. Irfan is already taking Jas's hand, ready to run now that we have what we need.

But this journey is about more than finding the stone. It always was.

"Stay back," I tell them. "There's something I must do."

Amir hollers for me not to go, but I'm already sprinting. When I am ten paces away, a few Charts turn their heads at the sight of me.

Whispers infiltrate their ranks. Now, instead of reverence, they stare at me with morbid fascination, though a few stick out. Young

Charts. Ones whose minds haven't been lost to my father's rule.

More Charts arrive, their boots like drumbeats as they approach. Several stallions shuffle behind them, attached to a carriage.

Father's Head Chart dismounts his steed and leaves the sea of bloody coats, approaching me. I freeze in place.

He's seen me on many occasions inside the palace. I recognize his roughly shaven beard and cutting, beady eyes. He stops suddenly, eyes widening when he notices my face. Then his gaze drops to the stone. He gapes as he stares into the red wishes within.

Before he can speak, someone leaves the carriage. I keep my chin high as the Charts part like curtains and Father steps forward. I haven't been gone from the palace long, yet he looks upon me like I am a stranger, scepter in hand, the snake head perpetually hissing.

"Daughter?" he asks, voice catching.

I erase the tremors from my voice. "Hello, Father."

# 39

## Ria

Amara wrenches open the doors leading to the dungeons, and we're thrown inside. The bowels of the palace are dank and smell like packed dirt. I catch sight of Samvir, the raja's snake, slithering before us. He looks as if he's guarding the cells with scrutinous, sharp eyes.

What is he doing here?

I make out the outline of Shima, tucked into the corner and barred in a cage. She looks sleepy. Amara must've given her a dosage of the sleeping drug, too.

Saeed and I are both unbound and pushed into adjacent cells. The whole way here Saeed and I were unconscious, until finally we reached the palace and awoke groggy.

I don't know how this night can get any worse.

The Charts and Amara retreat upstairs, and silence envelops the space between Saeed and me. He runs a hand over his face. My stomach twists at the sight of him—curly-haired, primly dressed, noble-looking despite being thrown into the back of a carriage like a common thief. Saeed is a true prince, in every sense of the word, from the honey in his eyes to the regal way he carries himself. He is nothing like me.

But he, like Rani, is also a mirror of me—a person who's loved and lost, a person searching for his way, a person who didn't understand the truth of who he came from.

"Tell me," he says. He's still dazed from the effects of the serum, but I hear the plea in his voice. "Who are you?"

My name won't leave my lips. "I'm no one."

His gaze burns into mine. I close my fingers around the shared bars between our cells and let my forehead fall against it. He takes two strides toward me and presses his warm fingers to my chin, lifting my face up. "You aren't no one. You're a princess."

"I'm a fake princess. *Rani* is your real betrothed. You love *her*."

"I thought I did," he says in the softest voice imaginable, so soft I almost don't hear him. "I told myself my love would last forever. But it did not. I told myself my heart was Rani's. That it could not belong to anyone else. But now . . ."

"Now?" I say, hating the broken sound of my voice.

He steps back infinitesimally. My lips part. *Tell him*, I think. *Tell him how you feel.* But I can't think straight. He's so close I can feel the warmth of his breath, see the heat blooming across his cheeks.

"Please indulge me, Princess," Saeed begins, "how did you and Rani come to meet?"

"I'm a thief," I reveal. "I don't know much about palace life. I only just met Rani on Diwali night. And then we decided to switch places."

A soft gasp escapes his lips. Though I won't admit it aloud, I like the incredulity written on his face, the way his lips are frozen in shock.

That look is worth more than all the rupees in Abai.

Despite what I just said, Saeed doesn't pull away. Neither of us do.

"Despite everything," Saeed says, "I never held any ill will against Rani. Her choices are her truths, just as yours are. And . . . I think I knew, deep down, that you were different. I saw it in your movements. The way you hold yourself. The moments you chose to act, how you spoke up against your father. I don't understand, but I know you, and I forgive you, as well."

"But . . . I lied to you. I pretended to be Rani when I'm not. My name . . . is Ria."

The silence is like music, and we wait for the right beat, the right chord. Then Saeed smiles at the revelation and speaks my name, my true name. "Ria." He's really seeing me for the first time. A girl born in dirt instead of jewels. But the way he speaks my name makes it sound like that's perfectly all right with him.

Steady footsteps echo in the distance, and we both shoot apart just as Amara appears.

She flicks her gaze to Saeed. "Son, don't get too close. The muck from the street thief will rub off on you."

Saeed reddens. "Mother, please. We know you want the Bloodstone."

"It's time to confess," I tell Amara with as much courage as I can muster.

Her voice is like poison. "You want a confession? Here it is. Do you think the raja would've looked for the Bloodstone if I hadn't suggested it? It was a fable to many, but I grew curious. A little over four years ago, I began taking trips to Retan, meeting with scholars who studied magic. The scholars' ancestors were saints, able to communicate with Amran and learn the properties of all magics. They recorded this knowledge in their ancient texts, which are heavily guarded. One scholar in Retan's capital taught me about the Bloodstone, a lifelong obsession of his that led him to believe he knew a key detail of its location: in water. It wasn't difficult to ask him for more information." She glances at her cuffs. "Many scholars theorized that Queen Amrita, the last known royal to have the stone, hid it. She knew its magic was dangerous. That even those who controlled it could become ill from abusing its power."

*Queen Amrita.* Mama Anita had mentioned her before. She'd died young . . . had she wasted away from using the Bloodstone? I shiver. No wonder she wanted to hide it. "Then why do you want it?"

"Its effects do not matter if one has the perfect antidote," Amara explains.

"You're delirious, Mother," Saeed says.

"Silence!" Amara snaps, her calm evaporated. "With the raja's resources, the Charts, and his maps, I knew it could only be a matter of time before he found the stone . . . and eventually, he would give it to me himself."

She plants a hand against Samvir's forehead. He nearly looks . . . relaxed. Controlled.

"You—you're controlling *Samvir*, too?" I remember the way his scales flickered between red and black that day in the rafters. A snake's scales are supposed to reflect the emotions of the person they're bound to, or in my case when I first got to the palace, close to. The red must've been a warning . . . a sign that Samvir's mind was being controlled by another.

Amara nods, like she wants me to go on.

"And . . . the raja?" I croak.

She smiles. "Do you think the raja would have obeyed me without this talisman? Helped me search for that precious Bloodstone? Appointed me his adviser?"

My body chills. "You made him this way, didn't you? Hungry for war. *You* manipulated him, the same way your father did to you!"

She looks like she might leap at me, claws and all, but she holds back. Paints on a sweet smile. "I might have started it, but the raja's hunger for power only grew from there. I merely made him realize his true potential.

"Samvir has been a great help," she continues, patting the cobra's head. "I would have more control over the raja if he were here himself, but the snake will do. Cheer up, dear impostor Rani. None of this will matter once I have the Bloodstone."

"To find the mythical Soul Master," I say. "We know all about your plan to bring your husband back from the dead. It's delusional. It's—"

Amara's growl cuts me off. "I've learned more about magic than you know. You see, when I first met the scholars, I was impatient. I needed a temporary way to see my husband again, before the stone should ever be found. They showed me how to use these cuffs to reconnect with my lost husband. The Retanian scholars taught me ways nonmagic folk could combine the cuffs' magic with a special item—in my case, roses—to reconnect to a loved one. Kumal's possessions heightened the magic. Then, I only needed to burn the petals so I could enter his memories."

"That's why you had his belongings," I realize. "You were trying to speak to him."

"Indeed. But as you now know, this magic was not strong enough. People cannot communicate through memories. Not even mindwielders," she adds bitterly. "But I have a solution. With the stone, I'll get everything I desire. *I* will have power. I will have my husband back. This will be over soon."

I squirm, yanking on the cell bars. "Over? What will be? The raja probably has the stone right now. The stone *you* want. Whatever you're planning to use it for—you won't even be able to touch it."

Amara only sneers. "Worry not, dear girl. I have greater plans."

She stalks toward the staircase, her hair rippling like flames.

"You're not telling us the whole truth," I say.

"I don't have to," she says. "My life is a story that began in tragedy, but I *will* get my happy ending."

Amara disappears up the staircase, leaving us in endless gloom.

# 40

## Rani

Once, everything I said turned to gold. Now my words are empty, hollow, and my chest feels that way, too.

"Rani." The raja frowns. "Why would you leave the palace? And what are you doing here? You must go to safety. This battle-field will soon be a dangerous place." Lust for war fills his gaze. He is ready for battle.

"I left on Diwali night," I say. I turn around and find Amir, Sanya, Jas, and Irfan watching carefully. I'm unsure if they can hear me, but even so, I can barely force the words past my lips. Spilling the secret in front of those I've betrayed feels like breaking my own bones. "R-Ria is in the palace."

Father's eyes look foggy. The name doesn't seem to mean anything to him.

"You must hear me, Father. I'm your daughter. *One* of your daughters. One of your twins!"

The raja's brows furrow. "Twins," he murmurs. For one

second—one fleeting moment—that lust falls from his face, and he looks at me with perfect clarity. He reaches out to touch my cheek. Father has never given me such a warm gesture, not since I was a child.

He wraps his hands in mine, enveloping the stone.

Then, in a cold voice, he says, "I have no twins, Rani."

"Please," I say, tears rising. How could a king—a *parent*— forget his own children? Unless . . .

I am helpless as the raja takes the stone from my hands. No, I was so wrapped up in my thoughts I practically offered it to him. He passes it to the Head Chart, who turns away, headed for the carriage.

"Wait!" I call, moving to rush after the Chart. "Father, this isn't right. Using the stone will only harm you. War will ruin our kingdom."

Father puts out one arm, stopping me in my tracks. His eyes are flinty. "This stone will save our kingdom, Rani. You speak of things you do not understand."

"It's you who doesn't understand," I say, voice breaking, desperate to convince him. The Head Chart has disappeared into the crowd of soldiers, the Bloodstone with him, and I swing around to face my father fully. "I can prove it, Father—"

"*Enough*, Rani!" he thunders.

I shrink back, despite myself.

But I promised the Master of Fire I would stop this. I promised Amir. I promised *myself.* Even if he refuses to listen to me, I have to try.

"Listen to me!" Father's eyes widen—at my audacity, no doubt—but I do not give him the chance to speak. Instead, I need him to remember me and Ria. The reason he split us up in the first place.

The prophecy.

"Do you remember looking into the Fountain of Fortunes before I was born?" I ask him. "There was a prophecy. *Sisters of the snake shall be born from Abai's royalty, twins of opposing forces, one of light and one of dark . . ."*

As I recite the prophecy, Father's brows lift.

"Twins," he mutters. He blinks again. Is it working? Could he actually be remembering?

I barrel on. "Do you remember us? You weren't always a blood-thirsty king. When I was young, you protected me. These soldiers behind you are children—they're even younger than I am! Would you have me go to war with Kaama? Just for an endless grudge?"

For once, my father seems taken aback. He spins to look at the soldiers gathered around us, his mouth opening and closing silently as he looks at the young faces. He seems almost . . . con-fused.

"Why would you let Amara convince you to lower the con-scription age? You could have said no. You have no right to let these children risk their lives."

"I—I don't understand, Rani. Why would Amara ask such a thing?"

"Because she's your adviser," I tell him. "You appointed her on Diwali night."

Father looks gaunt. "Daughter . . . I haven't appointed a new adviser in years."

Murmurs fill the air. "You haven't appointed a new adviser . . . in *years*?" I repeat. The Charts whisper. They know Amara was appointed not long ago.

"You don't remember," I realize at Father's blank face. Which means Amara's up to something. Something I never foresaw.

I take a step closer to him, wrapping my hands in his. Our gazes connect. I feel my magic twining with his, the power singing in our blood.

As snakespeakers we have a special bond, can feel each other's magic. But it's like his is being blocked by something. I sense it inside him, like a cloud, misty and faraway.

I might not have Ria's thieving instincts, but I can tell when something is amiss.

"I need to leave. Amara did something to you, and I must stop her. Do you understand, Father?"

". . . Yes," Father says slowly. "I—I do." Clarity marks his voice. He might not remember *everything*, but he's remembering life with me. Perhaps that is the first step.

I grip his shoulders. "Let me prove it to you. I'll find Amara, figure out what she's doing. But what of the Kaamans? Aren't they coming?"

Father expels a breath. I hold mine.

He surveys me, then drops his shoulders and gestures for the Head Chart to come forward. The Chart now holds the

Bloodstone in both palms, cradling the ruby jewel. It looks off, duller than I remember.

"Perhaps I should take the princess back to the palace, with your permission, Your Highness," the Head Chart says. "That way you can speak to the Kaamans at their arrival."

Father nods. "Thank you, Two Thirteen. But hurry," he says, placing the Bloodstone onto his scepter, like a crown on the snake's head. "If what you say is true, Rani, you must find Amara. Now."

The palace halls are an oddly welcome sight after the dirt roads of Abai's villages. The carriage ride here was no easy feat, and I convinced the Head Chart to bring the crew with me. The whole way I felt Sanya's ice-cold stares, Amir's discomfort, and Jas's keen eyes. Even Irfan eyed me like I was a puzzle to piece together. The story had poured out of me: who I truly am, the switch on Diwali night. I could practically hear the name swirling inside Sanya's mind: *Snake Princess. Liar.* Jas was there to calm her, as if she'd known, deep down, that I was different than I claimed.

"I'm sorry I lied to you. All of you," I told them. Sanya looked away, but Amir's gaze rested on mine. He hadn't seen the real me, Princess Rani, until this night, when I spoke to Father. I wouldn't blame him if he feared me like he fears the raja.

Now, standing in the entrance corridor, I feel oddly at home again in the palace walls. It is like seeing the world through fog, at once blurred and entirely familiar. No matter how I'm dressed, I stand confidently. Proudly. "We need to find Ria."

I harness my snake magic and clear the cobwebs from my mind. Shima lingers in the recesses of my brain. Usually her voice latches on, echoing into my eardrums, but right now I only feel a faint buzzing. *Shima*, I call out with all my might, *where are you? Where is Ria?*

Something crackles in my mind, and then her voice takes shape. *The dun . . . geons . . .*

"The dungeons?" I repeat, just as I turn to find servants gawking at me. They seem utterly befuddled by my looks. Of course. I am dressed in rags.

"By order of the princess," I tell them, "please take these denizens of Abai to the infirmary. They have business to attend to." I make my voice clear, yet soft. No longer the Snake Princess they once believed me to be.

"Infirmary?" Sanya retorts. "I'm not following a princess's orders."

"There's no time for fighting," Amir says, as if sensing my urgency. "Do you . . . sense something?"

"It's Ria," I say. "I think she's in the dungeons."

"Is she in danger?" Amir asks, voice laced with concern.

"I'm not sure." I look at Irfan, then Sanya, Jas. I can't put them in harm's way, either.

Amir steps up. "I'll come with you."

I smile. "Jas, Sanya, please ready the infirmary. They may be hurt."

Jas nods, resolute. "We will see you there, Princess Rani."

"And Irfan," I add, "you know the palace well. Perhaps with the help of a servant, you could find Amara."

"Of course," Irfan says.

Jas and Irfan take their leave, but Sanya remains rooted to the spot. For a moment, I'm afraid she won't listen. That she'll run off, escape, all because of me.

As I turn away, Sanya calls, "Wait."

I look back at Sanya, her fists clenched like she is steeling herself.

"Was it all an act, helping us villagers? Something to make you feel better about yourself until you got what you wanted?"

I think of how I began my mission. Amir, just a means to an end but no longer. I couldn't have imagined the place he'd hold in my heart. The place Jas held, Irfan, even Sanya.

*No more lies.*

"It began that way, yes. I lied to get what I wanted. I was selfish. I wanted to prove to my father that I was capable of ruling this land—but I wanted to help Samar, too. He was my tutor, and I needed to fulfill his dying wish."

I wring my hands. "And now . . . now you truly are my friends. My people. I don't expect your forgiveness, but I do need your help."

Sanya takes a measured step forward, gulping. "You know, you changed my brother for the better. You might be the Snake Princess, but I . . . ." The mask of hate she wore in the carriage begins to melt, replaced by an honest look. "I trust you."

Amir smiles.

She leaves, and I grab onto Amir's hand, pulling him through the maze of halls. I've been to the dungeons only once with Father as a child, but the bleak walls and weeping prisoners were enough to frighten me for months.

The door to the dungeons is sealed. "Locked," I tell him.

"I could try to pick it," Amir suggests, but I shake my head. This is a special bolt. Only Father and those he permits can enter with the proper key.

"There's gotta be another way." Amir's brows frown in thought. "Like the back end of an alley. People think alleys are dead ends but not always. You just have to get creative."

"A back end?" I wonder. Of course. There is always another way in—for *servants*.

"You're a genius!" I tell Amir. "There *is* a back end. Servants use their designated staircases to bring down food for the prisoners. Come on."

Within minutes, we find the servant staircase and rush down the narrow steps. The deeper we go, the murkier and darker it gets, until we reach the final level, the lowest of the palace.

The dungeons reek of filth and grime. I dash ahead, finding Shima in the dark through our connection, and cradle the bars before her. Her head is tilted down.

"Shima, what's happened?" I reach through the bars to feel the cool, supple skin of my snake familiar. Once my only companion, she looks tired now, her eyes barely holding recognition when she sees me. "Shima, wake up."

The snake begins to lift her head, but before she can speak, Amir's voice echoes through the dungeons.

"R-Ria?"

I spin to find Amir before the cell bars, and there—there is my sister, rising up from her crouched position. Relief fills me with warmth as soon as I see her.

"You're here. You both are," she says.

I rush over to her, taking her hands between the bars.

"Saeed," I greet, noticing him in the cell next to Ria's.

"So you really are twins," he says, eyes widening at the sight of us. His lips part as he gazes at Ria. How much has she told him about our little charade?

"It's true," I say. "Ria, thank Amran you're safe. Who did this to you?"

I know the answer before it escapes her mouth. "Amara. Sleep serum," she spits. But her eyes lighten when she finds Amir, and they hug as much as they can with the bars between them.

"I'm sorry, Amir. I'm sorry I left you. We were gonna leave, go far away from this mess." Tears glisten in the corners of her eyes.

"It's okay. To be honest, sneaking out of the country started to seem a little boring." Amir gives her a grin.

She lets out a surprised laugh and regards Amir, his torn clothing. "Where have you been? Did you find the stone?"

"The raja has it," I confess. "But the real matter here is Amara. She—"

"Has been controlling the raja," Saeed fills in, startling me. He stands a little taller, looking at Ria resolutely. They tell us everything: Of the cuffs Amara wears and the powers they wield. Of Saeed's visions, his memory magic. Of Amara's plot to keep Saeed from discovering her plan.

"The cuffs, they're the Memory Master's talisman," Ria says, voice grim. "She's had them this whole time. She could manipulate any one of us."

"I cannot believe this. Saeed saw Amara . . . but what is she planning?" I fret.

"She wanted the stone. We think we know why," Ria says. "We discovered these strange letters—"

"Letters?" I interrupt.

Saeed nods. "We found them in her chambers. They were recently written . . . to my father."

Amir crosses his arms. "I don't understand. What does this have to do with the stone?"

Saeed shudders in a deep breath. "My father . . . he's dead. But she kept writing letters to him. It was like she was pretending he was still alive," Saeed continues. "Like she wanted to bring him back from the dead."

My heart thuds. My mind whirls. "That's impossible. Even the Bloodstone cannot bring back people from the dead."

"Exactly," Ria says. "But we found something else in her chambers. A page from a book about magic. It spoke of a mythical seventh Master. The Master of—"

"Souls?" I finish. That was a story Amara told me when I was just five summers old. A scary tale to get me to go to bed, she'd likely thought, though I'd found it humorous, about as real as a ten-foot monkey.

"I don't get it," Amir says.

"I know what Amara's up to. She's going to use the stone to find this Master, bring them to life somehow. Then . . ." She inhales. "She'll get the Master to reap her husband."

I shiver. Just the idea of bringing to life a seventh, fabled Master is preposterous. But only someone like Amara would go through with it.

"We must find her," I say.

Ria shakes her head. "There's no way out of this cell. There must be magical barriers."

I nod, glancing at Amir's fear-flecked face. He's probably thinking about all the snakes in this place, or worse, the way I can control them.

"Father sealed this place with snake magic," I say. "If anyone tried to escape, they would be magically taken into the Snake Pit and eaten alive, with no public execution."

Amir gulps. "Dead without a spectacle."

I look away from him.

Ria's brows arch. "But *we* have snake magic, too."

"Father's magic is strong. I cannot counteract it. But if we called the Pit to *us* . . ."

Ria stills. "Is that even possible?"

I envision the layout of the palace. "The Snake Pit doesn't nec-
essarily take up space; it's a magical dwelling for the snakes that
exists out of the confines of space and time. But Father has always
said that prisoners are beneath the snakes. What if he meant they
were *literally* beneath them?"

Ria gapes. "As in . . . we're *beneath* the Pit?"

I nod, quickly reaching through the cell bars and taking her
hands in mine. "We can break out of here together, with Shima's
help. Use her to connect to the snakes in the Pit."

"I—I can't control all those snakes." She shivers, probably
thinking of her caretaker, the one who perished in the Pit's depths.

"Think of the prophecy," I say. "Your magic is strong. You've
learned much of it in these past weeks. Right?"

Ria bites her lips but nods.

"Call upon your magic. Command the snakes to guide us into
the Pit," I tell her. I think of Tutor, of magic and harmony and
peace. I close my eyes and call up the magic hiding in my bones,
willing it to be unleashed. For the magic to swell up, fill the chasm
between us, ready to burst.

Nothing.

My arms grow heavy like lead. Only silence remains—dark,
vast silence.

Why isn't this working?

*Be brave, Rani.* Tutor was brave. Jas was brave. Amir was brave.
Why can't I be, too?

Ria glances at the prison cage bars. I imagine all her fears mingled with mine: never escaping, our friends dead at Amara's command.

"Snake magic can't overpower Amara's cuffs," Ria says, and the admittance makes me step back. Reassess. Remember what our magic can do, combined, powerful.

"We need to think not of our magic but of the people who guided us here. Isn't that what this is all about? Creating our own destinies but remembering the paths others have taken before us?"

Ria blinks. She takes my hands, letting her eyes close. I do the same.

I think of all the people who guided me here. Tutor, Samar. Jas. Sanya. Irfan. Amir.

When I peek my eyes open, our hands are like candles cupping a flame, a warm glow emitting from them.

I say the names aloud this time, and Ria adds on. "Aditi," she says. "Saeed."

"My parents," I croak.

I feel Shima inside my mind, stirring to life, the magic between us reignited.

The dungeons begin to shake.

Everything in the room trembles. I stumble back on the quaking floor, before tightening my grip on Ria's hands and standing up firmly. Then a blinding flash of white, bright as diamonds.

When I open my eyes, Ria, Amir, and Saeed are next to me, sitting on the floor of the Pit. The walls are black as obsidian, lined with serpents and flaked with blood.

"It worked," Amir says. "Now . . ." He turns to Ria, who looks sickly.

"I think I'm gonna vomit at this smell."

*Sensitive much*, Shima mutters.

"You're awake!" I say.

*Somewhat*, Shima says, struggling to lift up her body. *You must command the snakes, Princess Ria and Princess Rani. They answer to power and authority alone.*

A flicker of a shadow. And then a voice that does not belong to Shima.

*Return to me . . .*

Ria turns, face blanching. "Did you—"

Before I can answer, the Snake Pit bursts open.

The entire group soars up, balancing on a puzzle of interlocking snakes. They twist and slither around us, bodies pushing us relentlessly upward. I take Ria's hand.

We land in the throne room, and the snakes part like gauzy curtains. We all leap onto the marble floor before the snakes recede back into the Pit, and the hole stitches itself shut.

"Thank you," I tell Shima. "I've missed you."

*And I have missed you.*

"We need to find Amara," Ria says. "Saeed, can you go with Amir and look for her in the east end of the palace? Rani and I will search the west."

"Of course." Saeed leads Amir out of the throne room. If anyone can talk Amara down, it'll be Saeed, and Amir is as quick and silent as a viper. Still, I feel a flicker of worry for them.

*Over there.* Shima's sharp eyes are on the courtyards. Ria and I rush outside with Shima and search the grounds, Ria taking the left side and me the right. My eyes land on a figure in the shadows, unmoving.

I take a step forward. Two. "Who's there?"

There's something in the grass. My chest tightens when I see it—*him*. The Head Chart's red coat comes into view. His face is stone.

Dead.

Someone turns and steps into the light, and I catch their eyes widening.

"You startled me, Princess," Amara says. Next to her hovers Father's snake familiar, Samvir, his scales flickering from red to black. She pastes a tight smile onto her face. "I was just on my way to—"

"What did you *do*?" I snarl.

"Only what I needed to."

My gaze falls to Amara's free hand. "No," I say, pointing. "Impossible—"

But it is here, illuminating her features, her red lips, her red hair. Her pupils reflect two rubies in pockets of darkness.

The Bloodstone.

# 41

## Ria

Voices sound from the other end of the Western Courtyard.

I turn, finding Rani and Shima. My sister is standing across from a woman with flaming red hair. My breath hitches. *Amara.*

"Rani!" I cry, rushing over. I reach Rani's side and Amara's eyes widen at the sight of us.

Shock, then a scowl, crosses Amara's face. "You're *both* here," she snarls. "I should've known you'd find your way back, Rani." She swivels her gaze to my sister. She breathes heavily, clutching something fiercely in her hands.

"The Bloodstone?" I whisper, glancing at Rani. An ache forms in the back of my skull.

"That cannot be," Rani says. "My father has the stone. *I* found it."

"I suppose I should thank you. I should have known a snake-speaker would be the one to find it. Doesn't it look marvelous?" Amara twirls the stone in her fingers.

"I *saw* the Bloodstone," Rani interrupts, looking horrified. "I saw the stone for myself, *touched* it—"

"Yes, you did," the woman sneers, placing a hand on Samvir's head. "*This* stone. I had the raja's Head Chart swap it with a fake and bring me the real one. It was simple to get a soldier up my sleeve who'd do my biddings for me. I didn't even have to control him, especially when I offered that he could have any wish he'd like." She moves to the side, revealing a body on the grass behind her. I gasp.

"You gave him empty promises and then killed him," Rani says, voice shaking.

"Well, I couldn't have him interfering," she purrs. Her cuffs shine like the Abai sun. "Many moons ago, in Anari Square, I got a ruby cut for myself, based on the ruby in Queen Amrita's portrait. It was the perfect replacement."

She holds the stone up, marveling in its beauty.

Shima hisses at the woman, spitting anger. *Snakes do not obey you, Amara.*

Even though Amara can't hear her, she gets the message. "It seems your *pet* needs a lesson."

"She's not a pet!" I snap, turning to Rani, who nods her head in agreement. But Amara flings out a hand, ready to use her cuffs on Shima. The snake dodges her and leaps into the air, fangs out, ready to attack. Just a second away from Amara, Shima strikes before she hits an invisible wall. She falls to the grass in a heap, motionless.

"SHIMA!" I cry, buckling to my knees. I reach out and touch the snake. "Shima, no! Please be okay." I feel her pain, as sharp as a fresh burn, but it simmers into anger.

*I . . . will be fine,* Shima says. She lifts her head. *You must face her, Princesses. You are more powerful than you realize.*

I look up at Amara, anger causing my words to waver. "What did you do?"

"The Bloodstone is more than a wish-granter, you see," Amara says with a sly smile. "Anyone who holds the stone is protected from attacks, a safeguard, if you will. You cannot hurt me. The foolish Head Chart tried to take the stone back and look what happened to him."

I fist my hands. "We might not be able to hurt you, but we know what you want," I snap. "Looking for the fabled Soul Master would destroy the balance of magic."

Amara chuckles. "Yes, I desire to bring my husband back, but you've come to the wrong conclusion. There is something else. What I am doing is much greater."

Rani shakes her head. "What else, Amara? War? Whatever your game, whatever your reasons, this is wrong. You used your magical cuffs to control our father. To make him the way he is. You *wanted* this war with Kaama."

She tuts. "Kaama's always been to blame. Yes, the raja was taught how to be a fierce and ruthless ruler from a young age, but I had to push his war hunger even further. *I* had to forge letters between the kings. I sent mail to the Kaaman royalty, writing as King Natesh. I had to give the raja a fake threat from King Jeevan to make it seem as though the Kaamans were ready. *I* had to spur on the war."

I reach back into my memory. The night of the engagement party—the letter from King Jeevan. The penmanship was so familiar. Only now do I realize why. It's the same handwriting on the war plans in the raja's office. *Amara's.* She must've used her control over the mail chariots to her advantage.

My mind races. Why would Amara do this? I think of Amara's husband—Saeed's father, Kumal. The great Kaaman Warrior. He died on a mission for his country.

"You can't blame an entire nation for his death," I cut in.

Amara reels as though I've struck her. "He was on a routine mission to weed out Abaian spies when he was *abandoned,* left for dead. He was promised security, but those Warriors didn't protect him." She shakes her head. "His own country didn't care to keep him safe. Why should I ever trust them again?" All the pain and grief she has suffered plays there on her face, so clear I feel as if I can read her whole story.

The father who used his power to manipulate and abuse her.

The husband who loved and protected her.

The man who risked his life for his country.

"Kumal's own family wouldn't take me in," Amara says now. "No one cared. You're telling me about blame?" She stares straight at me, clucking her tongue. "Don't you blame your parents for giving you up? Don't you blame your kingdom for what it's done to people like you? *Ria.*"

The air is thick with silence. My stomach quivers. "How'd you know my name?"

Amara purses her lips. "Haven't you wondered why your parents never acknowledged you? It's because you're not in their memories anymore, thief girl. It is because of *me*."

"*You* made our parents forget about us?"

"Well, it wasn't my idea," Amara drawls. "Your parents knew you had to be apart because of the prophecy, but they knew their resolve would never hold if they were to remember their other child, lost to the world. So they asked me—no, begged me—to perform a complex charm . . ." Amara glances at her cuffs. "In exchange, they would betroth my son to their remaining child. They asked that I erase the memory of the other twin from my mind, as well. But I thought I'd keep that memory alive, just in case. It seems I made the right choice."

I leap at Amara, screaming obscenities. Rani holds me back while Amara laughs. No wonder the raja allowed Mama Anita to be killed in the Pit. He didn't even remember her.

"You see, I was taught early on that none of us are born worth anything," she says. "We must seize influence and power. And that—that has been my game all along."

I think of everything Amara did. Erasing the memory of me from my parents' minds. Using the cuffs to manipulate the raja.

This whole time, I'd thought the raja and queen had pretended to forget about me. That I'd been beneath their attention, as if I'd never existed in the first place. My history, all of it, gone.

Fury ripples through me.

Amara's eyes are bloodshot. "I have something greater than just Kaama's destruction in mind. Greater than bringing back my husband. When he's alive once more, no one will harm him ever again."

"But you said yourself that Queen Amrita grew ill from using the stone!" I tell Amara.

"Of course. But as I mentioned in the dungeons, there is an antidote: The lifeblood of Amran, kept inside this very stone. Once I extract a droplet of his lifeblood and pour it into my veins, I will be immune to any ill effects."

"No," Rani whispers.

Amara's grin is feral. "Once I am protected with the antidote, I can finally make my wish without repercussions. You see, the Retanian scholars revealed to me a forbidden truth. I can wish to be more than mortal. Do you think I will merely call upon the Master I desire? No. I will make the greatest wish of all. I will become the Master of Souls."

# 42

## Rani

Amara's words echo in the warm air.

I'm frozen in shock. My bones turn to ice.

No one has ever become a Master. The thought is blasphemy.

"No one will be able to control me," Amara says. "I will become the Master of Souls, someone who can reap the dead. I shall bring back Kumal, and then *no one* can harm my family. I'll be indestructible."

I shiver. "You cannot cross the boundaries of life and death. The Master of Souls—that's just a myth!"

"Any myth can become reality with the help of the Bloodstone." Amara thrusts her arm out, directing the stone at us. We're thrown back from its power, its sheer strength. I land on the threshold of the throne room, my body on fire. It feels like a flame licking up my arms, and I grit my teeth against the pain.

"Rani . . . ?" Ria ekes out. She lies on one side of me, Shima on the other.

"We . . . have to stop her." I groan.

"It's impossible," Ria says. "She can't be stopped."

Despair creeps over me. It's true. With the Bloodstone, Amara is all-powerful. She's untouchable, unstoppable. We can't give up, but what else is left to us?

I look up, to where Amara, standing in the distance, starts closing in. *Ten feet away. Nine.* Her cuffs glow, and Samvir patiently slithers at her side.

I glance backward, into the throne room, looking for anything that can help, and my eyes land on where the Pit remains sealed. An idea flickers to mind. We opened the Pit once, from the dungeons. Why not again?

"We cannot attack her, but perhaps we can trick her." I whisper my plan to Ria and glance at Amara. Six feet away now.

"We can't let the snakes harm her," Ria says. "We just need them close enough so that they startle her. She'll have no way out."

I agree. My resolve unfurls like a flower, rising to the sun, claiming its own light.

We help each other rise and step back toward the sealed Pit.

"What're you two doing?" Amara says as she reaches the threshold of the throne room. She halts, her gaze dropping to the throne room floor.

"On three," I tell Ria. I take Ria's hand into mine, squeezing it hard as she stares at me quizzically, recalling every emotion I've felt with her. The fear and terror, love and warmth.

"One . . . two . . . ," Ria says quietly to me, barely a whisper.

I focus on the Pit, on the snakes beneath the ground, on the magic in my veins—magic I share with my twin sister. There are so many snakes—the magic boils inside me, twisting and writhing and threatening to erupt.

I yell, "Three!"

We release each other's hands and face our palms toward the ground. The Pit rips open from our combined magic, and the snakes rise, their voices echoing and thundering through my bones. The snakes move higher, higher, until they create a veil, a wall of green taller than Ria or me.

I let out an audible gasp at the power I feel thrumming through my veins, feeding between Ria, the Pit, and myself, creating a surge as strong as a tidesweeper's endless storms.

"We invoke the name of the Snake Master. We summon the snakes of the Pit," I say, my hands beginning to shake. Ria echoes me. "Help us. Defend us."

A chorus of hisses. Snakes of all colors and sizes slither with the direction of our hands, and we step forward, bringing them closer to Amara as they split off and begin to surround us all.

"Stop this!" Amara spits, but she cowers back at the sea of serpents. I tug Ria forward, beginning to circle Amara, until her back is facing the Pit. The snakes move onward with our command, hissing so loudly the sound is overwhelming.

*Sssstop*, they say, directing their words at Amara.

Their bloodlust floods me, tin and copper that feeds into my own rage. My thoughts join with theirs until I am a part of the mass around us, an endless loop of strength. I never expected this power, and I feel my and Ria's control slipping, the hunger overtaking everything.

Amara flinches from the snakes around her and falls back. The snakes are breaths away from her now. She clutches the stone tighter.

Snakes leap out and attack Amara's invisible wall. Some vipers hiss as they are thrust back, but other rise up to replace them, continuing the onslaught. Snakes thrash toward her and coil onto the ground, shrieking with fury.

We step toward Amara, nearly close enough to reach out and touch her.

"Amara!" Ria speaks up beside me, her voice strained. "Give us the stone!"

At her side, Samvir looks as if he is awakening from a slumber, and he joins the snakes, a cobra among vipers.

"Stay back! You can't have it." She gestures again with the Bloodstone, flinging a hand out, and the snakes billow away from her as though hit by a massive blow. But they do not break.

Amara steps back again, eyes shining with greed. My gaze falls. She doesn't know what's behind her.

The Pit.

*Crack.* My eyes widen with fright just as the floor begins to crumble beneath her. The Pit . . . it's breaking.

"Rani . . ." Ria's eyes widen. The whole ground shakes. We might have been controlling the snakes in the Pit, but the Pit itself is alive.

*It's been promised a new offering.*

Our control over the Pit snaps, breaking entirely.

Amara's arms shoot out as she struggles to regain balance. Her cries are muffled as she loses her footing. Everything slows: time, the world around us, my very breaths. The snakes below are writhing like worms. With hunger, thirst, promised wishes.

My breaths stop entirely.

I've promised them something without realizing. A new kill.

They want Amara.

I move to grab her, but I am too late. She clutches the stone to her chest as the Pit yawns open and catches Amara in its teeth.

# 43

## Ria

Death has a certain smell. Rotting bones and acrid blood, half-eaten bodies and choked-out last words. I smelled it on the streets of Abai, on hopeless nights in alleyways. I smelled it in the palace, a reminder of all the loss that's taken place here.

I can smell it now.

"Amara!" I rush to the edge of the Pit. I peer inside, Rani next to me, watching the Pit's infested insides. The snakes squirm and twist, but there's no sign of Amara. Now that the rush of power has left me, I feel almost dizzy.

"W-where is she?" Rani says.

I smell blood in the Pit and reel back, covering my mouth. "You don't think she's . . ."

Rani can't say the word. Neither can I.

I lean in. There's no sign of a body. The snakes continue to squirm, searching for their meal. How could Amara just disappear without a trace?

My voice quivers. "Can you see her?"

Rani shakes her head, her breaths running short. "No," she whispers, tears filling her eyes. "This isn't how people die in the Pit. I know. I've seen it with my own eyes."

The snakes' voices fill my mind, speaking as one.

*She is gone. She is gone.*

"What do you mean, gone?" I ask.

*She disappeared before she could reach the bottom. We have never seen such a phenomenon in the Pit,* a snake says.

"And the stone?" Rani shrills.

*Gone. Gone. Gone.*

Shima slithers out from the Pit, shaking her head, and I feel her confusion inside me. She glides onto my arm. I step back and hear the hole closing, stitch by stitch, until it's gone.

Fear pulses through my veins. *What happened to her?*

Footsteps approach the throne room doors. I tense up just as they burst open, and two figures appear before us.

Saeed. Amir. They look out of breath, Amir's cheeks red, Saeed's eyes wide.

"We found the queen and a servant tied up in an upper chamber," Saeed says. "It looked to be my . . . mother's work." His voice is strained.

"Aditi?" I squeak out. Saeed nods.

"They're safe now, both in the infirmary," Amir says, eyes locking on Rani's. "Where's Amara?"

"It's . . . a long story." I look at Rani.

"You might wanna hurry." Amir's eyes flicker to mine. "The raja's back."

The king stands before Rani and me, wearing a look of surprise.

"So this is true." He offers a prayer. "You're my . . . twins?"

Rani, the raja, and I are standing in a hall lined with portraits of past rulers. Rani called this place the Hall of Eyes. I can see why.

"My name is Ria," I reveal, voice shaking. "I've been here, at the palace, since Diwali night. You just didn't know it."

"How can this be?" the king wonders.

"Amara took your memories of us away because you asked her to," Rani explains. "I know this is confusing, but perhaps we should start at the beginning. Diwali night . . ."

The raja wears the same look of bitter shock Saeed had when we told him and Amir the truth of Amara's disappearance. Saeed didn't take it very well, but Rani promised him we'd find out the truth. Now he and Amir are on the way to someone named Jas in the infirmary. Rani asked them to relay a message—something about needing a draft of medicine.

We tell the raja about the moment we switched places. His expression doesn't change as we discuss Amara's confession of controlling the king with her cuffs; how she swapped the stone for a fake with the help of the traitorous—and now dead—Head Chart; our battle to get it back before she fell into the Pit.

He grinds his teeth when he hears the news. "And where is she now?"

"She's gone," Rani says. "I'm sorry, Father, but she disappeared."

*Or escaped*, Shima reminds me from her resting place by my feet. She's exhausted, all the snakes are, and I feel it in my bones.

"And my Head Chart? Was she controlling him, too?"

"Amara said she didn't have to control him to get the help she wanted," I say with a gulp. "At least not fully. We found him dead in the courtyard."

The raja—my *father*—takes a tentative step toward us. Rani and I move our arms together so our snake birthmark comes together. He stops short as the truth illuminates his features.

"For years," the raja reveals, "it was as though there was another voice in my mind. A bloodlust for battle that would not relent."

Rani bites her lip. "It was Amara's. She's been controlling you for longer than we knew. Using you to help her get the stone, with the Charts' assistance, and destroy Kaama in the process." Rani steps toward her father, placing a hand on his shoulder. "When you were at the river, it seemed like her hold on you began to break. Perhaps she could only fully control you when you were near."

The raja links his hands together. "While she is certainly to blame, my bloodlust was not entirely a result of mind control. You see . . . there were people before us, rajas and ranis, who believed King Amrit's bloodthirst was warranted. They *wanted* war at the end of these hundred years. As did I.

"It turned out that Kaama's king had been receiving letters from me—letters I had never written. I wonder if Amara had planted them, using the couriers, to spur on the war to come."

His face is solemn. "Once we realized how we'd been tricked, we agreed a battle was not the answer. Not tonight."

"But the pact said that blood must be spilled after a hundred years," Rani says. "Or a curse would befall our bloodline."

"Blood has been spilled," the raja says. He offers his left palm, where a jagged cut crosses his skin. "King Jeevan and I both offered our blood to the battlefield. But I think . . . it may be time to leave the past where it belongs. We have all been manipulated, by past hatred and by those who would exploit it for their own benefit."

"You mean you sacrificed your own blood, instead of spilling blood from battle? That's . . . brilliant," Rani says.

"So what will happen?" I ask eagerly. "Will you agree on a new truce with the king of Kaama?"

The raja considers me for a moment, something softening in his features, before giving a decisive nod.

"It won't be easy—there is much to be resolved, and much hate between us. Kaama and Abai have a lot to discuss."

Rani nods resolutely, her eyes shining. "But it's worth it."

"Yes," the raja concedes. "Your mother—she should know these developments. Where—?"

"Oh! She's in the infirmary."

We move hastily to the royals' infirmary wing. The king, Shima, and my sister hurry inside, immediately drifting to the queen, who lies on a cot. Somehow she looks pristine despite what's happened. I try to move past the curtain, but something roots me to the spot.

*Meet your mother,* a voice tells me.

*She wouldn't believe a peasant like you is her daughter*, another says. So I watch from the curtain's parting, nervously peering inside.

"Mother," Rani says, anguish marking her face. She lifts the queen's wrists, both rope-burned. "I can't believe Amara did this to you."

"Rani, what is going on? Natesh, why are you back so soon from the—"

"I'm sorry, Maneet, but it must wait for later." He looks back at me, then Rani's gaze follows.

"Mother . . . there's someone we want you to meet."

Rani draws the curtain aside, her body blocking me from view of the queen. "Are you ready?" she whispers.

I shake my head.

"You need to do this," she says. "No more fear."

I shiver but nod. Rani returns to the room. I shuffle out from my hiding spot, and the queen gasps. "How—"

"Before you ask, it's not a trick, Mother," Rani says. "Amara erased your memories of it with her cuffs, but you gave Ria up when we were just babies because of an old prophecy."

The queen gulps. "I would remember my children. I would remember—"

She stops and looks at me, the real me, for the first time. Meekly, I step closer. I swear I see something flash in her eyes. Recognition?

"Natesh, what is the meaning of this? *Twins?*"

I think of how the raja arrived back at the palace and found me and Rani. He saw me. He saw his daughter.

"I know we've all done things we're not proud of," I begin. "I stole to survive. I lived on the streets until I found my twin. Then I pretended to be Princess Rani." I pause. "You both gave me up to a midwife," I say, and Rani raises her brows. She doesn't know this part of the story yet. "There was a prophecy that I'd grow too strong, destroy the kingdom with my powers. The strength of my magic might've been true, but the outcome wasn't."

"We were both locked into lives we never wanted," Rani continues solemnly. "This was our opportunity for escape. Father, we've all been separated for too long. Now . . ." She squares her shoulders. "We have magic, both of us. If we work together to return your memories . . ."

The king shakes his head. "Snake magic, despite being deeply tied to memory magic, has never returned anyone's memories."

"But maybe it can," I supply. Everyone's eyes swivel to mine. "Amara took your memories away with her cuffs. But what if they weren't fully erased? What if they were . . . locked away?"

"In their minds?" Rani wonders.

"No. Inside *us*." I take Rani's hand, reminding her of the times we combined our magic to access our memories. Once, during the engagement party, we even saw our *parents'* memories. The moment they looked in the fountain and heard the prophecy. The moment they decided to give me up for my own good.

"You mean Amara's magical cuffs didn't erase memories like she thought. She merely extracted the memories and kept them in another place without realizing!" Rani cries. "We just need to find a way to take the memories out of us and give them back to our parents."

I pace along the floor, thinking. "Shima, do you think you could help?"

*As the raja said, snake magic does not return memories. But . . . my snake venom might.*

"Snake venom?" Rani repeats, glancing at me.

It takes a moment for the words to spur an idea. I recite what I learned while in the palace: "Snake venom was what Amara used to control Saeed's dreams. Visions," I correct. "He has some of the Memory Master's powers."

The king gasps. "But that's not—"

"Possible?" I finish. "I thought so, too." I gently place a hand on the queen's arm. I think it's the first time I've ever voluntarily touched her. Though her gaze is still one of hesitation.

The raja and queen exchange a glance.

"Amara used the snake venom tincture to block Saeed's visions," I explain. "But if your memories are already blocked, maybe snake venom—specifically Shima's, since she's bound to us—will have the opposite effect and *release* the memories."

*Can you do it?* I ask, heart slamming against my chest.

Shima is hesitant. *The risk is great,* she warns. *But it may restore the raja's memories.*

After Shima gives me the instructions, I guide the king onto a cot. Understanding dawns on his face. He knows what needs to happen.

Shima lowers her head to the raja's wrist, sensing the magic, the life, thrumming in his veins.

Then her fangs sink deep. His eyes shut from the pain. The darkening venom swirls through him, turning his veins black.

When he lets out a cry of agony, the queen snaps up and holds on to his shoulders. "What's happening?" she asks frantically. The raja shakes, but Shima continues to inject the snake venom.

My heart skips. Tears fill my eyes at the sight of him. I dig deep down, hoping he can see, *feel*, what I feel. Even Rani's lips quiver, unspoken apologies ready to be let loose.

My sister clutches the raja's hand. "I remember what I felt during my Ceremony," she says, as if trying to reach him. "The pain. It was as if the world would crush me in its palm. Hear me, Father. You're all right. You're *safe*." She steps closer. "I wish I'd never yelled at you. I wish we had only understood each other better."

Shima releases herself from the raja, venom dripping to the infirmary floor with a hiss. I don't know if it's because of Rani's words or Shima's retreat, but the raja stills. When his eyes open, they land on mine with an emotion I have never seen from him.

Love. Remembrance.

"Ria," he says. "Rani."

"You remember." I'm shivering. My father. He *knows* who I am.

"You did it, Shima!" Rani says.

*You mean I reversed the curse?* she says. *I've always wanted to say that.*

The raja lifts himself from the cot. There's something new in his eyes: recognition. Reclamation. "The fountain, the prophecy . . . I remember it all. You were right, Ria. We did give you up to the palace midwife. She delivered you both. And we trusted her to care for Ria even as our memories faded. Amara helped us do that." The raja shivers. He looks at the queen. "But what of Maneet's memories? Administering snake venom in such a way to a non-snakespeaker would be fatal."

Rani purses her lips. "I think I have an idea."

An older woman named Jas stands in the infirmary an hour later, holding a vial of green liquid between her fingers.

"Is that it?" Rani asks the woman, and she nods, looking at me with curiosity.

"I am learned in all medicines," Jas tells the queen, who's sitting on a freshly made cot, the raja by her side. "Including snake venom tinctures. This is a diluted dose . . . if all goes as it should, this will help restore the memories piece by piece, rather than attempting it all at once."

It was Rani who introduced me to Jas, a woman I've learned was Rani's old tutor's wife. The way she offers Rani a motherly gaze makes me wonder how close they've grown these past few weeks. I smile at the thought.

Jas hands the queen the vial, and she glances at the raja and hesitantly takes a sip.

The queen shuts her eyes against a sudden burst of pain, and I shoot forward on instinct, clutching her hands. "M-Mother," I say for the first time, "look at me. Remember me."

A ghostly pallor replaces the queen's brown skin. Her eyelids flutter.

"She will need rest," Jas says. "The liquid is still powerful for a non-snakespeaker."

"Thank you, Jas," I tell her. The woman nods, gives Rani a parting hug, and leaves.

I don't let go of my mother's hands. I wait, watching her eyes shut, her breaths slow. I don't know how long it takes—three minutes, ten, twenty—but Rani stays with me through it all. I watch my mother's chest rise and fall with each breath, terrified that in the next moment she'll go silent and still. Eventually, I hear a gasp of air.

The queen of Abai's breath shudders out, and her eyes snap open. As she straightens her spine, her gaze lands on us knowingly, and her cheeks flush.

"My twins," she says, glancing between us. She bursts into tears.

"You remember me?" I say, lips wobbling.

"The memory was simply locked away, not erased," Rani says, looking at me with a smile. And right now, with my parents' memories returned, we are beginning to unlock our true lives, piece by piece.

Mother's wrinkles deepen as she frowns, wiping the tears from her cheeks. "How are you both here? Alive? The fountain foresaw one of your deaths."

"'The girl of light will perish at the other's hand, while the victor survives,'" I recite. "That was just one path. One future. But we can make our own futures."

I will myself to mimic Rani's strength, to call up that bravery lying deep in my bones. Because now we'll both need it.

I've always called myself the girl from nowhere, the girl who passed through Abai's poorest villages just to survive. But now I have to act like a princess. For *real* this time. Maybe I can be a girl whose story is greater than she ever imagined.

"Tutor taught me something I'll never forget." Rani takes my hand and says, "We can be more than what the stars wish for. More than we ever dreamed." She says the words as if reciting.

She doesn't need to say more, because she's right. We can be more than the fountain's foretelling. We can change our fortunes—our future is ours to choose, and ours to dream.

"Our daughters are right; the prophecy was only one path," the queen says. I peer up at her. My mother, a woman whose gaze once drew shivers down my back. Now her eyes tell a greater story than she ever could with her own tongue.

*I'm sorry*, they say. *I'm sorry I forgot everything.*

"A princess never hesitates," Rani replies. She stands firm. I'm struck by how easily all these words leave Rani's mouth. How years of training have led her to this moment.

"My twins," our father says, his eyes shining with pride. "The true princesses of Abai. Our future queens."

"That is, if you'll stay with us, Ria," the queen says. "We would understand fully if you choose not to."

I swallow. I think of what being queen would be like. Living in this palace, forever. Will Saeed stay, with his mother gone? My heart pangs. I wonder if he'll still want to be with me after all this is over or mend our relationship despite my lies.

"I . . . I want to stay." The thought of becoming queen is overwhelming but strangely familiar, like the task has been threaded in my bones since I was a child. But Mama Anita knew—that my destiny lay not in the hands of the stars but in my own. And I would forge that path myself.

Now it's my turn to be who I truly am. Past and present. Princess of Abai, and a thief. Both.

"Then it's settled," Rani says. She takes hold of my hand once more. My sister doesn't need to say anything else.

Being royal never made me special. Never made me different, or better. But the two halves of me have always been there—thief and princess. The only difference now is they've come together. Maybe they always were.

# 44

## Rani

It is a warm winter night at the palace.

I pace the length of the Stone Terrace. Downstairs, the throne room is bustling with nobles and guests invited for a night of feasts, marking the beginning of a new era in Abai. What I once feared, I now embrace. I grew up believing only snake magic existed, but I was wrong. The world is full of magic, and that is a beautiful thing.

After Amara's disappearance, Father apologized, over and over, for what he and Mother had done. He promised that now was the time for change. To rewrite a long-written history.

It was the beginning of everything to come.

We are preparing negotiations with Kaama, trying to navigate the muddy waters of endless resentment. The Charts are searching for Amara in case she is still, somehow, out there. So far, there has been no word.

I attempt to block my once-future mother-in-law out, focusing on other matters. Life has changed in many ways: The palace is no longer a cold choke hold, much like my new clothing. The servants' quarters have been expanded at Ria's and my demand; each servant has a full bed and free hours in the day to themselves. I've assigned Irfan, Sanya, and Jas their own rooms. I've spoken to Irfan very little as he's readjusted to life at the palace and, despite his past, he's staying with Father's permission, though an uneasy tension lies between them. Ria has given Aditi her own special room, promoting her to be her personal helper. The servants are free to wear whatever they please—Ria's suggestion. I proposed that Jas be their teacher, thanks to her education at the prestigious Retanian Academy.

I think of the lessons earlier today; Jas and I taught physics, Saeed's favorite, until Amir interrupted and took to less theoretical tasks. He brought the children to the gardens for sword lessons, and later, showed the kids "magic tricks." Making coins disappear and reappear with smooth, liquid movements. "It's good if you wanna get a few extra rupees . . . or impress someone."

I tried to hide my smile. *Always a thief. Always.*

Although this week hasn't been all smiles. The day after Amara's disappearance, I held a formal meeting with Father and Ria. I could tell it was like a weight had been lifted off Father, now that Amara wasn't the one spurring his actions. I no longer saw those eyes craving power.

"I wanted a weapon. Something so powerful it was legendary," he said. "But in my haste, I failed to see the truth. And now Amara has the most powerful object ever seen on the continent."

Ria and I told Father of Amara's true plans: to resurrect her husband by becoming the Master of Souls. Avenge Kumal's death.

"I wish it were not true," Father said. "Amara fooled us all. She was your mother's closest friend. It seems her desire for the stone made her forget the people around her."

The future looked bleak, but one thing comforted me above all else: that it could always be changed. The fountain is a sooth-sayer, yes, but futures can be influenced. The fountain estimates, intones your paths—your *possibilities*. Our fates are ours to decide.

Now, in the palace, I am dressed in a fancy lehenga threaded intricately with red and burnt gold. For once, it does not feel like a weight—or a burden. I wear it because I want to. Because I am Rani. Because I am me, and though I share my title, my name is mine alone.

"You requested to meet, Your Highness?" a voice proclaims from the entrance. Irfan stands there, dressed in more formal clothing than I've ever seen him wear, and he bows.

"No need for formalities," I tell him, laughing. We both take a seat on the swing set. "There's a lot we haven't gotten the chance to discuss," I relent after his silence.

His silver eyes narrow. "Like what?"

"Like your past as a Chart. I know apologies will never be enough for what life was like under my father's rule. He's . . . changing. It will take time, but . . ."

I pause as he places his hand to the scar on his chest. Irfan's gaze sharpens. He looks as if he's seen a ghost.

The ghosts of his past. Red coats, cruel smiles, cold numbers.

I waver. *Perhaps he still despises me for my blood.*

But instead of hatred, his tone holds warmth. "The raja hasn't punished me for deserting my post. Why?"

"I'm no snake girl," I tell him. "You couldn't condone the cruelty of the Charts; how can I fault you? Father was war hungry. He channeled his thoughts into his soldiers. And though he is at fault for many things, we now know why he wouldn't relent in his judgments. Because of the woman with the real Bloodstone, Amara. My father is indebted to you. As am I."

"Thank you," Irfan says, albeit a bit bashfully—an interesting expression on such a hardened face.

"You know, Irfan," I start, "the moment I met you, I knew you were different. You thought you could forget your past, so . . . why did you keep the Abaian crest?" I think of the coin in my hand, the one that helped me connect Irfan and Father.

Irfan stares straight ahead. "A reminder," he clips. "I learned a lot as a Chart, even worked in a division where I was taught how to forge weapons. I brought my knowledge with me to the Foothills, to help people learn how to protect themselves."

Silence descends on us like fog. I only lift my head when Irfan speaks again.

"I remember you." His voice is tender now. "You were probably thirteen. I saw you peeking into the courtyard from the throne room. You hated it."

My eyes swell with remembrance. It was the first Charts' ceremony in recent memory. Father told me I could not watch; he brushed me aside, telling me to wait inside, but I peered out anyway. I shuddered when I heard their oaths. Mother shut the doors soon after, right before the screams. I never understood the cries of pain until now.

"I joined the Charts voluntarily," Irfan reveals. "I had no money and nowhere to go. I thought it wouldn't be so different from training to become an Amratstanian Sentinel. The branding was painful, but I had no other choice at the time."

"If I could mend your heart with magic, I would," I tell him. I would heal Irfan's. I would erase his self-deprecating thoughts, his worries.

"Spoken like a true rani," Irfan laughs. "How is the queen, anyway?"

"She is healing in the infirmary," I say. I have visited Mother every day for the past week. She's still recovering from the return of her memories.

"There you are," a different voice interrupts. I spin to find Amir dressed so meticulously, it's like looking at a different person. But his true self is still there: the scar, the callused hands that felt like honey on my own skin. "Sanya's looking for you," he tells Irfan.

Irfan takes his leave, and I stand at Amir's silence. We've talked only a handful of times since the fateful night we returned to the palace. Sometimes I still look at him with hope—but I do not know if he can ever see past the princess in me. If he can see in

Rani that same girl who meant something to him.

"Your family knows how to throw a party," he says, taking my silence as permission to step in. It's dark, the only light coming from a few torches and the stars.

"I think *I'm* the one who did all the party planning," I laugh, stomach warming.

"Don't tell Ria that," he jokes. "She was proud of her first official party."

"How is she?" I ask, even though I saw her a few hours ago.

"No more thieving, that's for sure." I don't realize how close he's moved toward me until his arm brushes mine.

"I should never have lied to you."

"You had no choice," Amir says. "I knew there was something off from the start, but I couldn't put my finger on it. And then when you told me, I didn't want to believe you were a princess. Out of reach."

Carefully, he opens his fist, revealing the timepiece from his father. "I don't want to waste any more time." He takes my hand. "Do you want to dance?"

I nod. Music thrums through my body, carrying itself up through the Abai air.

He doesn't say a word. His hands move to my waist. But it's not the dance I expect; it's the kind of dance when lips touch, when the world is long forgotten.

I relish the smolder, the heat of it all. The fire burning deep within me—somewhere I didn't know existed. I was so used to the ice I built around me that I didn't see the heat scorching in my soul.

I'm breathless when he pulls back. But he doesn't let go. Not yet. Not ever.

So we lose ourselves in the beat of the music.

# 45

## Ria

The celebration's in full swing. People filter in and out of the throne room, their multicolored suits lighting up the palace like lit diyas. I'm wearing an emerald lehenga (I've decided saris are Not My Thing), wearing the color with pride, a color no longer denoted to a lesser value. Even the palace itself has changed, with garlands of gold and green leaves strung around the palace pillars. I've changed too: my face looks different than it did a few weeks ago when I lived on the streets. I glance down at my bangles, bright enough that I would've never worn them while thieving. Bright enough to assert myself as princess but also a color of illumination. Of fire. Like saffron, unassuming but worth its weight in gold.

I leave the throne room, legs ready to carry me wherever I want. I think back to days in Nabh: a piece of naan in one hand, legs outstretched, ready to run at the right moment. I imagine tossing Amir his food. How unaware I was, thinking my life was one long dirt road, leading to nothing but heaps of unfulfilled dreams, like litter thrown to the wayside.

No—I'm Ria, not Rani, a girl whose speed and quick thinking got me through the toughest months of my life. I'm no one but me.

I pass by Aditi, who's playing with a few other kids, and she gives me a wink.

"Lynx," she says.

"Mouse," I greet in return. I've checked on Aditi in the servants' infirmary these past few days before she was let out. She had rope burns on her wrists, like the queen's. It seems the infirmary had its fair share of visitors this week; I even ordered the Charts to search for Amara's snake venom supplier and bring him back here, and now he's recovering in the infirmary, too, after much blood loss. We're waiting for him to heal fully in case he might have more information on Amara.

*Amara.* The night she disappeared, Aditi told me, "I stood up to her, you know. Before she tied me up. I told her she was messing with the wrong princess. I'm not afraid of her anymore."

Now Aditi giggles and smiles profusely as she tosses her chunni in the air. She's right. She isn't afraid anymore.

The courtyard is empty except for a few Charts, and I'm reminded of how stiff-backed and menacing they once were, of how wary and rigid they still seem. At least the age registration has been reversed. No more children will be conscripted into the Charts. No one else will be conscripted against their will.

There's still lots that needs to be changed, with the raja's and queen's help. I imagine the seas beyond, a sweeping current of cobalt. Once, the sea was all the freedom I craved. Now, with our parents' memories returned and Rani at my side, I'm truly free.

*Free as you'll ever be*, a voice chimes.

I spin to find Shima hidden in an alcove of the palace. She slithers out of the shadows and onto the grass. *Enjoying the party?* she asks.

"Yes," I say. "You?"

*Could be better. But I like the decor. Very chic.*

"Hmph," I laugh. "You have ridiculously high standards." A cool wind hits me and I shiver, remembering how much has changed in the past moon.

"I've been meaning to ask . . . you didn't . . . *know* Mama Anita, did you? When she came to the palace?"

*If you're insinuating I was one of the vipers in the Pit when your caretaker passed, you are wrong. Samvir, your father's snake familiar, was the executioner.*

My stomach coils.

Shima continues, *There is a light in the darkness, Princess. I was the one who led your friend Aditi to her caretaker, in the dungeons, during her last moments.*

I shake my head, confused. "W-why?"

*Because I sensed something about the woman*, the snake says. *And now I know what. I knew, when I forged my blood bond with Rani, that there was a secret buried deep in her veins.* The snake eyes me, watchful and steady. *And it was you.*

I step back. "Me?" I think of what the snake said—the blood bond. Forged through the Bonding Ceremony, a tradition between serpent and human. I feel it with her now, that strange tug and pull.

"Shima . . . ," I say. "I have a question."

She raises her head.

"When we were rising up in the Pit," I tell her, "I heard a voice. Do you know who it could've been?"

Shima's voice is grave. *He has been in the Pit for ages, biding his time, one with the walls and shadows.*

"Who's *he*?"

*I believe you already know.* Shima shivers. *It is strange. We no longer feel his presence since Amara's disappearance. Saeed's mother, on the other hand . . . there is something different about her. She is changed.*

"Changed?" I repeat. "Wait . . . can you sense if Amara's alive?"

*We snakes do not know for certain. But we do know that only someone of great power could have escaped such a dark place.*

I gulp. "Th-thank you, Shima."

Above, laughter pours out from the Stone Terrace. Leaning against the edge stand Amir and Rani, their hands intertwined. It's been no secret how Amir feels about my sister; the way he looked at her daily was no puzzle to figure out. Their embrace warms my chest. If I'd never met Rani, I might've always stayed with Amir, escaped Abai. Never fulfilling my own destiny, never finding Saeed.

I'm still wearing the engagement ring. My parents haven't

reprimanded me for it, and neither has Rani. Saeed's still wearing his, though we haven't spoken of it yet.

I head to the Stone Terrace. I can't help my surreptitious smile when I find Rani and Amir wrapped in each other's arms.

I politely knock on the wall. "Am I interrupting something?"

Rani groans against Amir. "Ria, I know you used to be a thief, but do you have to steal away a private moment?"

Amir chuckles, his eyes finding mine. "Some things never change."

I grin. "If you two lovebirds are gonna keep doing this all night—"

Amir removes his hands from Rani and raises them in the air. "I'm leaving, I'm leaving." As he exits, he playfully pushes an elbow against my arm, and I push back.

When he's gone, I move to where Amir was standing a few seconds ago, eye to eye with Rani.

"Are you happy here?"

"I should be asking you that question," she replies with a short laugh. "But yes. Very."

"Me too."

"When I left," Rani continues, "I never thought my life could change this much. Never saw that I could be . . . something else."

I think of all the people she met on her journey, people now staying at the palace with us: Amir's sister, Sanya. The older woman, Jas. The former Chart, Irfan. "And yet . . ."

"We're still princesses," she laughs. I join her, letting the sound settle against my skin. Then she turns to smirk at me. "Mother says I'm older."

"By ten minutes!" I quip back.

We double over with laughter. It's still strange, getting used to this whole sisterhood thing, but now I wonder how I ever lived without it.

Some time later, Saeed finds us on the balcony, wearing a watery smile that brightens when his eyes find mine. I don't know why my heart suddenly does backflips.

"Good evening, Your Highnesses," he says, bowing.

"You know you don't have to do that, right?" I say.

"Force of habit."

I pull him inside, away from the balcony. Rani shoots me a knowing grin, which I pointedly ignore. I notice a few locks of his hair are a shocking white, curling above his brow. He hasn't bothered covering them.

"I like your hair. It suits you."

"Seems the symptom is permanent." He shrugs. "I thought I'd embrace it."

"You know," I tell him, "you don't always need to hide in your room. We can *talk* about what happened." We've only met up a few times over the past week, and even then, Saeed's been somewhat distant.

He sucks in his cheeks. "I know, it's just . . . my mother. She's gone. Where is she? What magic could have done that?"

"I don't know," I say honestly.

"I see her in my visions. I think she's alive, Ria."

"Saeed—" I start.

"I know, I know. She disappeared into the Pit. But my visions haven't led me astray so far, have they? I don't know where she is, or what she is doing. I only hope she stays far from here."

I remain quiet at that. I can't even imagine the pain Saeed's gone through.

"That's why I was looking for you," Saeed says. "I'm officially leaving to search for her. Tonight."

"Tonight?" My voice sounds strangled. "Why?"

"I can't just stay here, knowing she could be out there. Perhaps my visions could help me find her. You must understand."

I nod. "I—I do. But I want you to be safe." I step closer to him, wrapping my hands in his. He thumbs the engagement ring that I haven't taken off.

"I will. I'll be back," he promises, "as soon as I have information."

Our eyes connect, and it's like I'm back at Rani's engagement party, the moment he told me he loved me. I'm frozen as he leans down to place a kiss on my forehead. My heart leaps.

"Saeed . . . stay tonight. You can leave in the morning, have a fresh start. Please."

Saeed's brows crinkle. But I don't have to use my snake magic for me to convince him.

He sighs. "Okay," he concedes. "Who am I to disobey Princess Ria?"

I grin. "I'll find you soon. Save a dance for me?"

Saeed's eyes soften. "Of course, Princess."

When we part, I swear I'm floating back onto the balcony and to Rani. I tell her about Saeed's plan, his visions of his mother.

"What if she's really alive?" I whisper.

"We'll work together and find her. Have faith, sister." Rani shakes her head, letting her long, raven hair hang loose. And then, she turns to the railing. Our kingdom.

It's nowhere near perfect. Nabh is still the Dirt Village. Anari is still the opulent capital. It's everything in between that's changed.

Outside, I see everything I once knew, and know still: merchant carts, dirt-lined roads. The stalls opening each morning, the vivid shouts and cheers of children. The part of me that only knew Abai's villages and alleyways isn't going anywhere.

Once, I was satisfied with only rupees in my pocket and an empty heart. Now I feel just the opposite.

There's still a lot to be discussed with my mother and father, like the Vadi Orphanage, the treatment of children with magic. No more suppressing who we are. As a princess, I have a voice. And I'm gonna make mine heard.

"Do you believe all twins could do what we did that night?" Rani ponders. "Facing Amara and our parents, bringing back their memories?"

"Nah," I say, grinning. "Just us."

Gently, she presses open my hand and brings her palm against mine. I startle, pulling back. It's still so odd, everything that's happened. I want to tell her how I feel—that I *do* see her as my sister, that having a twin has changed my life. But I'm still me. Ria. The thief girl. And trust doesn't come easy for me.

"I've always wanted a real family." I gulp. "Now that I have one, I—I'm too scared to admit it."

"You don't have to fear any longer. Your family isn't only your blood. It's the people who are around you. I didn't know then, but Tutor was a part of me, a part of *my* family, the same way Mama Anita was part of yours."

Rani's words light a fire inside me. It's true. I've had my family with me all along.

"So . . ." Rani half smiles, holding out her hand. "A truce?"

"I don't really wanna hear that word again," I laugh. "But yeah. Something like that."

With a featherlight touch, I take her hand. It's the first step toward a world where I don't have to worry about what food I'll eat or what clothes I'll need to steal. The first step to really changing things, for good.

From the courtyards, the celebration escalates. A tinny sound echoes across the grounds, followed by a shower of light. Fireworks are bursting through the air, raining down on all of Abai, a light to end eighteen years of darkness.

We are the princesses of Abai, standing before our kingdom. Together.

# Epilogue

She wakes in the darkness.

The cave is dim and disparaging. She rises from the ground and crouches over a pond of water in the cave, examining her rippling reflection. Reddened lips. Red as blood.

Her last memories return to her. Falling into an abyss . . . a deep voice . . .

"*I have waited a long time for this,*" someone says. She looks up before realizing the voice has come from within herself. But it is not her own anymore. She feels it slip up her spine and entwine with her very spirit, the same way it clung to her the moment she fell into the Snake Pit.

Something shimmers from the corner of her vision. She reaches for the object and wraps it in her hand. A stone, red and pulsing, beats in her palm like an aching heart.

"Are you the one who saved me?" she asks, her voice entirely her own.

*"Why don't you take another look? Tell me, dear Amara . . . do you see?"*

When she leans down to glance at her reflection once more, she sees her eyes—*his* eyes—serpentine and deadly.

"Yes, Master." She grins.

# Acknowledgments

Writing a book is a years-long journey. We started this book back in 2016, when the world was much different than it is today. But Ria and Rani have always stuck around, and we're so grateful that people can now read their story. We're extremely thankful to the following people for helping us along the way and cheering on *Sisters of the Snake*:

Our parents, Aneil, and all of our family and friends who have supported us on our writing journey from high school to university and beyond. Thank you for always being by our side.

Enormous thanks to Pete Knapp for being the first person to champion our books and truly understand them. *Sisters of the Snake* would not exist without you! A million thanks also to the whole PFLM team.

Kristen Pettit, for all the enthusiasm (Shima!) and expertise, and for being such an incredible editor with brilliant ideas. Clare

Vaughn, for fielding emails, answering questions, and having the magical touch on this manuscript. To everyone at HarperCollins who has helped guide this manuscript into becoming a real book, including Jon Howard and Megan Gendell on the production side, and also Team Epic Reads and all the tireless sales, marketing, and publicity folks. A huge thanks to HarperCollins Canada for their never-ending support, including Maeve, Ashley, and Marisol! Yay Team Frenzy!

Huge thank-you to cover designer Chris Kwon and artist Fatima Baig for bringing Ria and Rani to life. We seriously couldn't have asked for a better, more *stunning* cover and jacket design. *heart eyes* for days. THANK YOU for bringing our book cover dreams to life.

To our Toronto writer crew for all the fun hangouts and publishing chats. Y'all are awesome!

Sona Charaipotra and Dhonielle Clayton, thank you for always being incredible mentors and great people to work with!

Thank you to Sabaa Tahir for motivating us to write a story about twins way back in March 2016. *An Ember in the Ashes* helped us realize we could one day write high fantasy, too.

Huge thanks and lots of love to everyone who took the time to read and blurb this book.

To the PitchWars 2016 crew, especially Laura Ingram Lashley for suggesting the title! Shout-out to Judy I. Lin for the sprints and fun chats. And thank you to our amazing mentor Stephanie Scott, revision wizard and all-around amazing person and Instagrammer!

Thanks to Beth Phelan and DVPit for giving us a voice and championing diverse stories. To all our book blogger friends who've supported us on the journey thus far, and who've been with us since the beginning.

To the 21ders: We couldn't have asked for a more incredible group of authors to debut with. Thanks for all the Slack chats and messages while we go through this wildly amazing publishing experience together.

Finally, thank you to all the readers who've picked up this book and given it a chance. We hope you had as much fun reading Ria and Rani's story as we had writing it!